Praise for Lexi Blake and Masters and Mercenaries...

"I can always trust Lexi Blake's D
breathless...and in love. If you want sensual, exciting BDSM wrapped in an awesome love story, then look for a Lexi Blake book."

~Cherise Sinclair USA Today Bestselling author

"Lexi Blake's MASTERS AND MERCENARIES series is beautifully written and deliciously hot. She's got a real way with both action and sex. I also love the way Blake writes her gorgeous Dom heroes--they make me want to do bad, bad things. Her heroines are intelligent and gutsy ladies whose taste for submission definitely does not make them dish rags. Can't wait for the next book!"

~Angela Knight, New York Times Bestselling author

"A Dom is Forever is action packed, both in the bedroom and out. Expect agents, spies, guns, killing and lots of kink as Liam goes after the mysterious Mr. Black and finds his past and his future… The action and espionage keep this story moving along quickly while the sex and kink provides a totally different type of interest. Everything is very well balanced and flows together wonderfully."

~A Night Owl "Top Pick", Terri, Night Owl Erotica

"A Dom Is Forever is everything that is good in erotic romance. The story was fast-paced and suspenseful, the characters were flawed but made me root for them every step of the way, and the hotness factor was off the charts mostly due to a bad boy Dom with a penchant for dirty talk."

~Rho, The Romance Reviews

"A good read that kept me on my toes, guessing until the big reveal, and thinking survival skills should be a must for all men."

~Chris, Night Owl Reviews

"I can't get enough of the Masters and Mercenaries Series! Love and Let Die is Lexi Blake at her best! She writes erotic romantic suspense like no other, and I am always extremely excited when she has something new for us! Intense, heart pounding, and erotically fulfilling, I could not put this book down."

~ Shayna Renee, Shayna Renee's Spicy Reads

"Certain authors and series are on my auto-buy list. Lexi Blake and her Masters & Mercenaries series is at the top of that list... this book offered everything I love about a Masters & Mercenaries book – alpha men, hot sex and sweet loving… As long as Ms. Blake continues to offer such high quality books, I'll be right there, ready to read."

~ Robin, Sizzling Hot Books

"I have absolutely fallen in love with this series. Spies, espionage, and intrigue all packaged up in a hot dominant male package. All the men at McKay-Taggart are smoking hot and the women are amazingly strong sexy submissives."

~Kelley, Smut Book Junkie Book Reviews

Live, Love, Spy

Other Books by Lexi Blake

ROMANTIC SUSPENSE

Masters and Mercenaries
The Dom Who Loved Me
The Men With The Golden Cuffs
A Dom is Forever
On Her Master's Secret Service
Sanctum: A Masters and Mercenaries Novella
Love and Let Die
Unconditional: A Masters and Mercenaries Novella
Dungeon Royale
Dungeon Games: A Masters and Mercenaries Novella
A View to a Thrill
Cherished: A Masters and Mercenaries Novella
You Only Love Twice
Luscious: Masters and Mercenaries~Topped
Adored: A Masters and Mercenaries Novella
Master No
Just One Taste: Masters and Mercenaries~Topped 2
From Sanctum with Love
Devoted: A Masters and Mercenaries Novella
Dominance Never Dies
Submission is Not Enough
Master Bits and Mercenary Bites~The Secret Recipes of Topped
Perfectly Paired: Masters and Mercenaries~Topped 3
For His Eyes Only
Arranged: A Masters and Mercenaries Novella
Love Another Day
At Your Service: Masters and Mercenaries~Topped 4
Master Bits and Mercenary Bites~Girls Night
Nobody Does It Better
Close Cover
Protected: A Masters and Mercenaries Novella
Enchanted: A Masters and Mercenaries Novella
Charmed: A Masters and Mercenaries Novella
Taggart Family Values

Treasured: A Masters and Mercenaries Novella
Delighted: A Masters and Mercenaries Novella
Tempted: A Masters and Mercenaries Novella

Masters and Mercenaries: The Forgotten
Lost Hearts (Memento Mori)
Lost and Found
Lost in You
Long Lost
No Love Lost

Masters and Mercenaries: Reloaded
Submission Impossible
The Dom Identity
The Man from Sanctum
No Time to Lie
The Dom Who Came in from the Cold

Masters and Mercenaries: New Recruits
Love the Way You Spy
Live, Love, Spy
Sweet Little Spies, Coming

Butterfly Bayou
Butterfly Bayou
Bayou Baby
Bayou Dreaming
Bayou Beauty
Bayou Sweetheart
Bayou Beloved

Park Avenue Promise
Start Us Up
My Royal Showmance, Coming June 4, 2024

Lawless
Ruthless
Satisfaction
Revenge

Courting Justice
Order of Protection
Evidence of Desire

Masters Of Ménage (by Shayla Black and Lexi Blake)
Their Virgin Captive
Their Virgin's Secret
Their Virgin Concubine
Their Virgin Princess
Their Virgin Hostage
Their Virgin Secretary
Their Virgin Mistress

The Perfect Gentlemen (by Shayla Black and Lexi Blake)
Scandal Never Sleeps
Seduction in Session
Big Easy Temptation
Smoke and Sin
At the Pleasure of the President

URBAN FANTASY

Thieves
Steal the Light
Steal the Day
Steal the Moon
Steal the Sun
Steal the Night
Ripper
Addict
Sleeper
Outcast
Stealing Summer
The Rebel Queen
The Rebel Guardian
The Rebel Witch

LEXI BLAKE WRITING AS SOPHIE OAK

Texas Sirens
Small Town Siren
Siren in the City
Siren Enslaved
Siren Beloved
Siren in Waiting
Siren in Bloom
Siren Unleashed
Siren Reborn

Nights in Bliss, Colorado
Three to Ride
Two to Love
One to Keep
Lost in Bliss
Found in Bliss
Pure Bliss
Chasing Bliss
Once Upon a Time in Bliss
Back in Bliss
Sirens in Bliss
Happily Ever After in Bliss
Far from Bliss
Unexpected Bliss

A Faery Story
Bound
Beast
Beauty

Standalone
Away From Me
Snowed In

Live, Love, Spy

Masters and Mercenaries: New Recruits, Book 2

Lexi Blake

Live, Love, Spy
Masters and Mercenaries: New Recruits, Book 2
Lexi Blake

Published by DLZ Entertainment LLC

Edited by Chloe Vale
ISBN: 978-1-942297-93-2

Sign up for Lexi Blake's newsletter
and be entered to win a $25 gift certificate
to the bookseller of your choice.

Join us for news, fun, and exclusive content
including free Thieves short stories.

There's a new contest every month!

Go to www.LexiBlake.net to subscribe.

Family Trees

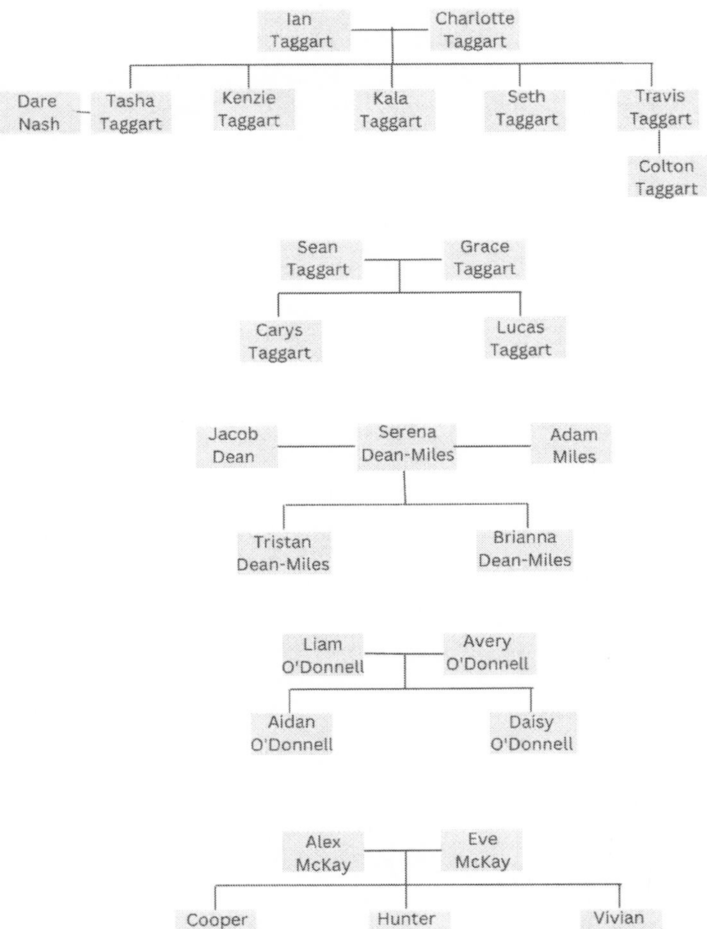

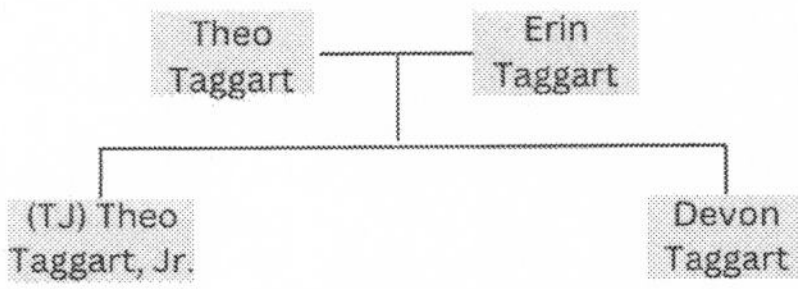
Theo Taggart
Erin Taggart
(TJ) Theo Taggart, Jr.
Devon Taggart

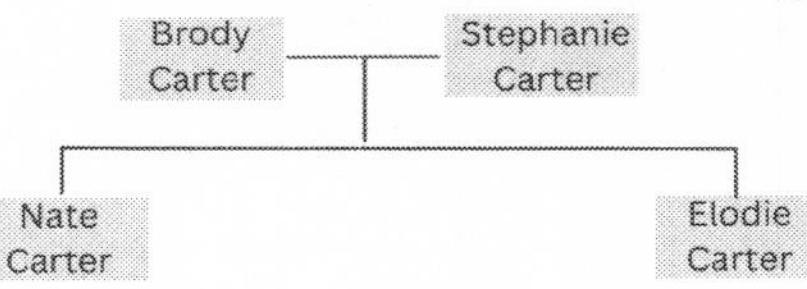
Brody Carter
Stephanie Carter
Nate Carter
Elodie Carter

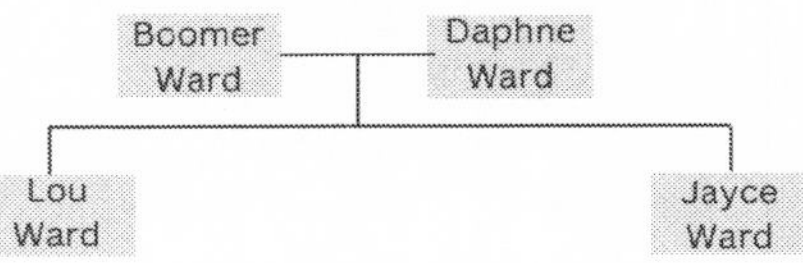
Boomer Ward
Daphne Ward
Lou Ward
Jayce Ward

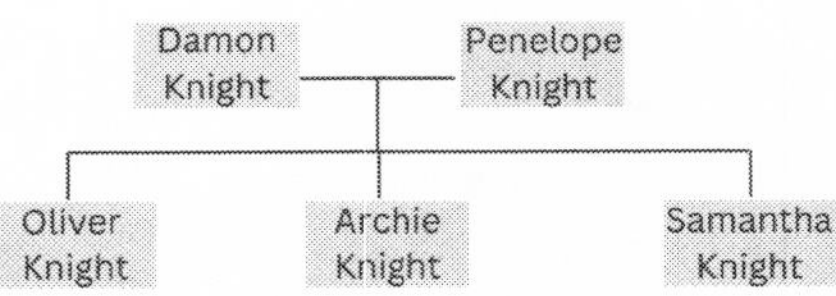
Damon Knight
Penelope Knight
Oliver Knight
Archie Knight
Samantha Knight

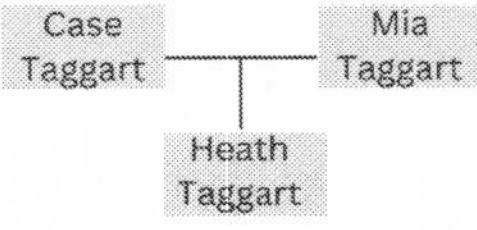
Case Taggart
Mia Taggart
Heath Taggart

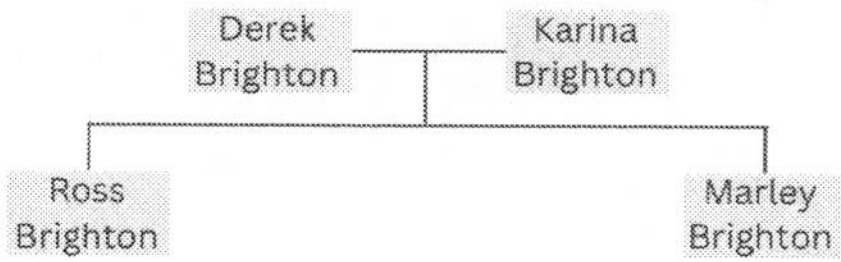
Derek
Brighton
Karina
Brighton
Ross
Brighton
Marley
Brighton

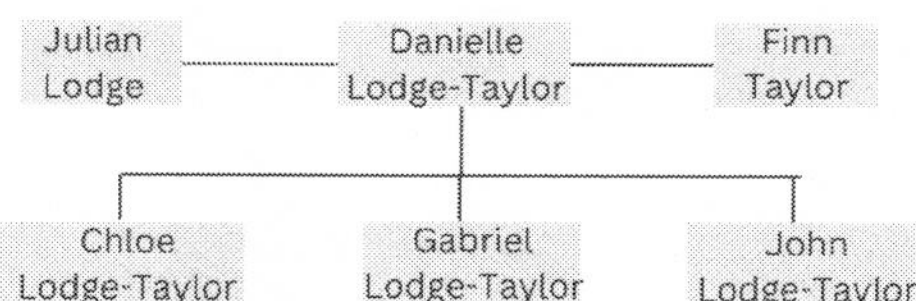
Julian
Lodge
Danielle
Lodge-Taylor
Finn
Taylor
Chloe
Lodge-Taylor
Gabriel
Lodge-Taylor
John
Lodge-Taylor

Acknowledgments

I've had a soft spot for Louisa Ward since the minute she knocked on Boomer's door in *Delighted.* I guess I saw the tiniest bit of myself in her. Not that I'm as smart as Lou, but there were expectations placed on me from a young age. I started writing stories very young and by the time I was in high school, I had two plays produced, including my high school's fall production. This led to a bunch of people in my life believing fully that I would be an award-winning writer by the age of 20.

It took a little longer than that, and I felt the heavy weight of that expectation—and the disappointment when I didn't fulfill the promise of my youth—heavily. I kept writing but I started writing novels, but I was slow and they weren't what most of the people in my life considered truly artistic work because I wrote romance novels rather than the intellectual plays and poems of my youth. I felt that judgment, too.

It's funny that we consider ourselves grown at the age of eighteen. I suppose we're technically adults, but most of us will be weighed down with the belief that what others think about what fills our souls should have some influence on us. The truth that we learn as we age is that what fills our souls should inform who we have in our lives and who we shouldn't. Lou understands this from her youth, so maybe she's what I wished I'd been. She had so many expectations on her and yet she decided to go on her own path. No matter what anyone thought.

It took me a little longer, but I got here. I no longer worry about what people think about my work. The fact that it satisfies me is all I need in order to find pride in it. I was lucky because I had champions who stood by me while I worked it out, who always knew where I needed to be and helped me find my way. I was born to write romance and that's enough. In finding out that truth I learned another.

I'm enough.

And as Lou will find out over the coming pages, so are you, dear reader. This is for everyone who is doing what makes them happy, who is proud to be part of this amazing romance writing and reading community we've built.

Prologue

"Are you sure I can't kill him?"

TJ Taggart sighed because he should have known it was a bad idea to bring his cousin Kala into this particular scheme of his. It had been suggested by several members of Johnson High School's senior class that a new "most likely to" category be created just for Kala Taggart. Most Likely to Murder Someone.

Luckily the administration had shut that right down. Probably because, like the rest of the world, they were afraid of Kala. He'd heard some talk about how relieved the entire staff would be when all the Taggarts were off to college and they never had to deal with that military mafia family again.

Their description, not his.

They would be waiting forever. His family was massive, and there always seemed to be a new addition.

"If I thought I could get away with it, I would do it myself," TJ said under his breath as they both watched the boy in question walk across the quad toward the main building. Unfortunately for him, Kala was the only way to go when it came to taking down an asshole. His sister, Devi, would try to kick the guy in the balls, but Kala understood they needed something truly awful in order to end this thing between Lou and that fuckwad walking across the quad like he owned it.

"I can get away with it," Kala returned.

"I think Lou's been through enough without losing her best friend to juvie." Dennis Sims walked up to a group of soccer bros. Assholes, every one of them. He wasn't sure why the boys' soccer team seemed to only recruit jerks he wouldn't leave alone with a girl for a single second, but there they were.

"I thought you were her best friend."

An ache went through him. Louisa Ward was…everything. Lou was his whole heart. Sometimes he wished he'd never met her because before he had, he'd never thought he was lonely. Now when she wasn't around he felt his singularity. "I think she's my best friend. I don't know that I'm hers."

Kala wore her normal uniform of ripped jeans, combat boots, and a leather jacket, even though it wasn't cold enough for one yet. Her hair was shiny blue, and she sighed in a way that reminded him of his uncle, her dad. This was Uncle Ian's patented "dumbass said something and now I gotta fix things" sigh. "You could change that. All you have to do is say Lou, let's get down and dirty. She's in love with you, TJ."

She thought she was, and maybe it was true, but she was a grade ahead of him, and Lou Ward was an academic force of nature. She was so fucking smart, and he was…TJ. People got excited when he made a C instead of a D. People praised him for finding out he'd read an actual not-comic-book book. He'd only read it because Lou was reading it. "She's going to college, and I don't think she needs to be stuck with a boyfriend who won't go to college at all."

"Tell me you're not still thinking about the Army." Kala frowned his way. "You're not dumb. I know I say it all the time, but insults are my love language. You can go to college. You can go, and then if you still feel the need to get your ass shot off at least you'll be an officer."

He'd gotten this lecture from more than one person. "I don't want to. I want to get in, learn some things that will help me get a job when I get out, and start my life. Lou is going in a different direction. She needs way more than I can give her."

Kala's head shook. "Your loss, man."

Yes. It was his loss because he would never be the man who

kissed her and touched her and slept beside her. He wouldn't be the man to smooth back her hair and hold her hand.

But fuck all, neither would Dennis asshole Sims.

His cousin was being something of a hypocrite. "And why do you always give me shit about the Army? You're planning a whole career at the Agency."

"Not the same thing. The Agency is cool, and no one will yell at me all day. Well, except Kenzie." Kenzie Taggart was Kala's twin, and while they seemed different on the surface, he happened to know they had a lot in common. They both wanted to be spies.

But his Lou would end up at some think tank or working at an elite university. She would be safe in her ivory tower surrounded by people who could keep up with her. She would change the world someday, and he would be so proud of her.

He would still be in her life. That was the important part. He fucked up all of his relationships. He hadn't kept a girlfriend for more than three months. Lou was too important.

So he was going to keep his hands off her because he couldn't lose her.

It would be easier when she was in college. She started at MIT in the fall. He would call her and text her and miss her like crazy, but it would be easier to not fuck things up if she was hundreds of miles away.

Kala's eyes narrowed. "They're breaking up. We can catch him on his way to first period. He's got a class in the east wing. Let's go."

Naturally Kala had everything planned down to the second. It was precisely why he'd gone to her when he'd found out what Dennis had done. He would have simply jumped the fucker and gotten suspended. Kala understood that revenge was a delicate art form.

But the most important thing was to get him to break things off with Lou before she got hurt.

"You can't kill him." Cooper McKay jogged up, one hand on his backpack. He was taller than TJ by a couple of inches but didn't have TJ's muscular build yet. At seventeen he was still all long limbs and odd angles. "Kala, let me handle it. TJ, don't you dare jump his ass. You get caught fighting again and they will expel you, and your mother will be the one doing the murdering."

Cooper had been the one to tell him what was going on. Cooper played baseball and had some of the same friends as Dennis the Douche.

"I'm not going to kill him, but he's not taking Lou to prom," Kala stated resolutely. "Not after making that bet."

TJ felt his hands fist at the thought of the jocks placing bets on who would get some on prom night.

Dennis Sims had bet he could get the nerdiest girl in school to give up her virginity.

Over his dead body.

"See, you look like a dude who's about to get expelled," Cooper said like he'd known it all along. "Have we thought about talking to Lou and letting her handle it? Maybe we could go to her parents."

Kala's eyes rolled. "Yeah, let's break Lou's heart and bring her parents in so we can all end up in some therapy session. Fuck that. We can handle our own shit."

"The last time you tried to handle your own shit, you got kidnapped," Cooper pointed out.

TJ waited for Kala to explode, but she merely turned a chilly smile Coop's way. "Yeah, and I learned a lot about myself. You feel free to go crying to our parents all you like, Coop. I'm going to pull up my big girl panties and get the job done. If you don't…"

"Hey, I'm sorry." Cooper reached out, grasping her hand. "I shouldn't have thrown that in your face. You're right. Let me come with you. Not for your sake. To stop TJ from losing his shit. And I know you're a black belt in several martial arts, but you just had your nails done."

No one knew how to talk to Kala like Cooper. She sighed, her I'm-going-to-give-in sigh. "Fine, but we have to hurry. He's in a class with Lou for second period."

They caught up to Dennis, who was walking into the east wing. Dennis was a senior, a year older than TJ, and in excellent shape.

That wouldn't help him if TJ decided to take him out. He'd been called a pit bull in a fight, and he didn't have a problem with that. Pit bulls could be quite sweet when they were treated right, and they could handle business if they weren't.

Dennis's blue eyes widened when he realized who was behind

him. "Hey. How's it going, Kala?" He nodded Cooper's way. "Hey, man."

He ignored TJ entirely.

"You're going to gently explain to Lou that you won't be taking her to prom," Kala said, not waiting for niceties.

Dennis frowned, obviously surprised at the turn. "Why would I do that?"

"Because I'll break every bone in your body if you don't." He'd already planned out how he would do it, too. He'd sat up last night thinking it through. He would start with the small ones and work his way up.

Dennis was suddenly interested in him. "What the fuck, Taggart? Is this about the whole 'you don't want her but no one else can have her' thing you have going? You're an asshole, you know."

"We know about the bet," Kala stated flatly.

Dennis's gaze immediately went to Cooper.

Coop held up his hands and shook his head, his expression utterly unapologetic. "Damn straight I told them. Don't think I'm one of your jock friends who treat girls like trash. Lou's a friend of mine. I wouldn't let you do this to any girl, much less someone in my family circle."

"Guys, that was locker-room talk. I like Lou." Dennis flushed a nice shade of pink. "That hasn't gotten back to her, has it?"

"No, and it's not going to. I already talked to the assholes you made this bet with and explained if Lou found out, I would be visiting them." TJ hadn't taken Kala on those talks. They'd sat down and made their plan to cover all of this crap up. Lou could handle some jerk blowing her off. He wasn't sure how she would take the whole school knowing they were making bets on her virginity.

So he'd handled the problem.

Dennis's head shook. "I get it. I was an asshole, but the truth of the matter is I like her. I'm not going to make anyone pay up on that stupid bet, so you can back off. You know you're the reason she can't get a damn date, Taggart. You've got the whole school terrified of you. Do you think that's good for her? Is she's supposed to be alone for the rest of her life?"

She wouldn't be, and he would have to deal with that someday. Not today. "Break it off with her. Gently. I don't care what you tell her but make it sound good."

His expression went stubborn. "And if I don't? I know you Taggarts think you run things here, but you're all freaks."

"Hey," Cooper began.

Kala waved him off. "That's fair. Dennis hasn't even met my dad. He has no idea how freaky we can get. But he's going to find out if he doesn't break things off with Lou. Today."

"Fuck you. I'm not scared of you," Dennis announced. "I think I'll tell Lou about this conversation right here and see what she thinks. I know she feels awkward because she's younger than the rest of us, but she's a cool girl. I think it's being around you assholes that holds her back. I think she'll do better with my friends. We'll show her what normal looks like. Yeah, that's a much better plan. I'll tell Lou who you people really are."

"And then I'll release the proof that you cheated on your trig final and get your scholarships revoked," Kala said, cool as a cucumber.

And that was why he'd brought in the beast. Kala knew shit no one else knew. She kept track of the people around her, the ones who could potentially hurt her. Dennis had been running around talking about the free ride he was getting to LSU, but that would go away in a heartbeat if he was caught cheating.

Dennis's jaw tightened. "I didn't cheat."

Kala smiled, a predatory expression. "Ya did, and I have proof. You paid a hacker you found on the Internet to hack Mr. Fender's system and copy the exam. You were smart enough to not score a hundred, but you did not earn that 93."

Lou had scored a hundred, naturally. She'd been helping Dennis study. It was how they'd met.

"You can't possibly know that," Dennis replied.

"Who do you think the hacker was, asshole?" Kala asked.

Dennis had been a moron. He'd actually asked some people how he could get his hands on the exam, and TJ had caught wind of it. He hadn't liked how Dennis was sniffing around Lou, and so he'd put out the word that there was a way. Not that he told Dennis himself. Getting word out through mutual friends had done the trick, and now they had his ass in checkmate.

The key had been to let him actually get the grade so there was nowhere for him to go.

"And I'll send it to the school anonymously," Kala continued. "You could talk and try to get me in trouble, but I'll turn everything over and no one will believe you. I've cleaned my tracks up. As far as the Internet trail goes, you sent two hundred bucks to a dude in Turkey to handle the problem for you."

"Fuck." Dennis's eyes closed, and when he opened them again there was resignation there. "Fine. I'll break it off with her. I should have known better than to try to hang with anyone in your group. You're all toxic. Good luck to all you fuckers. May I never see any of you again after we graduate."

He stormed off.

TJ really wished he'd gotten to punch the man.

"I'm not toxic," Kala said, her lip pouting out.

Cooper frowned down at her. "Seriously? You're hacking teachers?"

One shoulder shrugged. "He was getting close to Lou. TJ and I might have baited him a little. We wanted something on him in case I needed to get rid of him, and sure enough I did. You know I've got something on most of the assholes here. Information is far more effective than TJ's fists."

She was going to be a ruthless spy.

And that was why his ass was going into the Army and Kala would be in the elite circles of intelligence.

Story of his life. The women around him were all smarter, more ambitious, better than him.

Cooper was looking at Kala like he was going to eat her up. For all his Superman morals, he got truly wound up when Kala did something smart and slightly shady. She was Cooper's own personal kryptonite.

"I'm going to go to class." Anything to get away from the teen lust that was suddenly filling the hallway. "You two… Bye."

He turned a corner and practically ran into Lou. She barely managed to keep her books in hand.

"Hey." It felt like the whole world softened when she was around. "Sorry, sweetheart. I was trying to get away from whatever Kala and Coop are doing and not paying attention. You okay?"

She smiled up at him, tucking a piece of golden-brown hair

behind her ear. "What did she do now? I thought they were mad at each other."

"I don't think that would stop them." TJ fell into step beside her. This was pretty much where he always wanted to be.

He wanted it so much he couldn't ever risk not having it. Despite her big brain, she was so young. Barely sixteen and already graduating as the valedictorian of the class. He would be almost nineteen when he graduated because his parents had been advised to hold him back from starting kindergarten. Yup. He'd been too dumb to start school with everyone else.

"And you have to stop calling me sweetheart," she said with a curl to her lips. "Dennis isn't exactly my boyfriend, but I don't want him to get the wrong idea about us."

Guilt flashed through him, but he shoved it back. It was better for her to be a little hurt now than utterly be humiliated. Even if Dennis had been honest that he truly liked Lou, it would have gotten out if she'd gone to prom with him.

If she'd slept with him…

"Will do," he promised. "No more sweethearts. Only LouLous."

Her nose wrinkled into the cutest expression. "Weirdo. I'm going to be late. See you at lunch."

"Wouldn't miss it." He watched as she walked away.

It was better this way. This was how it had to be.

* * * *

"I just…I thought he liked me." Lou took the tissue Kenzie offered her.

She'd been crying all day over that jerk face. At least in the privacy of her own room, she could let it rip.

This was what she got for being full of herself. She'd eagerly accepted Dennis's invite to the prom because it meant TJ wouldn't have to step up and offer to be her date. That had been in the works, or so she'd heard. It had been a relief when Dennis had asked her. Everyone would know she and TJ were going as friends. And everyone would know that wasn't what she wanted.

She was pathetic. She wasn't really crying over stupid Dennis.

She was crying over TJ. Always, always TJ. Theo Taggart, Jr.

She'd met him and suddenly understood why girls went crazy for boys. Though she'd only ever truly wanted TJ. She'd thought if she spent time with Dennis, maybe her heart could change.

Kenzie settled in beside her. "Do you want Kala to kill him?"

"Already offered." Kala sat on her other side.

Lou sniffled. She'd been positively energized this morning thinking about the fact that she had a date. Maybe this would prove to her that she wasn't forever cursed to love a boy who couldn't love her back.

And then Dennis had stopped her after trig and explained that he'd forgotten he'd promised to take someone else to prom and crap, he felt bad, but them's the breaks. Or something like that. It had been fast and he'd practically run away from her, leaving her standing in the middle of the hall with tears in her eyes.

"I think he found someone he wanted to go with more than me." It was hard to be the youngest person in her class. She'd only legally been able to drive the second half of her senior year. Not that she hadn't practiced. TJ let her use his car so she could get some time behind the wheel. He would take her and his sister, Devi, out of the city and patiently teach them.

Her mom got too nervous. Her dad often fell asleep because he was the chillest human on earth.

TJ was a close second. She'd never told him how comfortable she was with him, how the energy he gave off calmed her. TJ was solid. Like her dad.

TJ could calm her down when she got wound up. He brought her out of her head when she thought too much. She enjoyed who she was when she was around TJ.

But while TJ was perfect for her, she wasn't the right one for him.

"I could kill her, too," Kala replied. "Just have to find out who she is and the hit will be in."

"We're not killing anyone," Kenzie said, sitting up straighter.

Lou blessed the day these two came into her life. She'd been twelve when the older girls had taken her under their wings, and Lou had friends for the first time. Kala especially, but Kenzie had been there for her, too. When her mother had married Boomer Ward, she'd become a part of this big found family. Boomer worked with the twins' parents at their company McKay-Taggart. It was more than a workplace. Suddenly Lou found herself accepted by some of the coolest kids she'd ever met.

They weren't weirdos like everyone said. Sometimes she caught people whispering about how Kala would be the person most likely to go to jail.

Kala would never go to jail. She would totally get away with all her crimes. And if she didn't, Lou would break her out.

"But we do need to think about a new date for Lou," Kenzie mused and looked over at her sister. "Are you still boycotting?"

"I wish you all the best, sis. Have your magical night," Kala said, letting her head fall back. "It's a hard pass from me."

Kenzie stared her sister's way. "You're going to let Cooper go with someone else?"

Her eyes closed. "I don't own him. If he wants to participate in some dumb ritual, he's free to."

"It's not a dumb ritual, and I'm participating with the man I'm going to marry," Kenzie announced. "We're making memories."

That got Kala snorting. "Yeah. You're going to end up with dumbass Dalton Bernard."

Kenzie seemed to think about that for a moment. "Well, I like him for now. I only say it because I'm pretty sure Dad has a minor heart attack at the thought of me marrying someone named Dalton. It keeps his mind off what I want to do after college."

Join the CIA. That was what they wanted. And Kala had promised that one day there would be a place on that team for her.

Everyone seemed to think she would end up a professor somewhere. How surprised would they be when she followed her best friend all the way to the Agency? Everyone seemed to think she was some sweet, brainy girl who could do no wrong. Kala's mom often talked about what a good influence Lou was on her girls.

Would Charlotte Taggart be surprised to know that she'd been the one to figure out how to remotely set off the fire alarms so Kala wouldn't have to spend all day in detention? She'd set those fuckers off one after another until they'd released all the detention kids, and Kenzie and Lou had picked up Kala and spent the afternoon at the mall.

The school had a smart system. Lou loved smart systems

because she was almost always smarter.

"So are we going to strong-arm TJ into taking you?" Kenzie asked.

That sent her stomach in a spiral. "I already told him no."

Kala's eyes opened, and she and Kenzie were suddenly both looking her way. "What?"

Like she couldn't tell TJ no. Well, she never had before. "He caught me crying at lunch, and I told him what happened. He offered to take me, but everyone would know he was doing it as a pity date. I'm fine. I don't need to go to prom. I'll keep Kala company."

"It's not a pity date," Kenzie insisted.

"TJ's a moron, but I do believe he cares about you," Kala said. "If he asked you, it's because he wanted to. Look, I don't think any of us needs to find true love at this point. We're too young and we have things to do, but I do realize that Lou's feelings for TJ haven't changed since the day she met him."

"His feelings haven't changed either," Lou pointed out, sorrow welling.

They were friends. He'd never felt more for her. He'd been gentle with her when she'd professed her love last year out at the lake house. Kala had snuck some beers down to their campsite, and Lou had learned she was a lightweight.

This isn't a good idea, baby. I don't think we make sense as a couple.

Of course they didn't. He was gorgeous and athletic, and she was…smart. Yeah. Guys loved that about her.

"I don't think he understands his feelings." Kala sat up, groaning. "You handle this part, sis. I'm going to vomit if I have to keep going."

Her bestie wasn't a feels girl.

Kenzie was. Her strawberry blonde hair was in a ponytail, giving her Malibu Barbie vibe's as she leaned in. "What Kala is trying to say is TJ might be scared of what he feels for you."

TJ wasn't scared of anything. TJ knew exactly who he was and what he wanted to do with his life. He was going in the Army with the plan to make Special Forces as soon as possible. He would find a hot wife and settle into being the hero he was.

She would be his kids' weird aunt.

"I think TJ is worried he's not enough for you," Kenzie continued.

That was where she was wrong. "I've told him he is."

Kala's brow rose. "You did? I was not aware of this."

Lou sighed. "Last summer I made my play for him, and he turned me down. He said he couldn't see us as a couple because we were so different, but if that was true we wouldn't work as friends. We're amazing friends, so I don't get what he was saying."

Kenzie and Kala were staring at each other, doing that silent communication thing they so often did. Lou would swear they could communicate through a series of small facial expressions.

Lou needed to make herself plain or Kala might decide to find a way to force TJ to love her. "He's not attracted to me. It's the only explanation."

"It's not the only one," Kenzie countered.

"No, but it's the most logical." Kala's face settled into a frown.

"I thought it was because he wanted to go into the Army and Lou's going to Massachusetts," Kenzie said.

"But if she just laid it out and he said he couldn't see them as a couple? That's fucking bullshit." Kala stood and started to pace. "He said that? Said those words?"

And this was why she hadn't mentioned it. "Yes, but don't get mad at him. I'm not. He likes me, but it can't work because he doesn't find me attractive. He's…I mean, he's TJ. There's a reason every girl in school wants to be around him."

TJ dated a lot, but he never stayed with one for long.

Logic stated that TJ was never going to love her. They could be friends again, but maybe she needed the time. Maybe it was a good thing she was going away.

"He's an asshole if he can't see how amazing you are, Lou," Kala said.

But he wasn't. He was kind to her. He'd protected her like she was his own sister. He was good to everyone, and when he walked into a room, he brought along sunshine. He was goofy and sweet, and she loved him.

"It's okay. I don't want you to be mad at TJ. He's your cousin."

"Yeah, well, you're my sister." Kala slumped down beside her,

her head dropping so it was on Lou's shoulder. "I hate that you're hurt, and right now it feels more like TJ hurt you than that fucker Dennis."

TJ didn't mean to hurt her. "I wish all the best for him. So we're going to pretend like I didn't tell you and life will move on. I will not be attending the prom. I will be staying home and watching movies and eating pizza. Want to join?"

"Well, now that sounds like fun," Kenzie said with a frown.

"You have a dress and everything," Kala shot back. "Like Lou, I made my play a couple of months ago at another dance and I'm done. I don't care what they say. This is not the best time of my life. It's not. But it's coming."

There was a knock on the door, and then her dad stuck his head in. "Hey, sweetie, I brought some snacks."

Her dad always brought snacks. She sniffled and sat up. "Thanks."

Her dad was a big blond hunk of man who looked like he should be on a muscle magazine rather than carting around a teen girl charcuterie complete with string cheese and grapes and Slim Jim's. Her dad was six foot seven inches of pure muscle, though his badass look was always tempered by some dog at his side. There were two following him around now. He was fostering one super-sweet but mangy looking mutt who kind of cowered behind him, and the other was a creaky old Chihuahua Lou treated like a baby half the time. Her father loved animals, as evidenced by the four goats, two horses, and multitudinous chickens on their property. And then there was the sleeping baby on her dad's chest. Her baby brother. Jayce.

She was so happy for her mom, so happy she'd found someone who could love her, who deserved her.

He sat the big board down, and there was a deep crease between his brows he only got when he was worried. His hand went up to the sling he had around his torso. Since Jayce had been born, her dad had taken to carrying him around most of the time.

"What can I do?" her dad asked. He looked to Kala.

"Already offered. I'm not allowed to murder anyone," Kala said with a sigh. "But I am allowed to hang with her that night. How about you make some of your pizzas for us, Uncle B?"

Despite the fact that there wasn't an ounce of blood between them, Kala had grown up calling Boomer Ward uncle. Like Lou called Kala's dad Uncle Ian.

Was it so surprising that a guy like TJ viewed her as a sister?

"Anything you girls want," her dad promised.

There was only one thing she really wanted, and she wasn't going to get it. Did she have to give him up entirely? Could she not have the man she loved in her life even if he couldn't love her back? She managed a smile. "Thanks, Dad."

She settled back as Kenzie started talking about something going on with her friends.

Kala's hand found hers, squeezing.

She was good. Dennis would mean nothing to her in a couple of weeks, and she would move on with her life.

Kala was right. They had a plan, and that was what she would focus on.

Not TJ.

Chapter One

Dallas, TX
Twelve Years Later

Lou stared at the man across from her. "I'm going to be honest. When we matched on the app, I didn't think it was actually you."

The man across from her smiled, and she had to admit he looked good. He'd been a cute boy in high school, but he was obviously a man now, his lanky form having filled in with muscle. And the beard on his face suited him, too. "Well, I knew damn well it was you, and I was excited. It's been a long time, Louisa. You look amazing."

Dennis Sims wore a dress shirt and slacks despite the fact they'd only agreed to meet for a coffee. It was obvious he'd taken care with his appearance.

The last time TJ had been in town he'd spent the entire time sitting in her living room in sweats and a Cowboys T-shirt playing video games with her. He'd needed a haircut but hadn't been willing to get it until the day before he reported back, so he'd looked a bit scruffy.

She'd still thought he was sexy as hell, but she was done mooning over that man. They seemed to have moved into a long-term married couple phase without any of the sex that should have come before it. He came into town on leave and spent all his time with her. He didn't even bother to drop his stuff at his parents' place. He showed up and took over the guest room. He worked around her house, fixing things up, and they watched TV together and he hugged her like he didn't want to let her go and then marched back on with his life. Years. She'd spent years like this, and she was done.

She remembered the last time she'd seen TJ. They'd been in a conference room in Sydney, Australia. His team had clashed with hers, and they'd had some serious tension between them. She'd been stupid and had read his cues wrong and embarrassed herself again by trying to kiss him.

Baby, this is still not a good idea. Nothing's changed.

But she wanted it to, and if she didn't try her life never would. She would watch her friends all find love, and she would end up alone with five cats. And probably a couple of dogs and goats. So when he'd tried to get her alone to talk about their tension, she'd told him no.

Don't think this is over, LouLou. Not even close.

But it was. It had to be.

Watching Tasha Taggart fall in love had given her the push she needed.

Hence the dating app. She'd been on three dates and then matched with Dennis, and curiosity had gotten the better of her. Not that she was going to do anything with the dude who'd dumped her for prom, but she was curious. She was viewing this as a good test date.

Surely at some point she'd meet someone she wanted to have sex with.

Or she could find a Dom at The Hideout.

"What are you doing these days?" Dennis asked. "I was surprised you were still here in Dallas. When I've thought about you over the years, I have to admit I saw you in New York or LA. London, maybe. You got your doctorate, right?"

She'd finished her doctorate in mathematics at the age of twenty-two and become one of the youngest professors in the history of the University of Texas Austin. Then Kala Taggart had walked into her office and offered her a spot on the team.

The CIA team her best friend had been trying to land forever. The last two years of her life had been about the Agency.

Not that she was going to tell Dennis that. Her life was highly classified. "No, that was fine for college, but I always wanted to be close to my family. My parents are here, and my little brother. He's twelve, and I don't want to be some picture on my parents' wall to him. So I'm working at this think tank run by the guy who built 4L."

"You work for Drew Lawless?" Dennis looked impressed.

Which was exactly what her cover was supposed to do. When she'd joined the team, they'd all needed covers, with the exception of Cooper McKay and Tristan Dean-Miles. They had the military to cover for them. Lou, Kenzie, Kala, and Tash had never belonged to the armed forces. But they did belong to McKay-Taggart. Kenzie and Kala and Tash all worked for their dad's firm in various roles. Lou needed something more. There wasn't a position for doctorate in mathematics and expert in mechanical and computer engineering at a security firm. It was a cover that worked on short ops—like the one they'd recently run in Sydney—but anyone who knew her would question it.

No one was shocked to discover she was the head of technology, research, and development at one of the edgiest think tanks in the country. Especially given her family connections to the man who ran it.

It came with a good salary—way better than the Agency—and a spectacular lab where she created tech to help her "sisters" save the world. All in all, not a bad gig.

"I do, though he's not around a lot. I've only met him a couple of times. His wife and kids seem nice." Andrew Lawless was connected to the Taggarts by marriage. His sister had married Case Taggart a long time before, and the billionaire hadn't minded stepping in to help out Ian Taggart's Agency team. Especially since he got first dibs on a lot of Lou's work. "His main focus is 4L. He kind of lets us do what we want."

Dennis's head shook as though he'd known it all along. "Wow. I knew you would go places. You were so smart."

Not smart enough to go to prom with though. Still, he was feeding her ego. She knew she shouldn't take the compliments seriously, but it felt good to have a man looking at her like he wanted to date her. "How about you?"

"I'm in banking. I work in investments," he replied. "I work for a billionaire, too, but mine is some old dude on a board somewhere. Not as cool a job as yours." He seemed to get serious, taking a sip of the Americano he'd ordered. "I'm glad you said yes, Lou. There's something I've wanted to say to you for a long time."

Even though she hadn't thought about him in forever, the rejection still hurt. "Is it about prom?"

He nodded slowly, as though he wanted to think about every word he was about to say. "I was a jerk in high school, and I would like to apologize to you."

She nodded. "You're forgiven. It was a long time ago."

His head shook, and a look of deep regret came over his face. "You don't know what you're forgiving me for. That shouldn't surprise me. You were always such a sweet girl. You never could see… That doesn't matter. Louisa, I made a stupid bet about you back in high school, and I regret it. I regretted it right after I did it. It was locker-room talk, and I wouldn't have gone through with it. I kind of asked you out on a bet, and then I realized how much I liked you. I need you to understand that I am not that dumbass kid anymore, and I would kick my own kid's ass if he ever did anything like this. Not that I have any kids. I'm single and child free at this point. But I wouldn't want my kid to ever act that way."

"A bet?" She frowned his way. "Tell me you didn't bet you could get me to sleep with you on prom night. Because that would be cliché and gross."

He winced. "Like I said, I wasn't going through with it."

She had to laugh. "Okay, well, I'm glad that you didn't because then I would have let Kala murder you."

"Oh, she threatened it, but then she had some crap on me that I didn't want anyone else to know and between her and that fuc…TJ, it became clear that I wasn't going to be able to explain anything to you."

"What did she do?" She wasn't angry. Curious. It was a day for curiosity. She understood exactly what Kala had been doing. She'd seen something that would have hurt her best friend, and she took care of it. Sometimes she thought Kala would have done well on her mother's side of the family. The one that ran a syndicate in Moscow.

"She blackmailed me. Which on the surface is bad enough, but then I found out the reason she had shit to blackmail me with..."

Lou could finish that sentence. "She baited you and then used it against you. It's classic Kala. And I'm kind of glad I didn't know people were betting on my virginity then. Today I can roll my eyes and not care, but I think it would have hurt then. I would have felt everyone laughing at me."

"No one laughed at you, Lou."

"Oh, they did." It hadn't been easy always being years younger than the people in her class. Maybe that was why she'd been so drawn to TJ. He'd looked at her, talked to her, included her in things. Made her feel special. "I assure you there were girls who laughed at how awkward I was and boys who thought it was fun to fuck with me. Until Kala explained what she would do to them if they didn't leave me alone."

"No," he corrected, "that was TJ. She might have talked to the girls, but I assure you it was TJ who threatened to beat the shit out of anyone who looked at you sideways. Sometimes I think I took that bet just to have a reason to go after you. I could say I was standing up to a bully."

She stared at him.

"Yeah, now that sounds dumb," he admitted, "but you know things look different from the outside. It always felt like TJ was protecting you from everyone when most of us only wanted to know you. Maybe not when we were freshmen, but by the time we were seniors, everyone was kind of in awe of you. And terrified of the twins. I know Kenzie seemed sweet, but she could throw down when she wanted to."

She still could. It was funny how everyone underestimated Kenz. It was something she used to perfection in their job.

"I'm kind of glad I never have to see them again," Dennis continued. "Do you know whatever happened to them?"

"Yes, they work for their dad," Lou replied. And run dangerous missions on the regular. They were part of Lou's team. Her family.

But more and more she was realizing the friendships she had weren't enough. She wanted what her mom had with her dad. What Uncle Ian and Aunt Charlotte had. What Tasha and Dare had so recently found.

"I heard he was a psycho, too, so I'm not surprised."

And she wasn't going to find anything special here. "Well, Dennis, it was good to see you. I should get back to the office."

He winced. "You're still friends with them."

"The best of," she replied.

"I'm sorry. I suppose it still stings," he said, "and before you point out what I did would have stung like hell if you'd known, I'm truly sorry, and I don't want you to go. I won't say anything else. I'm sure they've changed since high school. We all have."

Adulthood had refined Kala's personality. And she had access to way more weapons now.

"Hey, how is your dad?" he asked. "I remember how cool he was."

Dennis had met her father a handful of times and they'd gotten along, but then Boomer Ward got along with everyone. Still, she had to admit Kala did piss a lot of people off. If she refused to talk to anyone her bestie had bulldozed at some point, life would be a very quiet place.

The real question was why TJ had threatened him. She understood Kala, but she remembered how TJ had acted that day. Which made her wonder. "He's good. He's volunteering with a bunch of animal rescues, and I'm pretty sure he's why my brother wants to be a vet. When did this thing go down with Kala? The one where she blackmailed you. You don't have to tell me what it was. I'm sure she caught you cheating on an exam."

Kala liked having intel on people she viewed as potential enemies, and that was the majority of the population. The thing was she never used that to her own betterment. Only her friends. Sometimes Lou wondered if Kala buried herself in her sisters and friends so she didn't have to look in the mirror and acknowledge Cooper McKay was the love of her life.

"That morning before first period."

Then it had to have been before she'd run into TJ and made that dumb joke about him not calling her sweetheart. He'd known, and he'd let her walk into it.

And then he'd gallantly offered to take her instead.

Kala had probably strongarmed him into that.

She hated this feeling. "That tracks. I kind of still wish I didn't know."

"That I was an asshole? Sometimes I wish they'd told you because I think I could live with being the guy who made you angry. It's been really hard being the guy who broke your heart. I didn't go with anyone. I skipped because I didn't want to walk into that hotel ballroom and see you with TJ."

"I didn't go with him."

"No, you stayed home with Kala. They kept you to themselves. I would bet they still do. I meet with an old group of friends for drinks once a month. We've talked about you a lot. You could come next time. You'll see there were a lot of people who looked up to you."

But she'd had everyone she'd needed back then. Did she have them now? It was such an odd feeling to know what she wanted was right there but never be able to reach out for it, to take it for herself. She had to admit that if TJ was her actual boyfriend, she wouldn't need anyone outside of her circle, but here she was. She had friends who felt like family, and not one of them could give her the love she knew she needed. So it was time to expand. "That could be fun."

His smile kicked up. Yeah, there was a reason she'd said yes to him all those years before, and it hadn't all been about the fact that someone, anyone, asked her out. When he wasn't a high school boy jerk, he was quite charming. "So you are not with TJ? Like with with him. I don't care if you're his friend. I can handle that now. But I don't want to step on his toes either."

"TJ and I have never been together that way. He's in the Army, and I only see him from time to time." She would see him less now that they were in a fight. He hadn't called in weeks. He'd probably found a girlfriend. Well, that wasn't the word she should use. He'd found a sub to top for a while. He tended to go silent for weeks at a time and then she'd hear a rumor he'd been playing. He never acknowledged it to her, never mentioned it and never brought one home, but she knew. When he was at The Hideout he always took dungeon monitor duties and watched anyone she played with closely. He could be a dick about it.

But she knew there were nights at a place called The Club.

There was only the tiniest ounce of her that kind of wanted to see what TJ would think of her dating Dennis. But only a little. It was time to end this somewhat toxic cycle in her life. "But I should tell you I don't know anything could work out between us. I would like to see some of the people from high school, but…"

"You want to go as friends," he finished for her.

"I wouldn't say we're friends," she corrected.

"Not yet." He sat back and looked her over. "I meant what I said, Lou. I liked you then. I like you now. I agree to all your terms. Come with me, and we'll see what can happen when TJ Taggart doesn't come between us."

"Lou, I need to talk to you."

She turned, surprised because she knew that voice. Zach Reed was standing right there in the middle of the coffee shop. Zach shouldn't be here at all. He should be at CIA headquarters. Zach was the team's military liaison, and when they weren't working, he went back to DC where he coordinated with other teams as well. So why was he here? "Zach? How the hell did you…"

"It's work," he said with a grim twist of his lips.

Of course. She grabbed her bag and shot Dennis an apologetic look. "Sorry. Work calls. Something must have broken down. But I will join you at the drinks reunion thing."

"That would be great. I'll text you, and maybe next time we can have lunch," he offered. "It was good to see you."

"We should hurry, Lou," Zach said. "It's about the LT Project. It's in trouble."

A shiver went down her spine. It was an old joke between their parents and TJ. They still sometimes called him the littlest Tag, though he certainly wasn't. That was how they often referred to him when they spoke in code. He was LT. TJ hated it, which was probably why the twins loved it.

TJ was in trouble?

What if he hadn't found a woman and gone dark for a few weeks? What if something had gone wrong on a mission?

What if someone was after him?

She ran out, following Zach and completely forgetting about Dennis.

It looked like things weren't over between her and TJ. Not yet.

* * * *

Somewhere in Germany

In his dreams, things went differently. It was weird. TJ knew he was dreaming, knew his body was hanging by chains waiting for the next brutal assault, but in his head he was in a completely different place. A place where the pain couldn't touch him.

With her.

He walked into one of the smaller rooms at The Station, the BDSM club in Sydney where his unit had collided with Lou's. Somewhere in the club there was a pissed-off Canadian operative, and he rather thought Tash had some serious explaining to do to the dark-haired dude she seemed to have some connection with, but none of that mattered.

Lou was here, and she'd thrown herself in his arms when he'd called for her, and all was right with the world.

She turned, looking up from her laptop and smiling. "Hey, is everyone still alive? It looked like it was getting pretty heated down there."

That was what happened when the left hand didn't know what the right one was up to, but that was the Agency for you. He would rather be working for Lou's team, but he was still a grunt for the most part.

He moved in and hugged her, unable to keep his hands off her. He shouldn't have been able to see her for another couple of months, but here she was. He fucking hated that she worked for the Agency, but at least she was safely behind a computer. She wasn't a field operative, at the whims of bosses who wouldn't care if she lived or died as long as the mission got completed. She was the brains of the team, and they wouldn't let her do anything dangerous.

The minute she was in his arms it was like the world slowed down and made more sense.

She settled her head against his chest. "It's all fucked up. I don't know what Tash is going to do. She's in love with him."

With her target? That wasn't a smart thing, but then he'd been in love with a woman he couldn't have for a long time. "Something tells me my aunt and uncle are already working their magic. Are you okay? Did we scare you?"

"Well, I was scared Kala was going to kill someone. I think she took down two of your men, and Coop got a couple, too. Tristan was up with me, helping me get the lights back on and trying to figure a way out."

No, Tristan had stayed to protect her, and that was exactly what he should have done. "It's all okay now. Uncle Ian will take over, and Chet can suck a dick, for all I care."

"Isn't he your boss right now?"

"Nope, that's that asshole Mike. Chet is nothing more than an Agency hack, and he'll loathe the fact that my uncle will insist on me sitting in on the meeting we're about to have. But I don't care. It means I get to be near you. I missed you."

"Missed you, too." Her head tilted up, those big brown eyes kicking him right in the gut. She was the most beautiful woman he'd ever seen, and it kind of turned his stomach to think he'd ever been with anyone but her.

He'd never been with her. He couldn't trust himself not to fuck it all up.

He stared at her for a long moment, the air between them heating with unnamed emotion, and that was when she went up on her toes and her lips almost met his.

This. This was the part he didn't want.

Fuck it all. It was his dream, and when he woke up he would have to deal with the fact that a mercenary thought he was good target practice for his cattle prod.

In the dream, he met her lips halfway. In the dream, he didn't let his fear rule him. In the dream, he became everything she needed.

Her loving Master.

Having to watch her with his friends nearly killed him, even when he knew there wasn't anything sexual about it. That wasn't the way it would be between them. He wasn't going to spank her and tie her up and leave her aftercare to Kala Taggart. Fuck, no.

He was going to spank that sweet ass, tie her up, and fuck her until neither one of them could see straight. He would keep her in a privacy room until the club closed, and then he would bring her out and they would have the whole place to themselves. Eventually he would let her run around in her own sweet skin, everyone's eyes on her so she knew how gorgeous she was, but it would take him a while. He was possessive when it came to Lou.

In the dream he didn't step back and shake his head. He didn't say, "Baby, this is still not a good idea. Nothing's changed."

He kissed her, his hands cupping her cheeks and sliding into her hair so he could twist it and deepen the kiss, moving his tongue inside her mouth. Hers reached out, tentative at first, and then dancing against his own. He could feel his cock swell, lengthen, getting ready for that moment when he finally, finally found some fucking relief.

Pain made him shudder, and in the dream he dropped his hands, losing Lou. She looked at him, tears in her eyes.

The way she had that night.

"Who is The Jester?"

He didn't want this. He wanted Lou. He tried so hard to hold on to the dream, but pain flared again, this time to his back.

"Sergeant Taggart, I have to insist. Who is the arms dealer known as The Jester?" a heavily accented voice asked.

TJ groaned as he forced his eyes open. They'd mostly beaten his torso, so he still had full range of vision. Woohoo. That meant he could see the tall, lean man who was torturing him.

What he couldn't see was the man asking the questions. He managed to stay out of sight. He was a dark, deep voice constantly asking one thing.

Who is The Jester?

This was the part where if he was in a movie, he would start in with name, rank, and serial number.

Instead, he did what he was now trained to do by the Agency. Which was talk and play as dumb as he possibly could. "Jester? Like in medieval times?"

It wasn't hard since he knew very little. All he knew was that twenty-four hours ago he'd been hanging with some friends in a bar in a town outside of the Ramstein Air Base in Germany, waiting to catch a ride back to the States. He'd spent weeks debriefing after the clusterfuck situation in Australia had left his team without a CO. One minute he'd been drinking a beer and the next he'd woken up god only knew where and this fucker was treating him like a punching bag.

He'd been roofied, and his cousins would never let him hear the end of it.

"The Jester is a new player in my world, and I would like an introduction," the German who he couldn't see explained. "But you know that very well."

Oh, they were under several misconceptions. "I know absolutely nothing. I am dumb as dirt when it comes to this."

And he'd been dumb as dirt when it came to Lou. God, now he could see it so clearly. He should have kissed her that day.

Being close to death brought life into sharp focus, and his meant nothing without Louisa Ward.

"I don't think so, Sergeant Taggart."

TJ's gut twisted. They knew exactly who he was, and he'd been targeted. But he couldn't figure out why. Yes, he often worked with Agency teams, but he wasn't a spy himself. He was the Special Forces version of a grunt. Oftentimes he barely knew why they were doing what they were doing. "I don't know what you're talking about, man."

There was the sound of a throat clearing, and then pain bloomed over every inch of his skin as his captor lit him up.

He was never again going to make fun of that chick at The Hideout who liked a Dom to tase her pink parts. That woman was tough. She might be a goddamn national treasure when it came to having a high pain threshold. He needed to talk to her about getting on one of the teams because if she'd been here, she would smile and ask for another.

He just wanted to see Lou again.

Although not getting hit with the prod came in a close second.

Something was going on. Something he didn't understand, and he had to figure out what these assholes wanted because he wasn't going to die here. Wherever here was.

His shoulders ached, and his hands had long gone numb from holding his whole body weight.

Why would they think he knew some dude on the Internet who called himself The Jester? Or that he would know what "business" his captor was in.

"Sergeant Taggart, I can do this all day." The guy's English was good, but his accent was German and thick. "All week, even. No one knows where you are. I've used your phone to send some texts to your fellow team members letting them know you're taking the week off to spend some time with a woman you met at the bar. My team, you see, is good at crafting a fiction when they need to. We sent pictures as well. No one is going to look for you, so you might as well tell us what we want to know."

"I would if I had any idea what you're talking about."

There was the sound of murmuring, and that was the moment TJ realized there were at least three people in the room. The torture fucker, the one who spoke, and apparently someone who didn't want TJ to hear his voice.

The actual boss.

He twisted his head around, trying to see into the shadows, but the light was so bright.

"All right, perhaps you might…remember…more if I let you know how much we know. The Jester is what we call, in our line of business, an information broker. I assume you know what that is since in addition to your work for the Army, your team often backs up the CIA."

He knew exactly what an information broker was. His aunts used to be the best in the business. Chelsea and Charlotte Denisovitch had made a name for themselves selling secrets. But they didn't anymore.

TJ had to consider the fact that he might know more than he thought he knew. His family still had ties to the Denisovitch Syndicate, though he'd never actually met any of them.

"I work on classified missions, but that doesn't mean I understand the ins and outs of them. They tell me who to shoot and I do it. That's all I am. You've got the wrong guy."

"Oh, we don't think so. We happen to know that you met with The Jester a mere month ago, and lying about it won't help you." There was the sound of fingers snapping and then his torturer moved briefly into the shadows, coming back with a tablet in his hands. He held the screen up.

It was a grainy picture of two men walking down a European-looking street.

But it was clear from the photo that one of the men was him.

The other man's face was concealed by the heavy hood of his jacket.

"This is you walking with a man we've identified as The Jester. You were in Berlin, meeting him six weeks ago."

Six weeks ago he had been in Berlin, but this meeting hadn't happened. "I was in debriefs the entire time I was in Berlin. This is a deep fake."

"I don't believe it is. I believe you are protecting your real boss, but that will only buy you pain."

"I didn't meet with anyone except my team in Berlin." And shortly after, the team had been called to Australia to babysit a Canadian operative. The mission that led to his CO getting offed by his cousin.

"All right, Sergeant. It seems you need other motivation. It is unfortunate, but a reality we are prepared for. We will secure it and speak again. Enjoy the accommodations in the meantime," the voice said. "Klaus, dose the sergeant and secure him in his cell. We'll decide between his mother or sister. He can watch us use them, and then we'll see who he values."

"Please not my mom. My mom… Don't hurt my mom." His mother would kill these fuckers if they touched her. She'd been a deadly soldier most of her life, and he would still put her up against most of his teammates to this day. But Devi… His sister wasn't as well trained. She knew some self-defense, but Devi would get hurt.

"Or perhaps the little mouse you hang out with when you're home. What was her name?" There was a whisper. "Oh, yes, Louisa. She works for a think tank. She might be an extra prize herself."

Fuck. Not Lou. He couldn't be the reason Lou got hurt.

He kicked out, his mind going red at the thought of Lou in these bastards' hands.

Then he felt the prick of a needle against his bicep, and the world went dark.

Chapter Two

Lou hustled into the conference room at the McKay-Taggart building. It was usually empty on a Sunday, but the conference room held the twins and Cooper McKay.

It was Cooper who looked up bleary eyed as she strode through the glass doors with Zach.

"There better be a good reason I'm here on my day off," Coop said, yawning behind his hand.

"He's grumpy because play at The Hideout last night went into overtime," Kala said with a smirk. "I told you that beam wasn't going to hold that rigging."

She'd skipped her regular Saturday hangout at the BDSM club her friends ran in favor of sitting at home with Bud 2 and watching old reruns of *Mission Impossible*. The sixties version. She'd been up and out of the house before the twins had woken up. But she didn't have time for a rundown. "TJ is in trouble."

That got everyone sitting up straight.

"What do you mean? I texted with him a couple of days ago," Kenzie said. "He was hanging out at Ramstein. He had a lot of paperwork to do after his CO got whacked. He blamed Kala, despite the fact that we kept her murdering him out of the official reports, but he knows her pretty well."

"The dude was going to kill my sister. I would have fucked up Chet, too, if he hadn't cried like a baby," Kala said under her breath.

Chet Whittington had been a CIA operative who'd gone bad, and TJ's CO had been in on it with him. They were both dead now, and she'd taken some comfort in it since Chet had openly declared he was at war with the Taggarts.

"What did you text him about?" Zach sat down at the head of the table where he'd placed his laptop. He flipped it open and started typing.

"About him coming home," Kenz explained. She bit her bottom lip. "He had a couple of questions."

Lou could bet on what those questions were. "Did he want to know if I was still mad?"

Kenzie sighed. "Yes. He wanted to know how to talk to you. He feels bad."

"He should," Kala declared. "He's been fucking up Lou's life for more than a decade now."

She wasn't here to talk about her love life or lack of one. "It doesn't matter. What does matter is the fact that until twenty-four hours ago, TJ had been planning to come home for a couple of weeks. Cooper, did TJ text you?"

There was something about the tight set of Coop's jaw that let Lou know he was hiding something. He'd been completely relaxed until he'd seen her. It wasn't the first time Coop had felt bad for her about something TJ had done.

Cooper sat back. "TJ is fine. He just changed his mind about coming home."

A brow rose over Zach's eyes. He was slightly older than the rest of them. At twenty-nine, Zach was the team's Army advisor. He was in charge when it came to the military teams they used as backup, but they all looked to Zach when it came to the physical aspects of a mission. "Did he send you pictures?"

Coop unlocked his phone. "Yeah. Does Lou need to see this?"

"Yes, Lou needs to see this." She reached out and looked down at the screen. There was TJ, smiling next to a gorgeous blonde. They were at some swanky ski resort looking cozy and all coupled up.

Change of plans, brother. I'm going to hole up with this cutie for a couple of weeks. See you soon.

That picture made her ache, but she pushed the feeling aside. "And you think this is real?"

Cooper frowned. "Why wouldn't it be real?"

"Because it's Devi's birthday in a week. When was the last time TJ missed his sister's birthday for anything other than work?" She stared at the picture. It looked real, but reality wasn't what it used to be.

"I've got the same picture and almost the same text," Zach said, turning his laptop toward her. "Have a look."

"TJ wouldn't miss Devi's party." Kala was sitting up now. She pulled her cell, putting it to her ear after sliding it open and pressing the screen. "Has anyone actually talked to him? Not text."

Lou was staring at that picture, trying to find the holes. There were always holes.

In the picture they sat on a big sofa, TJ's arm around the blonde's shoulders and her legs crossed over his. Where was it taken? She opened a piece of software she'd developed with Tristan Dean-Miles and imported the picture, setting the program into motion.

It scoured the Internet and social media for similar pictures, looking for anything that could ID a position. It would take into account the sofa itself, the placement of the big windows behind the happy couple.

"I haven't talked to him, but we usually text," Cooper admitted.

"Did anyone call Tris?" Kenzie asked.

"Tristan is not reachable at this time," Zach said. "And you know I can't talk about it."

Tristan hadn't returned to the States with them after the Australian op, but that had felt normal. At least of late. When they'd first started working together as a team, Tristan had taken every opportunity to come home and spend time with his long-time girlfriend, Carys Taggart, and best friend Aidan O'Donnell. They'd been a trio since they were kids, and when they'd hit high school, they'd openly dated. All three of them. Tristan and Aidan had decided not to fight over the girl they both loved.

And then something had happened. Tristan had withdrawn. He

was working on a project, and he claimed he couldn't share it with the team.

Something dangerous. She worried about Tristan, but she knew she could get him in serious trouble if she started trying to solve that mystery. The Agency was using him and his unique skills for some kind of long-term mission.

She hoped it didn't cost him the love of his life.

"We don't need to bother Tris," Lou said as the program narrowed it down to three different possible locations where the picture itself had been taken. She took those results and started another, more detailed search before loading the pic into a program she'd designed to find even the best of photographic manipulations. "I can take this thing apart in a couple of minutes. And don't call Tasha. She's with Dare and her mom looking at condos."

"I'm going to miss my sister, but I will not miss how loud those two are. They go at it hard." Kala stood and walked around to move in next to Lou.

She'd lived with Tasha, Kala, and Kenzie in a four-bedroom house they rented in the suburbs not too far from Ian and Charlotte Taggart since she'd left her job in Austin. They also had a small apartment in DC they shared when they were called into the office, so to speak. She would miss Tash, but it would be nice to have more space.

And they *were* loud.

"What have you got?" Kala asked.

A notice popped up, and Lou had her answer. "It's been manipulated. It's not even Germany. Look. The program found the original photograph on a social media site. It's from someone named Annie Jackson. She posted it four years ago while she was on her honeymoon in Aspen with her husband, who is roughly the same size and body shape and skin tone of one Theodore Taggart Jr."

Her tone was even. Like she was working any case. But her heart was beating in her chest. Someone had TJ. Someone had taken TJ, and they were doing a halfway decent job of covering their tracks.

"Yes, I need to activate a tracker." Kenzie had her phone to her ear. "My ID number is…" Her voice trailed off as she walked out of the conference room.

"If they're good at all they'll have pulled his tracker. If they know he's Special Forces, they'll look for one," Zach said, sitting back. "All right. So they've tried to cover his kidnapping. That means they want time with him. What would TJ know?"

"He's been on over sixty highly classified missions. It could be anything," Cooper said. "He's worked with a bunch of different agents over six continents. I can go over his mission briefs if you get me the clearance."

"I'll call Drake." Zach pulled his cell. "Coop, I want you to reply to him. Something douchey like *get in there, brother.* I don't know. Whatever a frat bro would text, that's what you should do. I'll do the same after I talk to Drake."

Drake Radcliffe was their Agency liaison, and he could get them into any files they needed.

"Hey, we're going to find him." Kala put a hand on her arm.

Who would want TJ? Yes, he'd worked on a lot of covert ops, but he wouldn't have the information his Agency handlers did. Of course, if they knew his friends were Agency, they wouldn't have tried to throw them off with simple texts and pictures.

Kenzie walked back in, a grim look telling them what they already knew. "The tracker is in a landfill in Germany. They threw it out. The last location they show is a bar a couple of miles outside of Ramstein. I would bet that's where they picked him up. It's been a little over twenty-four hours, so I think it's still early."

It wouldn't feel like twenty-four hours to TJ.

What were they doing to him? Was he hurt? Was he being tortured somewhere out there?

It didn't matter that he couldn't love her the way she needed. She loved him, and she couldn't leave him.

"Lou, he's going to be okay," Kala promised.

But she couldn't know. She couldn't know what he was going through, if he was already…

She shoved that thought away because it was too terrible to contemplate. She couldn't imagine a world without TJ. She could let him go, but she couldn't ever let him die.

Why would they want TJ? Who would want TJ?

She heard a dinging sound, letting her know someone had unlocked the security system and was coming in the lobby doors.

Kala's head turned. "Were we expecting anyone else?"

"I haven't called anyone." Zach stood, his hand going behind his back, likely feeling for the semiautomatic Lou knew he kept there.

"They know the code." She wasn't going to let him get into a gunfight because whoever was coming through probably had one, too. "Some people come up on the weekends to work while it's quiet."

Lou got to her feet, but Cooper was already at the door.

His eyes widened at whatever he was seeing. "Aunt Erin? Are you okay?"

TJ's mom was here? Lou moved to the door and realized why Cooper was so shocked. Erin Taggart was dragging a body. A big body.

"Oh, hey, kids. I'm glad you're here. This asshole's heavy." TJ's mom was dressed in jeans and a T-shirt, her red hair up in a ponytail. "I didn't want to leave him downstairs for the security guard to find. Howard's getting up there in years, and his heart's not what it used to be. Definitely didn't need two bodies to deal with."

"Mrs. Taggart, is there a reason you're dragging a dude around?" Zach asked. "Is he dead?"

Erin looked down at him, wincing. "I think so. I was a little enthusiastic. It's been a long time since someone jumped me. So now I have a dead body, but the good news is I have all you young, strong kids to help me deal with it. Kala, look, I brought you a dead asshole. Do you think your dad has any more room in that backyard of his, or am I going to have to haul him to the lake house?"

"Why?" Lou asked. Sometimes the older generation's motivations evaded her.

"Did you hear the part where he jumped me?" Erin asked.

"Okay. The better question is what happened. Like more than he jumped me and I was cranky," Kenzie corrected because she knew how the OGs worked. Sarcasm powered their parents through life, and they weren't above joking about a dead body. They kind of lived for it.

"I was coming up to get some paperwork done because Theo's got a bunch of guys over playing board games. It was a lot of talk about wings and birds. I do not get that. So I hopped in my Jeep and grabbed some lunch—which I dropped because of this asshole—and that might have played into the whole 'squeezed his windpipe a little too long' thing. Also, I'm embarrassed because I should have realized I was being followed. Don't get old, kids. It sucks. I really wanted that burger. Theo's on a health kick."

"Have you searched him yet?" Lou asked.

Erin shook her head. "Nah. Like I said, I didn't want to freak Howard out. And there are still lawyers in the building, despite Big Tag scaring most of them off. Couldn't risk one of them finding me and wanting to call in the cops. So I decided I would drag his nasty ass up here and call Tag. Maybe it was random, but he got into the building, which makes me think he's a pro."

"Why would someone want to assassinate you?" Zach asked.

Erin shrugged. "I don't know. I'm a fucking delight."

There were probably a bunch of people she'd pissed off over the years, but Lou didn't think this was about Erin Taggart. "Check for his phone. I'll have an ID asap."

Kala stood beside her, staring down at the body. "What are you thinking?"

"That some dumbass thought Erin would be an easier target than TJ's dad." Lou turned to Erin. This was not a conversation she'd ever dreamed she would have. "I think someone has TJ, and they're trying to get him to talk."

Erin's eyes went steely, and her stance became militaristic, shoulders going back and feet planted. "And what are we going to do about that?"

"We're going to get him back." A terrible plan hit her brain. Or a brilliant plan. "And I know exactly what to do."

* * * *

"You want to do what?" Ian Taggart looked at Lou like she'd told him she was growing fairy wings or planned on becoming a street performer.

Both of those things ranked high on the Uncle Ian bad-life-decisions scale. She wasn't joking. He had an actual scale and everything.

"I want to let this dude kidnap me. Not him, exactly, since he's dead and I don't think I have the energy to *Weekend at Bernie's* this thing. But someone who looks a bit like him. Someone these guys will believe is a mercenary," Lou explained.

"I told you she had a plan," Kala said under her breath.

Kala's father frowned her way. "You also told me this was about TJ's unit."

Kenzie shrugged. "Well, I was worried you would tell us to stand down if you found out about the texts. I needed to get you here so we could prove this isn't TJ flaking out and disrupting your nap time."

Kala nodded her twin's way. "We all know this is your sacred napping time, so getting you here was crucial."

The twins had run to their parents while Lou, Cooper, and Zach had spent the last two hours figuring out what the situation was. Apparently, they'd come up with a story to get Big Tag moving faster, and it had worked. And Erin had DoorDashed a burger and fries. Murder had not set her off her lunch plans.

In this case, Lou couldn't blame the twins. After all, Ian and Charlotte Taggart were their day-to-day Agency bosses. While Drake and Taylor Radcliffe handled things directly with Langley, the Taggarts often went into the field. Lou's team was still considered experimental, and there were a lot of eyes on them.

The Taggarts had strode in, and when she'd seen Ian and Charlotte and the twins followed by Tasha, something had eased inside her. Of all the team members, Lou spent the most time working with Tasha. They were the behind-the-scenes operatives, making sure everything moved smoothly.

This was her team. She trusted them. They would get through this. They would get TJ back.

Her plan would work.

"I don't like it, and I know for a fact TJ would say no." Cooper had made it plain what he thought of her rescue plans.

"Well, then TJ shouldn't have gotten his ass kidnapped." Kala was on her side at least.

Tasha had her laptop in front of her, staring at the documentation Lou had managed to put together. She sat beside her mom. "What TJ wants or doesn't isn't our problem. Getting him home is."

Tasha had left her fiancé behind with her infant nephew and two well-trained dogs. It was good to know Dare supported his future wife's career.

It hadn't taken long to figure out that the man who'd thought Erin would be an easy target had been a mercenary connected to several mafia families. Lou had managed to use the information she'd found on his phone to link back to some groups on the Dark Web, including one that served as a sort of marketplace for all kinds of criminal services. A Craigslist for murder and kidnapping. They'd left out reviews, though, and that seemed like an oversight. She thought a couple of good ten out of tens, *Great assassination* customer reviews would liven up the site.

"I'll go." Theo Taggart had left his game behind and hauled ass up to the office when his wife had called. While Erin was cool as a cucumber, Theo was pacing like a caged tiger. "One of us can pose as a mercenary responding to the ad and turn me over. I'll go with them, and I'll get my son out."

"It's not that easy, Uncle Theo," Kenzie said.

Zach's head shook. "You weren't on the list of targets."

Lou had managed to break the dead guy's codes and access his portfolio on the aforementioned criminal jobs' site that someone somewhere should take down. She'd found the job and Dead Dude had been given three potential kidnapping options. Erin or Devon Taggart or one Louisa Ward. They'd put together crappy files on all three of them. All Erin's had was her address, place of business, and age. Not once did it mention she was former Army intelligence and worked for a company that solved security problems across the globe.

They'd listed Lou herself as working for the think tank, given her address, and posted a couple of pictures they'd gotten off her social media. No mention of her work with the Agency. It was a half-assed job.

Devi was luckily in New York for a couple of days with her best friends Daisy O'Donnell and Brianna Dean-Miles. Given who Brianna's father was, they had a guard with them. Adam Miles was known for developing software that had taken down many criminals. He was a high-value target, and so were the members of his family, so they always had some security around them. Another bodyguard was now on the way, and Devi was in a very quiet lockdown. They wouldn't have a chance to get TJ's sister.

So that left Lou.

Theo's head shook. "I can't believe they thought Erin would be an easier target than me."

She wouldn't have been that much easier. Theo Taggart had been on the same CIA team as Lou's dad, and he'd been a badass. Erin was only slightly more ruthless than her husband. Of course if the mercenary had gone after Theo, he would likely be alive and she would have gotten a whole lot more intelligence.

Luckily she'd found a text giving him a location in Bavaria and a time two days away. It had to be the drop-off.

"They didn't do any research," Charlotte said with obvious disdain.

Erin winked her husband's way. "Misogyny for the win, babe. And I'm with Lou. If TJ wanted to keep the ladies in his life safe, he shouldn't have gotten kidnapped. I can go in if we don't want Lou going."

"Mrs. Taggart, that is not your call." Lou would normally call her Erin. She didn't use aunt or uncle with these Taggarts. Probably because even as a kid her relationship with TJ hadn't been familial. Not from her end. "This is not a McKay-Taggart mission, and the information you've learned here should be considered classified and only given to you out of respect. You will not be going in because you are not the one on the team."

Erin's lips curled slightly. "Then you're really ready, and you definitely know what you're doing. Proud of you, kid."

"Does she?" Big Tag asked. "Know what she's doing that is. From an emotional standpoint."

Erin sighed. "Yes, she does."

"I'm not sure about that," Cooper replied with a grim frown.

Erin sighed. "If this is about the whole 'Lou loves TJ and TJ strings her along' thing, it's more complicated than that. And it doesn't matter. I know even at my angriest with Theo, I would have saved his life. I wouldn't have been able to live with myself, and I damn straight wouldn't have been able to leave it in someone else's hands. I lost him for almost two years, Tag. I don't want that to happen to my son."

"I won't let it." She'd felt the flush of embarrassment go through her when Erin had mentioned the unbalanced nature of her relationship with TJ, but she shoved it aside. Everyone knew she loved TJ and he considered her a kid sister. Nothing had changed. It had simply gotten put out in the open.

And Erin was right. No one else could do this job the way she could.

Erin's gaze went soft. "I know, sweetie. And I also know you're way more competent at this than my son thinks you are. I worry one of the reasons he's held back with you is he doesn't think you can handle his world."

That made zero sense. "I work for the Agency. I live in his world."

"In a support role," Theo pointed out.

"I assure you, Lou can handle herself in the field. I made sure of it." Big Tag sat back, seeming to consider the situation. "Do you honestly believe I would put a woman on a team if she couldn't handle herself?"

She'd had to pass all of Big Tag's tests, despite the fact she wasn't normally supposed to go into the field. She was there to do a lot of the mental and technological lifting.

Tasha didn't look up from her screen. "Dad put Lou and I through all the same training as the rest of the team. We're competent in hand to hand and have used all the weapons. Lou's good with a knife, and she's excellent at finding weapons in the field. She's surprisingly creative."

"Big Tag used to send pretend assassins to keep us sharp," Lou explained.

Big Tag grinned, a predatory look. "I sent in new hires. If the girls killed them, then they weren't ready for the job."

"I know Lou can handle herself," Cooper said. "But I have to reiterate that this is not what TJ would want. He wants her safe. Look, you're right. He's under a couple of misconceptions. He thinks Lou's job is safer than it really is. He thinks she simply sits behind a computer and never has to defend herself or her team. I've kept up the delusion because I worry what he would do if he thought she was in actual danger. He can be unreasonable when it comes to Lou."

Lou was confused. "He's Special Forces. I'm Agency. I don't see a whole lot of difference. He should know better. We don't work the way other teams do."

"But he's a young meathead male. He hasn't gotten the dumb out of his ass yet," Big Tag explained.

"Really, brother?" Theo shook his head. "What he's trying to say is TJ hasn't learned he has to trust his partner yet. He's young and untested when it comes to this. Probably because he's too afraid to risk losing you."

There was only one problem with that scenario. "I'm not his partner."

"Aren't you?" Theo asked. "I know the two of you haven't gotten physical yet, but you are the constant in his life. You're all he talks about. He's never once brought home a woman to meet his family. He comes to holidays and birthdays with you. When he was first deployed, he made me promise to watch out for you."

"He made us all promise that," Cooper agreed.

A heaviness hit her, a weariness the adrenaline couldn't wipe out. He loved her, just not the way she needed.

Were they both stuck? Was she holding him back every bit as much as he was holding her? They'd met and it had felt like her soul found its other half, but something had gone wrong because the attraction TJ needed wasn't there. Something essential was missing, some spark that would have lit their lives together. It didn't mean they had to live in this weird limbo forever.

She was taking a step, making dates and plans with people who weren't TJ Taggart. She'd spent all this time desperately holding onto their friendship, but maybe she needed to step away from that, too. Maybe what they both needed was a clean break.

After one last sacrifice. One last mission.

"And that's why I think we should come up with another plan. We know where they're supposed to meet. We go and follow them back," Cooper offered.

"I'm going." She wasn't about to let Captain America protect the women. She didn't need protecting. "I didn't join this team to be safe. Uncle Ian, Aunt Charlotte, what's your assessment of my plan?"

"That your father's going to snipe me," Uncle Ian said.

"And that it's the only way to go." Aunt Charlotte looked thoughtful for a moment. "I've got some calls in, and my sister is working this from another angle. It's obvious they want something from TJ, and they think pulling in one of the women in his life will make him give it to them. Chelsea is trying to figure out what he could possibly know. I've brought her in as a consultant, so she has clearance. She agrees that they've tried to cover his disappearance, which means they want him alive for now. If they don't know who Lou is, we know we're not dealing with the top-tier intelligence world."

"No, we're dealing with criminals of some kind, and criminals like to kill and torture people," Zach countered, looking Lou's way. "I will support you no matter what, but you need to know going in that you could get hurt. I know you're trained and you've backed up field agents before, but this is different. You're risking a lot for him."

The sad truth was she would risk everything for him. "I know."

Zach looked to Ian, his brow rising. Lou wondered if he realized how much like Ian he'd become over the time they'd worked together. "I'm going to recommend Lou's plan."

"I back Lou as well," Tasha said.

"And me," Kenzie agreed, giving her a thumbs-up.

"I don't know why we have all this drama. I'm not going to let my best friend die." Kala sat back like it was no big deal. Just another day at the office. "She'll be fine because I won't let it be any other way."

All eyes went to Cooper. He took a long breath. "Yeah, I'll back Lou."

Big Tag looked his wife's way.

"Lou is ready, and we have several advantages because we know things our opponents don't know," Charlotte pointed out. "Lou is smart, and she won't be in there for one second longer than we need to confirm that TJ is there and how to attack the complex."

Big Tag clapped his hands together. "All right. The decision is made. Lou is going in. Zach, I want you to figure out who we send in as her kidnapper. We're going to hope they don't know this guy personally."

"They don't." They'd caught another break here. "They found

him on the Dark Web. I'm pretty sure they picked him because he was located in Austin, and it wouldn't take him long to get to Dallas. He also said he had access to a private plane and could get the target to Germany in forty-eight hours. They might have a picture of him, but he looks like every other white athletic dude in his twenties. He's very basic. Blandly attractive."

"So we're sending Coop," Kala quipped.

Coop groaned, but his lips curled up. "I'm extremely attractive, thank you, but I will take her in. I'm roughly the same height and coloring. He's got a scar on his cheek. Kenz can fake that with makeup."

"Shouldn't we talk to Boomer?" Theo looked pale, like he couldn't stand the thought of sending one of the kids in.

But they weren't kids anymore. "My father knows the risks I took when I agreed to do this job. They are the same ones he took. My father does not ask me about my job because he is my father and not my boss. So no, we will not be calling my dad because I am an adult who has passed all the tests and who is competent at her job."

Erin chuckled. "Forgive my husband. He's a lot like my son. He wants to protect everyone he cares about, even when they don't need to be protected."

Theo ran a hand through his short, cropped hair. "I'm sorry. I know Lou is well trained. But I also know TJ will want to die if anything happens to her."

She wasn't sure about that, but she did feel for Theo. She'd kept herself calm, a bit cold, but seeing TJ's dad so worried thawed her heart. She got up and walked to the man who'd been such a part of her teen years. Theo had been the fun dad, the one who took them to concerts and never made fun of the pop bands. He'd sang along with them all.

She walked up and put her arms around him. "I will bring him back. I promise."

Theo hugged her tight. "You come back, too, Lou. You be careful and cautious and wait for the right time. We'll be there. We won't let you down."

They never had. Not once.

And she wouldn't let them down. She would get TJ back and then she would finally be able to move on with her life.

Chapter Three

There was movement outside the door, and TJ prepared himself for pain.

The last…he wanted to say day, maybe day and a half…had been surprisingly quiet. After they'd announced they were going to give him a reason to talk, they'd chucked him in this windowless room and left him on his own. He'd passed out for an undetermined amount of time and when he'd woken, he'd managed to find the light switch. He'd been surprised when it worked, and more surprised to find himself in what looked like a somewhat normal room. There was an industrial-looking cot he'd been laid out on with sheets and a blanket. The nightstand was bolted to the cold concrete floor. Not that he had anything to put on it. He had access to a toilet and rudimentary shower, though there were no toiletries. That was it. No windows. No desk or table. Just a small, cell-like room with concrete walls and a solid-looking door.

He'd tried the door, of course, but the banging from the other side had let him know he wasn't alone. There was a guard on the door at any point in time. They brought in bland food for him twice a day. MREs with tepid water, so they were even worse than well-done MREs, and weren't those words he'd never thought he would put together.

Sometimes he blamed his Uncle Sean. He'd grown up around a highly celebrated chef. It made it hard to get used to MREs.

God, what was happening to his mom? It was awful, but TJ hoped and prayed they went after his mom because she had the best chance of surviving an attack. Devi or Lou… He didn't know what he would do if that door opened and they dragged him out and showed him his sister or Lou tied up and helpless.

He didn't know what they thought he knew. He had no idea what they were talking about.

He had nothing to trade for their lives.

What was he going to do if he had to watch his sister or Lou die?

Make shit up. He could do that. Sure, he knew this Jester guy. His real name was Ian Taggart.

No, that wouldn't work. They wouldn't believe it was his uncle. He was too high profile. He needed someone tough, someone who would be on guard because the minute Lou or Devi went missing, they would know something had gone wrong. They wouldn't think either woman was going off on their own for the weekend or ditched plans.

Would they know the same about him? Or would they think TJ's kind of a flake. That sounds like something TJ would do.

Fucking TJ.

He knew how his cousins referred to him when they thought he wasn't treating Lou right.

Would they leave him here? They might, but they wouldn't leave Lou and they wouldn't leave Devi, and that was all that mattered.

It was the worst revelation in the world. Now that he was here, now that he was facing never seeing her again, he knew he'd been stupid.

He should have taken Lou the minute he realized she didn't want to live in an ivory tower. When she'd made the decision to work with his cousins, he should have taken that as a cue. It didn't matter that they would have to have been long distance. Hell, they didn't. He could tell his uncle he wanted to be on the team and his uncle would make it happen. It wasn't like he didn't work with Agency teams all the time. He could have had Zach's place on the team, but he hadn't thought he was ready.

He never thought he was ready.

There was shuffling outside the door, and TJ turned his whole focus that way. The light above was dim, the bulb locked under a covering he hadn't been able to dismantle. He'd tried since he'd looked for any weapon he could find. He'd been willing to use that bulb as a knife if he'd had to, but to no avail.

He didn't have a weapon, but while his bones ached, he could fight. He wasn't letting them hurt a woman he loved. Not a chance. He would get away or he would die, and either way his sister and Lou would be safe.

He wished they hadn't parted the way they had. Adrenaline started to pump through him, and he moved to the side of the door to give himself the best chance to jump whoever was about to walk through that door.

"Move it, lady," a deep voice said.

His stomach turned. They were bringing someone.

The door came open, and his worst nightmare was real.

Lou. There was a hood over her head and her hands were tied in front of her, but he knew who it was. He'd bought her the emerald green sweater she was wearing. It was cashmere and cost way more than he should have spent, but he'd known how good it would look against her skin, how it would bring out the gold in her eyes. She wore it with a skirt that went down past her knees and boots that had a square heel.

They pushed Lou through the door, and his instincts kicked in. He didn't take the chance to jump the guard. He couldn't because he had no idea what shape Lou was in.

What had they done to her?

What had he done to her?

He caught her before she could hit the hard floor, gathering her into his arms even as the guard stood in the doorway.

"Now we have someone to torture instead of you, Sergeant Taggart. Perhaps you should take the next few hours to explain to your friend why she's going to suffer. Or you could take this time to change your mind and talk."

"I'll talk," he promised. "I'll tell you everything. Just let her go."

Lou shook in his arms. She was crying. She was probably so scared. He held her close.

"We'll be back this afternoon. Take this time to truly decide. You have no idea what we can do to her," he vowed, and the door closed again. He heard the sound of a heavy lock sliding closed.

His whole world narrowed to the woman in his arms. "Lou? Baby, are you okay?"

He fumbled, getting the hood off her head. Her glasses were askew, but they hadn't taken them from her. Normally she wore contacts. If they'd taken her glasses, she would have been even more vulnerable. He smoothed back her hair. It was usually neatly kept, but she'd obviously been through some things. It was tangled, but her face looked untouched. Her eyes looked up at him, brown with flecks of gold. Tears slipped from them, caressing her cheeks.

"You're alive."

He held her close. "Yeah, but we're in trouble, baby. I'm going to get you out of here. I promise. I'm going to do everything I can to make sure they don't hurt you. You have to be ready. Kala will know something's gone wrong, and they'll look for you. Did they find…"

Her head came up and her eyes flared, a clear warning. "Yes, they found me. I'm here, aren't I? They didn't find Devi, though. She's out of town. I think they were looking for either her or me."

He certainly hadn't meant finding *her*. He'd been about to ask about her tracker. They'd found his, but they'd obviously known he was Special Forces and taken the chance he might have one. Not every soldier did. It was both a strength—his CO could potentially find him—and a weakness if anyone got control of their codes. Then anyone could track potential high-value targets. There was a chance they hadn't checked Lou.

But she didn't want him to mention it.

Which meant they hadn't, and she was worried they were listening in.

Fuck. They couldn't talk. Not about anything important. He couldn't talk about the team, couldn't assure her someone was coming. Why else would they be giving him a couple of hours with her if they weren't watching? Weren't listening to see if he would talk now that she was here.

"Are you okay?" He could ask that question even though he knew the answer.

Her head nodded slowly, her voice going low. "Yeah. They didn't hurt me. Not yet, though there was a lot of talk in German. I got the gist. I think the boss isn't here and they want him here for the interrogation. That's why we have a couple of hours. They're expecting him around 1500."

He started to work the rope binding her wrists, easing them off. Three p.m. "I don't know what time it is now, Lou. I've been drugged a couple of times. I have no idea where we are."

Or what they want from me. Or how to save you.

"I think it's around noon," she replied, her voice still low. "And I think we're somewhere close to the Austrian border."

He wasn't sure how she would know that, but Lou was ridiculously smart so he would take her word for it. Not that it helped to know where he was since he had no way out.

He felt utterly helpless. "I'm so sorry. I would give anything to not have you here."

A brief hurt flared across her face, and then her hands were free and she scrambled to her feet. "Well, that shouldn't surprise me. Have they hurt you?"

"I didn't mean it that way."

She shook her head. "It doesn't matter."

"I meant I can't stand the thought of you getting hurt."

"Yes, that might have been mentioned a couple of times before." She frowned and then turned to the door, moving to it and pulling on the handle.

"Baby, I've tried. I can't open it."

"What is going on?" Lou asked. There was anxiety to her tone that hadn't been there before. When she'd talked about what she'd learned from their captors, she'd been cool and calm. Now there was panic in her eyes. "I was at home and this man came to the door. I tried to fight him."

"Who else was there?" Lou lived with his cousins. As far as TJ knew, right now Dare was staying there, too, until he and Tasha moved out.

"I was alone. My roommates left for the week. They had some time off and went to visit friends in Seattle."

Roommates? Like he didn't know who they were. And he didn't know of any friends in Seattle. And that didn't explain where Tash and Dare were. It was weird, but she was probably in shock. "But someone will look for you."

She shook her head. "Not for days. My mom and dad are out of town, too, and I took a couple of days off. No one will look for me until Wednesday when I'm supposed to be back at work."

But she texted with her parents all the time. "Surely when your dad sends you some funny meme and you don't reply, he'll know something's wrong."

"They have my phone. Like they have yours. I thought you were holed up with a woman in a ski resort."

He shook his head. "Everyone believed it?"

"What are they supposed to believe, TJ? It wouldn't be the first time."

He couldn't believe they were talking about this now. Did she not understand the danger they were in? But hey, he could throw down. He was kind of sick of always being reminded how he disappointed Lou. "Yeah, I think it would. It would definitely be the first time I blew you off for some other woman. Say what you like about me, but I always put you first, and I am honest with every woman I've ever dated. And quite frankly, that's not many, and not a single one has been serious. Certainly not as many as my cousins make it out to be. And I definitely wouldn't have missed my sister's birthday. We had plans, Lou. When was the last time I skipped out on plans with you?"

"This is stupid. I don't know why they thought I could make you do anything. From what I heard in the car, that's what this is about. What do they want from you?"

He hated how cold she seemed all of the sudden, but that was what happened when Lou got overwhelmed. She didn't cry until after the crisis, and then only when she was alone or with him or Kala.

That was why a real scene could work for her. Not some demo, but a scene where he was completely focused on her. He could spank her and she could cry and cry, and then he would hold her and all that anxiety would be gone and he would have given her some peace.

He wouldn't be around to give her any peace at all.

He felt his jaw go tight and he moved in, whispering directly in her ear. "They want to know who The Jester is. I have no idea what they're talking about. I think he's some kind of arms dealer. They have a picture of me walking down a street in Berlin with him. But I don't know him, Lou. That picture's a fake."

He felt her head nod against his. "Okay. We need to buy some time, but I know they're listening. We can't say anything about you not knowing. We shouldn't say much at all."

She was right. And maybe all that crap about no one missing her was just that. Crap. Someone would miss her. If she was alone, Coop would come over to make sure she didn't need anything. Tristan's sister, Brianna, was over there all the time.

Someone would hear Bud whining. Tasha would drop by, and she would know Lou would never leave the dog by himself.

They had to buy time and not give away the fact that he had no information to give them.

He would make some up if he had to. He would send them to someone who could handle himself. He just had to figure out who that was.

She backed away from him. "I also heard them talking about how I'm not your girlfriend and it would have been better to bring Devi in. I worry if they think I'm not the person to make you talk, they'll move faster to get rid of me."

"Do you honestly believe I would let that happen?"

"I don't know."

He was overwhelmed and not thinking straight. The last couple of weeks had been pretty fucking awful, and he hadn't had her around to help him find his center. They were at a breaking point. He'd tried so hard to keep his hands off her so he could stay in her life, but all he'd managed to do was put them in this shitty position. "You are my whole world, Louisa Ward. Girlfriend doesn't begin to cover how I feel about you. I didn't think we were ready. I didn't think I was good enough for you, but that doesn't matter now. I realize that. I should have listened to you. You always were so much smarter than me. They want to know how much they can get me to do if it spares you a moment of pain? I can show them."

He did what he should have done years and years ago. He

leaned over, ignoring the ache in his muscles, and slid a hand around her neck, holding her still.

Her eyes flared as he stared down at her.

"TJ," she began.

"Tell me you don't want me and I can step back."

"You're the one who doesn't want me. You don't have to do this."

"I should have done this a long time ago. I don't think you're going to listen to words. I think I have to show you. This might be my last chance."

"TJ," his name came out of her mouth again, this time softer, a plea, but he didn't know for what.

To kiss her? To walk away from her? All he knew was she hadn't told him no, and that was what it would take to stop him. He lowered his lips to hers and attempted to satisfy over a decade's worth of longing.

Soft. She was so fucking soft. And warm. He let his hands find her waist and gently explored her lips. He loved her lips. They were full and plump, and he loved it when she smiled or frowned or pouted. He loved her every expression, and damn, but he loved how they felt beneath his own. The world went fuzzy around him, narrowing down to her. Only her.

He'd always known if he put his hands on her, his mouth on her, his cock in her, that he would be beyond obsessed, and he felt it overtake him like a wave.

This was it. There would be no going back. If they survived, he would do anything he had to in order to be what she needed him to be. It was still a terrible idea and he could lose her, but now, in this place where everything was ripped down to its core, he knew he had to try.

He had to have this moment with her. No matter what came after.

He would have his one moment with Lou and then he would do whatever he could to save her. Even if it meant sacrificing himself.

TJ felt the moment she gave over. Her chest crushed against his, and her arms went around his shoulders, clutching him like she would never let him go.

It was all he needed. He let his tongue surge inside her mouth, drinking in the way she tasted, the silky glide of her tongue against his. It wasn't awkward in any way. This was the opposite. This felt like something they'd done a million times, and yet it was new and fresh and always would be.

He kissed her over and over, his brain going fuzzy. Nothing mattered except Lou and the way she smelled and tasted and felt. His hands slipped into the thick, soft waves of hair that brushed her shoulders. She usually wore it up, but it was down now, and he played in it, tightening and releasing to lead her where he wanted her to go.

She followed every cue, moving with him in an effortless dance.

In the back of his head, he knew this was one of the dumbest things he'd ever done. They were trapped and needed to find a way out. They should be getting ready to fight their captors.

But he couldn't stop. He couldn't not give them this one moment—not when he'd been the reason they wouldn't have a lifetime together.

He held her tight against his body. He didn't care that his muscles ached and still burned from where the darts had bitten into his flesh as they'd tased him over and over. The pain was nothing more than a reminder that he was alive in these moments, that he had to make the most of every single one.

"Do you know how long I've wanted you?"

"Don't. I don't want to talk about it. If you insist on trying to convince me the last ten years were about you protecting me, then this ends now," she said, fire in her eyes. She stepped back.

And he didn't like that. He reached out and gripped her wrist. He'd always thought Lou could be a heinous, glorious brat if she ever gave the lifestyle a real try.

"Don't want to talk about how much I want you? Don't want to talk about how much fucking time I've wasted for both of us? You need to understand that if we get out of this, everything changes."

"Nothing will change," she vowed, her gaze going steely. "You're scared. That's all this is."

"Then you don't have anything to worry about, baby. Tell me you don't want me and I'll back off. We can sit here until they come for us, and then I'll do everything I can to make sure you survive this. But if there's even the tiniest part of you that doesn't want to die without knowing, then don't make me walk away."

"There's nowhere to walk to. We're caught here," she pointed out.

And they always had been. Since the day he'd met her, he'd been caught somehow. First out of fascination for the girl who knew so much, and later for the gorgeous young woman she'd become. Lou had been his. Only his, even when she dated other guys and he tried to find someone on his level that he could feel half what he felt for her. "Yes, we are. So what are we going to do about it?"

She pulled her wrist from his hand, and for a moment he thought she was going to fight him, to retreat and leave him aching. He would die aching for her.

She turned and slid the glasses off her face and set them on the nightstand. And then stared at him while she pulled her shirt over her head.

Fuck. His whole body went hard.

"This is the stupidest thing I've ever done," she whispered. "I'm going to get such a lecture."

He wasn't sure who would lecture her, but he didn't care. All that mattered was the fact that Lou was half naked and saying yes.

Everything changed after this. They would die or be together, and he wouldn't let her go. He would move fucking heaven and earth to stay with her, and he would find a way to be what she needed. He tugged his own shirt overhead and tossed it to the side.

Thank god she wasn't wearing her glasses because otherwise she would see every wound he'd taken. Even without them, she gasped.

He didn't want her sweet sympathy. He caught her hand again. "No. Not now. I'm fine, and I won't have you holding back on me. This might be the only time we're together, and I want everything from you. I want you to take everything I can give you. Pretend we're in the club. We're at The Hideout and I've carried you off to a privacy room, and you obey me there. I might be a dumbass in every other aspect of my life, but not there. There I give you what you need."

Her gaze softened. "TJ," she began.

He twisted her wrist gently, turning her so she was held against his chest, her round ass nestled to his cock. He leaned in so he could whisper against her ear. "No TJ here. You call me Sir."

Her breath caught, and for a second he worried she would refuse, and the sweetest huff came from her mouth. "Sir."

That was what he needed. His cock twitched, so fucking eager. One arm wound around her waist. He had no idea how long they had, but he needed to make it good for her. "Tell me yes, Lou."

Her head fell back against his chest. "Yes. Yes, Sir."

His arms tightened, and he knew he would never let her go. Not until the very end.

* * * *

Lou's body felt electric.

This…this was what had been missing with the others. Not that there had been many. She'd had a boyfriend in undergrad. Neil. He'd been as studious as she was, and they'd been excellent study partners who'd tried sex a couple of times, and it fizzled out when he'd moved to Cal Tech for his post-grad work. Not that it had been all that hot in the first place. And then she'd had a brief relationship with another professor at UT Austin, which had been easy to walk away from.

TJ's hand moved up to cup her breast. His big, manly hand. She felt his lips against her ear. "You're so fucking gorgeous, baby. I want to see your breasts. I'm going to get my hands on them, put my mouth on them."

She'd been worried when her glasses had fritzed out as they'd entered the compound. Up until then she'd had Kala in her ear. The glasses were an updated version of the ones she'd designed a couple of years back. They were smart glasses, a technological leap forward from the ones on the market today made possible by a combination of CIA funding and a whole lot of Drew Lawless cash. Those glasses looked perfectly normal, but they sent back all sorts of information to her team. They could listen in and see everything she saw. They sent coordinates, and she could even access the Internet when she needed to. She could hear what Kala said through micro receivers concealed inside her outer ear.

Not that she could hear anything now since they'd stopped

working. That was when she'd realized she might be in trouble.

TJ pulled at the straps of her bra. It was a solid bra. She hadn't dressed for seduction, but then she never did. She dressed for comfort and practicality. She'd dressed for the German weather, which would be chilly.

She kind of wished she'd let Kenzie dress her in something pretty. It was the only time she was ever going to be with the man of her dreams and she was in cotton undies and an industrial-strength bra.

This was all part of the op. That was what she was telling herself as TJ's fingers found her nipples. Her ridiculously hard nipples. He rolled them and tugged, and she kept telling herself this was their cover. One of the things she'd overheard her captors saying was they would be able to tell if they had the right hostage based on how TJ reacted. They'd wanted someone else. Erin or Devi, but the mercenary had brought her.

Cooper had brought her, and he'd played the asshole mercenary to the hilt. He'd even walked away with twenty grand.

She should be worth more than twen…

That was a cock. TJ's cock. It rubbed against her, threatening to send her brain right where her glasses had gone. To a useless place where all that power meant nothing.

Now she understood. For years she'd had Ian Taggart telling her not to think with her pussy. It had seemed like such a logical thing to do that no one should ever need a reminder. Like breathing. It happened naturally. No reminder needed. But now she understood because for the first time in her life her pussy was telling her brain to go to hell.

Her pussy was wet, and she could feel the blood starting to pool there. It drained from her brain and took away all her thought processes. Lust. It was lust, and it was making all the decisions for her.

When TJ's hand slipped under the waistband of her skirt, she couldn't breathe.

He kissed her neck as his hand slipped lower. Her nipples were so hard she swore she could feel the damn things pulsing. Like the rest of her skin was deliciously sensitive to his every touch.

Dumb. Dumb. This was so dumb. Her team would be here.

Their captors were obviously jamming cell signals, but it wouldn't take her team long to figure that out, and they would use aerial photography to search where she would…

She clenched her teeth as TJ's fingers slid over her clitoris. It was there. She could feel the orgasm playing around the edge of her consciousness. It wouldn't take much, and it usually took forever. She usually had to find a way to smile and finish herself off after her partner slipped away to the bathroom, but she was not having that trouble today.

She usually thought too much, couldn't shut off her brain.

That thought drifted away as he pressed gently down and circled the button of her clit with perfect precision. Just hard enough she could feel what was coming, but not enough to send her over the edge.

"Baby, you're so fucking wet. How did you get so wet so fast?"

"I'm sorry." Embarrassment threatened to swamp her. She was. She was liquid down there, and it didn't compute. She wasn't this girl. She could take or leave sex. It was something people seemed to need, but she'd always been a weirdo so she hadn't questioned it. "I don't. I don't do that."

Her body didn't flare to life under some guy's hands. Her pussy didn't… It didn't need the way it did now.

His hand pulled out, and before she could apologize again, he picked her up and carried her to the utilitarian bed. He set her down, that gorgeous face looming over hers. She loved his face, the blue of his eyes and that square jaw that always seemed to have some sexy scruff no matter how often he shaved.

He'd kissed her. Really kissed her, not some brush of his lips over her chin or forehead like she was a child. He'd kissed her like she was a woman he wanted, and he couldn't stop himself. The world could have burned down around them and it wouldn't matter because he was right. She had to know.

"You do that," he insisted. "You do it for me. You get wet for me. Your body knows who it belongs to, and I'm going to reward you, Louisa. Do you want to know how?"

His voice had gone dark and deep, and everything inside her responded to this part of him. This part she'd never met before. He was chill, never taking anything too seriously. He was kind and sweet and funny.

He was dark and deep, and looked like he could eat her alive.

"Yes." She did want to know. She wanted to know everything this man could do to her. In that moment he wasn't the boy she'd loved forever. He was something new and different, and she wanted to explore him.

His lips kicked up in the sexiest smirk. His shirt was gone, and she could see a couple of bruises on his body but mostly golden skin. Damn, she wished she hadn't taken off her glasses but they were thick, and she didn't want him to look down and see her in them. The glasses might be smart, but they also helped her see.

"I'm going to get my mouth on you, baby." He got on his knees and pushed up her skirt.

The skirt she'd worn for a specific purpose. It was way easier to hide things in a flouncy, flowy skirt than in skintight pants. She had four different weapons on her, and not one of those assholes had thought to check her. They'd seen what she'd wanted them to see—a terrified, helpless girl.

Who couldn't possibly know how to hide not only two microdosers with enough sedative to take down a horse, but also a slender but deadly knife made of material that folded in on itself, and a baton that did the same. The thin material was light and didn't weigh her down, and because of how the fabric folded and moved, wasn't easy to detect.

And there was C4 and a tiny detonator in her boots.

She was loaded up and ready to go.

TJ didn't seem to notice all the crap that Kenz and Kala and Tash had helped her hide in the fabric of her skirt as he pushed it up, revealing her legs and the not-so-pretty underwear she wore. The soaking wet underwear. His eyes widened as he looked down at her, thumb brushing over the wet patch.

She had to hold her breath because that stroke sent a flash of lightning through her and another pulse of arousal.

"All of this is for me, isn't it, baby? You don't react like this to anyone else, do you?"

She never had. All her damn life it had been TJ. Even when they were thousands of miles apart, he was the center of her universe. She had to stop, had to find balance and a way to have a good life without him, but she couldn't think about that now. Her mind was probably blaring warning signals, but her body wasn't listening. Red flags be damned, she was going to have this. Here in this one place, she was going to be what she'd dreamed of. His lover. His submissive. And that meant there was no room for lies. "Yes. Only you."

She worried it would only be him forever.

He leaned over and put his face right against her pussy, breathing her in.

That shouldn't be so damn sexy. It should be weird and awkward. It shouldn't make her hips want to tilt up, make her want to grip his shoulders and force him to give her more.

He dragged the panties off and maneuvered them over her boots. "I'll get you naked in a minute, but I can't wait. I have to know. Years I've gone not knowing the most important thing." His face tilted up, and there was fire in his gaze. "How you taste."

And then she couldn't breathe or think or do anything but feel the heat of his mouth on her pussy. He devoured her. His tongue parted her labia, dragging along her sensitive flesh and making her vision go fuzzy. Fuzzier than normal. She needed contacts when TJ was half naked on top of her.

No. She couldn't think that way…couldn't…

His tongue stroked over her clitoris, and a finger slipped inside her pussy.

That felt like heaven. He seemed to settle in, finding a place for himself between her legs. She'd never once felt so wanton, so fucking sexy. She'd had full-on sex and it hadn't felt like this. Nothing else in the world mattered except the slow stroke of his tongue, the way his fingers curled up inside her, seeking that spot no one had truly stroked before.

It was all it took. She couldn't hold it back, that feeling that had started to build from the minute he'd looked at her with that dark, dominant gaze, rushed through her veins like a drug.

And she was already an addict.

TJ wasn't done. He ate her pussy like a man on a mission. Like a starving man. Like a man who'd longed for this one taste all of his life and he finally, finally found relief.

His tongue delved deep, lapping her up. His hands pressed her thighs open. "I need more."

"Dear fucking god, what the hell am I seeing, Louisa Ward? Tell me that is not my nephew. What have I said about fucking on a mission? Tell me you are not fucking the fucking target in a fucking cage."

All thoughts of pleasure fled as those words came through the receivers in her ears. They were connected to the glasses but worked as long as they were in close proximity. Which they were.

"Baby, what's wrong?" TJ's eyes were wide, and he scrambled to his feet. "Did I hurt you?"

Her team had made it way faster than she'd imagined. They'd obviously taken out the jammer, and now they would be able to see through the glasses. That were sitting on the nightstand giving whoever was watching a spectacular vision of her…everything. She was fairly certain her gynecologist hadn't seen as much of her as her team just had.

What had she done?

"I'm sorry. It's not a cage, exactly. It's more of a room," she said, knowing the person on the other end of the line could hear her fine.

That person being her boss. Ian Taggart. It had been his grumpy voice that had come over the line.

"Are you okay? I didn't mean to hurt you, Lou," TJ was saying, and she could still see her arousal glistening on his lips.

What the hell had she done?

"Do you think I needed to see that, Lou? Do you think my eyes can handle that? They can't. I'm going to turn in my Agency credentials because I am obviously a horrible mentor if I haven't even taught the smartest member of my team to not have sex while in captivity. I will never fucking recover from that. Your father is going to murder me, and he'll eat me all in one meal. Good god, tell my nephew to get his dick under control."

Her whole body was red. She was sure of it. The pleasure was still kind of low key there, but it was warring with righteous embarrassment that the man who was kind of a bonus dad had caught her having sex with his nephew. In the middle of a mission.

"Give me that," a familiar voice said. Kenzie, she would bet. "Way to finally find your freaky side, Lou. While my father bleaches his eyeballs, you need to blow that door. Tasha has taken over the CCTV cams, and Kala is already on her way in with Coop and Zach. You've got one on the door. Take him out, and your prize is his M-15. Kala and Coop will be coming from the hall to your right. Zach is going into the west side of the building if you need him. They're waiting for my go, and I won't give it until I know you've got the door open."

She pushed TJ off and forced herself to go cold, letting her training take over.

Kenzie was right. It was go time.

Chapter Four

TJ had no idea what was going on. One minute he'd been in heaven. He'd had his mouth on her, tasting her freaking orgasm. He'd realized what he'd been missing all along. He'd thought he had zero to offer her, but her reaction had proven him wrong. Those smart boys she liked to hang around with hadn't made her come.

And the next she was pushing him off and talking like there was someone else in the room with them.

She grabbed her glasses, shoving them on her face even as her hands went to her skirt, seeming to search for something. "I'm coming. It'll only be a… Kenz, this is not the time."

Kenzie? Her glasses. Damn it. He'd forgotten that sometimes Lou's glasses were more than glasses. Sometimes they were gateways to whole worlds. Worlds where his family got a front row seat to his sex life.

"Lou, tell me they didn't see us."

She stopped, her head coming up, and she was truly adorable when she was horrified. "Your uncle says he's going to bleach his eyeballs. We have to move."

His uncle was here? "We're not doing anything until I understand what's going on."

She simply tore a hole in her skirt and pulled out a piece of metal that she then managed to fold into a deadly looking stiletto. Not the kind one found on shoes. Lou didn't wear those kinds of shoes. She was more of a boots and flip-flops chick, but she held that knife like she knew what she was doing.

Which she didn't because she was an analyst. She was the Agency's version of Bond's Q—the super smartie who made the weapons but didn't use them.

"I'm here to rescue you," she said, sitting on the bed and putting one leg over the opposite knee. She used the knife she'd made—the one that seemed to deny the laws of physics…maybe it was physics, he wasn't sure, but he knew something that folded up in a skirt shouldn't be that solid—to pry open the heel of her boot. There seemed to be a secret compartment there.

"Who sent you? Wait. I don't have to ask. Uncle, if you're listening, I'm going to kick your ass. You should know better." How dare they put Lou in danger. She wasn't a field operative. She should be safely behind a computer screen. He hadn't kept his hands off her for fucking years so she could die trying to rescue his sorry ass.

Lou winced as though hearing something loud. "Could you two leave the family drama for later? Yes, I hear you. No, he can't, and I'm not about to tell him that." She pulled something out of the boot and jammed the compartment door closed again. "We need to move. By now they'll surely have heard us since I said I'm here to rescue you out loud. Rookie fucking mistake."

Because she shouldn't be here. He needed a plan because she was probably right. Adrenaline started to pump through his veins. The fight was about to start, and the only thing he could do was try to save Lou. "You stay behind me. We're going to barricade ourselves in as best we can."

She frowned his way as she stood and approached the door. "Why would we do that?" She slapped her hand against a space near the handle and the lock that kept them inside. "Though you should get down. Fire in the hole."

Fire in the… What the fuck? TJ moved, crossing the space between them and tackling Lou, taking her to the floor and covering her body with his in a frantic play to protect her from the explosion that was coming.

And it was perfectly quiet.

He looked down at her. "Fire in the hole?"

She bit that plump bottom lip of hers. "It sounds cool in the movies. And you didn't give me a chance to hit the detonator."

It was too small a room. They would get torn apart. Had she run around Europe with C fucking 4 in her boot? "Lou, don't you…"

Her hand tightened and there was the sound of a puff and then the door was swinging open. Her lips curled up. "It works. You see I modified the chemical structure slightly so I can use less and it makes far less noise. It's also about where you place it. Oh, shit. We need to go."

"*Was machst du*?" a deep voice said. "*Steh jetzt auf*."

The guard. The guard was here and would probably kill Lou. He felt the muzzle of a rifle at his neck and reacted. He let his instincts take over. He brought his right arm back, catching the gun before the fucker could fire. He heard the rifle clatter to the floor as he rolled off Lou and kicked up because there was no way the dude wasn't coming after him.

"Run, Lou," he commanded as he started to get to his feet.

And got punched. Pain cracked across his face, but he had to ignore it. He brought his knee up, trying to take out the guy's balls. The mercenary groaned but proved how well trained he was because he didn't move. He was so big. TJ was big. Six foot three and two hundred ten pounds, but this guy had at least fifty pounds on him. He kicked again and brought his arms up to break the hold because the guy's hand was as massive as the rest of him. It was almost fully around TJ's throat.

Not that he would let something like a lack of oxygen stop him. He saw it play out in his head. He would pop his legs open, putting his opponent off balance, and then he would roll the fucker, grab the gun, kill this guy, and hope he could find Lou wherever she was hiding.

He was about to put his excellent plan in motion when something warm sprayed across his face, and the dude who was currently trying to crush his windpipe stopped and got the dumbest look on his face. There was a knife in his throat. A slender, delicate knife sticking right out of what TJ suspected was a much-needed artery.

Then a feminine hand came in and pulled it out, spraying blood everywhere.

He looked for his cousin or one of the members of her team.

Lou reached down, holding a hand out. "We have to go."

Lou. His sweet LouLou had stabbed a man in the throat. She'd killed a guy. She'd killed the guy *he* was going to kill. She hadn't even given him a damn chance. "I was going to take care of him."

Her eyes widened, and her mouth dropped open. "Are you kidding me?"

He pushed the now solidly dead asshole off him and reached for the M-15. "No, I am not. I could have taken care of him without all the blood. Do you know how hard that is going to be to get out of that sweater? It's cashmere. That sweater was expensive."

She looked down and frowned. "Oh no. It's my favorite."

"I'll buy you a new one." What had it taken for Lou to do that? Adrenaline was getting the better of him. "Baby, I'm sorry. Let's get out of here. Stay behind me."

Those brown eyes of hers rolled, and she suddenly had a baton in her other hand. His sweet, too-precious-for-the-world baby had a bloody knife in one hand and a wicked-looking baton in the other, and she'd snuck them both into a mercenary compound in her skirt. Come to think of it, she'd likely designed both weapons along with apparently making a quieter freaking C-4.

Fuck, she was hot.

He was standing in the middle of a paramilitary compound with the love of his life in danger and he had a hard-on because Lou doing bad shit did something for him.

She turned, her gaze narrowing on him. "Try to keep up, TJ."

She jogged out the door, looking like an avenging goddess-warrior queen bitch. The bitch part wasn't something he would say out loud. She might take offense, but for him she looked like the baddest bitch he'd ever seen, and he'd been raised around a whole lot of them.

Suddenly he was seeing Lou in a whole new light, and he wasn't sure how to handle it.

He only knew he damn sure wasn't letting her go.

He gripped the M-15 like it came naturally. Which it did. "When did this become a CIA op?"

"When we realized they had you. No one bought the whole TJ's screwing around thing," she said, stopping at the end of the hallway. She flattened her back and closed her eyes, seeming to listen to something in her head.

Or one of his cousins was in her ear. He could guess what had happened. She'd figured it out, gotten on the Dark Web and discovered the plot to take her in and either allowed herself to be taken, or had one of the guys pretend to be a mercenary and haul her in. She'd come loaded with all kinds of devices that would keep her connected to her team and discovered they were jamming the signals.

"When did comms come back online?" he asked.

"I suspect when Kala or Coop killed the jammer. And it all came back at the worst time possible. You should know your uncle might never recover."

He didn't care about the whole "we kind of made a sex tape" thing. "Good. Then he understands."

That got her head to turn his way. "Understands?" Her expression went blank, and then she nodded. "Coming from the east. Yes. I have him. He's safe but the guard is dead. Yeah, I know."

She knew? Knew what? He didn't like being on the outside. Normally he would be wearing a headset and would be able to hear all sides of the conversation.

"I'm on it," she promised and then started moving again, going to the left down the corridor. They were in some kind of industrial complex with concrete walls.

"Hey, did they take out the cameras?" He hustled to keep up with her, noting the CCTV cams that dotted the hallways.

"No, Tasha took them over. They can't use them, but we can," she explained. "Tasha's taken over back at base since your uncle is apparently traumatized. You should know your parents are there. They flew out with us. Your mom kind of murdered the first guy sent to take her out, so we subbed Coop in."

That would buy him some points on the maternal front. His mom hadn't killed anyone in a long time, and he thought sometimes she missed it. "I want to argue with you and tell you how fucking dangerous this was, but I think you've been holding out on me."

She stopped. "Holding out on you?"

"You know I thought you were an analyst. I had no idea you were out in the field."

"I'm not, for the most part."

There was something he'd been wondering about. "I heard some rumors about what went down at the end of the Australia op. Did you kill my CO?"

She gave him the brattiest look and started walking again.

That got his blood churning, though he wasn't mad, exactly. This version of Lou did something for him the sweet, soft one never had. He always wanted to protect her. He wanted to give to her.

What if she liked it when he took, too?

"I'll take that as a yes, then." He kept up his careful protection of her back since she seemed to be plowing through. Likely because Tash told her it was okay, but he wasn't taking any chances.

"I didn't kill Mike. Kala did. He was going to turn over Tasha to the bad guys. The only reason Chet didn't die was he cried like a baby, and Tasha couldn't handle it. So I hogtied the asshole and had to babysit him while Tasha was nearly dying. It took everything I had not to murder him so I could get to the hospital."

"I can see it was hard on you, baby. How many kills?"

She sighed. "It doesn't matter."

"It does."

"None, okay. I've always been backup. I've clipped a couple of guys, captured a bunch in well laid out traps, but I never killed anyone before. Up until now the people I was backing up didn't require me to kill anyone."

There was an edge to her tone that made his voice go low. "Baby, you are begging for it now."

"Begging for it?"

"Yeah, and I'm going to give it to you," TJ vowed. "As soon as we're alone, you're going to understand that while I love that smart mouth of yours, you can only push me so far."

"Push you?" Her lips formed a flat line, annoyance plain in her eyes. She stopped for a moment, seeming to listen to the person in her ear. "Yes. I am. Blame him. He's the one who's not being serious."

Oh, he was serious. He was incredibly serious about her and putting them on a steady footing. But she was right about one thing.

He needed to stop arguing with her and get her out of here. After he'd made one thing clear. He stepped up and slid his hand to grip the nape of her neck. When her eyes flared and her head relaxed against his hand, he knew he had her. "You're going to get me out of here, Lou. It's your op, but I'm your soldier. I'm yours. Do you understand me?"

She nodded, her eyes on his lips.

"What does base want from us?" It was what he would ask any CIA agent he was working for. He would ask for a mission brief, and then he would follow the agent's lead because he was support. He didn't normally move into the agent's space, force her head back so his lips could hover over hers.

"They want us to try to catch one of the guards on our way out. Kala said when she and Coop got to what they thought was the central office, it was empty. They're taking all the data they can find, but they want someone to question."

"Because my mother killed the guy they could have questioned and you killed the other one," he whispered, feeling the way her breath hitched.

"I had to kill him. I didn't have a choice."

"Yes, you did. I had him."

"You didn't have him."

Fuck all. Professional Lou was bossy and stubborn, and he only knew one way to shut that smart mouth of hers up. It would be okay because Tasha would tell them if they were about to die. Of course she would also see what he was about to do.

And he didn't care.

He kissed Lou, parting her lips under his, letting her feel how hungry he was for her.

"Are you fucking kidding me?"

He broke off the kiss and frowned the intruder's way. No one had mentioned Zach Reed, but here he was in all his glory.

TJ stood at attention, giving Captain Reed the respect he deserved. Zach had done what his family had wanted him to do. He'd gone to college before joining up, so he'd entered as a commissioned officer. "Sir, I'm not kidding, sir. I was asking Agent Ward what her orders are. In our own unique way."

"We do not have a unique way. We don't have a way at all,"

Lou said, her face beautifully flushed, and then her attention was on Zach, her jaw tight. "Base wants someone to interrogate, so Tash wants us to go out the back. There are a couple of guards there."

"You got what you need?" Zach wore all black, a balaclava covering most of his face. He'd pulled the part that covered his mouth down, showing a chiseled jaw.

He wasn't asking TJ. He was asking Lou. She nodded. "Yes. I equipped before I blew the door. I just need to get hands on someone. It would be better to not have to deal with a wounded prisoner."

"Then lead the way," Zach commanded. "TJ, take our six. Tash, we're heading out and will need extraction in less than five."

Lou dropped her weapons, running for the door.

TJ started after her, his heart pounding. Why the fuck was she running?

Zach held a hand out. "Let her do her job. She's right. We would shoot first and then not have a chance to ask questions."

He watched as Lou burst through the doors and a guard turned, startled.

"Help me," Lou said, sounding breathless.

The man who was holding a deadly weapon reached out for the sweet, covered-in-blood-so-she-looked-wounded woman.

Who reached up and cupped his neck with her right hand.

"And there it is. Nighty-night, buddy." Zach walked out of the doors.

TJ followed. She'd had a doser? How the hell many weapons did his baby have on her? He rushed her way because the dude she'd sent to nappy time was trying to stay on his feet by holding on to her. TJ got to her before she hit the ground, sliding on his knees so she didn't touch the concrete.

Her left hand came up, gripping his bicep, and she looked into his eyes. "TJ."

She was gorgeous even with all the blood on her… And she was going fuzzy on him.

He gritted his teeth. "You had two dosers, didn't you, baby?"

"I'm so sorry. I slipped them on my hands while you were getting redressed." She twisted so now she was the one holding him. "It's why I didn't touch you when you kissed me."

"You could have mentioned…" He couldn't quite get the words out because those drugs worked fast. The Agency always had the best drugs.

"Yeah, Coop, you're going to have to come to me. Your dumbass Romeo cousin got his ass dosed, and he looks heavy," Zach was saying.

But TJ kept his eyes on Lou as the darkness took him.

* * * *

Lou looked down at the boy asleep on her lap. Boy? Would she always see that smiling, sunny boy when she looked at him? The one her twelve-year-old self had fallen in love with? Nope. It was a man sleeping on her lap. Well, his head was on her lap. The rest of him was laid out on the middle seat of the SUV Cooper drove toward wherever they'd managed to set up base. They'd argued about tossing him in the back with the now tied up guard, but Lou wasn't about to let him bounce around back there. Even if it would have made the others comfortable.

"Lou, are you okay?" Because TJ's body was taking up a whole row of seating, Kala was the one bouncing around in the back. Zach had tried to give his shotgun seat to her, but Lou had known that would be too far away for her bestie, who probably had a hell of a lecture building up.

They'd all seen her. Well, only base had seen her, but they all knew she'd done something with TJ. Something dumb. So dumb.

What had she been thinking?

Her glasses were off so everything was hazy, but she was close enough to see every inch of TJ. She knew she should still have them on, but Tasha could reach them through the radio in the car now, and then Lou wouldn't have to listen to Big Tag complaining in the background.

"Of course." She wasn't, but now wasn't the time.

"Uh, you want to tell me what happened?"

"Kenzie didn't already do that?" Tasha would keep what happened private, but Kenzie would immediately tell her twin.

"All I got from Kenz is that Dad is broken and it had something to do with TJ's dick. As you were the one in the room with my cousin at the time, I have to worry it's about TJ's dick doing something bad. Does TJ still need his dick?"

"Kala." Cooper didn't take his eyes off the road, but he proved his hearing was excellent. "You don't know what happened."

"That's what I'm trying to find out," Kala replied. "If I find out he tried to force himself on her, I'll make sure he can't do it again."

"He wouldn't do that." Lou couldn't quite take her eyes off him. He was so beautiful, and now he had it in his head he owed her or something. They'd been in a high-octane moment. It didn't mean a thing.

"He definitely wasn't doing that," Zach said with a long sigh. "She was not fighting him off in the hallway."

"What the hell were you doing in the hallway, Lou? In the middle of an op?" Kala sounded kind of like she was begging to get the right answer to that question. "What made Dad go blind, Lou? What made him go blind?"

Yep. There was horrified begging that came with the revelation that something terrible had happened, but she wasn't ready to face it. "Your dad is being an asshole. TJ at no point had his dick out. It stayed in his pants the whole time."

Kala bit her lower lip as though thinking the problem through. "Lou, did you keep your skirt on?"

"You know we should be getting ready for the debrief." Cooper always tried to stay professional.

Kala didn't let up. "That is what I am asking. I happen to know Lou likes briefs. Cotton briefs. That's her jam. So the question is did my cousin debrief you, and that is what made my dad blind?"

Zach actually gasped. It was such a surprised sound coming from the normally rock steady, let-nothing-get-to-him captain he was. "Oh, fuck. It was bad when I thought this was about TJ taking a leak or something and the glasses caught his dick swinging. Did the big boss see you and TJ doing it? Holy crap. You and TJ did it in his interrogation cell?"

"We'll never hear the end of this," Cooper said with a shake of his head. He turned onto what looked to be a main road. They were somewhere in Bavaria, green forest rising all around them.

The forest where fairy tales were born.

Some fairy tale she had. Even her one and only encounter with the man of her dreams had turned into a nightmare. "Maybe he won't want to talk about it. You know he sometimes buries trauma deep. He's always telling us to swallow pain down like real men do."

"You've met him, right?" Zach asked.

"Lou, my father is going to talk about this moment until death takes him." Kala sat back, propping her feet on the sleeping guard. "He will bring it up at every meeting, every party he ever goes to for the rest of his life, so we need a reasonable explanation because we have to avoid this at all costs. So let's think, people. Why would Lou get caught without her undies? I need solutions."

"I don't think there's another explanation that Big Tag will accept," Zach said with a shake of his head. He'd pulled the balaclava off his head and stowed his rifle and tactical vest. Cooper had done the same, so there wouldn't be questions from the locals about a paramilitary group wandering the countryside.

"So we really think Lou and TJ were going at it?" Coop asked. "We don't want to, you know, come up with something else."

"Yes, some other reason," Kala insisted. "Did one of the guards like punch your pussy and you needed TJ to make sure your pelvis wasn't broken?"

"Yeah." Coop got into it. "I told Big Tag I was worried because those guys seemed rough with her. We can work with this."

She was slightly offended. After all the sex she'd been around because her friends were perverts of the highest order, and this was what she got from them? Like sex was for everyone but Lou, who should stay sweet and pure and never have a single physical need of her own. "Well, if that's the option you choose, you're going to have to explain why TJ felt the need to use his tongue during his very thorough examination."

Kala went a bit pale, and Coop stiffened.

That felt better. If she was going to do the time, she wasn't apologizing for the crime. Well, she also wasn't going to tell them the real truth. That she'd gotten so caught in the moment she hadn't thought about anything but how that man could make her feel. "The glasses went out when we entered the compound. I wasn't sure how long you would be."

"So you went straight for oral?" Kala had a hand to her head.

"This is worse than I thought. We should keep driving. I didn't like this job anyway. Coop, let's go to one of those countries my dad doesn't believe exists. Oooo, Luxembourg. He thinks it's a European joke."

How should she explain? "No, I didn't go straight for oral. I didn't go… TJ was hurt and I was nervous, and we might have gotten emotional. Honestly, I needed to give him something to do because he wanted to talk too much."

"That's why you had sex with TJ?" Zach had his head turned, a brow cocked over his eyes. A judgmental brow.

"I didn't exactly have… Not in a full-on sense. It was more like a distraction in a lot of ways." Yes, that was what had happened. Sure. She hadn't been ready to keep her legs spread, to let him shove his cock in without anything close to protection. Nope. That hadn't happened.

"You distracted him?" Cooper asked. "You couldn't have like given him a riddle to solve or something?"

"You should think about that because my dad will ask the same questions," Kala pointed out.

"He can ask away. I'm sure it wasn't the best way to do it, but I also couldn't come straight out and tell TJ not to talk because they were listening in." She was lying to everyone. She could have found a hundred ways to get him to stop talking. "And don't blame him for that. He's hurt. They used tasers on him." She'd seen the dart marks where they'd burned him from staying on far too long. She shifted his T-shirt, letting the rest get a look at the burns on his abs. "We don't know what else happened to him while he was in there. He was traumatized."

"He didn't look traumatized when he had his tongue down your throat in the middle of the hallway in a hostile environment," Zach pointed out.

"You kissed him again?" Kala asked.

"He kissed me." And it had felt like… It had been so much more than she'd dreamed. She'd seen another side of the man, and she liked it. TJ was always sweet and solicitous. He was funny and kind.

He was dark and dominant, and when he'd given her commands, she'd felt something she never had before. She was a founding member of The Hideout, but she'd didn't play often. Mostly she put on the most modest fet wear she could find and hung out in the lounge. She'd taken the classes and was happy to be used for demonstration purposes, but she'd never taken a Dom or had sex in the club. Kala always did her aftercare.

When TJ had stopped her in the hallway, she'd had a vision of them at the club, on her knees, with him looming over her before they performed a scene that would give them both exactly what they needed.

"Look, Kala. It was a high-pressure situation, and it got emotional," Lou explained.

"Oh, god, that's even worse. Yeah, talk about the emotion when my dad starts in on you. That'll make him run," Kala replied.

She wasn't getting any help from there. "How far away are we?"

"Not far enough that I can come up with any other explanation," Cooper replied. "We're in a cabin about a mile from here. Do we think TJ needs a medic? Big Tag might want to move quickly."

"He's asleep, not half dead," Zach insisted. "We're not moving out until Big Tag tries to get something from our friend in the back. In the morning, we'll take TJ home to the States. I've already gotten permission to move Sergeant Taggart to our team for the next three months so we can protect him."

That wasn't all they would do. They would watch him, question him.

Kala seemed calmer now. "Did TJ say anything?"

I'll get you naked in a minute, but I can't wait. I have to know. Years I've gone not knowing the most important thing. How you taste.

Yeah, she wasn't about to share that with her bestie. Luckily, from what she could tell, they'd only gotten the visual show. By the time the glasses came back online, it had mostly been moans and licking sounds that would probably make her boss stab his own ears.

Lou's body still felt like a live wire. She could feel his hands on her, the long, slow slide of his tongue over her tender flesh. She tried to force the memory away. She'd always told herself she would regret never spending a night with TJ Taggart. Now she worried this was a case of "watch what you wish for" because she might never get that one moment out of her head. "I tried to keep him from talking too much, but I got the feeling he didn't know what they thought he did. I'm not sure. I didn't want him to give too much away. I needed to buy time."

Kala's head shook. "I don't think that's going to work on my dad, but you try. When we get there and he rushes you—because he will—let me handle him. I'll show him some shock and awe."

TJ turned on his side, his face rubbing her thigh. Somehow her skirt had come up, and she could feel the brush of his scruff along her skin. "Lou, baby, you feel so good."

"TJ," she hissed.

But he was more than half asleep. He curled his arm around her leg, holding her tight. "So fucking good. Waited forever."

"Nope, you didn't," Kala argued. "If you had waited forever, we wouldn't be going into battle."

Up ahead she saw the road winding around and a small cabin at the top. "I'll handle it. It's my mistake."

It hadn't felt like a mistake. It didn't feel like it right now while TJ was wrapped around her like she was his favorite toy.

"The fact that he's able to talk through those drugs is impressive," Zach said. "Our other guy is still out, right?"

"Yeah, and still breathing and everything. He does not have my cousin's capacity for sedatives. I'm pretty sure his mom started randomly shooting him with darts when he said he was going into the Army before college. Uncle Theo has bad luck with getting dosed, so she wanted her son to be prepared," Kala explained. "Aunt Erin is parenting goals."

She was only half joking about that. Lou happened to know Erin hadn't been happy with her baby boy following in their footsteps. She'd wanted him to go to college.

She'd asked what colleges she might be able to get TJ into that were close to MIT. Erin had thought if he could be around her, TJ might get over his "I'm not smart enough for college" thing.

She'd been wrong. Everyone always told her TJ would come around. Well, they'd told her that in high school and college, and then they'd told her to give up on him and get a life.

Just as she'd started to take good advice, he'd pulled her back in.

"Baby, I'm so tired," he whispered. "Can we go to bed?"

Kala made a gagging sound.

Lou brushed back his hair, looking down at him. His eyes were closed, and he looked oddly peaceful with his big body stuffed into a too small space. "I'll make sure you get into bed."

"Stay with me." He rubbed his cheek against her leg. "Stay with me, and in the morning, we'll do it right. We're together now, LouLou. No going back."

But they weren't, and they would be going back. He was going to wake up and regret everything he'd done.

This was it. This was the break. This was the end for them, and she had to find a way so they weren't the most awkward duo in the history of time when they saw each other at family functions. Or the club.

Sir. She'd called him *Sir* and it felt real and natural. Her whole body had gone soft and submissive.

She needed to cry but she couldn't start. If she started, she wouldn't stop, and she could only handle so many emotions at once. No. She was going to suck it up, go a little cold, a bit numb.

She could still feel the way the knife had slid into that man's neck, feel the fine hot spray of his blood as it hit her cheek.

A shiver went through her.

"Don't be scared, baby. I'm going to take care of you," TJ whispered. "I won't let them hurt you."

"Sure you will, TJ," Kala said with a sigh. "Yeah, you're going to save Lou, dumbass."

"Don't." She wasn't sure why, but irritation flashed through her. No. She did know why. "Don't call him dumb."

Kala's eyes widened. "Oh, shit. You're into this."

"I am not." She couldn't be. "Like I said it was emotional and stressful, and we gave in. It was probably inevitable, but it won't happen again. He's going to wake up and be horrified, and I need to figure out how to get around the whole 'it's not you, it's me' speech I'm likely going to get. When's the first flight out?"

"Oh, it's not that easy," Zach promised. "We've got a debrief after Romeo here is fully awake, and then Big Tag is going to have a talk with our friend. We don't leave for at least twenty-four hours and we're on the smaller jet, so I'm sure we'll all get to listen in on your therapy session. Shit. He's already out. I thought we might be able to smuggle Lou in."

Cooper pulled up a long, private drive that led to a big cabin. If one didn't know what to look for, it would appear to be an inconspicuous ski chalet, but she could see the signs that this place was heavily fortified and secured.

Big Tag stood on the lawn along with his brother and sister-in-law. Tasha was on the porch, biting her bottom lip, as though she knew there was about to be a huge scene. The door opened, and Kenzie practically sprinted out, racing to the car.

Big Tag stood there, his hands in fists at his hips. He was the biggest, baddest authority figure in her world, and he'd now seen how much she enjoyed oral sex.

She'd never enjoyed oral before. It was weird, and she couldn't get comfortable or relax enough to enjoy it.

But TJ hadn't allowed her to get self-conscious. He'd overwhelmed her with pleasure, so she didn't think about anything but him.

Cooper stopped the car, and Kenzie was right there, hauling the door open.

"Lou, are you okay?"

"Yes, Lou's okay. Lou's probably the loosest, most relaxed one here since she's so recently discovered my nephew's tongue," Big Tag announced, his eyes wide. "That is not something I should ever have to see, Lou. What the hell am I going to tell your father?"

"Nothing because it's classified," she tried, easing out of the car, though she didn't want to leave TJ. She wanted to sit there until right before he woke up, longed for this warm time when he seemed to want her because he thought they were back in that place.

Big Tag ignored her reasonable suggestion. "I have to tell Boomer because your bride price is now heartily reduced. I'm sure he was going to trade you for goats or something."

"I think we'll handle Lou. No goats required." Theo Taggart stopped in front of her and put his hands on her shoulders. "You did good, kid. Thank you for bringing our boy back."

"Thank you, sweetheart," Erin agreed. "Now let's get him to bed. I take it he walked right into a microdoser."

"He didn't know I had them. He was trying to stop me from

falling, and I grabbed him. Not his fault," Lou explained.

"You know what is his fault?" Big Tag asked, but she knew a rhetorical question when she heard one. "My hysterical blindness."

Kala strode from the other side of the vehicle, her finger pointing her dad's way and a look of righteous indignation on her face. "Don't you dare, old man. Don't you dare start shaming Lou. You have no right. How many times did I walk in on you and Mom doing… I still haven't figured out the purpose of some of those positions. How many?"

Kenzie seemed to pick up on her sister's distraction ploy. "Yeah. One time you asked me how I thought I was made and to shut the door and you went back at it. We could all hear you. You were a sexual terrorist."

"You knew your parents loved each other," Tag argued. "How else would you know?"

"Any other way," Kenzie shot back. "And by your own words, now we know how thoroughly TJ adores Lou. So good for them."

Big Tag's head shook. "No. It's on the list. Thou shalt not fucketh thine rescuer."

Kala's eyes rolled. "You just made that up, and you didn't have any problem when that French agent saved Zach from getting his ass poisoned by SVR."

"I totally fuckethed her," Zach agreed, helpfully. He leaned against the big SUV, as though ready for some entertainment. "It was payback. My life. Her orgasm. Also, think about the tenuous relationship we have with her country. Now it's better, and all because of my dick."

"I didn't have to see that," Big Tag countered, ignoring Zach.

This was ridiculous. She walked right up to the big guy. He was intimidating, but she'd been around the man since she was a kid. "I'm sorry, Uncle Ian. I made a decision when I thought the comms would stay out for a while. I thought we were being listened in on, and I couldn't come out and tell TJ what was happening. He was talking too much so I distracted him."

"With your vagina," Tag said, his head nodding like he was still trying to process the trauma.

"Dad," Kenzie said between clenched teeth.

"With my vagina. I forgot to bring in a laptop, so TV was out of the question, and it was pretty sparse in there," she admitted.

Tag stared at her for a long time. "Fuck."

"We did not quite get there." Sometimes the key to Big Tag was to go with it.

He didn't take the bait. His expression softened. "Is that how you're going to play it?"

"I'm not playing. It was an op, and I might have made some bad decisions but it was still successful." Lou was going to accentuate the positive.

She was going to stay calm because she could feel anxiety building. It was creeping up along her spine, and soon it would wrap itself around her lungs and she wouldn't be able to breathe.

"Not if that's the way you're playing it," Tag said with a frown. "All right. Go get some rest. We debrief at 1900. And Lou, you need to think about how you're going to handle TJ when he wakes up because he didn't know you were distracting him. He thought it was real."

She watched as Theo and Erin carried their sleeping son up the stairs to the porch.

"He thought we were going to die, and he needed comfort," Lou explained. "That was all it was. I'm sure if we'd sent someone else in, he would have come on to them, too."

"Not me," Kala pointed out.

"Lou." TJ's head was slung back, and his eyes were open now. "Lou."

"Yeah, he sounds very not serious." Tag sighed. "He's drugged half to death and still calling for you."

"Hey, Lou. He seems worried about you," Theo called out. "Can you come let him know you're still here?"

She wanted to run. TJ was going to wake up horrified.

So maybe it was best to be right there to assure him nothing had to change.

Yes. That was why she followed them upstairs, responding every time TJ called out her name. That was why she helped his mom get him down to his boxers and tuck him into the bed.

That was why she crawled in next to him when he begged her to come closer. His arms went around her, and he quieted finally.

"Lou," he whispered, nestling his head to her chest. "Mine."

Yes. He would be horrified when he woke up. She would let him get good and asleep and then ease out so they were on a proper footing when he woke.

In a minute she would do it. He was so warm, and the day had been…she wasn't even sure what to call it. It had upended her whole world, and she had no idea what happened now. Except for the apology she would give him.

But she would deal with that later. She yawned and fell asleep wrapped in his warmth.

Chapter Five

She could feel the blood on her hands. It coated them, and she knew her aim had been true. She'd hit the man's jugular, and he was dead before he hit the floor.

She could see his eyes as they went blank, something essential fleeing with death.

She'd done that. She'd ascertained that it was the guard or TJ, and there hadn't been a second's hesitation.

So much blood.

"It's okay, baby. It's just a dream," a familiar voice whispered.

And then she felt his lips on her neck.

She was pinned down, but in the sweetest way. There wasn't any blood in this place. In this place TJ became someone new. She became someone new. In this place they didn't have to have their long history between them. They were simply a Dom and his sub. They knew their roles and what was expected of each, and things were simple.

"I'll make sure you're okay," TJ vowed right before she felt his lips brush hers.

He'd only kissed her once, and now she was addicted to it. Her whole body shifted to consciousness, ready to leave crappy dreams behind. This dream was better.

His tongue ran across her lips, demanding entry, and she gave it to him. He deepened the kiss, his tongue a powerful presence even as his hands were moving down, cupping her breast.

He kissed her until she was sure she was drugged with wanting.

There was a brief knock on the door and then it opened, Big Tag standing there with what looked like two mugs of coffee. "It's time to… Why? Why are you doing this to me?"

Shit. She scrambled to get TJ off her because somehow he'd managed to maneuver her bra off so her left boob was hanging out. She struggled to right herself.

TJ calmly stood and walked to the door, seeming not to care that his penis was erect and pressing against his boxers. He slammed the door right in his uncle's face. Then seemed to rethink. He opened it again, took the coffee, and slammed it again.

And locked it.

"See, if you'd done that the first time, we wouldn't have this problem," his uncle said through the door.

TJ ignored him, handing her the mug and frowning. "You might as well take that off. It's cool. The door's locked, and he knows not to come in. Let me see you."

"I'm pretty sure you've seen more than enough of me." She straightened her clothes. What had happened? Why the hell had he kissed her like that? Was something still wrong? Maybe they'd done more than use a taser on him. "You know we're out of that place, right? We're at a safe house here in Germany. Your parents are here. Should I go get them?"

He frowned her way like she'd said something completely unexpected. "Do you want my parents to watch us fuck? Because you should know my mom *will* critique us, and I don't know we're ready for that as a couple yet."

She forced herself to stand. His dick was right there. It had kind of found the exit in his boxers and was poking out as though looking for her. His heat-seeking missile. God, he was hot. Even with all those bruises, he was the most gorgeous man she'd ever seen.

"Keep looking at me like that, baby, and I'll give my uncle something that will really freak him out." TJ's lips had kicked up in the sexiest smirk. He set his coffee down.

"Hey, I was trying to get you two up because we have a debrief in five." Big Tag's voice was only slightly muffled. "So you should hurry through whatever it is you think you need to do but probably shouldn't around delicate old people."

"You might only last a couple of minutes, old man, but I'm going to need more time. We'll be down in an hour," TJ offered.

"We're ready now," Lou corrected. It was obvious something was up with TJ.

When she started to move to the door, his big arm clotheslined her midsection, and she found herself falling back on the bed, TJ on top of her. "What's going on?"

"We're supposed to be in a meeting." She wasn't sure what to say now that they were here. It had seemed so obvious before, but now he loomed over her, and there was zero way to miss the sexual tension between them.

There hadn't been sexual tension between them before, she realized. There had been comfort and ease and friendship. This thing between them, the live wire that now threatened to shock her, had been utterly missing.

"They'll wait. I made you a promise."

She shook her head even as her pelvis seemed to tilt of its own accord, sliding over the hard edge of his erection, and it felt so damn good. It felt like heaven. "I'm not holding you to anything. It was a moment out of time. We're back in reality now, and we should probably try to forget it happened."

He frowned down at her. "Forget? Forget that we're together now?"

How often had she dreamed he would say those words? That he would look at her and finally see her and know they were supposed to be together? Now. He picked now, just as she was starting to date and move on with her life. "No. I'm sorry, but I was supposed to go in and make sure we were ready for extraction. I was worried you would say too much and blow my cover. So I apologize if I gave you some false signals."

"False signals?" If he was offended by her words, he didn't show it. "Like the way your pussy is already wet and ready for sex? Like that false signal? You have a well-trained vagina there, Ward. Do they teach that in spy school?"

He wasn't taking her seriously at all. "You should get off me."

"No. I think this is a conversation best had with some real intimacy because I don't think you understand what happened back there."

It was clear she didn't understand anything, but she'd made a plan and she was sticking with it. "I do. You were emotional. You thought you were going to die, and you clung to someone you're comfortable with."

A brow rose over his eyes. "You make me sound like a scared little boy. I didn't cling to you. I had my tongue up your pussy. That's not clinging. That's a fucking mission statement. And don't think we're not going to talk about the whole weapons cache and all your badass knife skills. Baby, most of the reason I stayed away was because I didn't think you could handle my needs. That was my fault. I didn't talk to you. I should have, but I was worried if we tried and failed that would mean you were out of my life, and I couldn't handle the thought. I decided that sex wasn't worth our friendship."

It wasn't anything she hadn't heard before. He'd always told her he thought she was gorgeous, but he couldn't risk their friendship. She'd thought it was BS meant to keep her in his orbit for as long as he wanted her there.

Lou sighed. That wasn't what she truly thought. What she'd always known was that it couldn't work if TJ wasn't all in. "And now?"

"It's totally worth it. Let's fuck, baby. Let's fuck for a couple of weeks and then maybe I'll be able to sit through a debrief without my balls aching." He started to lower his head toward hers.

She couldn't let him kiss her. She rationalized the earlier kiss. She'd been half awake, but if he kissed her now, it would mean something. "You can't say those things to me."

He stared down at her like she was speaking a different language. Or perhaps he'd expected her to fall at his feet the minute he touched her.

"Who else would I say them to?"

"Any of your numerous girlfriends." That was better. It was a good reminder that TJ Taggart never kept a woman for long, and falling at his feet would make her look like a moron later on. She already hated the fact that everyone knew how dumb she'd been.

He shook his head. "There weren't that many, and it's not like you've been celibate, baby. I know you were sleeping with that dumbass at MIT, and I suspect you were having an affair that first year teaching at UT. So don't pretend like poor Lou sat in the background waiting for TJ to notice her. I always, always noticed you. I dropped everything to make sure you were taken care of."

This had been their problem for years. He didn't trust her in his world. Even though she'd literally lived in his world since she was twelve. She sometimes thought she understood his world better than he did. "I didn't need taking care of. I can take care of myself."

"Can you? Because from the way you reacted to me eating your pussy like it was my job, I don't think you take care of yourself very well."

That wasn't what she'd meant at all. "You can't talk like that."

"But I can," he countered with a smirk she shouldn't find so attractive. "I'm good at it. I think I'm way better at it now that we've gotten through our awkward phase. I'm feeling some things I've never felt. I'm going to be extremely possessive when it comes to you."

Maybe she should state this plainly. "We are not a couple."

If that bothered him, he didn't show it. He seemed to prefer staring down at her like he was memorizing the way she looked in this one moment. "Then what are we?"

"We're Lou and TJ. We're what we always are, always will be."

His head shook, and he leaned over to brush a kiss over her forehead. "No. I was friends with the sweetest girl in the world, and I will admit to being the dumbass who worried we wouldn't be compatible in the long run because you would need your intellectual equal, and we both know I'm not it. But you've held out on me. You've hidden a whole fucking lot of your personality from me."

What did that mean? He was irritating her in a way that made her feel anxious. "Hidden? Are you talking about the fact that I can do my job?"

He seemed to consider what to say for a moment. His hips were nestled between her legs, reminding her of all the things he hadn't done to her yet. "I'm talking about the fact that you put yourself in danger, and I don't know that I like that. Except I did think you were hot when you blew that door. That did something for me. I don't know. I'm all twisted and need some time to process, which is why we should lock the door and fuck for a really long time."

She pushed at him again. "You can't do this to me. You don't get to play with me that way."

His gaze turned slightly savage, an expression she'd never seen on his face before. "I'm not playing. Look at me. I'm not playing games with you. I never would. It's time. I knew what I was going to do even before you dropped into my lap like the best gift ever. I knew if I survived, I was going to try with you. I've spent so much of my life denying myself because I thought I wasn't good enough for you. I thought I couldn't possibly give you what you need, but I was wrong. You do need me. Tell me if a single one of those men ever gave you a real orgasm."

A flash of heat went through her because he was right. Sex up until now hadn't been some amazing thing she couldn't live without. It had become something to get through so she could get to the cuddling part. She didn't want to cuddle up with TJ. She wanted to explore with him, and that was dangerous on so many levels. "That's not what I build a relationship on."

"And, as my uncle would say, that is why you fail." He stared down at her for a moment, his expression going serious. "I know I've given you reason in the past to think I didn't have romantic feelings for you, but that's bullshit. I wanted you to have the life a person like you is supposed to have."

Yes, this had been one of his arguments, too. She needed to be locked away in the academic equivalent of a white castle where she would dance around in that magical world and solve math puzzles all day. It was what everyone expected her to do. "And what is that?"

"You were supposed to get your doctorate and grab a place at a university and live in that world where you would be safe and protected and you would find someone as smart as you are and live this charmed life. There wasn't a place for me in that life."

It was what she'd told him she wanted, what she had wanted for the longest time. Maybe right up until the moment Kala had shown up in her office and offered her the Agency gig.

Would there have been a place for him in that life? Or would he have gotten as ground down as she would have if she'd followed him and become his sweet Army wife, setting up a home wherever they landed.

It was a good life for a lot of people, but she'd always known it wasn't for her. She'd never once offered to follow TJ. She had been willing to let him follow her.

Had she been willing to do to him what men had done to women for generations? To set him up in a little house and expect him to worship her while she got to have the career of her dreams?

The thought caught in her brain, but she shoved it to the side to examine later while TJ kept talking.

"But now I know you walk around with weapons and play fast and loose with your safety, and there's damn straight a place for me in that life. I was willing to let you go for your own good, but you've made that impossible now."

She wasn't sure she was following him. "Let me go?"

"Yes. Let you go." He smoothed back her hair. "If I'd followed you to MIT like everyone thought I should, where would we be? I don't think we would still be together, and that is what I didn't want. I never wanted to be your schoolgirl crush, the one you look back on fondly while you marry the man you're on equal footing with. I want to be that man, and now I know I can because you need two things from me."

"And what are those?" Lou asked.

"You need someone watching your six at all times."

"And the other?"

"This, baby. You need this." He lowered his head and his mouth was on hers, and she couldn't work up the will to stop him.

His body pressed hers into the softness of the mattress, pinning her there in a way that felt wicked and decadent. Like he'd tied her down and there was nothing she could do but accept whatever her Dom gave her. Somehow when he kissed her like that—like she was the only woman in the world—her brain shut up, and she could feel in a way she'd never been able to before.

When he kissed her she turned into someone else, someone sexy and submissive.

Someone she couldn't be in the real world.

His tongue slid along hers as his cock pressed against her thigh.

She was already so wet. He wouldn't have any problem taking her then and there. And then maybe she would understand why her friends were obsessed with sex. Why Tasha practically glowed after spending a night with Dare. Why her mom's whole life had changed when she'd met Boomer Ward all those years ago.

She was in so much trouble because she couldn't trust this. He was still in shock. He would change his mind. "This is a way for you to process what happened to you. Can't you see that? This is a trauma response."

He snorted and kissed her again. "If you're so worried, then let's get married. We can elope. It won't surprise anyone. They've all been sitting around waiting for me to get smart enough to admit I can't live without you."

Married? The word was enough to bring her out of the dreamlike state his close proximity could put her in. She pushed against him. "TJ, get off me. Right now."

He rolled to the side, covering his eyes. "It was too fast. The marriage thing was too fast, wasn't it? See, it feels like it took too long for me to ask."

"You didn't ask. You suggested it as a way to deal with my feminine hesitation. Yes, it's insane that I would question the motives of a man who has told me for years he doesn't want this with me." She forced herself to stand on wobbly legs. It had been such a day. She'd been running on pure adrenaline most of the time, and she was out of fuel.

"I never said I didn't want you. I said it wasn't a good idea. I no longer care about good ideas. I care about the fact that when it was all on the line, you were the only thing that mattered. You are my world and you always have been, but we found something we needed. It clicked. It finally clicked for us, baby, and I don't want to waste another minute."

She needed to cry, but she couldn't. It had to wait until she was alone, until they were safe and no one could hear her. It was odd since it was something she'd learned from her mom when she was a kid. Her mother would find a quiet place to cry, thinking Lou wouldn't notice. Even after she married, it had taken a long time for her mom to be open about her darker emotions. Lou, it seemed, had taken that lesson to heart.

She was going to lose him. She was going to lose him because she hadn't been strong enough to resist.

"Hey." He sat up, reaching for her hand.

She would have moved out of reach, but he was fast. He looked up, seeming to search her face.

"Baby, are you okay? That was a lot, and you haven't cried yet, have you?"

"I don't do that anymore." She tried not to. When she was younger she would bottle things up, a leftover habit from when it had been just her and her mom, and she couldn't put more on her mom so she would let it build and build and then spend hours in her closet, crying.

TJ had found her once, and he'd climbed in with her and held her hand for the longest time.

"If you haven't then you need to." He tangled their fingers together. "Today was a lot, and I would bet you still haven't processed the fact that we nearly lost Tasha. It's been a hell of a couple of weeks, and you haven't purged at all, have you? You've been shoving it all down so you don't worry your friends."

He was correct on all points. There was a storm brewing, and if she didn't do something about it, she might explode. Except she couldn't. She'd tried. The week before, she'd even gone into her closet with a book that was sure to make her cry and she'd ended up sitting there feeling numb.

"We had a fight. A pretty big one. That has to have thrown you. I know it did for me. I don't like not being right with you. Come here. Let me hug you."

That was the last thing she needed. The lines were too blurred right now. She liked them nice and neat, to know exactly how to behave and what to expect. She didn't have that with him now. Now all she had was chaos. "A hug isn't going to work, and we have other things we need to do including going downstairs and proving to everyone we can still be professional."

"Yeah, I don't care what they think. I only care about how tight you seem. I can do this any number of ways. We were interrupted earlier today. We didn't get to finish."

"I'm not having sex with you so I can cry." But it sounded so good. If only she could manage the mental hurdles it would take to justify it.

He patted his lap. "Then let's try this a different way. Over my knee."

"What?"

"You heard me. Place that sweet ass of yours over my knee and we'll see if spanking does it for you." His voice had gone deep again, like it had in the cell. "You know it works for a lot of subs, and don't tell me you're not a sub. When it comes to sex, you are absolutely submissive. It's why it didn't work with those other men. You need a dominant partner when it comes to sex, and a calming influence outside of it. Lucky for you, I'm both. Come on, Lou. You know you need this. Or we can go for a jog."

That sounded terrible.

Did she want to go into that meeting as wound up as she was?

It was an actual ache in her chest, and if she did nothing she wouldn't be able to sleep because the voices in her head would be so loud, telling her she'd done everything wrong, that if the mission failed it would be her fault, that she would screw everything up and be alone.

She knew it wasn't real, but those old anxieties never let her down. They were always there unless she found a release valve.

A stupid idea played through her brain. What if he was right? What if this was exactly what she needed?

"Or I could call my uncle in and get you a session with someone," TJ offered as though it was the worst thing he could think of.

She felt a wave of disappointment go through her. "Can I have some time to think about this?"

"What is there to think about?"

"Whether or not we should take on that kind of relationship. I assumed when you basically offered me a session, you would be acting as my Dom and not my friend."

"You want me to…" His brows had risen and then he nodded. "Yes. That is what I meant. As your Dom and not your friend. You need a physical release to gain an emotional one, and I'm here for you. I don't think we should wait until we get back to the club, though."

Now there was something she hadn't thought about. There

might be a way out of the chaos. "We could keep it to the club."

"Seriously? This is where you want to go with this? You want us to do this thing where we pretend we're not together outside the club."

It might be the only way she could handle the situation. "What happens in the club, stays in the club."

A weary expression came over his face. "Baby, I don't know if we're going to the same clubs, but I can see you need this. Let me see if I understand what you're offering me. I top you in the club and don't touch you outside of it?"

"If I need a session outside of the club, we could have protocols for that, too."

"Do I get to fuck you, Lou?" TJ asked quietly.

God, how could he talk to her like that? How could his gorgeous mouth be so filthy, and how could she love it so much? "I don't know if that's a good idea."

"So I do all the work and get nothing that I need?"

She didn't like the sound of that. "What do you need?"

His eyes were back to that dark, possessive look she'd never seen before this day, the one that pinned her and made her think twice about pushing him aside, the one that made her feel like he was looking at her for the first time. "I need you. I need you all the time, but you're going to punish me for being foolish, and I can't blame you. I have gone behind your back and pretty much threatened every man who ever looked at you with wretched death if they fucked you over."

"You did what?"

He shrugged. "I did. I hated the idea that you were with someone else, so I made sure they knew what would happen if they screwed around on you."

That brought her to something she'd liked to address with him. She couldn't forget what she'd learned. "Like you did with Dennis?"

"Dennis?"

"My prom date."

A satisfied smile came over his face, like he was recalling a nice memory. "Oh, yeah. Kala and I got that asshole good. I still wish I'd ruined him. Hey, how did you find out about that? Even back then I was good at covering my tracks."

"Because I'm dating him."

Fire flashed in his eyes but his jaw tightened, and he seemed to take a steadying breath. "That didn't take long. I guess you meant what you told me in Australia. All right. Good, then I'll get to kill him like I wanted to. My folks have a big backyard. It's waiting for a couple of bodies. You know it's not a Taggart homestead if there aren't a couple of places you're never supposed to dig."

He was doing an excellent job of distracting her from her anxiety since now she was more irritated with him than she was worried about the future. "You can't do that."

"Watch me. I assure you I can and have. Not killed anyone, exactly, but I do keep tabs. Hey, now that I know you're kind of a freak, too, have you ever surveilled the women I hung out with?"

"No." Who did he think she was? Or the better question was who the hell was he?

"Well, you don't have to worry about that since I'm not planning on seeing anyone except you, so you will be responsible for my celibacy if we aren't allowed to follow our instincts and do what Doms and subs do." He held up a hand. "But you need time. When you make the decision, let me know." He stood and dropped a kiss on her forehead. "I'm going to take a shower. You want to join me?"

"TJ." His name was a warning. For who was the question.

He held up his hands, and he had that cute-boy look on his face, the one the girl inside her had never been able to resist. He was careening from sexy, possessive asshole to the boy she'd always loved. It was disconcerting. "I was thinking about saving water. You should think about saving time because this thing between us is inevitable."

"It never has been. I'm supposed to believe you just up and decided to…" She'd been about to say fall in love with her, but he hadn't mentioned love. This was about lust. "Want me because I killed a man."

The truth slammed into her. She'd known it as an intellectual fact. She had been the one to stab him and therefore was responsible for a human death.

She'd killed a man. It wasn't like she'd never seen it done. She had. She'd backed up all of them at one point or another. She'd helped dispose of bodies.

But she'd never done the deed herself. She'd never had blood on her hands. Fresh warm blood from a man whose eyes had faded as she'd watched.

"All right. You can hate me for this later." He sat down and offered up his lap. "Right now, Louisa. Over my knee."

It was oddly easy to do. She felt like she was in a fog. It was all right to kneel and place herself over his lap, to let him drag her skirt up and her panties down, exposing her naked ass to the air.

And somehow when that first slap came, she felt the walls shake.

The pain was…not really pain. It was sensation and heat.

He slapped her ass a dozen times, but he was holding out on her.

"Harder."

"Lou," he began.

She was over his knee, but she felt the power she had. "You promised me. You said you would do whatever it took. I need more. Or should I get another Dom? There are at least two others here."

Cooper and Zach, neither of whom she would ever ask for a session. She was being a bitch, but she knew she was on the cusp of something and couldn't stand the idea that he would hold her back.

His hand found the nape of her neck, fingers sinking into her hair and tugging. Just enough to light up her scalp. Just enough to make her damn pussy clench. "You better tell me to stop if I'm really hurting you. I can't trust you if you won't put boundaries in place."

"I know what I need."

This time when his hand came down, fire lit through her. Again and again until tears squeezed out of her eyes and a sob caught in her throat.

He picked her up and turned her over, not bothering to fix her skirt. She was sitting in TJ's lap with her ass hanging out and it didn't matter. Not if they were who they said they were—a Dom and sub. They could keep this contained, and maybe they would find a way to still be friends on the other side.

He wrapped her up, and she let out all the poison.

* * * *

TJ knew damn well he was in trouble.

Despite the fact that she'd let him spank her and hold her, when she'd been done, she'd thanked him for the discipline and gone into the bathroom to clean up. And locked the door.

When she'd come out, he'd felt like she was further away than ever before.

He was so in love with her, and she didn't believe him.

"You alone in there?"

His mom. That had been a lovely surprise when he'd awakened. His parents had been there witnessing him once again doing stupid shit. He was surprised they hadn't picked up his sister so this could be one big family reunion. "Yeah, come on in."

He was dressed and felt reasonably human. The debrief had been rescheduled for later, and he could hear Kenzie and Kala arguing about something in the background as his mom strode through the door. She looked tired, but then she'd been awake for more than twenty-four hours and worried she could lose her only son.

How much had it cost her to send in Kala and Cooper and Zach instead of going on her own? His mom could be a control freak. "You okay?"

She sighed and sank down on the sofa by the window. "I'm just glad you're safe. We haven't gotten much out of our friend downstairs, but your uncle will explain all that in a little while. If he can see by then. I know I should tell you and Lou to keep the sex thing private, but I love seeing Big Tag act like a fainting Jane Austen character. I need to get him some smelling salts and a fan. We could put one of those chaise lounge things in his office so he can pass out on it."

He'd had enough of his uncle's antics. They weren't helping him with Lou. "The second time was completely his fault. He should have waited for someone to open the door, but he walked right in."

His mother laughed but then sat back, going serious. "How is Lou? She looked wound up. I hear she had to take a couple of guys out."

And she didn't look surprised by that new information. "Did

you know what she was doing for the team? You knew I thought she was strictly an analyst."

His mom had curly red hair she usually kept in a ponytail or a bun, but now was around her lean shoulders. She wore a white tank top and tactical pants and combat boots. She hadn't been in the Army for over twenty years, but it was still ingrained in her being. "Well, you've also thought she would get bored and go back to her ivory tower, leaving you outside to pine for her, so I didn't think the truth would do that much for you."

"What is that supposed to mean?"

His mother studied him with intelligent eyes. She'd been in the military, but she'd worked intelligence. She hadn't been a grunt like him. "It means you've loved Lou for a long time, but you didn't want to be in love with her."

He wasn't sure he'd understood the difference until a few hours ago. "I've always loved Lou."

"But you didn't think you deserved her love. Because you think you're not smart enough for her." His mother summed up ten years of his life in a neat packet. "You're not, of course, but that doesn't matter. She's smart enough for both of you. She doesn't need you to mentally challenge her. She needs you to balance her, but until you see that, there's not a lot I can do. I know because I couldn't see it either."

"Couldn't see it?" He was curious because it wasn't like his mom to get real deep. That kind of talking was his dad's territory. If his mom was willing to open up, she thought this was important.

"Couldn't see what your dad could possibly see in me. I was older than him, harder than him. I was pretty broken when we met, and I didn't want to love him because I would get my heart broken when he inevitably found a woman worthy of him. And then he died. That's what it took. He died and I was pregnant, and I had to sit down and look at my whole life and figure out what I wanted. You know I almost gave you up. I never thought about not going through with the pregnancy, but I did think about finding another home for you. I didn't think I was worthy of you, either."

"Mom, that's ridiculous. You're a great mom, and Dad is still madly in love with you. It's not the same."

"Isn't it? I often get distracted by the fact that you look so much like your dad, I think you're another him. But you're not. You're so much like me, baby boy. I thought because you didn't have the same problems as me growing up, you would be different. But I've learned some patterns are ingrained in us from birth. It doesn't matter how much love and support you have, you'll never be perfect, and that's okay. Did I tease you too much? I need to know if you thought I was disappointed that you weren't smarter. Because I wasn't. You're exactly who you need to be, who this family has always needed you to be."

She must have been terrified because there was actual emotion in his mom's voice. Not that she was cold. She wasn't. She loved her kids, her husband, her family, her friends and her gun, Bertha, and in that order. Everything else could burn for all his mom cared. She was focused on a few people.

His dad was the opposite. He was sunny and happy and always willing to lend a hand.

"You never made me feel dumb. I did that to myself," he replied.

"I teased you," she said, biting her bottom lip.

He couldn't stand the fact that she was sitting there wondering if she'd fucked up. He knew that was what she was doing because it was what he would do. He didn't need an imperfect childhood to have self-doubts. "And I would know you were pissed at me if you didn't. Mom, this isn't your fault. My problems with Lou go back a long way. I didn't fit in with her when she was in school." How to explain this? "I couldn't keep up, and I think if she hadn't been so close to my cousins, it would have ended there. I would have thought she was a nice girl, but not for me. Then we kept getting thrown in together and we fit, but not all the time. I don't know. Every way I think to explain it makes me look like the asshole who strung her along. But that wasn't what I was trying to do."

"Are you sure about that? Tell me what you think would have happened when you left the Army. When you come home and work for McKay-Taggart, did you see yourself alone or was that when things would be right between you and Lou? When it was right for your timeline?"

"See, right there. Asshole. But I can't convince anyone that I didn't plan that far. I'm not smart enough to have a damn plan,

Mom. I never have a plan. I only knew I couldn't hurt her. I wasn't sure I could love her the way she needs to be loved, and I wasn't sure she could handle what I need from her. I can be…"

She held up a hand. "You don't have to say it. I understand. In that you do take after your father and your uncles."

"Okay, that's gross, but it's also true. She's never had an aggressive bone in her body. She's always been the quiet, sweet one no one else seemed to see for anything except how big her brain is."

"She was a treasure for you to hoard," his mom pointed out. "Because you're a possessive little shit from time to time. It's okay. So am I. Again, I thought it was because my childhood was so deprived of real affection that when I found it, I had to hold it close. I sometimes got super jealous when women would hit on your dad."

"Well, one of those women erased his memory for years and caused you to think he was dead for a long time," he pointed out. "You do have cause, Mom. I don't, but you're right. She was mine and it was safe, and now it's not and she's still fucking mine but it's different. And it probably doesn't matter because she doesn't believe me. I offered to marry her."

His mom winced. "Too soon, kid. She probably thinks you're in a trauma response."

Well, at least his mother could figure Lou out. "I'm not in a trauma response."

"You could be. If I were Lou, that's what I would worry about. You pushed her away for so long. It's going to be hard to get her to let you in. You've done some damage there."

The words were a kick in the gut. "I didn't mean to do damage. I was trying so hard not to. But she held back on me, too. She assured me the life she wanted was not something I could be a part of. She never said the words, but we both knew I wouldn't fit in where she needed to go. Except apparently where she needed to go was with my death-defying cousins, and right in the middle of it. She knifed that dude so perfectly I almost cried a little."

"She held back on you?" His mother's brows rose. "Did you happen to sit her down and say 'hey, Lou, you know how most of my family are total perverts who like to spank their partners and their partners are on the pain-slut side?'"

He felt some sympathy for his uncle in that moment. "You do

not have to put it that way. Still your son."

She shrugged like it was no big deal. "Have you?"

"Of course not, but we belong to the same club."

His mom bit back a laugh. "I'm sorry, baby. Yes, you belong to the same…club."

The Hideout was a club. It might not be freaking Sanctum, but it was a club. "So it's not like she doesn't know I'm a top."

"And what does Lou do? Because I've heard she doesn't play a lot."

"Sometimes she'll scene with a Dom if I've cleared him, but that's always for demo purposes. I would never let…"

His mom pointed his way as though he'd made her point. Which he had. "There it is. There is your possessive little shit coming out. You would never let what, TJ? Don't lie to me because we both know the truth."

"I would never let one get close to her," he admitted.

"Why?"

"Because I'm a possessive shit."

His mom nodded. "Yes, and now it's time to make that work for her instead of against her. Look, I love Louisa. I want her in my family for so many reasons, but the number one reason is she fills something inside you no one else can, and I don't think they ever will. But I'm worried you're on your last chance with her. She's dating."

He couldn't possibly forget that fact. "Yes, fucking Dennis Sims. I saved her from him once. I can finish the job this time. That fucker will think twice once I've paid him a visit."

"Yeah, that's probably not going to work, but I'm sure you'll try."

He didn't see why not. "I've scared them all off when I've needed to. Damn. See, that sounds better in my head than it does when I say it out loud. I didn't mean to hurt Lou."

"And she didn't mean to hurt you. I know everyone dumps this on you, but she didn't fight for you either. She accepted what you were willing to give her, and likely for the same reasons. But she's not in the same space you're in, and that's a problem. She's convinced herself you don't want her."

"I think I've proven I want her. Uncle Ian knows. I don't see why Lou wouldn't."

"History has taught her something different," his mom said. "Like it did for me. Hey, babe, I think it's time you took over."

His father strode into the room, a big smile on his face. His father had been through so much, but he could still smile and let his happiness infuse the world around him.

TJ's heart squeezed when his dad leaned over and kissed his mom.

They had been—were—such great parents. He should have learned how to be in a relationship from them. Everything he wanted was what they had. It was there in the easy way they loved each other, but there was something deep and dark about their love, and fuck all, he wanted that too.

He wanted his wife to look at him the way his mom looked at his dad.

Wife? He wanted Lou. Only Lou.

How was it so clear now?

Maybe this was a trauma response, but damn it, he was going to make that trauma his bitch and ride that fucker right into the relationship he wanted.

His mom stood and smiled up at his dad for a moment. "Can you take it from here, babe?"

"You think he's ready? I don't want to put Lou through the wringer if this is all about adrenaline. Maybe we should give him a couple of days," his father said.

In a couple of days, Lou might decide to give that fucker Dennis a shot at getting in her granny panties. He was the only one getting inside those cotton atrocities. The pussy that hid behind the voluminous fabric belonged to him, and it was time to let her know. "I'm not waiting. I don't care why the revelation has happened. I only care that I'm in love with Lou, and I need to remind her that we were always supposed to be together."

"Okay, then we should talk about how to handle a skittish woman. I think I remember most of it," his father said, sliding into the seat his mother had vacated. "I definitely remember how Boomer got her mom. I think the key with Lou is going to be a whole lot of manly wiles. Have you heard the term male cleavage?"

His mom made a vomiting sound. "See, this is where I leave

you, baby boy. I'm happy to have you back. Listen to your dad. He knows what he's talking about. I'm going to go and make fun of your uncle. But, TJ, we have some serious things to talk about in that debrief. We need to figure out what they want from you because until we solve this mystery, you're both in danger. They'll know they can get to you through Lou. And they'll know I can still kill a man with the strength of my thighs."

"I wish I didn't know that," he replied with a shake of his head.

"Hey, I'll want to see some of that strength later, baby." His dad winked up at her.

"If you need a soundtrack for your man makeover, let me know." Her lips had curled up, the words an obvious secret joke between them.

That was what he wanted, and he could only ever have it with Lou because that kind of deep connection came from soul mates, and she was his. He'd just been too scared to let them be what they needed to be.

Or maybe he hadn't been ready and now he was.

"I think I fucked up, Dad."

"From what I saw on that tape, you didn't fuck up," his dad replied. "She seemed to enjoy it."

He hadn't meant to make a sex tape, but then that had been Lou's fault. She'd known everyone would be able to see through those highly inventive glasses when they inevitably cleared the jammers. "We don't ever have to talk about that again."

"You might not want to talk about it, but you should probably do it again and often. You'll discover that women as smart as Lou often forget their own bodily needs and often have a hard time turning off their brains long enough to enjoy sex," his father explained.

Yep, they were having this talk. Well, his family had always been strangely open. "She wants a D/s only relationship."

His dad snorted at that bit of news. "Then you're already halfway there. This isn't going to be hard, son. Now, let's game-plan."

He leaned in, willing to learn from the master.

Chapter Six

"Okay, you seem weirdly calm for what happened." Kala entered the dining room with a mug of something warm in her hands. "I kind of thought I would have to come and drag you out of wherever you would be hiding."

"Why should I hide?" Lou was weirdly calm. Not weirdly. Pleasantly.

Well, except she was horny. She'd joked about being horny before, but now she thought what she'd meant was lonely with a side of "I wish I wanted to have sex more."

Now she understood. She wanted. Longed. Needed.

The spanking had been enough to get her through the initial anxiety, but she'd had to stop herself from seeking him out again. Luckily she'd seen his mom disappear into the room he was in, and that had been enough of a deterrent.

"Because it's what you do when you need to cry. Depending on which way the wind is blowing, I either find a sub and beat his ass or I let Coop beat my ass and then have a couple of drinks. You hide in your closet and reread the sad moments in romance novels."

Her best friend knew her well, and yes, more than once over the years Kala had snuck into her hidey-hole and brought her some tea or a soda or smuggled in one of the Buds so she had a dog to cuddle.

"Well, my closet isn't here, and I didn't bring a book."

"So what worked, Lou?"

There was an air of expectation to her best friend, the one that told her she was willing to be stubborn as hell until she got some answers. Kala Taggart had been like a sister to her. They hadn't started out that way. At first she'd been the cool older kid who didn't mind hanging with someone younger. She'd practically worshipped Kala the way she had TJ.

Because they'd been the first friends she'd ever made, the first of her peers to accept her for who she was, to love her for who she was.

She loved Kala on every level. She loved her for the complex, irritable, loyal, stubborn woman she was. "You don't want to know. What's in the mug?"

Kala sighed and slid it her way. "Chamomile tea. So you did the deed."

She was twenty-five years old and they were talking like she'd lost her virginity and brought shame to the family line. It was annoying. "Not exactly. I let him spank me and it worked, and I feel better now."

Mostly better. She was still kind of dreading the moment TJ would walk in and she would have to be professional with him.

Kala's eyes widened. "No. You didn't. Please tell me you didn't decide to have a D/s relationship with my cousin. Did you use the words *we can keep it to the club*?"

Lou wasn't sure what the problem was. "Is that so surprising? You've always told me I should find a top to play with. Now I have."

Kala's head fell back on a groan. "That's what the dumbass guy who needs to make up for shit is supposed to say."

"Nah." Kenzie bounced in, setting her laptop on the already crowded table. "That's what the chick who can't let herself believe that it's real is supposed to say. Wait until I tell Mom. She'll say you're coming along nicely."

She wasn't coming at all, and that was the problem. Now she had a taste for it. "I'm ready to explore D/s, especially as a coping mechanism, and I think TJ is perfect. He doesn't have a permanent sub and he's kind of part time, so it's not like we would be in each other's space too much."

Kenzie looked at her twin, and they had one of those telepathic talks of theirs. She could almost read it.

When did Lou get delusional? Kenzie would ask.

Dad would say when her vagina took over, Kala would reply. Lou could tell. It was all in the way her brow curved up in a "what are you going to do about it" expression.

So what do we do?

Lou wanted to answer that one. *Absolutely nothing. Not a thing. Just let it be, Taggarts.*

Obviously we have to fix the problem for her. Yup. That was the look on Kala's face.

"You can't kill TJ." That was Kala's solution to everything.

Kala's lips tugged up in a genuinely amused expression. "It would solve a lot of problems."

"We could also talk to some of the military dudes we know," Kenzie mused. "Maybe get him assigned to Antarctica."

"You are not messing with his career." It was absolutely the last thing she wanted. She stared the twins down. "Do you understand me? I know I'm the quiet one, but you mess with TJ and you mess with me. He's your cousin. He's a freaking Taggart."

"So is Lucas, but he can be a pretentious asshole sometimes. Honestly, having that Taggart name makes you more and not less likely to be a massive ass. I should know." Kala could be very self-aware.

Lucas Taggart was Sean Taggart's son and a rising star in the culinary world. And he wasn't an asshole by anyone but Kala's standards. "He wouldn't let you run an Agency op in his kitchen. That does not make him a bad person. And TJ is confused right now. He's been through something terrible, and I'm his friend. He needed some comfort."

"So you're like a blankie?" Kenzie asked.

Out of the corner of her eye she saw Big Tag starting to walk in. He pressed through the French doors, moving toward the front of the table.

"A warm, soothing vagina blanket," Kala countered. "She's TJ's vagina blankie."

And Big Tag turned without saying a word and practically ran back toward the kitchen.

She was starting to worry about him. "Stop saying the word *vagina* around your dad. He can only take so much. And I meant what I said about TJ. Don't try to screw with his assignments."

"Dad already did," Kenzie explained. "He's sticking with us for the next three months. We're heading back to Dallas in a couple of hours, so I guess you'll get in some club time together. I don't know. It could work. It works for Kala and Coop."

It did not. Not in any way. They were the most dysfunctional… She couldn't call them a couple. Pair. Or was that her and TJ?

Except all of the sudden, TJ seemed to want to function. A lot. He wanted to function all over the place.

"So you're hedging your bets." Kenzie slung a leg over one arm of the chair she sat in, regarding Lou thoughtfully. "You think TJ's going to change his mind, but you can't quite not give it a shot, hence the keep-it-to-the-club thing."

"She's scared." Kala got serious. "And she's got every right to be. Why should she open herself up to him? He's always denied her before, always friend-zoned her. Poor baby got tased a half a dozen times and suddenly he needs his blankie. Well, what happens when the taser sting wears off and he wants a normal life again? What happens when he wakes up and decides he wants someone else?"

Were they still talking about her and TJ? She knew Cooper had drifted in and out of Kala's life for years, knew he'd said some things that had hurt her when they'd been kids. But since he'd joined the team, Cooper seemed to spend all his time trying to get close to her.

And in the club, they could be savage.

Did she want that with TJ? Did she want to screw him so badly that she would toss out all the rest?

"What happens if he's awake now and doesn't want to go back to sleep? What happens if he finally found the one piece that didn't fit, and now it's the right time?" a deep voice asked.

For spies, they really should know better than to talk about sensitive subjects in the middle of a room that opened to all the other rooms. TJ stood in the archway that led to the great room and the stairs to the bedrooms. He leaned against the wall, his hair a bit scruffy and damp from a shower.

A shower he'd offered to take with her.

Longing welled up. All the man had to do is walk into a room and she longed. She wanted.

Would satisfying that longing be enough? Because despite his words, he would go back to his job at some point, and he would remember all the reasons they didn't fit.

"Was the piece that suddenly fit her boobs?" Kala was relentless.

"I haven't gotten a really good look at those yet," TJ admitted. "I saw them briefly in the compound, and I almost had that sucker off her when your dad walked in. Can you keep a leash on him? He's wrecking my suddenly important sex life."

"TJ," she hissed under her breath.

He gave her a heart-stopping grin and crossed the space between them. "There's no bullshit with this family. You should know that. We're not polite. We're not circumspect. When we're in love, we're pretty much ruthless as fuck, and then when we get what we want, we're the absolute best partners in the world."

Good for whoever he ended up with. "We're not partners."

"Yet. But that's where the ruthless part comes in. Up until now you've dealt with a man who loved our friendship so much he was unwilling to risk it. Now I am, and you'll see the other side of me. Come sit on my lap."

"Is there a reason Dad's dry heaving?" Tasha asked as she walked in followed by Zach and Cooper.

"What did you two do?" Cooper slid in beside Kala without even looking for another seat.

"I am not sitting on your lap." That was a terrible idea. They were supposed to be professional.

"It's a nice lap, and there aren't enough chairs," he pointed out. "My parents are on their way in, and Dad's back isn't what it used to be. I think we should take one for the team." He leaned over. "I might be able to slide my hand under those panties of yours and make this meeting more fun, if you know what I mean."

The words sent a shock of arousal through her system.

"Zach, you need to find an extra chair or my dad is going to pop a couple of blood vessels in his eyes," Tash said with a frown. "I'm not joking. I don't think he can take much more of this."

"Like he's never walked in on you and Dare." TJ simply slid that big, gorgeous body of his onto the seat next to hers, sliding an arm around the back. Possessively. Like she was his and it was a foregone conclusion that he would get his way.

Tasha's eyes narrowed even as Zach went off to find that chair that would apparently save Big Tag. "Not even once. Dare respects my father's boundaries, and so do I."

TJ and Kala snorted at the same time.

"I was not aware the man had boundaries until today," Kenzie remarked with an eye roll. "He should understand that when Ben Parker and I finally have our epic happily ever after, we're doing it all over the house. Everywhere. No place is untouched, and that is for Mr. Bear, who got stuck under my parents and was ruined for all of time."

"You did swear you would avenge him, sis." Kala gave her twin a quick fist bump. "But as for TJ, well, I'm watching you. Ruthless, my ass."

"I don't need for her to believe me," TJ promised, leaning in again. "Honestly, it might be better if you don't believe me. I'm just your friend TJ. The same sweet guy you've always known. You can indulge me because there's no way I would trap you and tie you down and fuck you until you can't remember any man except me. Sweet TJ would never do that. I'm sure we'll be watching movies and petting puppies in no time at all because sweet TJ won't be thinking of every single way he could have you. Every minute of every day."

Who the fuck was he and why were her panties wet again?

"I can still hear you, and now *I* kind of want to vomit," Kala complained.

"I'm actually thinking of betting for him now." Kenzie was looking at TJ with new respect.

"We are not doing that." Lou needed to shut that shit down or she and TJ would be at the center of The Hideout's infamous betting book.

The whole stupid thing had been her idea because she'd read way too many romances set in the Regency where all the finest clubs had betting books. It was mostly dumb stuff like whether or not Sally Sub could take three hours of foot tickling—she couldn't.

Or who would punch hardest. She'd modified a punching bag with sensors to register the strength of a punch, converting the power to joules and then to pounds-force. Zach's punch was the equivalent of being hit by a refrigerator dropped from a second-story window.

But Kala's was almost as bad.

Lately, their dumb bets had taken on relationships and how fast certain people would hit the sheets.

"I say she holds out until TJ comes to his senses," Tasha said.

That hurt, but at least someone had faith in her.

"I don't have any senses," TJ promised her. "And that makes it sound like Lou isn't hot. Like oooo, I'll wake up and realize I got the girl with the glasses when I was going for the popular one. I never did. I might have been stupid and insecure, but she's always been gorgeous to me. I think she will be even more gorgeous when I get to properly see her boobs. Honestly, and the rest of her."

"TJ." She had no idea who she was dealing with now. What had his mother said to him?

"Well, it was too fast. I didn't get a chance to do the whole stare-at-you thing. I had to get in there with my tongue," TJ began.

"There is not enough Scotch in the world." Big Tag shook his head and looked like he was ready to flee again.

"Get in there." Theo Taggart pushed his brother along.

"You need to make him stop," Big Tag complained. "Your son is the one doing this. This is not Lou's fault. Lou is a nice girl."

Lou is a nice girl. Lou is a smart girl.

"Lou would never do these things," Big Tag continued. "It's TJ's fault."

"It is definitely TJ's fault," Kala agreed. "He's saying all these nasty things to her like we don't have ears."

Zach reappeared, frowning. "There are no more chairs. Not any that I can get in here. It's okay. I can stand."

"TJ perving on Lou is probably the worst thing that happened all week, and that includes him getting his ass kidnapped." Kala pointed her cousin's way. "If I'd known you were going to get all handsy with my bestie, I would have gone in myself and murdered you right there."

"That's the way, baby girl." Big Tag found his seat. "You protect the smart one at all costs."

The smart one. The nice girl. The girl who everyone came to with their problems because she was the sensible one. Louisa Ward always made good choices.

"I don't mind standing." Erin had joined them, her hands on her husband's shoulders.

"You can join me, baby," Theo said, bringing her hand to his lips.

Big Tag didn't have a problem with that, and he'd almost certainly walked in on Tash and Dare at some point. They all had. They were not circumspect in any way and the walls were thin, so she'd definitely heard some nasty talk coming from Tash's fiancé.

It was only her. Lou, who was supposed to stay sweet and single because she was so smart she shouldn't have any physical needs at all.

She pushed back her chair, and all eyes were on her for once. It was weird. She was always in the background, always in the shadows.

She stared down at TJ. "You said something about your father's back. We should help the older generation out, shouldn't we?"

A slow smile spread over his lips, and he moved so she could maneuver onto his lap.

His comfy lap. Comfy except for the erection she could already feel against her butt.

"See," he said as his arm went around her waist. "Isn't that better?"

How long had they played these roles? Lou, the academic, and TJ, the soldier, and never the twain shall meet. Good as friends, but they didn't fit together anywhere else. Except she fit fine on that man's lap.

She leaned over, whispering far more softly than he had. "It's like we're in the club. That's all. You gave me something I needed. I think I might need this too."

She might need her friends to see her in a different way because maybe, just maybe, then she could see the possibilities, too.

"That's enough for now, sub," TJ replied.

His uncle groaned again.

But she could have sworn, right before his head hit the table, that the man smiled.

* * * *

"All right. Now that we all have seats or laps and our boy in danger has what is apparently his favorite blankie, can we get serious?" Big Tag asked. "We've got a flight in less than two hours, and I've got to hand our hired idiot over to German intelligence. They want a word, but all I've gotten out of him so far is that he works security for a man named Friedrich Huber. The man's a known arms dealer. He runs guns in and out of Africa and the Middle East."

TJ knew he should probably send his uncle a death stare, but he was kind of right. Lou was like a blanket. He wanted to wrap himself up in her and she smelled like fabric softener, and damn that was sexy to him.

He hadn't realized how much his family would help him by pointing out how nice Lou was. He understood why she'd slid onto his lap, and it wasn't all about wanting to be there. It was about wanting everyone else to think she could be there.

He would use that. He'd meant what he'd said. He could be ruthless when he needed to be. He'd always carefully hidden that part of himself, preferring to be Lou's golden boy heroic type. It was precisely why he'd never mentioned all the assholes he'd warned off her. He was Lou's friend, the one she could count on to always do the right thing.

Now he needed to access the bad boy she brought out in him.

He let his hand find her knee, running up her skirt, but careful to keep the motion slow and hidden.

"I'm sending a full dossier to each of you," Tasha said. "But it's not anything that will set the world on fire. It's a fairly typical crime story. He's from a lower-class background. Mom died, and Dad abandoned him. In and out of prison in his youth. There are a couple of Italian mafia groups that work in Germany, and he became associated with them."

"From what we can tell, he moved from running drugs to guns, and when his mentor died, he moved in to lead the operation. The Italians actually took down most of the family he worked for a few years back, leaving something of a power vacuum that Friedrich was happy to fill," Big Tag continued. "So the question is why do they want TJ? All I got out of the guard is that he wants to go home and something about another arms dealer the boss wants information on."

"He's called The Jester," TJ murmured, staring at the way Lou's neck curved into graceful shoulders. How had he never simply spent hours staring at her? He'd watched every movie she'd ever asked him to when he could have been watching her. "From what I can tell, he's a new presence in the arms world, and our friend either didn't like the competition or he wants to hire the fucker."

"Yes, that is the name the guard used. The Jester. Dumbass," his uncle agreed.

His dad cocked a brow his uncle's way. "Really? It's better than The Broker?"

Oooo, he was glad his Aunt Charlotte wasn't here. She'd gone by The Broker when she'd been the world's premier information collector. She and her sister, Chelsea, had ruled that world for several years.

"Nah, The Broker was brilliant. It's self-explanatory," his uncle countered. "You know exactly who you're dealing with when they introduce themselves as The Broker. And it's sexy. What is The Jester supposed to mean? Does he think he's funny or something? Is he like trying to be The Joker but didn't want to deal with copyright infringement?"

His mom was saying something snarky and the others were watching the byplay of the older generation, and that meant he could move a little more. He got his palm between her thighs. Warm skin. Soft skin. He'd spread her wide the first time, but now he wondered what it would feel like if she'd wrapped her legs around his neck and been surrounded by the soft core of her sex.

"Lou, next time find someone with more information, please."

Lou shook her head like she wasn't quite following the conversation. "What?"

His uncle had been the one who'd dragged her attention away. His uncle's eyes narrowed as though he knew something was going on but couldn't quite figure out what it was. "I said the guard was low level. He didn't have much information. I got everything out of him I could, but next time, find me someone higher up. The dude who's guarding shit usually doesn't know much."

"Well, it's not like I had a lot of choices. He was the only person I saw on my way out," Lou replied, wriggling slightly. Yeah, that felt good. "And honestly, that was beyond the parameters of my mission. I was supposed to get TJ out. I did. Why didn't you ask Kala to chase down the CEO of this organized crime thingee?"

She was so cute when she was flustered, and there was zero doubt that she was flustered. It was there in the breathy quality of her voice and the way her chest hitched as his hand climbed up her thigh. And the fact that she'd used the word *thingee*. Lou tended to be precise. She was a smarty pants of the highest order.

He was the dude who wanted to get into her smarty pants, and suddenly that seemed like enough. He spent his whole life backing other people up. Why couldn't he back up the person he loved most of all?

He'd spent all this time thinking he was a grunt and not worthy of her, but didn't the smarty pants of the world need comfort too? Didn't they need someone who took care of them and gave them the affection they clearly deserved? What would another smarty pants do right now? Probably spend his time paying attention and trying to look…smart. That's what they did. When he thought about it, another smarty pants would actually clash with what Lou needed.

He was almost to the apex of her thighs when she put a hand on his arm.

Damn it. So close.

She bit her bottom lip and closed her eyes and then removed her hand.

When he let his fingers slip under the band of her panties, she spread her legs slightly.

Yeah, this was what they needed. She would almost certainly pull away after, but he would pursue her with far more willpower than he'd ever used to push her away.

"I made it to what I suspect was the main office. No one was home," Kala admitted. "Coop and I tried the computers, but most of them had been bricked. We only got one to give us data, and I think it's the one that controlled CCTV. They had good protocols. Once we burned the jammer, the important people took off. I would bet there are tunnels nearby that aren't tracked by CCTV."

Kenzie nodded. "Yes, I found some records of excavation at that site right before World War II. This whole area was ground zero for the Nazi movement. It was heavily bombed later in the war, so it makes sense that they had underground shelters. The tunnels would have led back to the village a few miles away."

"It would have made sense to know that before we went in," his uncle pointed out.

Kenzie frowned. "Sorry. I was trying to figure out what we were going into, not where they would run."

His mother's eyes rolled. "Yeah, says the dude who pushed these kids to plan and execute a delicate rescue op in less than forty-eight hours."

"Yes, to get your son out," his uncle shot back, and then seemed to give up the argument. "TJ, you haven't explained how the hell you got captured."

He'd been dreading this, but now it didn't seem so bad because he could feel the heat of Lou's pussy. She was fucking wet already. She responded to his touch like she'd been made for him.

How had they not been doing this for years and years?

"I was out with friends and got roofied at a bar. Woke up to a bunch of tasers and like bright lights and shit." He slipped a finger over her clitoris and felt her stiffen. She was so good at this. Perfectly quiet, and aside from the slightest flush of her skin, she looked like she was concentrating again.

Such a good girl. Yeah, they could play with that.

"Are you serious?" Zach asked, shaking his head like he couldn't quite believe it. "You let yourself get roofied?"

He wasn't taking that from him. From anyone. He wasn't a part of this team and never had been. He worked differently. "I'm not a spy, man. There's zero reason for anyone to kidnap me unless they are interested in how our comms work or need a lesson in sharpshooting. Otherwise, I'm pretty meaningless, so I don't sit around wondering whether someone spiked my drink when I got up to hit the head."

"You're useful for your last name alone, man," Cooper pointed out.

The Taggart name meant something in military and intelligence circles, but there were far more important Taggarts to be had. His cousin Heath might be a Taggart in name, but he was also heir to the 4L fortune, along with their Lawless cousins. Luke and Carys Taggart would someday inherit his Uncle Sean's restaurant empire. And Kala and Kenz were important in so many ways.

He was just TJ.

"That's not why they brought me in." He circled her clit, feeling her wriggle slightly as though trying to find the exact right spot. The good news for her was he was actually quite good at multitasking. He looked to his parents and uncle while he stroked Lou over and over again. "I woke up, and after a couple of rounds of pre-game torture, they explained that they wanted me to put them in touch with the man known as The Jester. I had no idea who the fuck that was, however, they did not believe me. They have pictures of me walking in Berlin with a man I've never seen before. They have some bad intel. Did someone go into the interrogation rooms?"

So wet and hot, and it was all for him. He played with her, light touches and strokes that would keep her on edge.

How much fun would they have in the club? She'd agreed to bottom for him, and he was going to show her what a good choice that was. When they were in the club, he wouldn't have to hide what he was doing. He could be open about fucking her. No one would question him in the club once she had a collar around her throat.

"Kala and I did a sweep, but it was clean. They obviously have excellent protocols," Cooper explained.

"What I don't understand is why they didn't try to make a damn stand." His uncle sat back. "They ran immediately."

"That bothers me, too," his mom agreed. "We sent in a small team because we thought they had the best chance of getting around their security. We weren't ready for a prolonged fight. From what I could tell from watching surveillance, they had at least ten armed guards. But they didn't even try to fight. They ran and fast."

"Which means they had something to hide and thought it was a strike team coming after them." His dad was staring at him with a frown. Like he knew what he was doing and was hitting him with that "what the hell, TJ" look.

If that look was supposed to intimidate him, then his father shouldn't have told him to please Lou sexually every chance he got. Maybe his dad didn't think this was the right chance, but TJ took things seriously. "I never got a good look. I think the man who interrogated me was Friedrich. He had a German accent. But I think someone was with him. I heard whispering. Like there was someone bigger, someone they didn't want to expose, but he was running things. He wasn't speaking German, but it also wasn't English. I'm not sure. Definitely a European. They explained that they'd made it so my friends would think I was off with a woman."

He'd been so worried they would believe it. He rested his head against Lou's shoulder. Outwardly it would look like he was being affectionate. But the motion covered his arm moving, so he could slip a finger in her pussy. Thumb on her clit, rotating while that finger slowly drove inside her.

"Can you not be professional?" Kala complained. "Do you have to be so huggy?"

He was going to have to shut that down. She could be territorial when it came to Lou, but he wasn't going to let that stop him. If Kala was happy being sexless and alone because she couldn't forgive Cooper, that was her choice, but he was going to make sure Lou didn't make the same one.

"Like Mom and Dad don't do this all the time during a meeting," Kenzie shot back. "They made out in front of the Joint Chiefs of Staff once."

"And we all swore we would do better," Cooper shot back.

TJ rather thought he was doing better. This was better than some rando make-out session.

"I knew you wouldn't do that." Lou sounded only a bit hoarse. She placed both of her hands on the keyboard of her laptop and glanced down as though staring at something on the screen. "When Zach got the text, he brought it to me, and I knew it wasn't you."

Her screen was a blank Word document, and then she typed.

Harder.

Oh, she thought she was in charge, did she? Still, she'd been awfully sweet to defend him, to know exactly who he was. He pressed down and rotated. "I'm glad someone knew me. You knew I wouldn't blow you off."

"I knew you wouldn't miss Devi's birthday," she replied, eyes still on the screen.

He eased off.

Damn it.

"I wouldn't blow you off, Lou," he said quietly.

"I have a memory burned into my brain that says you would," his uncle added.

It feels like you are now. This feels like punishment. Should I get to my own seat?

It sucked that she was the only one who could communicate, but then he rather thought she liked that. He stroked her again and felt her relax. They were going to have such a talk after this, but first he had two jobs to do, and only one of them involved his mouth, unfortunately. "Anyway, after a pretty full day of seeing how much electricity they could run through my body, they decided I wasn't going to give in. That was when they explained to me that they were going to the States to pick up something that would make me talk. I'm going to admit that I tossed my mom straight under a bus."

"You did what?" his dad asked.

Lou's pussy tightened around his finger, and he knew she was close. So close to coming for him, and she was going to be a good girl and keep it quiet. She wouldn't let anyone know what he was doing. His cock was practically throbbing, but he ignored it. His cock would have to wait. He had a play to run.

Make Lou crave him the way he craved her.

His mom merely smiled and winked his way. "Thanks, baby boy. It was fun. I hadn't gotten jumped like that in a long time. And you know there are privileges that come with age. I didn't even have to bury the body on my own. All the fun. None of the responsibility."

Lou's fingers moved on the keys, but then no one would think anything of it. Lou was always somewhat distracted during a debrief, always looking something up or making some kind of note.

So close. Please don't stop.

His dad nodded as though understanding. "Ah, they floated some names out, and you begged them not to hurt your mom. Your delicate flower of a mother."

"Damn straight I am. Tag, you need to send me and Liam back out in the field. I have a taste for killing again," his mom quipped.

"Well, Li's got a taste for his recliner, so good luck with that," his uncle replied.

His parents had filled him in on how things had gone down from there. Cooper had played the part of the mercenary and Lou had been taken in, and voila, now they were here.

And he still had zero idea who The Jester was and why anyone would think he was involved.

What he did know was how to blow Lou's mind.

He pressed down on her clit and she gasped slightly, holding herself still as he moved his thumb against her, stroked inside her with his finger.

His uncle closed his laptop and rubbed a place between his eyes as though the day had been far too much for him. "All right. TJ, I'm going to need a thorough written report."

He felt the moment she came. It was there in the way she shivered. In the way her fingers pressed against the keyboard, but nothing like actual words came out. Just a bunch of *r*s and *p*s. Her lips pursed, and then she relaxed.

He should have known he would get punished for getting kidnapped. Paperwork.

I'll type it up. Promise.

Like she could read his mind. "I'll get right on that."

"And I'll call in to Langley and see what I can find out about The Jester," his uncle promised. "And someone fucking find Tristan."

"He's on a secondary assignment, sir." Zach stood and faced the big boss. "I've tried to get in touch with him, but I was told it was beyond my paygrade."

So Tristan was working some kind of black ops for another team. Even his Uncle Ian wouldn't be able to get information on where he was.

"I don't like the sound of that," his mother said. "I'll call Adam and see if he knows anything."

Kala was staring at him across the table. Like she knew what was happening.

He didn't care if everyone knew. All that mattered was Lou was relaxed, and she sat back in his arms.

He gently withdrew his hand from her undies, sliding along her thigh.

"We're wheels up in two hours," his uncle announced. "Zach,

help me escort our friend to German intelligence, and for god's sake TJ, if you're going to hump her leg do it before we get on the plane. It's the small jet. I can't…I just can't, damn it."

His uncle stalked out.

His dad shook his head and leaned over, whispering something his mom's way.

That got her smiling again. "Seriously? Did you teach him that?"

His dad kissed his mom. "Maybe. Maybe we should go and see if I'm still any good at it."

"And I'm out of here." Cooper stood. "You know I get enough of this from my own parents. I do not need it from you."

"Or you," Kala said under her breath as she stared his way, proving she'd known exactly what was going on.

TJ shrugged because he didn't care. He wasn't sure why everyone was acting all prudish. They'd grown up surrounded by parents who liked to show their affection way too much. "And yet here I am."

He fought the urge to bring his fingers to his lips and taste her again. There was only so far he could push. Especially since his father knew exactly what he'd done.

"I should get ready to go." Lou hauled herself up, gathering her laptop and crushing it against her chest.

Probably so no one would see her nipples were hard.

"Did I miss something?" Kenzie was looking around like she'd skipped the best part of the soap opera playing out in front of her.

"I don't know." Tasha slipped her cell into her pocket. "I think TJ was rubbing her leg or something. Should I schedule a physical for TJ?"

"I don't need…" he began.

His dad pointed a finger his way. "Yes, you do. You are not going to be stubborn about this. At the very least you'll let one of the docs look at you. You went through something…"

"Don't you dare say the word traumatic." He was sick of that word. He was fine. He didn't need a doctor.

Lou looked up at him, her eyes big and wide behind her regular glasses. "Please let them look at you. I would bet Aidan or Carys can do the basic physical if that makes it better."

Fuck. He hated physical exams. “Okay.”

She nodded and then turned and walked away.

His mom watched as Lou left. “Wow, son. You have a button and she pushed it.”

“That is not how I explained it,” his dad hedged. “It was kind of supposed to be the other way around.”

Kenzie frowned. “Seriously? Here while we were talking? Ewww.” She frowned. “Now I’m sad. Everyone gets to do perverted things except me.”

She flounced off.

TJ sat back. He did have a weakness. He would pretty much do anything Lou wanted.

Except let her go.

Chapter Seven

"Yes, you heard me right the first time," the big boss was saying. "No. It wasn't one of the twins. They were perfectly well behaved. I raised them right. I'm going to have a long talk with Boomer when we get back. I can't blame TJ. He was raised by wolves."

Lou felt herself blush because Big Tag was talking to Drake Radcliffe. She could barely hear him because she'd taken a seat at the back of the jet, hoping if she sank down maybe people would forget she was here. And that she'd pretty much had not one, but two orgasms in public.

Her dad was going to kill her.

Or he would hug her and tell Big Tag to leave her alone. That was the scenario most likely to happen. Her dad kind of treated her like a princess who could do no wrong, and that could lead to some serious spoilage, but her early years had tempered her. She would do anything for her dad.

Something flew across the cabin, hitting Big Tag right in the noggin.

"Hey, I meant Erin. I know you're a delicate flower," Big Tag shot back.

It was usually funny to watch the Taggart brothers squabble, but she was feeling… She wasn't even sure how she was feeling. She'd avoided TJ after she'd fled the conference room. She'd spent those last hours in Bavaria helping Zach make sure the handover of the guard to German intelligence went smoothly.

All the while she could feel TJ's eyes on her.

When they'd found their seats on the luxurious jet, she'd picked one of the single seats instead of the doubles, or the comfy couch-like seating Tasha and Kenzie were currently occupying. Kala was sleeping in the lounger across from Lou, having taken the seat before TJ could.

Cooper was in the cockpit along with Zach, who could fly the plane but not the way Coop did. Cooper had been fascinated with airplanes since he was a kid. He'd gotten his pilot's license at sixteen, though he'd been flying with supervision before then.

They were the only team who had their own plane and pilot. Mostly because the plane wasn't the property of the Agency, and Ian Taggart was allowed a kind of freedom with this team no other handler had.

No wonder everyone called them the Princess Team.

Big Tag and Theo were arguing and she heard something about leaving the kids alone and Big Tag saying he wished he could leave them alone, but they were on his freaking team, and poking to make sure they were alive was his literal job.

She wished she could sleep, but she worried if she did she would see that blood on her hands again.

Or she would dream about TJ and make an idiot of herself by drooling and calling out his name.

Kala's eyes came open, and she yawned. "You okay?"

She was getting a lot of that today. "Sure." She leaned over and snuck a peek at the front of the plane.

TJ was sitting by himself on the couch across from where Kenzie was napping and Tasha was working on her laptop. He sat there, staring out the window at the night around them.

He looked sad and lonely and remote.

"You're not okay." Kala stretched and leaned forward. "You're weird, and I'm wondering what's going on in your head. You know no one really believes you two were playing at the conference table. What did he do to you? Try to pull your skirt up and touch your thigh or something? You know you can punch him in the face. Or tell me and I'll do it for you."

She wasn't ready to have this conversation with her bestie, but she suddenly remembered one she did need to have. "I didn't think you needed my permission to do that."

Kala frowned. Lou could tell a lot from Kala's frowns. Some people had a bunch of different smiles, but Kala's mood could always be mapped by her frowns. This one was her "what do you know that I should have hidden better from you" frown. "I don't know what you're talking about."

It was good to have Kala on the ropes for once. She wasn't truly pissed about what Kala had done in high school, but she wanted to make sure she wasn't still doing it. "I had a date with Dennis Sims right before this mission."

There was Kala's "I should know this, but I don't" frown. "Going to have to refresh my memory."

"Prom."

And a "yeah, I got caught" frown. "I told that asshole what would happen if he told you." She shook her head. "Wait. You had a date with that asshole? How did you have a date with him?"

"We matched on a dating app and I was curious," Lou admitted. "And I don't think he's an asshole. I think he was young and stupid. He seems nice now. He pointed out that you and TJ kept a lot of people away from me in high school."

Kala's eyes hooded. "I was trying to protect you."

Lou reached out and put a hand over hers. She'd been so young, and she'd clung to Kala. Now she realized how much Kala had clung to her, too. "I know and I appreciate it. You were right. It was better for me to think he was just a jerk. I would have been so embarrassed had I known the rest of it. I wasn't calling you out."

The hint of a smile hit her best friend's lips. "You weren't?"

"Maybe a little, but I do appreciate everything you did to protect me while we were in school. But we're not in school anymore, and I need you to be more receptive to me bringing other people into our circle."

"People like Dennis?" Kala asked.

"I don't know. Probably not. I met with him because I was curious, but I do know that I need more than this job. I'm lonely."

A sad expression crossed Kala's face. "I thought that was why we had each other."

"It's not enough and you know it, but I can't make you see that Cooper isn't the boy he used to be. He isn't the one who hurt you."

"Oh, that boy is in there." Kala shook her head and sat back, staring out the window into the darkness. "He'll always be there. He's going through a phase. Cooper McKay is always going to want a white picket fence and a wife who fits in with his friends."

Lou didn't understand. "You do fit in with his friends."

"The ones he has now, but that will change. And you should understand this. Otherwise you wouldn't be sitting on my cousin's lap again making my father nauseous."

Was it that different? TJ had never rejected her the way Cooper had rejected Kala, though she only knew bits and pieces of what had happened that night. Before that night it had been a thousand little things, but after, Kala had closed off a piece of herself, the part only Cooper ever got to see. "TJ hasn't changed. He's always been TJ."

"And he's always loved you." Kala let her head rest against the window. "Shouldn't you have this convo with Kenz? Or Tash?"

"Kenzie and Tasha aren't my best friend. I love them, but they're not you."

Kala grimaced and sat back up. "Fine. You want to know what I think?"

She wasn't sure. Kala could think some really shitty things.

Kala blew past her hesitation. "TJ has always loved you, but he didn't think he was worthy of you."

"Try again."

"No, that's real," Kala insisted. "You have no idea the conversations he's had with me and Luke and Seth. Probably his sister, but she would never tell. His sister loves you but she's one hundred percent team TJ, and that should tell you something."

"I never said TJ wasn't a great guy. I'm saying he's not my guy."

Kala sighed. "He's always been your guy, Lou. That's the problem. Okay, how about we get really fucking honest. This is my opinion and not something I've talked to either you or TJ about. You were great friends. If I'm honest, he was sometimes a way better friend to you than I was. I can be selfish and possessive when it comes to you because I sometimes think you're the only person in the world who gets me."

She wasn't. Lou thought Cooper got Kala just fine, but Kala couldn't get over whatever had happened between them that night when she'd gotten kidnapped as a teen. They'd gotten back to being friends but never to the caring they'd had when they were kids. "You were and are a great friend."

"I'm not sure about that, but I'm going to do things right now. You should know I never would have tried to stop you from having a relationship with my cousin," Kala admitted. "Never. When we were younger, I wanted you two together because that bound you to my family more. But it wouldn't have worked because you weren't ready."

"I wasn't ready? Don't you mean he wasn't ready?"

"No. I think you probably could have pushed him and made him ready when he was younger."

Lou was confused. "You don't think I tried."

"I don't think you tried hard enough. I don't think you flat out told him you needed more from him or you would walk away because it was too painful to simply be friends with him. I think you were willing to live a half life with him rather than risk the relationship to have what you both needed."

"So you think at sixteen or seventeen I should have walked away from one of the best relationships of my life?" Lou asked.

"No. I think you weren't ready. You were so freaking young. Both of you. I know you think if he'd seen you back then, really seen you, that everything would have fallen into place, but I think it would have fallen apart and he would be your childhood sweetheart. You would always have had feelings for him, but you would have moved on." She turned thoughtful. "Actually, put like that, maybe you should have. You could be totally over him and we could rule the club scene. We could run through some dicks, sister."

That was pure bravado on Kala's part. Kala didn't date. In college she'd had a couple of relationships that had ended with Lou talking her down from murder. She'd definitely had some men she'd slept with, but even that had dried up in the last couple of years.

Because then she'd been with Cooper all the time, working or at the club. She talked about cutting him out of her life, but the last few years had simply drawn them closer together.

"Think about it. We could take some leave, hit the British pub scene," Kala mused. "Or Italy. Maybe someplace tropical. We could run through all the hot tourists."

"I think I'll pass." She wasn't sure why, but this conversation bugged her. "This isn't about sex."

Kala's head shook. "But it is, and the last twelve hours should have proven that to you. I know it proved it to TJ. He's never viewed you as his physical equal. He's seen you as sweet and fragile, and the truth of the matter is you never viewed him as your mental equal. He was a cuddle bug to you. Cute and happy and he made you feel good. It was puppy love. What happened today was full-on adult dog something."

She had a way with words. "It was sex. It wasn't all that important. We both got emotional."

Kala obviously wasn't having it. "I could buy that the first time. Explain the conference room to me."

"That was… I don't know. I guess I hate the fact that no one thinks I'm a physical being. Everyone assumed TJ had made me do something and not that I took hold of his head and forced him to…do that." It still rankled.

Kala snorted. "I know you have physical needs. I also know damn well you didn't shove your pussy in his face and tell him to eat his fill. You are way more subby than that. Again, something he didn't take into account. There's a difference between being sweet and being truly submissive. Needing a dominant sexual partner to bring out your nasty side. Oww."

Kala leaned forward because her dad had gently smacked her with a rolled-up newspaper.

Big Tag frowned down at his daughter. "No using the word *sexual* in my presence. Bad Kala. Bad."

He kept moving toward the back of the plane.

"That's right. Run away, you crotchety hypocrite," Kala shouted.

"I should have brought my water spray bottle," Big Tag shouted back. "All the puppies need training."

Kala growled. "If he wasn't my boss…"

"He's your dad."

"Wouldn't matter," Kala replied. "He did teach me the fine art of survival of the fittest. I would take him out in a heartbeat."

She wouldn't. Kala loved her dad, but the obnoxiousness was one of their ways of communicating, and she wasn't going to let that get in the way of this seemingly important discussion. "We don't know that I have a deeply submissive sexual side. All of my play at The Hideout has been for demo purposes only. It never got emotional or really sexual. I never found a top I wanted to do more with. I guess it seemed weird to even try to play in front of TJ. He didn't play in front of me, though I know he does at the other club."

"I think he blows off steam at Lodge's place, and he tries to make sure Seth doesn't get murdered. Seth has a love-hate thing with Chloe Lodge. I can't tell if he loves to hate her or hates to love her. Either way, he could die."

Chloe Lodge was the daughter of the infamous Julian Lodge. Who might or might not have mob ties. Probably not. He probably put that out there to scare the crap out of everyone, but he was an intimidating man, and not in the lovable Big Tag way. The fact that Kala's brother had a weird thing for her was interesting. "I'm voting on death wish. But that doesn't change the fact that he does play. Do you know if he's ever had a sub?"

"No," Kala answered. "TJ never plays with anyone for more than a couple of nights from what I've gotten out of Seth and Lucas."

And that was what she really wanted to know. "So you watch TJ to make sure he doesn't hurt me. Kala, you have to stop that. You have to let whatever happens happen. I need to know that you're not going in behind my back and threatening the guys I date."

"I haven't done that since high school."

Lou stared at her.

Kala sighed. "Okay, college. But nothing since then. I showed remarkable restraint not introducing myself to that douchebag professor you were seeing that first year teaching."

He was only partially a pretentious blowhard. But they'd had so much in common. He'd understood her when she talked about abstract mathematical structures. He got her science jokes. He'd been her intellectual equal in every way. So why had he bored her? And she wasn't a fool. She'd known why Kala hadn't pushed to meet him. "You knew it wouldn't last long. You knew you were close to getting your team and bringing me on. Did you have a single doubt I wouldn't leave everything I'd worked for to follow you?"

"It wasn't about following," Kala argued. "It was about joining, and everything you worked for led here. We worked for. I guess I thought once you were on the team, he would see you differently."

Lou felt her jaw drop. "Are you telling me you want me with TJ?"

Kala shrugged in that nonchalant way of hers. "Nothing's changed. I still want you in my family."

She leaned forward and took Kala's hand in hers. Sometimes her best friend could be standoffish. She wasn't the most physically affectionate person, but she needed it. "I am in your family. Me not having the last name Taggart doesn't change that. I am never going to leave you. It's you and me for life, and no man is going to change that."

"Tash is already moving out."

"Of course she is, but she's still your sister." She hadn't been thinking about how poorly Kala handled change. Tasha had lived with them for the last couple of years. "She's never not going to be in your life. Just like I won't. But that isn't a good enough reason for me to force TJ into a relationship with me."

"Force?" Kala growled a little, a sure sign she was getting annoyed with all the emotional stuff. "Who do you think was right by my side when I threatened to ruin Dennis?"

"I know TJ was there, but that was high school."

"Was it? Do you know why Fred broke up with you?" Kala asked.

Fred. He'd been a guy she'd seen for almost two years at MIT. She'd actually considered he could be a good partner. Again. Lots of interests in common, and he seemed like a genuinely nice man. He'd explained that he'd found another woman and couldn't stay away from her. "He was cheating on me."

"Oh, if only it was that easy," Kala mused. "That feels sadly normal. No. He was planning on using your theorems as his senior project. I know because I hacked his system and monitored his ass the whole time you dated him."

Shock hit her. "What?"

"Yes. I suspect he downloaded your research, or you shared it with him."

"I most certainly did not. I talked to him about it, but I wouldn't have shared it." How many times had Kala saved her over the years?

"TJ made me do it. TJ met him and didn't like the vibe he got off the guy. He told me he didn't know how to keep watch on him, so I offered to do it. When I went to Fred, he told me to go fuck myself. Again, I showed an enormous amount of restraint. He was good, by the way. He could probably work black ops. It takes a lot to stare me down when I get going. He told me I would have to prove it and that with what his family gave to the college, they would always pick him over you. That was when TJ took over."

She wanted to be shocked, wanted to be able to tell Kala what she'd done was wrong, but it didn't feel that way. Kala was one of the world's predators. She could have gone another way had she not been surrounded by love and parents who taught her to use her instincts to help the people around her. Kala could have been one of the people they hunted, but she chose differently, and Lou couldn't blame her for focusing on the people she loved. TJ was different. TJ was sweet and happy-go-lucky and kind. "What did he do?"

Kala's lips turned up. "I still don't know, but I am fairly certain he only talked to the guy. I think he explained what he would do to him if he followed through with his plans. TJ can be intense when he wants to be, and he is intense about protecting you. I know I've been freaked out today, but I've thought a lot about it. Like I said, he's been serious about protecting you. Even from himself, but something changed today, and I think you met the TJ I've seen from time to time. I think you met the one who got Fred to back off, the one who dealt with every guy back in high school. The one who goes to clubs you're not at and picks petite brunettes every single time."

She couldn't buy it. "I was always willing to be with him."

"But you weren't willing to fight for him," Kala countered. "I think today he figured out that you're strong enough to fight for him. To fight with him."

"I don't want to fight at all."

"But life is a fight." Kala's voice went soft. "You knew that when you were younger. Before your mom married Boomer and you were stuck at that school, you knew it was all a fight."

Tears pierced her eyes when she thought about that time. It had been her and her mom against the world, particularly against her wealthy grandparents. "You know what's funny? My biological father was very much like the guy everyone seems to think I should be with. Intellectual. Ambitious. Focused on his legacy. He wasn't interested in me at all until I showed academic potential. He pushed me hard. Even at the age of four. After he died my mom was lost and my grandparents took advantage."

They'd paid for the best private schools, making her mother terrified they would pull the financial funding if she ever stepped out of line. Lou's life had been dictated by what her grandmother thought she should do, should be, should attain. She'd been pushed through school, her brain academically ahead but her emotional state lagging behind.

It had been a fight. Until her mom had found Boomer and she'd had the support she needed from this amazing family he'd brought them into.

And then it wasn't a fight at all.

Because Kala and TJ had fought for her. Without her even knowing it. "You can't hide things from me anymore. If you want me to fight, I have to know what I'm fighting."

"I just… You were so young."

"I'm not now. I know I was young when you took me under your wing. In some ways, you needed someone to fight for." Because Cooper didn't want her to fight for him. Kala needed someone to focus on. Kenzie had wanted her own world, her own friends. Lou had stepped into that place. "Do you have any idea how much I love you?"

Kala's head fell back, and her eyes closed. "Don't."

"Yeah, I'm doing it because you have to understand that me changing things up doesn't mean we change. Except for the whole Lou needs to be protected at all costs. I'm not a kid anymore. I can handle things. I won't ask you to not watch out for me. I need that."

And so did Kala.

"You changing things up means trying this whole D/s thing with TJ?"

"I don't know that it's a good idea." Because she couldn't seem to help herself around him, and she couldn't quite believe he actually wanted her.

Kala nodded. "Then you've made your decision and I'll support you. I need to tell him he can't come over, though. I'm pretty sure he thinks he's coming back with us."

Because he always came to their place when he was home on leave. It didn't make sense for him to rent an apartment, and while he loved his parents, he would rather stay with his cousins.

No. That was wrong. He wanted to stay with her.

The idea of TJ not seeing her when he was on leave was… It left a kind of hollow place inside her. Was she ready to give it all up? If she rejected him, could they find a way to be friends again someday?

Kala started to stand but Lou stopped her. "Don't. Tell him he can stay in the office."

Kala stared down at her. "Lou, don't be like him. If you don't want him, let him go."

The world seemed watery all of the sudden. Not want him? How could she not want him? The words didn't even make sense to her. TJ had always been the center of her universe.

Or maybe he'd been the easy thing to fixate on because he was always out of reach. Always sweet and nice, and he made her feel good when they were together. She'd halfheartedly tried to kiss him a couple of times and shrugged it off after.

Was she in love with TJ or with the idea of TJ because she never had to take that scary step with him?

"I can't imagine a world without him," Lou admitted. "But I'm having a hard time seeing us together."

"You're always together. You function like a team. He lights up when you walk in a room," Kala pointed out. "But up until today you were missing something necessary."

She knew exactly what her bestie was talking about. "Sex."

"Yup. Hot, sweaty, satisfying sex, and I kind of think you're the only one who got the satisfying part." She frowned suddenly. "Oh, shit. Was he bad? The way my dad talked about it I thought you were having a good time. Was he shitty at oral?"

Sometimes she wished Kala wasn't so open about sex. "That was not the problem."

"No, the problem is you're a big old scaredy cat, and that's okay. He's played a part in that." Kala eased back down. "So do what my mom would tell you to do. Take him up on his D/s offer and keep dating. See how that goes for you."

There was a light in Kala's eyes.

"You think I should keep dating? While I'm playing with TJ?"

"A D/s relationship doesn't have to be exclusive," Kala mused. "You told him you were going to date, so mean it. Show him it wasn't a ploy to get him in line. Keep it light with him. Prove you can be friends with benefits for a while until you either know it can work with him or you find the one you want to stick with."

"This feels like a trap." It was too good to be true. She would get to try with TJ while not giving up on her plan.

Not that she loved the plan. Dating kind of sucked. Her best date so far had been with a guy who'd bet he could take her virginity in high school.

"The thing about a good trap is you walk into it and you're stuck before you can think to walk back out," Kala explained. "An excellent trap feels like home."

"Okay, that does not make me feel better."

Kala considered her for a moment. "What would? Turning back time and not having today happen?"

"Maybe. I don't know." Did she want to not know? Maybe. The problem was she was fairly certain they would be spectacular in bed together. Or he was just really good and she would disappoint him.

"Well, that's not happening, sister. So do I go and tell my cousin he's shit out of luck and he's going to have to move back into his old room? I'm pretty sure Aunt Erin turned it into a home gym. He could probably sleep on the treadmill. Or he could sleep on Lucas and Seth's couch and wave at all the women who come in and out. Hopefully he doesn't catch a contact STI. My cousins are kind of gross."

"They aren't going to have the security he needs." Yes, that was what she should be thinking about. The op wasn't over until they figured out why someone thought TJ had a connection to an arms dealer. His mom had already had to kill one dude. Lucas and Seth were often distracted by their own manwhoriness.

Ian and Charlotte had a baby at home right now. Their

youngest, Travis, was finishing up law school and needed help because he was a single dad. She shouldn't put a baby in harm's way.

They had excellent security at their home. No one would know by looking at it, but there was a beyond state-of-the-art security system in the smallish four bedroom.

When she thought about it, staying close to TJ was the only way to do her job.

"He should stay with us. We can protect him."

Kala snorted. "Yeah. We can protect the delicate Green Beret."

There was something Kala wasn't taking into consideration. "Well, I had to do it today, didn't I?"

"You keep up that level of sass and this could be fun." She yawned. "And Lou?"

"Yeah?"

"I'll back off. A little. I love you, too. And I might vomit a lot, but if you did get involved with TJ and did the whole happily married with kids thing, I would be a great fun auntie." With that Kala yawned and closed her eyes again. "If my dad comes by, throw something at him. That old dog needs some sensitivity training."

She was asleep in moments, and Lou was left watching the night outside and wondering if she knew what she was doing in any way at all.

* * * *

If his uncle swatted him with a newspaper, he was going to get pissed. Luckily the man passed him by and then used it on Kala, proving he had a death wish.

"My brother is such an asshole. I have no idea how those kids haven't murdered him yet." His father sat back in the lounge chair. "I mean after he got these company jets, did we really need him?"

"You love the bastard," his mom murmured. She was looking over files. "They do, too. Although him doing it to Seth on stage was over the line."

His cousin Seth was a singer/songwriter—not what his Uncle Ian had expected. But like a good dad, his uncle often attended his son's performances. TJ had been there the time Seth had been experimenting with using a synthesizer and yes, it had been terrible, but he wasn't sure anything was so bad that his uncle had to go on stage, hit him with a rolled-up newspaper—something his uncle would never, ever use on a dog—tell him he was a bad musician and take the aforementioned awful synthesizer off stage with him.

Seth really should stick with guitars.

There were times he was so glad he was Theo Taggart's kid. Of all the Tags, his dad was the best.

"So when we get back, are you okay staying in Devi's room?" his mom asked. "When she comes back from New York, I'll shift some stuff around."

"I'm staying with Lou." Not that he'd actually asked Lou. Technically he was staying with his cousins in the weird room they called an office on the most uncomfortable sofa bed in the history of time. His sister's room was perfectly comfortable, but it lacked an essential element. Lou.

She was already pulling away, and he couldn't let that happen. He was going to be exactly who she thought he was. Funny. Nice. Helpful around the house. Right up until the moment he got a hand on her and then ooops, he wasn't sleeping on the sofa anymore.

His mom looked slightly surprised. "I thought she would distance when she obviously avoided sitting next to you."

She'd run like a scared mouse, but he wasn't about to let that stop him. "Yeah. I'm heading back to their place when we touch down. It'll make it easier to talk about the op. We still have no idea why they think I know this dude. We're supposed to get more information on the guy in the next couple of days."

"They were serious if they were willing to kidnap your mother in order to make you talk," his father pointed out. "So they have to have a reason to believe you're involved. You need to go over every op you've been on in the last couple of years, everyone you've worked with."

"I think we'll all be doing that over the next couple of weeks." Cooper was standing in the aisle, a mug of coffee in his hand. "Hey, TJ, Zach wants a word. Call me if the plane starts going down."

Shit. What did Zach want? He wasn't close to Zach. He'd worked with the man on a couple of occasions, and he reminded TJ a lot of his uncle. Zach was an authority figure with a capital A.

Some people went into the military because they didn't have another place to go or wanted to use the training to get good jobs. Zach had gone in because he was practically the poster child for the all-American soldier.

He got to his feet and marched toward the cabin, wishing he was moving to the back of the plane. At the back of the plane was a small kitchen and bathroom, but more importantly it was where Lou and Kala had set themselves up. He would think Kala was trying to ice him out, but she'd been the one to tell him he could stay with them the way he almost always did when he was in town.

Which was good because his other option was sleeping on Seth and Lucas's couch, and that meant watching at least one chick try to sneak out in the early morning hours. Sometimes two, but he'd seen as many as four sneaking away, and he didn't like to do that math.

Would that have been his life if he hadn't met Louisa Ward? Would he have ditched the military and worked for one of his uncles and screwed as many women as he could? The strange thing was he didn't find it appealing at all. He genuinely preferred hanging with Lou and Kala and Kenz, watching movies and playing games or taking Bud 2 to the dog park. He liked going over to Lou's parent's house and hanging with her little brother.

Had he screwed this up so badly he couldn't hope for that life now?

He glanced back when he made it to the cockpit door, but Lou wasn't looking up. She was leaning forward and talking to Kala, a serious expression on her face.

He wanted to go back there, take her hand, and show her where her place was, but his uncle might have a heart attack, and his father had counseled patience at this point.

He had weeks with her. Unless she freaked and kicked his ass out.

He knocked on the door and then entered when Zach gave him leave.

Zach was sitting in the pilot's seat, his masculine features illuminated by the lights coming off the instrument panel. "Hey, man. Have a seat. We're in full autopilot mode for the next couple of hours, and I thought we should have a chat."

That sounded bad. "In a captain to sergeant way, or a don't fuck up my team you nitwit way?"

A ghost of a smile hit the man's face, and he gestured to the chair beside him. "Can't it be both?"

TJ managed to slide into the copilot's seat. He wondered if Zach had changed seats since Cooper was the pilot and if he'd done it for intimidation purposes. Not that he was. "Sure, except you should remember this is my team, too. I grew up with them. They're my family, so you should understand I will never willingly put them in danger."

"And yet you did today." Zach was all business now. "Sergeant Taggart, did you or did you not stop down in the middle of a mission to kiss my asset?"

"She's not your asset. She's Lou."

"Do you think I don't know that? Do you think I don't know exactly how many missions she's run and what her kill rate is? Zero. It was zero until today, and I planned to keep it that way. You fucked that up. You are the reason she was forced to do something counter to who she is. She was supposed to get in, hunker down with you, and wait until comms came back online so she could blow the door and get away. You distracted her."

"That's not what she said." He'd heard her telling someone before the conference meeting that it was all a way to keep him from saying something he shouldn't. Bullshit. He didn't believe a word of it.

"You and I both know she's trying to salvage her pride." Zach obviously wasn't buying it either.

TJ hated the thought. "Because it's awful to kiss me?"

Zach's head shook. "Because your uncle saw it. Because he'll absolutely mention it to her father."

"I can handle Boomer." He would tell Boomer that he was going to marry Lou and protect and love her for the rest of his life, and the big guy would chill.

"How am I supposed to work with you if you won't admit that what you did today was reckless and counter to every bit of training you've ever received?" Zach asked. "I can understand what happened, but I cannot condone it, and if you expect me to then we need to move you to Langley and work this problem from there."

Fuck. He hadn't even considered that as an option. "My uncle won't let you do that."

Zach's head shook as though he was deeply disappointed. "Ah, but I'll go around your uncle. I'll go straight to Drake Radcliffe and explain the situation. That's why I am here, you know. I act as a check and balance to what is basically a family operation. There's no other team like this in all of the intelligence world, and I can't tell you how many people want us to fail. I will not allow you to be the reason we do. Cooper can't view this with an unbiased eye. He grew up with you. You're family. Kala will rage against you all day and in the end, she'll still let you close because you're her cousin and she trusts you. Tash is far too kind to even consider dumping her cousin in DC and getting out of it. So I have to be the bad guy. Are you going to make me be the bad guy, Sergeant?"

He had put Lou in danger. Crap. He'd been running on pure emotion, and he needed to get his head out of his ass and acknowledge the situation. He wouldn't take it back. Not the time they'd spent in his cell. They'd been as safe as they could have been there, but he'd kissed her and distracted them both in the middle of hostile territory. "I apologize, sir. I will acknowledge my mistake and not allow it to happen again. I'll accept any discipline you think is correct, but I would like to stay with the team."

Zach's lips turned down as though he'd kind of hoped for a fight. "It can't happen again. You shouldn't work with Lou."

He disagreed, but he wasn't going to argue with the man who was basically his CO right now. As long as he was working with the team, Zach Reed was his direct superior. "I understand. I hope Lou is able to go back to her former technical role. She did an amazing job today, but her real value is behind a computer."

Zach's brow rose. "You trying to say she's the goddess of information and your cousins are cannon fodder?"

"Not at all," TJ replied. "My cousins are forces of nature, and what they're doing with the Agency is going to change the way teams can work. But Lou is...special. She's a freaking gift, and I worry the Agency won't see how valuable she is."

"I assure you that your uncle and aunt understand, and so do I. Louisa Ward has a role no one else has. She's allowed an enormous amount of freedom to do what she does. She's already made some technical innovations that we've implemented in the field. The altered C-4 worked brilliantly, from what I could tell. What was your assessment of how the op went, Sergeant?"

"With the exception of my fuck up, I think it went well. Agent Ward handled the situation with professionalism." There was no way he wouldn't back up his girl.

Zach snorted.

TJ shrugged. "Once she realized the comms were back, she was all business. She didn't hesitate and showed strong instincts in the field. She was excellent at her job."

Zach seemed to think about that for a moment. "I didn't expect that either."

"What? That I would back up Lou? I suppose you don't know much about our relationship."

"On the contrary. I know pretty much everything about the two of you," Zach countered. "I'm the only member of this team who didn't get his diaper changed by Ian or Charlotte Taggart. I had to learn this team from back to front or I would have been out in the first couple of weeks, and I didn't want that. I studied them all, and I understand the dynamics of their relationships. I know Kala and Kenz will fight constantly, right up until the moment they need to move as one person, and then no one on earth can tell them apart. I should know because I've watched them fool their father. They do it simply to keep up the practice and never would tell him because they love their parents in a way I can't comprehend. I know that Cooper is still trying to pay for something he did as a kid. You want to let me in on that one? It's the one secret I can't crack."

He only suspected, but he would never tell if he did. "That's Kala and Coop's story."

Zach nodded, accepting the response. "I know that Tristan is a reckless asshole who is probably in over his head, but I can't convince him that not everyone in the Agency is trustworthy. I suspect he's working for a couple of teams, but I can't get the information I need to vet them and figure out how dangerous his side projects are."

The thought of Tristan working dark ops made him worry. "But my uncle knows, right?"

"No. He doesn't, and that's what scares me. If Drake knows, he's not talking, and that makes me nervous. We all knew he was doing some support work, but we thought it was for the military. I wasn't too worried about it until I tried to contact him for this op. I was told he was on a high-security mission and wouldn't be available for a few weeks. I worry Tristan is trying to prove he's as good as his father, and it's going to get him killed. Tasha is grace under pressure. She can handle anything and she never panics. And then there's Lou."

"Don't try to tell me you know Lou better than I do."

"Oh, but I do." Zach stared out at the dark night. "I know the Lou who lives for the thrill of the op. I know the Lou who's living out some of her childhood dreams right now. And I know you. You view Lou as this princess in a castle to be worshipped from afar."

He didn't like how intimate Zach sounded. "I assure you I worshipped her from up close, and I intend to do it again. Zach, if this is your way of telling me you have a thing for Lou, I need to make myself plain. I don't care what power you have over me. She's mine until the minute she cuts me out of her life and even then, I'll protect her. I don't care if something's gone on between the two of you. I love Lou, and I won't let you or anyone else stand in my way."

Zach's head fell back on a groan. "That's the last thing I need." He brought his head up, shaking it in a weary fashion. "Do you know how happy I would be if this team was like every other team? On other teams the mission is the only thing that matters. No one gives a fuck about their teammates because they don't know each other." He took a long breath, his face a bit ghostly in the light. "It's easier and maybe more efficient. This is hard because I care about every person in the field, and I know they care about me. I am not in love with Lou. That's not where my heart went, but that's neither here nor there. What is important is you're going to be working with us for the next couple of months, and that means I have to trust you."

"So you're not leaving me at Langley?"

He was well aware that he was on a timeline. He wouldn't be allowed to stay with Lou's team forever. He had to convince her because if he got sent away on assignment for a couple of months, he wasn't sure she would be waiting when he got back.

Zach waved him off. "Oh, that was an empty threat. I wanted to make it plain that if you put my team in danger again, I'll take care of you myself. I complain about them. I worry about them. I sometimes don't fit in with them, but they are my team, and I will do whatever it takes to protect them and this experiment of ours. So are we clear?"

He was jealous of Zach, jealous of the place he had in all their lives. "As crystal, sir."

Zach nodded. "Excellent. Keep your mouth off her in the field unless she needs CPR. That is for home or the club, and try to keep the drama to a minimum and we'll be okay. For now, you're going to have to do some of Tristan's work because I don't know when he's coming back."

He was worried about Tristan, too, and maybe it was time to start getting to the bottom of what was going on with his friend. If he was in Dallas for the time being, he could do some snooping. Maybe he and Lou could make it a project. "Is that all, sir?"

Zach finally turned his way. "You know she's been dating, right?"

"She mentioned she had a date with this asshole from high school. I think it was only one date, though she claims she's going to see more of him."

"She's been on four dates, including the coffee she had with Dennis Sims."

TJ wasn't sure he could handle this, but he plunged on anyway. "You've been watching her?"

Zach shrugged. "We all have. What do you want me to say? We're a freaking spy team, and she's everyone's best friend. We were all worried about her so we take turns vetting her dates, and if we sometimes happen to be around the spot she's meeting the dude at, well, it's just keeping our surveillance skills tight. But you should understand she's serious about it. I'm pretty sure she's got a date set up for some time next week."

"She'll cancel it." Though they'd be at home, they were still in the middle of something potentially dangerous.

"Should she?" Zach asked. "Or should she have a bodyguard? I mean someone was recently sent to take in your mom. I laughed at that. They came after Erin Taggart with one dude, and he didn't even try to snipe her from afar. I think that guy genuinely looked at her and said he could take her. They'll think the same of Lou, so she should be protected. I was going to talk to her about it. It's not like you're doing anything."

Zach wanted him to watch Lou date? "I don't know that I could handle that."

"Sure you can. You be professional and look good. You stand in the background, and every time she looks your way you send her a longing look like you're a rescue dog she's thinking of taking back to the pound. Cry a little, man. I know the older generation didn't have those tools to work with, but we do. Not too much. Just like a hint of a tear and she'll probably melt. I would also play up the trauma of what you went through. You have to hurt like a motherfucker."

He did. Every muscle ached. "I took some ibuprofen. I can handle it."

"Dude, you're not listening to me," Zach said. "Let her baby you. Let her take care of you, and thank her for it. And don't wear a shirt so she can see the scars."

His father had said the same thing. Was there a class he was supposed to take? Still, he'd promised himself he would let his ruthless side out. He had a plan, but maybe she should see all sides of him, and he could definitely handle some babying from her. "I can do that."

"All right. Then you're dismissed, and we'll meet up after we've had some rest. I want to pore over everything you've done, everyone you've seen or talked to in the last couple of years. Be careful and watch what you say to anyone outside of this team," Zach ordered.

"Well, my team is pretty much trashed after the Aussie op, so I don't think that will be a problem," he replied, working his way out of the seat. It wasn't easy. Planes weren't built for bulky dudes.

Zach wasn't done. "If someone calls and asks where you are, you tell them you're home for a family emergency and nothing else."

He didn't like the implications. "What's going on that I don't know?"

"I think there are some people in the intelligence community who don't like this team and don't like how much leeway we're getting. They're trying to withhold intel from us. Or hell, maybe Kala stepped on the wrong toes or Big Tag did in the distant past," Zach said with a sigh. "It feels like all eyes are on us, and you being tied to an arms dealer isn't going to help."

"I don't know who he is."

"It won't matter if we can't figure this out, so play your cards close to the vest you won't be wearing because you're trying to entice a girl," Zach offered. "Send Coop back. I'm ready for a nap."

"Will do." He opened the cockpit door and stepped out. Lou was leaning over in her seat as though she'd been watching the door, waiting for him to come out.

She immediately sat up, and her head was down, looking at her tablet.

TJ felt a rush of satisfaction. She might not be sitting next to him because she was a big old scaredy cat.

But he still had a shot.

Chapter Eight

Lou took the sheets out and wondered how TJ was going to fit on the couch for longer than a couple of nights.

Three months. He was here for at least three months, and he would be living here and going into the office with Kenz and Kala and hanging out every day. They would eat dinner and breakfast. Like they lived together. Like they were together.

Tired. She was so tired. The flight had taken forever, and she'd been to Germany and back in a forty-eight-hour period.

Kenz and Kala were already sleeping, but she had TJ to deal with. Kala had yawned and told her TJ had been her problem for a long time and if it was up to her, he could sleep with Bud 2.

Gorgeous, sexy, hurt TJ. He'd been perfectly sweet the whole flight, not coming back and trying to force her to his side the way she'd worried he would.

Maybe he was starting to come down from all the adrenaline of the last few days and realizing what a horrible mistake they'd made.

"Lou, Dare and I are going to stay with Mom and Dad. Put TJ in my room." Tasha stepped into the hallway. She'd changed into PJs but had her sneakers and a hoodie on.

"It's two in the morning, Tash. You don't have to do that." It had been a long flight, and they would feel that jet-lag for days.

Weariness threatened to swamp Lou, and she still had to deal with the man currently sitting in her kitchen.

He wouldn't even go home to grab some things. He'd merely gotten in the car with her and promised he would stop by his parents' place sometime tomorrow. He'd told her he had the only important thing.

A SIG. But then she could have told him her place was a veritable weapons' cache.

"We were planning on staying there anyway. His siblings are coming down in a couple of days, and Mom and Dad have way more room. Dare is outside waiting for me," Tasha explained. "I think he's been up most of the time I've been gone. It's the first time I've gotten called away on short notice. I need to make sure he's handling it okay. He's been staying with Mom and Travis, and he signed the paperwork on the condo so we'll be moving soon anyway. Let TJ stay in my room. He'll be more comfortable there." Tasha looked her over. "Do you know what you're doing with him?"

"Nope." She was honest with the Taggart sisters. Always. There were no prevarications between them.

Tasha nodded like she understood. "Then go with your instincts, Lou. Not your fears. You live in your head half the time. I know you've been dating recently, and you don't have to stop, but you could maybe see what a casual relationship with him would be like."

She clutched the sheets to her chest, though it looked like she wouldn't be using them. "I don't think anything between me and TJ is casual. At least not for me."

Tasha settled her backpack on her shoulder. "I don't think it is for him either. Otherwise he wouldn't have plotted with Kala to ensure you found a man who was worthy of you. I know I'm not supposed to talk about that…"

"She told me," Lou interrupted. "Apparently he's been doing this weird stalker thing for years."

Tasha studied her carefully. "And how does that make you feel?"

She knew how it should make her feel. Violated. Annoyed. Disturbed.

But she'd been in this family long enough to know that protection instinct was hard wired into their systems. She'd thought about it on the long flight over. TJ had stepped in when she was in trouble, when someone was going to hurt her. It might not have been right for him to do it behind her back, but then she hadn't exactly told him she'd gone into the system at school and changed his Algebra final from a 55 to 68, just enough so he passed the semester and graduated with his class.

She'd only told Kala that she routinely hacked the system to make sure TJ was okay. She'd never once mentioned it to TJ.

So maybe she was a stalker, too.

She damn straight would have fixed things for him if he'd gotten terrible assignments in the military. If he was being sent off to some place he wouldn't want to go, she likely would have stepped in, applied pressure here or there, and gotten him somewhere he would enjoy.

"Weirdly protected," she admitted.

Tasha smiled and stepped around her. "I know it's scary and it feels like you've got a lot to lose, but you don't. You understand that if it doesn't work, it's not like we're going to kick you out of the club. Him either. We're family, and we'll find a way to make it work even if it's awkward. The truth of the matter is when you genuinely love someone, you can get through anything, even heartache."

She hadn't even thought about that. If there was one thing she was secure in, it was this group she had around her. That was why she'd been worried when Zach had called TJ into the cockpit. Zach could be protective, too.

"I think we're going to try playing at the club this weekend. Neither of us has a play partner."

"Oh, my mom is going to find that endlessly interesting," Tasha said with a grin.

Lou was sure she would. Charlotte Taggart believed in using D/s as a way to ease into a relationship when things were weird between two people.

Was that what she was doing? Or was she trying to have some time with him before he came to his senses?

Either way, it scared the crap out of her, and it might be a moot point because he'd barely talked to her.

"Dare's waiting. I'll see you at the office, and call me if you want to talk," Tasha said as she headed out.

Lou heard her leave, locking the door and resetting the security system.

"Should I be worried?"

She turned and TJ was standing there. He'd changed from what he'd been wearing on the plane into a pair of gray sweatpants and nothing else. Not a damn thing else. Nothing to hide his sculpted chest and broad, muscular shoulders. Nothing covering his six-pack, and the sweats rode low on lean hips.

How long had she been staring? She shook her head. "About Tash? I don't think so. She and Dare are going to stay at her parents' place until they move. They recently bought a condo apparently. She says you can stay in her room."

Tasha was moving on with her life. Tasha was getting married, and she would happily settle down with the man of her dreams, and the man of Lou's dreams was standing right there and she had no idea how to reach out for him.

"You should get some sleep, LouLou. Don't look so terrified. I'm not going to jump you. I promise."

She breathed a sigh of relief. Sort of. He was waking up. He was coming out of the trauma response.

"Unless you want me to." His voice went deep, and his gaze suddenly seemed hot. "We could make that our first scene. Consensual non-consent is a bit advanced, but I can make it happen."

And her pulse was racing. "I'm not sure that's such a good idea, TJ."

"I agree. We should start with something more basic," he replied. "I was thinking we would have some fun on the equipment. Find our style. A little bondage. Some spanking. I'm going to be honest. I'll probably stay away from the violet wand. Too much like a taser, but we could try a TENS if you like."

Every word sent her into a weird panic cycle. First, there was arousal and curiosity. She'd always wanted to know what it felt like. And then she realized TJ would see her naked and self-consciousness struck. "I didn't mean that. I meant the whole club thing. The whole D/s thing might be a bad idea."

"Why?" He moved in but kept a few feet from her. His handsome face settled into a deep grimace. "I thought you were going to at least give me that. I know you're going to keep dating, but I thought I would have a shot. And don't tell me I'm going to wake up. I know that's what's going through your head, but it's not happening. You're dating. I get that. I won't stop you. I only ask that I get a chance, too. If you won't let us play together, then we could go on a real date."

That seemed even worse. At least at the club they would have boundaries and rules. There were plenty of people she knew who kept their relationships to the club. TJ would eventually leave and life would go back to normal, and if she didn't have a boyfriend and he wasn't involved, they could see each other at the club when he came home on leave.

Yes. That was why she'd gone this way in the first place. "Okay, but I think we should definitely start slow. Uhm, the non-con should wait until we know each other better."

His lips curled up. "It's weird to think we don't know each other. I know you better than anyone. At least parts of you. But now we get to explore this part."

He sounded like he wanted to, like he was excited about it. "But I'm serious about continuing to date. I need to look around. I need to discover what's out there for me."

His eyes went puppy-dog sad, and it took everything she had not to hug him. "Because you don't trust me to stay."

She had to be honest with him. If they were actually going to explore this thing between them, honesty was going to be necessary. "Because I don't trust any of this."

He moved in again, his hand coming out to brush back her hair. "And when you wake up a year from now and I'm still begging you to stay with me? What will you do then?"

He was pushing her, and she was too tired to think. "We'll cross that bridge when we come to it. Like I said, you can stay in Tasha's room. I think she already changed the sheets, but I'll leave these for you just in case."

She turned to go but he stopped her, reaching for her arm and bringing her back to him. "I'm sorry. It's too fast. I'll be good.

We're friends like we always were, but we're adding the club. That's all. I'm single. You're single. We're both interested in the lifestyle but don't have play partners. We can handle this and still be friends."

She wasn't so sure of that, but she also couldn't deny that she would regret it if she never spent a night with him. "Charlotte is setting me up with some men she thinks I should meet. I'm planning on going on those dates. You're okay with that?"

"Nope. I'm nauseated by that, but that is the last I'll say about it because I put us in this position. I will support you and care for you even if you don't pick me in the end. You'll always be my best friend. If you find a man you love, I will bury this feeling so it never makes him uncomfortable, but I need to be in your life."

Why couldn't he have said these words to her even a few months before? Why had he only said them after she'd finally pushed away from him? Was that it? Was it the chase he was interested in? Would she find herself right back where she was once she gave in?

"Again, I'm pushing when I should be patient. I'm sorry," he said quietly, letting go of her arm. He started to move past her but stopped. "Hey, could you look at my back? I'm worried one of the wounds opened up."

Her whole heart seemed to soften and worry infused her. He'd been hurt, tortured, and she was throwing him into a room and walking away.

"Of course. Let's get to where we have some light." She followed him to Tasha's room. Like the others in the house, it was small but cozy. Tasha's room was ultra-feminine. Masculine TJ looked out of place in the pastel-walled room with its queen-sized bed and dainty furnishings. There were family pictures in frames around the room, and ones of Tasha and her friends. TJ sat down on the fluffy comforter and gave her his back.

She breathed out as she studied him. There were welts all over, bruises that showed how brutal they'd been with him. "Are you sure we shouldn't get you to a doctor?"

"Aidan's coming over in the morning. Cooper's got some medic training, and he says it's all superficial. The shakes have stopped for the most part," he replied, sitting calmly while she brushed her fingers over the places where his skin had singed. "I was lucky. They wanted to keep me in pretty good condition. I think they figured out torturing someone I loved would be more efficient than hurting me. But we were lucky they didn't start in on you."

She hadn't been worried about that. "I've been tased before. I know it hurts, but I could have handled it."

He turned. "Who the fuck tased you?"

There was the protective bear. He wasn't thinking straight. "I'm on a CIA team, and I do go into the field. I've had all the training, and some of that included how to survive an interrogation. As to who tased me, it was some chick from Langley. I can't remember if she was a Black or a Green. One of the colors we use even on ourselves at times. She spent about six weeks going over all the horrible things that could happen to us and how to counter them. Including how to use a cyanide pill to take all those secrets to our graves. She was a sadist, I think. It disturbed her to no end that Kala smiled through all of it. I think it might have been Kala's favorite part of training."

He turned, and there was fire in his eyes. "I want to know who she was."

She needed to find a way to make him reasonable about this. "TJ, she was Agency. I'm Agency. She was good at her job, which was training us to deal with things that could happen in the field. You got trained, too, and not all of it was fun."

"I'm a soldier," he pointed out. "You're an analyst and technical expert."

She was more than that, and he needed to understand. "Yes, and I make things that we use to spy on other countries with. The crap that's in my head is valuable. I know how we operate, how everything functions, and I know what innovations I'm working on. Your uncle wouldn't let me on the team without the training. Same with Tash. Her last name alone makes her valuable. I didn't love that period of my life, but I did find it oddly freeing. I'm tougher than I look, tougher than I thought I would be. It made me realize I did spend way too much time in my head. My body is strong, too. My body can be used to help my team. I still work out. Kala and I spar from time to time, though I know she takes it easy on me. If I let my physical training go, your uncle would have my hide."

"My uncle needs to remember who you are and what you do."

She sighed, tired again. She didn't want to argue with him. "But he does. You're the one who doesn't. Did I prove that to you yesterday?"

"I'm always going to want to wrap you up and protect you, but yes, you did. You were magnificent, Lou. You were…" He grinned. "You were hot, baby."

She flushed. "I was doing my job. Now I think your back is all right. I don't see any open wounds. Did Zach dress you down?"

TJ nodded. "Oh, yeah. I'm to keep my mouth off you in the field."

Of course he'd gone there. She was sure she was a bright shade of pink. "Yeah, he might have mentioned something like that to me, too, and before you get all worked up, he's my CO in the field. I think he had to do it because Big Tag has been avoiding me. I have to call my dad tomorrow before Big Tag gets to him."

"He's not going to talk to your dad," TJ assured her. "I know he acts like an asshole, but he won't talk about what happened during a mission. But if you want to talk to him, I'll go with you. I'll explain what happened and what my intentions are."

That sounded like the worst idea in the world. "I'll handle my parents."

"You don't have to." TJ stood and started to dismantle the mound of decorative pillows that Tasha had on the flouncy bed. "My uncle will keep his mouth shut unless we're in a meeting. My parents won't mention it. If you want to give it some time, we can." He yawned. "We can talk about it, if you want. I don't know how well I'm going to sleep. I fell asleep on the plane, and my mom woke me up because I started punching out. I think I was having a nightmare."

Of course he was. "Was it about what happened in Germany?"

TJ laid back, and she tried hard not to think about how hot he looked. He was her friend and he was hurt, and he didn't need her to sexualize him. "I was trying to get to you and they kept hitting me with tasers. My body didn't work, and I watched them take you away from me. I couldn't do anything but lay there and shake."

She reached out and put a hand in his. "I'm fine. I'm right here and I'm not going anywhere."

"Will you stay with me until I fall asleep?"

That was dangerous, but she knew if she'd asked he wouldn't have hesitated. If she'd been hurt and afraid, he would hold her all night long. Tasha had told her to follow her instincts, and every single one of them told her to grant TJ his request. She stood and turned off the overhead light. "I'll stay until you fall asleep, and then I'll be right next door if you need me."

TJ got under the covers, taking the side of the bed closest to the door. "I don't know if I can sleep with you just sitting there. Maybe you could get in for a little while. Like we used to."

Used to? It hadn't been more than a couple months since the last time she'd fallen asleep next to TJ. They often stayed up super late when he came home on leave, and they talked until the wee hours of the morning and he fell asleep on her bed. She sometimes woke up cuddled against him.

She pretended they were together and that his arms around her meant something.

Would it mean something now?

"Sure." She was going to be letting the man spank her ass. She could lie next to him in a bed. She was already in her PJs, so she would be comfortable until she could sneak back to her own room. Lou climbed in next to him, keeping some space between them. "It's going to be okay."

"I'll make sure of it. I won't… I'm not going to hurt you ever again, Lou. Even if you never want me the way I want you. You should understand that while you're dating, I'm not going to see anyone else. I'm going to concentrate on being your friend and your temporary Dom," he said, his voice low in the darkness.

"TJ," she began.

He rolled her way, and his head was suddenly nestled against her shoulder. "I just wanted to put it out there."

They were quiet for a moment.

"I think there was someone else, someone in the background," he said quietly. "I know I mentioned him before, but I can't get it out of my head. He wasn't speaking German, but I couldn't quite catch enough to know what language it was."

"Don't think about it right now." She shifted so her head was against his, the intimacy reminding her of her childhood and how he would hold her when she was scared.

But there was something more to it now, something beyond innocent comfort. There was need and…there was something right about lying there.

His breathing became even, and one arm went around her waist.

She would give him a couple of minutes and then ease away.

But it was warm and cozy, and she liked the sound of his breathing and the way she felt with his arm around her. Safe. Protected. Beloved.

Just a minute more and she would get up.

She drifted to sleep, letting the darkness surround them like they were the only people in all the world.

* * * *

"Dude, someone fucked you up."

TJ looked at Aidan O'Malley. Aidan had shown up bright and early with his fiancée, Carys Taggart, in tow. She was currently hanging out in the kitchen with his cousins and Lou. There was the smell of bacon and coffee floating around, and he wanted to join them but nope. He had to follow Aidan's finger with his eyes and get his blood pressure checked.

"That's what happens when you're kidnapped by a Bavarian mobster," TJ shot back.

He sat on Tasha's bed, the comforter rumpled, and there was still an indentation on the pillow where Lou had lain her head.

"Have you had any headaches?" Aidan tilted his head up so he could get a look at the bump over his left eye.

"I feel fine with the exception of being sore as hell." And his dick hurt, but that wasn't the aforementioned mobster's fault. It was Lou's because she was so sexy and pretty and he hadn't been able to get inside her yet.

He probably wouldn't have a real chance until they went to the club.

Tonight. He needed to play it cool and not freak her out. Once they were on the dungeon floor, she would sink into the play and be in the moment. Like she'd been before when they were in the cell.

Aidan brought up a small flashlight. "I need to check your

pupils. I don't think you have a concussion because Cooper would have caught that, but I like to be thorough."

Cooper had in fact checked his pupils, but he'd suspected Aidan would put him through it all again.

Aidan was a second-year resident at one of Dallas's largest hospitals. He was working on becoming a trauma surgeon, while Carys was doing her OB-GYN residency or she would be in here, too, giving her opinion. Carys and Aidan could be playfully competitive, but some of that light was gone from his friend's eyes now, likely because Tristan wasn't with them. TJ remembered when all three of them would have been joking and teasing and Tristan would say that he didn't need medical school because he'd been forced to watch three hundred seasons of *Grey's Anatomy*.

"Do you feel groggy? Did you have a hard time waking up?" Aidan asked as he moved to the other eye.

TJ fought not to blink. "Well, I was definitely hard. Shit. Did I say that out loud? I'm jet-lagged and spent a good portion of the last couple of days drugged out of my mind. And not in a fun, chose-this-path way."

Aidan looked like a younger version of his father, Liam O'Donnell. He had dark hair that was always a bit too long and intelligent green eyes. He was wearing scrubs because he was going straight to work after he left. He glanced over at the bed, likely putting together the fact that both pillows had been used. He frowned. "You brought a woman here? In Lou's house?"

Did everyone think he was an asshole? He didn't spend a terrific amount of time with Aidan, but he thought the guy knew him better. "I would never do that. I wouldn't have done it before, and I won't do it now or ever."

Aidan's expression went blank, and then he seemed to figure it out. "Lou slept with you?"

"Lou slept beside me," he corrected. "And it's not like that's such a big deal. I spend a lot of time here and the couch sucks, so I sometimes fall asleep on her bed. I'm staying for a couple of months this time around, so Tash is letting me have her room. Lou kept me company, and she fell asleep."

"I do not get that," Aidan replied, pulling a stethoscope out of his bag. "I don't get the whole we're-just-friends thing."

Of course he didn't. He'd found his future wife at the age of…birth, practically. Aidan and Tristan had been trailing after Carys since they were freaking toddlers. "We're not. We're not just friends. Not now."

Aidan seemed to think about that. "I guess I don't understand the timing. If you loved Lou, why wait?"

"It wasn't right. It wouldn't have worked back then. Timing is important." He was a tad irritated by the other man's judgment. Aidan had it easy. Aidan hadn't ever worried there was something wrong with him. He matched Carys in every way. They'd literally fought over who had the highest GPA. Aidan never had to consider if he was the best choice for the woman of his dreams.

"Huh, I never thought about timing. My path always seemed set. I don't like the whole up-in-the-air thing." Aidan's expression shut down, going a perfectly polite blank. "So back to what I'm here for. I don't suppose you want to tell me the details of how you came to be injured. Beyond quips."

TJ wished he could say more. "Not really."

"So it's classified," Aidan said, his voice tight as he put a stethoscope to TJ's chest.

"Yeah. Sorry, man." TJ knew Aidan had a reason to get irritated by all the spy stuff. After all, it seemed he'd lost his partner and best friend to it.

Something had broken down when Tristan had joined the CIA team, and now it was so bad Aidan and Carys were getting married. Without him.

"I'm used to it. Take a deep breath. Can you at least tell me what they used on you? I would say a taser, but it could be a cattle prod," Aidan said, his tone going mild.

TJ breathed in and out before he answered, allowing Aidan to listen. "It was both. They were full-service torturers. I was also dosed with some kind of roofie. It was put in my drink, but I seem to have metabolized it."

"That all?"

"Oh, uhm, I might have also been accidentally dosed with whatever the Agency uses in those microdosers. You know the ones they put on their palms and oops, you're suddenly asleep," he admitted.

"Accidentally?" Aidan asked.

TJ shrugged. "It happens. I would explain it to you…"

"But it's classified." Aidan sighed and sat back, wrapping the stethoscope around his neck. "I would like to do some blood work, but superficially you're fine."

"That's what I told everyone. Sorry to bring you out so early."

"It's not a problem. Carys and I meant to come by at some point. Time…it seems to get away from me. We work. We sleep. We start again. Oh, and we plan a wedding that hopefully will actually happen this time."

Aidan had asked Carys to marry him two years before, just after they'd formed the CIA team. They'd set a date and then put it off. Once and then again.

As though they were waiting for something. Or someone.

"Do you think he's going to change his mind?" TJ asked, hoping he wasn't stepping on any toes.

"Tris? I think Tris is an arrogant, stubborn asshole who makes decisions without talking to his loved ones." Aidan sighed. "I don't know. I also don't know that it matters anymore. He was supposed to work Army intelligence, cyber intelligence, from safely behind a screen. It was something he could do here in the States, but he got pulled into…"

This was the in he'd been looking for. "He got pulled into the Agency. But again, I would think that's okay. For the most part he could be here like the rest of the team. Aidan, I'm worried about him. I thought he was just working with the twins and Lou, but he's involved in something else, something I'm not even sure Big Tag understands."

Aidan's jaw went tight. "Well, if Big Tag doesn't understand, then I don't know how I'm supposed to."

But there was something about the way Aidan stiffened. He wasn't a spy and he wasn't a good liar. But TJ also wasn't sure that going at him directly would get the answers he wanted.

And suddenly he wanted answers. He didn't like the idea that Tristan's Agency work could break them up. What would happen when he someday left the Army and came home to find a job? Would that break him and Lou?

He wouldn't allow it to. Not that they were together, although he had woken up with the sweetest bundle of femininity wrapped around him. He'd wanted to kiss her awake and pull that old *Mission Impossible* T-shirt off along with the boxers she used as PJ bottoms and start the morning right.

Instead he'd stayed still and let her slink away like she hadn't spent the night in his arms. When she'd brought Aidan back here, she'd pretended like nothing had happened, asked him how he'd slept.

Like a baby.

"The team doesn't know where he is," TJ gently prodded. "I was hoping you might. I know we're all worried about him."

Aidan started to pack up his bag. "No idea, man. Tristan has made it plain that his work is nonnegotiable. Carys and I understand and we're moving forward. I haven't seen or talked to him in months."

But there was a little tic as his jaw locked and then released.

Was Aidan lying to him? Why would Aidan lie? "You don't know what he's working on?"

Aidan stood up. "Sorry, man. You would know more than I do."

"And you have no idea why he would walk away from you and Carys?"

"It's not your business."

"Carys is my cousin. You know this family. It's all our business. I could beat the shit out of him for you." It was sometimes the way they handled things in the Taggart clan.

Aidan's eyes widened. "No. No, leave it be. Look, Carys and I dealt with this pain a long time ago. We're going to be fine together. It wouldn't have worked. Our paths diverged after college, and there was nothing any of us could do."

Except find a way. Something was off, and TJ had never thought about it before. He'd always thought they needed time to settle in, but what if that wasn't all there was to the problem?

The way Aidan explained the situation sounded oddly rote. Like he'd memorized the words and spat them out at the appropriate times. He supposed that wasn't so strange since Aidan probably got asked the question a lot.

"He's not happy," TJ said. "I don't know what he's telling you, but I've been around him a lot in the last year and a half and he's not the same."

Aidan picked up his bag. "Well, that's his choice. We've always been here. We didn't change the plans we've been making for years because we want a little glory. He's the one who walked away. Maybe he found someone else. Maybe he can't handle what it means to be in the kind of relationship we were in, but he's gone and won't be coming back. Not to us."

"Would you let him?"

Aidan's shoulders slumped. "No. Not anymore. He broke trust with us, and we're done. You do know everyone has asked us these questions, right? It gets to be a lot. How about I ask what you're doing with Lou. She's a good kid. She doesn't deserve to be jerked around."

Yup. That hurt. "First, she's not a kid. Not anymore, but she was in high school. She might have been super smart, but she was young and naïve. I never meant to jerk her around. I love Lou. I always have. I had no business messing around with Lou back then, and she went to college and our paths diverged."

"But they came back together when she chucked it all to join the twins' mad experiment."

TJ had to tamp down his irritation. "It's not an experiment."

"Forgive me if I'm bitter since that team is one of the reasons I lost my partner, but that's not the point," Aidan explained. "She's been on the team for two years and you didn't approach her. From what I understand you recently rejected her. Again."

Did everyone know about that? It had happened on a super-classified op. Did anyone know the meaning of the word discretion? "That was a mistake. I'm correcting it now. I'm in love with Lou, and the time is right. I'm going to convince her and marry her, and I hope everyone in the family will support me."

Aidan gave him a once-over. "Are you sure this isn't…"

"It's not fucking trauma." He was sick of this. "Look—support me. Don't support me. I'm getting my girl."

"And when your job takes you away from her when she needs you?" Aidan asked.

"Then I quit my job. She's more important than any career. I quit and I come home and get on my uncle's payroll and support her. Hell, I'll be a great stay-at-home dad. I've done what I needed to do. Now it's time to do what I want, and that's to be with Lou."

"All right. I'm glad to hear it," Aidan replied with a nod.

A slow clap came from the doorway. Kala stood there. She was dressed to go into the office, wearing black slacks and a button-down she managed to make look both badass and feminine. Her bright pink hair was in a neat bun. "Me, too. I guess I need a new nickname for you."

"Other than Fucking TJ?" He knew what they called him. "Yes. How about Lou's boyfriend. I'll take that one."

Kala chose to ignore that, turning to Aidan. "He okay? He might not mention it but there was a muscle in his left arm that was still twitching on the plane ride back. Should he go in for more tests? I don't know that he would actually tell us everything that happened to him."

"I told you," he argued. "And the twitching seems to have stopped. I feel fine."

Aidan settled his bag over his shoulder. "I'd still like to do blood work. Otherwise, I'm going to clear him for basic work. I don't think he should be on a team doing missions for a while."

"He's going to be here in Dallas for the forseeable future. I'll make sure he takes it easy," Kala assured him. "And Aidan, thank you for coming by. I know it's hard for you. If it helps at all, Tristan is being an asshole. And he misses you."

"That doesn't help. Not at all. But it's beside the point. Carys and I will always be here when you need us. No matter what dumb shit you're doing." Aidan turned and walked away.

Kala frowned, a mulish expression. "It's not dumb shit. It's superhero shit. I'm very misunderstood."

"He thinks the team is the reason Tristan left them," TJ explained. "He's bitter. I suppose I would be, too."

Kala walked in, sitting down on Tasha's bed. "Yeah, well, I think when Tris gets back from this secret mission of his, I'm going to hold his ass down until he tells me what's going on. I'm tired of this. I know my dad is, too. It was one thing when he thought Tris had cold feet and needed some time. But there's something else going on here."

"I think Aidan was lying to me," TJ admitted.

Kala sat up straighter. "About?"

"I asked him if he'd seen Tris recently and he told me no. I'm almost sure that was a lie." He felt comfortable talking to Kala. She'd so often been his partner in crime that it was easy to fall back into the groove.

"Something's going on and I don't like it," Kala said.

"Then we should do something about it." This was not a bad plan. If he brought Lou in, she might feel closer to him. Having a mission of their own might work in his favor. "Have we asked Lou what she thinks?"

"You're serious this time, aren't you?" She didn't wait for him to answer. "All right, Lou's wannabe boyfriend. We'll talk to her about it. I want to know where Tris is going and why his fathers aren't losing their collective shit. Uncle Adam knows something. He has to or he wouldn't be so calm about this."

TJ stood, feeling way more optimistic than before. This was a plan. He had three months, and Lou would be with him almost 24/7. She wouldn't be able to hold out on him. And the whole dating thing was going to fizzle out when he got her on the dungeon floor. She wouldn't be able to withhold her heart. "Excellent. Let's talk over pancakes. I'm starving."

"Uh, you are on your own for breakfast. I have to get into the office and pretend to work on whatever my dad gives me. The case of the missing puppy or something." She stood and looked down at her watch, grimacing. "He's going to bark at me all day."

"Then I'll fill you in on what Lou and I talk about." He was looking forward to a leisurely breakfast since Lou's hours were pretty much whatever she wanted them to be. She would go into her lab, and he would hang with her, making sure no one tried to take her. His father was sticking close to his mom, and his sister had a bodyguard, too. It was the way they would work until they were sure the danger was over.

Kala went still. "Uhm, Lou already left."

He reached for his jeans. "Did anyone mention she has a bodyguard? Zach put me on Lou duty."

"None of us got that memo," Kala admitted. "Though I haven't read through his report. He sent it out this morning. That man is way too thorough."

At least he knew where she was and that the building she

worked in had excellent security. Though now that he thought about it, so did the McKay-Taggart building and his mom had still gotten jumped. He needed to hurry. He should have explained all of this to her the night before, but he hadn't wanted a fight. "I'll catch her at her office."

Kala winced. "She's not there. I'm afraid something came up."

"What came up?"

"My mom might have called and set up a breakfast date for her," Kala admitted.

Oh, he needed to have a talk with his aunt. "What? She has a date this morning?"

Kala shrugged. "She's got a lot of time to make up for. You can still catch her at her office. Probably. Unless the date goes well."

"Kala, where did she go?" He was not playing games. "Lou is out there, and I know she's capable, but she needs backup. We have no idea if this danger is over or if they'll try again. They'll know damn well I'll trade myself for Lou."

Kala frowned. "I'm only telling you this because you're serious and you should understand that if she gets hurt, I'm taking your balls and hanging them on our Christmas tree."

Kala gave him an address, and TJ moved like his life depended on it.

Chapter Nine

Lou felt her cell buzz and glanced down. TJ was calling her.

She turned her ringer off. She would call him back when her date was over. She'd set herself on a path, and she was going to follow it. She was absolutely sure TJ thought he could kiss her and she would fall right into his lap. Then once he had her, he would go back to his old ways and hey, can't we be friends, Lou?

"Anything important?" Her date was a truly stunning man with golden hair that had the slightest hint of curl to it and piercing eyes. He had a jaw carved from granite and a smile that should have assured him a spot on the big screen.

She had zero idea what Charlotte thought she was doing with this Greek god of a man.

Except he was British. He had the sexiest English accent. She'd been surprised since he wasn't what she'd expected at all.

"It's just work, and I can handle it later." She could stare at this hunk in a three-piece suit all day.

But that was all he was to her—a work of art. He wasn't TJ. He wasn't warm and comfortable and soul fulfilling. Still, how could she know if she didn't try?

She'd woken up warm and happy until the minute she realized nothing had changed. TJ was still reacting to something terrible that had happened to him. He was still the man who'd turned her down time and time again. She'd eased out of bed, a kernel of anger thrumming through her.

He was in her house, giving her puppy-dog eyes and expecting her to fall in line. Everyone thought she would, too. This morning when she'd gotten the text from Charlotte, she'd been ready to come up with an excuse, but Kenzie had said something about TJ wouldn't like it.

It didn't matter what TJ liked. They had agreed. She would continue dating and they would play at the club. Only at the club. Outside of the club they would be friends.

This was what it felt like to be truly stubborn. She didn't like it. No wonder Kala was grumpy all the time.

So she'd told Charlotte to set it up and gotten dressed in her sluttiest dress—the one with the deep V-neck—and left as Aidan and Carys were walking in.

"Tell me about your work. Mrs. Taggart said you were involved in some kind of technical job."

He really was gorgeous. Every woman who walked by stopped and stared for a moment. A bunch of the men, too, since they were in Oak Lawn. The café was small and tasteful, with early morning light that showed off this guy's immaculate skin care regime. He practically glowed.

TJ had looked rumpled and adorable this morning, totally out of place with a pink comforter around his chest.

"I work in research and development with a company called 4L. And she mentioned you're an accountant, right? She said you and Phoebe met at a conference recently and started helping each other out."

"Yes. She's a bright one, Phoebe is." He leaned in, his eyes fastening on her. "But accounting is such dull work. I wonder why I went into it sometimes. Your work is much more interesting. And your family. I must say I find Mrs. Taggart's family utterly charming. How do you know them?"

The woman who worked the front counter refilled Lou's coffee. She was the only woman who hadn't looked at her date like he was a dessert and she was starving.

"I'll take another tea when you have a moment," the Brit said.

"And some more milk."

The petite woman sighed. "Right away, sir."

That woman did not like her job, but she seemed to be the only one working. It was lucky there hadn't been a bunch of customers. The woman with curly blonde hair walked away muttering something Lou couldn't make out.

"My father has worked for McKay-Taggart for over twenty years." She didn't go into the fact that he was technically her stepfather. This relationship wouldn't warrant that level of knowledge. While he was gorgeous, there was something cold about the man.

"Yes, my own father has been at the same firm for years. He works as the head of a subsidiary company in London. The main offices are here in the US. You would think I would have gotten to spend a lot of time over here, but with the pandemic and political situations being what they've been, I'm afraid I lost touch with some of the people I knew when I was younger. It's why I was happy to be able to work here in Dallas for a bit."

Though she knew this wasn't going anywhere, she had some time before she needed to get to the office and go over all the data and reports Zach had sent this morning. She found herself curious about the man in front of her. "I have to ask. You are not what I was expecting when Charlotte told me I would be meeting Miguel Garza."

He grinned. "Ah, well, we have immigrants in the UK, too, you know. My mum is British. She met my father when she went on holiday in Spain when she was a teenager. She told him she was trying to learn the language at the time. She wasn't. She was fluent, but she wanted an excuse to spend time with him. When he applied to university, he chose an English school, and the rest is history."

"And what does your father do? You said he works for a US company." She wondered what TJ was doing. Probably having breakfast, and not at a petite café with croissants and *pains au chocolat*. He would be eating Kenzie's pancakes and downing more than his share of the bacon. She always ordered extra so he could steal from her.

"He's in…landscaping." There was the slightest hesitation. It could be that he was embarrassed, though she didn't understand why. "I'm afraid the thing my father is best known for is his green thumb. You should see his garden. It's spectacular. I'll be honest. I've gotten many a woman from simply walking them through the garden."

His voice had gone deep and low. Seductive.

She was sure it worked on a lot of women.

And she recognized that voice. Well, of course Charlotte had sent her a Dom. He was giving her Dom eyes and that "do my will, sub" Dom voice.

The barista put a mug in front of Miguel and a small pitcher of milk. "Will there be anything else, sir?"

He glanced up. "Not at all."

"Good, because my shift is almost over," she announced and then turned to go.

Miguel sat up a bit straighter.

"I'm afraid I'm not great with plants. I love them, but I travel a lot and so do my roommates, so the watering part can get away from me." It was the slightest bit awkward, but she'd found most first dates were like that.

"I grew up surrounded by them," Miguel replied. "We had a country home I spent much of my childhood at, but even the house in London was filled with them. You seem a bit distracted, dear. Is anything wrong?"

She was hella distracted. "No. I just got back from a business trip, and I have to admit I'm a bit jet-lagged."

But only a bit, and that was a surprise. She usually had a hard time getting to sleep after a mission, but her ever-churning brain had locked right down when TJ's arms were around her. Like something deep inside her knew she was safe, and it was okay to sleep deeply.

"Ah, where did you go?"

"It was a quick trip to New York. My boss is usually in Austin, but he's got a place in Manhattan." It was her go-to excuse when someone asked where she'd been. Meeting her boss in New York.

He studied her for a moment. "New York is only an hour off. I wouldn't expect jet-lag from that."

She really needed a better excuse. "I guess I stayed up late, and I need to catch up."

He sat back, and suddenly the smooth charm was replaced with a keen, somewhat predatory look. "Or it could be the seven-hour difference between Dallas and say, Munich."

A chill went through her. "You're not Miguel Garza."

A satisfied smile crossed his handsome face. "Not at all, but you are the lovely Louisa Ward, and the job at 4L is a cover for what you really do."

She pushed back from the table. "I'm afraid I need to go. If you have questions, you should ask my boss. It seems like you know him, so I don't have to give you his number."

His hand shot out, gripping her elbow as she tried to walk away. "I don't think so, love. I'd like to leave Ian Taggart out of this."

She twisted her arm out of his grip. "Like I said, talk to my boss. I don't know who you are or what group you're with, but I'm not about to sit here and talk to you."

He sighed but sat back, looking like a superhot brat prince. "We can certainly do this the hard way, if you like."

She wasn't doing this—whatever this was—at all. She had a million questions, but she knew what protocol insisted she do. Get out of the situation and call base. She was reaching for her cell when she hit the door, pushing through to the street.

Well, that's what she meant to do. But the door didn't budge. It was locked.

She turned back and realized at some point the café had emptied. When she'd entered there had been a couple of people, but they had gone and no one had taken their places. Given the time of day, this place should have been packed.

Situational awareness. She was going to get such a lecture.

The man she should have known wasn't Miguel Garza stood, adjusting his jacket. "It's only you and me. I'm afraid I've taken over this nice establishment. No one is coming in or out. And that one will not help you. She's with me."

The woman who'd made their coffee was pulling the shades down. She turned off the *Open* sign.

A little panic went through Lou as the windows were covered. She was alone, and no one could see inside.

"Let's take a drive, you and I," he offered like this was a normal date and not a kidnapping.

"I don't think so." Adrenaline started pumping through her

system.

"I must insist." He nodded to the woman who now held a semiautomatic in her left hand.

"You should do what he says, Ms. Ward." The woman had dropped the flat American accent and sounded every bit as British as her coworker. "If you talk quickly, you might avoid his seduction routine."

The Brit frowned her way. "My seduction routine is practically perfect. Send the signal we've got the package and we're coming in."

She was the package, and she wasn't about to go anywhere with them.

"Don't bother with your phone," he said. "It's not going to work now. It won't work in the car, either. Neither will your locator. You're welcome for that. I happen to know there's a location device that was planted under your right shoulder when you joined the Agency. I don't want to have to rip that out. Don't want to leave a scar on a girl as pretty as you."

So he had a jammer working. It would stop her cell service and block her locator if anyone thought to look for her. Of course he wasn't counting on the fact that it would still show this location since it would be the last place it had pinged. At least her team would have a place to start looking. "Who are you?"

She followed him through the back of the café, the woman with the gun solidly behind her.

She had to wait for her moment.

"That isn't important," he replied, holding the door to the kitchen open. It was perfectly quiet. "What is important is the identity of a man known as The Jester, and your team seems to hold the clue to that."

She was confused as to why this dude thought she knew anything. "Give my boss a call. I'm strictly tech support."

"Oh, you're so much more than that. You're the real brains behind that team." He unlocked the door that led to the alley behind the building, and she caught sight of a limo parked outside. The woman moved around her, opening the driver's door and sliding inside. "Don't try anything, Louisa. I would hate to have to hurt you."

She was outnumbered, but now the woman was starting up the car, and her captor didn't have a gun in his hand. She wasn't going down without a fight. If she got in that car, she had no idea what they would do with her.

She wished she'd stayed in bed with TJ, wished her pride hadn't forced her to take this stupid date.

"You're perfectly safe," the Brit said, offering to help her into the car. "You have my word as a gentleman."

The Brit was a liar.

The limo purred to life.

She wouldn't get a better shot. She gave him a tremulous smile and started to hold her hand out like she was falling for his bullshit. At the last minute, she pushed out, catching him off guard, and took off down the alley.

"Help!" she screamed. "Help me!"

They were in broad daylight right off a busy street. Someone would be here. Someone would hear her.

If she could get to the street, he couldn't manhandle her back into the limo. He would be forced to retreat. And if someone shot her, then at least she wouldn't get taken away and tortured.

She ran, but she'd chosen poorly because of course today was the day she'd decided to wear heels. She wasn't a heel person, but she'd wanted to feel sexy and confident. Now she wanted to feel capable of saving herself. She stumbled, her knees banging against the concrete. How did Kala and Kenz run in those things?

Lou screamed again as she started to rise, but an arm went around her waist, hauling her back.

"Hush or I'll have to tell my partner that the woman you work for is actually two women. If you don't shut up and get in that limo right now, the fact that Ms. Magenta is twins gets out to the entirety of the intelligence community."

Her heart sank. The twins. He knew about Kala and Kenz? In the intelligence world there was only one Miss Magenta. The twins shared a single persona. They worked hard to never let the truth that there were two of them get out. But this man knew. How the hell did he know? And who was he working with?

"Are you going to force me to make that call?" The question was whispered against her ear.

She shook her head.

He hauled her back to the limo and gently forced her in.

Lou took a long breath and hoped she got out of this alive.

* * * *

"It's up ahead. You don't have to park," TJ said.

"Oh, do you not want Lou's date to know you had to call your mom because you don't have a car?" His mother was way too perky this morning. She had a bright look in her eyes she got when she was working a particularly good case.

His case. His mom was working his case, and it was making him grumpy because she was right. He didn't want whichever successful dude Aunt Charlotte had set Lou up with to know he had to call his mom for a ride.

It was also good to know his kidnapping had put a light in his mom's eyes.

"The boy's right, Erin. Slow the car down and let him jump." His mom wasn't the only OG he was dealing with this morning. Liam O'Donnell had been sitting in the passenger seat when she'd driven up. He'd explained that he was riding into the office with Erin for the week because his saint of a daughter Daisy needed to use his car.

Those words. Those exact words had come out of the man's mouth.

He wasn't sure Uncle Li had met his daughter. Daisy was a ball of chaos and nowhere close to a saint. It wasn't that Daisy was awful. She was lovely, but crazy shit seemed to follow her, and according to her father, she was responsible for nothing.

Liam had been his mom's partner for…well, as long as TJ had been alive. They'd been paired up when his mom had joined McKay-Taggart, and Li referred to his mom as his work husband ever since. Yep, husband not wife. It felt almost right to have the man witness his humiliation.

Because Lou had to have known walking out the way she did would hurt him.

"What are you going to do if Lou won't drive you back to the office?" his mom asked as she stopped at a red light.

Liam briefly put his newspaper down. Where did the man find a physical newspaper? He always seemed to have one. "That's a good question. Are you going to rent one of those scooter things?"

Excellent. He had two sarcastic parental figures to deal with. At least if his dad had been in the car, he would have gotten some sympathy.

And likely more advice. Was he dressed for this? He needed to get V-necks because he couldn't show off any male cleavage in this crew neck.

He thought about getting out and walking the block and a half. "She won't leave me. I'm her bodyguard. I called Zach, and he told me he informed her that she now has a bodyguard. Either she hasn't read his report yet or she's being mean. As Lou is the least mean person I know, I'm going with she hasn't opened her email yet."

Because she was too busy getting ready for her date with an accountant. During the wait for his mom, he'd looked up Miguel Garza, the dude his aunt thought would be a good fit with Lou. According to his socials, he was at least ten years older than Lou and thought pickleball was a real sport. He supposed the guy was attractive in a nerdy way, and he was way invested in *Star Trek*. Which would be a point in his favor when it came to Lou.

It wasn't happening. He knew he'd said it was fine, but she shouldn't be dating while they were working a dangerous case. He was putting his foot down.

"Do not put your foot down," his mother said with a shake of her head, proving she knew him well. "I know that look. Your father gets that look when he's about to be super stubborn. Don't do it. She won't handle it well."

Liam turned to her. "What would he be putting his foot down about? And why? I don't think TJ has that place in Lou's life. Has anyone told her?"

His mom grinned Li's way. "Oh, I didn't tell you. So when the kidnappers had TJ, his response to being in danger and Lou getting sent in to save him was to hump her leg. And in a way that Big Tag saw."

A booming laugh came out of Liam's mouth. "Are you serious? How did the big bastard take that?"

"Oh, it was so much Big Tag drama. There was talk of him

gouging his eyes out or bleaching them. I offered to sew them shut for him," his mom replied.

"You didn't even tell him Lou and I are together now?" His mom knew how to bury a lead. This dude was his mom's best friend and she hadn't even told him?

Liam shrugged. "She told me the important stuff. You let yourself get roofied and some bad guys think you know another bad guy."

This man had a reputation as McKay-Taggart's problem solver. The man who could put the wildest shit together to solve a case.

"Though she should have told me Big Tag got an eyeful," Liam continued. "He'll probably still be ranting about it this morning. So you finally fell into bed with Lou and now you think you need to put your foot down? Why would that be?"

"Because the men who kidnapped me got away, so she could still be in danger. She's my weak spot and everyone knows it," he replied. "So while I'm here, I'm her bodyguard."

Liam turned and looked at him. He was roughly the same age as his mom, with a hint of silver at his temples and intelligent green eyes. Though he'd lived in the States for the majority of his adult life, the man still sounded like he came straight out of Dublin. "Let me see if I understand. She had to go in and save your arse, but she's the one in danger. You know there is a school of thought where if you're the target of a bunch of maniacal killers, you maybe distance from your loved ones."

His mom made a gagging sound. "Don't even put that into his head. TJ, you would do that if your family was some precious middle-class clan who'd never had to bury a body. Oh, hey, did you thank Avery for letting the kids use your backyard?"

"Not a problem. I know Big Tag is full up, and our dog is a lazy bastard. He won't be digging our friend up. Though I did make them do it in the dead of night," Liam replied. "Couldn't have my sweet Daisy seeing that going on. That girl needs a bodyguard."

They were getting off the topic. "I'm not putting space between me and Lou to save her. That feels dumb when she's apparently perfectly capable of saving herself. But as her bodyguard, I have to have a say in her safety, and meeting a bunch of strange men isn't safe. My aunt should know that. She shouldn't be sending her off with random men."

His mom moved a couple of car lengths before the light turned red again. "They aren't random. I assure you that Charlotte wouldn't set her up with anyone who didn't pass a bunch of tests. This particular guy is a friend of Phoebe's."

"How would you know?" TJ asked.

One slender shoulder shrugged. "Who do you think does the actual vetting?"

A nasty sense of betrayal flooded his system. He sat back, letting that knowledge sink in. His mom was helping Lou find someone who wasn't him. His mom, who had always loved Lou, who told him on so many occasions that he would regret not taking a chance with Lou. He knew he'd screwed up.

Still, he'd thought his mom would be on his side.

"What'd you find this time?" Liam asked.

"He's allergic to dogs," his mom replied.

The light changed and his mom moved through, taking them closer to the small café where Lou was meeting a dude who couldn't be around dogs.

Lou loved dogs. Like was obsessed with them. All animals, really.

His mom loved him. "Aunt Charlotte doesn't know that?"

"I don't think it came up. He's successful and looks good on paper, but there's zero way our Lou doesn't have a bunch of dogs in her future. I also vet her online matches. Dennis Sims seems good on paper but he's still a frat bro, and that will come out at some point, and Lou is never going to be with a man who could have done that to her when she was a kid. Tell Kala I was proud of how she handled that." She stopped the car in front of the café and turned his way, her lips curling up in a satisfied smile. "I know everything. Everything, son. My intelligence work trained me for motherhood in a way you can't imagine. And if Devi thinks I don't know how her car got that dent last week, she hasn't been paying attention. Tried to avoid a duck? Who does she think I am? I can get into CCTV cams, child. I know she hit a fire hydrant because a hot guy ran by in shorts that would make a cheerleader blush. Duck, my ass."

Liam's head tilted up as though he was looking to the heavens. "I thank the lord my sweet girl isn't all that interested in boys."

He saw his mom's eyes roll in the rearview, but she didn't correct him.

Daisy wasn't interested in boys. She was a maneater.

Which didn't matter. He breathed a sigh of relief. "So you're not trying to find a nice guy for Lou?"

"Lou has a nice guy." She reached back and rumpled his hair like she used to do when he was a kid. "You should understand that I was planning on having a long conversation with you when you came home this time around. I was going to give you a month tops and then I was going all in because you can't keep her in limbo, baby."

Liam went back to his paper. "She's telling you the truth, son. Your mother's been planning this conversation. I've listened to it about a hundred times now. She's about to talk about how Lou deserves better."

His mom nodded. "Lou deserves better. And I happen to agree with you about timing. I don't think it would have been a good idea for you to follow her. I think you should have gone to college, but getting a minimum wage job and hanging out with your genius girlfriend wouldn't have served either of you. But it's time and you know it. So I'll be selfish because I want Lou as my daughter-in-law. She's good for you. You have to prove you can be good for her, and that starts with not walking in and making an ass of yourself. Go in there and do the busy work Zach assigned to keep you out of his hair, and you do it with a smile on your face."

"Yeah…wait, what?" It wasn't busy work.

His mom ignored him. "Be polite and sweet and talk a lot about dogs. I'll work this from another angle because we have to deal with Boomer."

"I can't imagine having Boomer as an in-law. You know I've had to feed the man at Thanksgiving," Liam complained. "My poor Avery had to buy out a Kentucky Fried Chicken after the man ate a whole turkey."

"Oh, I'm too smart to offer to cook. I've learned your lessons," his mom countered. "Theo and I are taking him to a buffet for lunch. We'll get him in a good mood so you can tell him what's going on."

There was a problem with that plan. "I promised Lou I wouldn't."

"You're not going to tell her father you're together?" Liam sounded confused. "I know Boomer doesn't have a reputation as a philosopher, but he's going to figure something's up when you're suddenly sleeping in Lou's bed."

"He's going to find out," his mom agreed. "Are you or are you not planning on playing with her tonight at your club?"

She really did know everything. "Yes."

"And who works with Lou's mother every day?" His mom seemed determined to poke holes in his plan. "Who is Daphne's prized apprentice?"

He sighed because once again she was right and proved his mom played chess and not checkers. Damn it. She was right. She was always right. "Marley Brighton, and she's going to be at the club tonight."

"Thank god my own sweet Daisy doesn't believe in gossip," Liam muttered under his breath.

No. Daisy believed in making as much of it as possible. "I can talk to her. Even better, I could have Kala talk to her."

"Won't happen," his mom argued. "Kala loves Marley's mom. She'll tell you to suck it up and be a man, though she'll use way rougher language. So you and Lou need to understand that everyone will know after tonight, and that includes her parents. Be forthright with Boomer. He'll appreciate it. If Boomer's happy and Daphne believes you're going to take care of Lou this time, everything will be fine. If not, one of Big Tag's kids will pull some serious shit and you two can have cover for a while. We can always count on the twins, though the boys turned out to be more trouble than I would have imagined. I'll never forget the moment Big Tag realized his son was singing to the lunch crowd at a Pot-Bellied Pig."

Liam snorted. "Serves him right after all the hell he gave that boy."

Somehow he thought Travis having a kid out of wedlock at the ripe old age of twenty-three was a bigger scandal than Seth following his musical dreams, but apparently his Aunt Charlotte couldn't cuddle a guitar. He glanced over and was surprised to see the blinds to the café were down. Shouldn't they be open? They weren't facing east, so it wasn't a sun problem.

"Hey. Have you ever been to this café before?" TJ asked,

unbuckling his seat belt.

"No, but they pop up all the time in this neighborhood. It looks like every other froufrou brunch place," his mom said. "Why? You getting a weird feeling?"

It was good that he didn't have to explain. His parents had taught him to trust his instincts. "I don't like the fact that the blinds are down. It's a beautiful day. Places like this value stuff like natural lighting. I'm going to go in. Do you mind waiting for a minute?"

"Not at all. I'll keep the car running. If you think she's in trouble, forget everything I said and hustle her out here. I'll deal with the fallout with Charlotte."

Liam leaned over. "And if they have a breakfast sandwich, I'll take one of those."

He should have known he would end up running errands. He eased out of the car, checking the area around him. It was pretty normal for this part of town. Oak Lawn wasn't known for its towering buildings. Most of the businesses here were small and independently owned and operated. So there weren't a lot of sniper positions. Still.

He moved in and frowned. The *Open* signed was turned off and the door was shielded by another set of blinds.

This was wrong. He felt it in his bones. He reached out and tested the door. Locked.

Fuck.

He pulled his cell and called Lou again. She hadn't answered before and he'd thought it was pure stubbornness, but now he had to wonder. Nothing.

He punched in another number.

"McKay-Taggart Security Services, how can I help you?"

Even though he couldn't see her face, that bouncy answer told him Kenzie had the phone she and Kala used exclusively for emergencies. It was one they used for cover and the only one he could be absolutely certain they would answer without fail. "I think Lou's in trouble. I need you to activate her locator."

"Lou's on a date, TJ. Don't be an asshole," Kenzie replied. "Look, I know it sucks to be rejected, but I don't think this rejection is going to stick. I think if you're patient…"

He did not need another lecture. "The place where Lou is

meeting her date is closed."

"They probably went somewhere else then," Kenzie argued. "I just think you should give her some space. I do think she loves you, but you can't push it."

"I have a feeling, Kenz. Activate her tracer or hand me over to Kala. Something is wrong."

"Fine," she said with a huff. "Give me a minute."

He tried to see inside, but those blinds were doing their job. He could have sworn he saw some movement, but he couldn't be sure. All he knew was his gut was telling him something was off here. Yes, businesses closed, but Lou would have texted Kala, and if Kala knew something, Kenzie did, too.

"Hey, what's going on?" That slightly deeper voice was Kala. "Kenz is pulling the locator. I gave you the address Lou gave me. It doesn't check out?"

"It's closed."

Kala hesitated. "Okay, then something's wrong because she didn't text me that her plans had changed. Hold on. Kenzie says her locator shows she's there. Wait. What do you mean? Try it again."

He started moving back to the car. "What's happening?"

"We've got some kind of delay," Kala explained. "The last time her locator pinged was ten minutes ago. There might be a problem with the satellite. Don't panic."

He wasn't panicking. He felt a cool, calm come over him. Lou was in trouble. He didn't get to panic. She needed him, so he would do whatever it took.

If this was all some crazy misunderstanding where she forgot to let her team know where she was, then he could take it out on her pretty ass tonight at the club. But for now, all that mattered was finding her and getting her to the office safely.

Then he would get to the bottom of all this mess. He wasn't going to let Lou get hurt.

"I'm waiting on the locator," he said to his mom through the open window.

Liam looked up from his paper. "Have you called her?"

"Twice, and she didn't answer," he replied. "I thought she was being stubborn, but now I wonder."

His mom nodded, her expression calm as well. "Who do you

want me to call? Ian or Zach?"

The fact that she was giving him the choice meant she trusted his instincts. "The twins will let their dad know. Call Zach. Tell him to take over the CCTV cams and look for Lou's car. It's not on the street, so it's probably in one of the lots around this area."

"Hey, I think we have a problem," Kala said over the line.

Fuck. "Hit me."

"The locator isn't working, and I can't ping her cell either," Kala admitted. "I can show her going into that building, but as of ten minutes ago, she disappears. Everyone else's locator is working."

And that wasn't a satellite problem. Someone had nullified her locator device. If they'd simply cut it out, he would know where they'd tossed it.

The thought of someone cutting up Lou threatened his calm.

"My mom is with me. She's talking to Zach," he began. "Uncle Liam's here, too."

And then he heard it.

"Help! Help me!"

It was in the distance, but he knew Lou's voice. He took off. There was a building between them. He sprinted, his whole being focused on making it to her.

He rounded the corner, his heart pounding in his chest.

Just in time to see a limo pull away. He ran down the alley, but he knew he was too late.

"Damn me. I can't get a shot from here." Liam was beside him, a gun in his hand. "We have to follow them."

Lou was in that limo, and he'd failed her.

TJ heard a honk and he realized his mom was behind them, and she'd brought the Jeep.

"Get in," his mom ordered.

Liam opened the back door. "You take the front, kid. This could get messy. Thank the saints my own sweet Daisy has never been kidnapped."

"Give it time." He got in the car.

The chase was on.

Chapter Ten

Lou eased the shoes off her feet. If she got another chance to run, she was going to take it. She'd learned her lesson. "Are you MI6?"

Her captor sat back, looking like he was born to ride in a limo. "Perhaps. Perhaps not. Can I get you a drink? I've got a whole bar in here. Excellent Scotch."

"It's like ten in the morning."

"He doesn't go by things like time or societal norms," the woman driving said.

"*Mantén los ojos en el camino y yo me encargaré de la dama,*" her captor said in perfect Spanish.

Keep your eyes on the road and I'll take care of the lady.

Lucky for her, it was one of the languages she was pretty good with.

"Really? Spanish? You want to use Spanish on the spy from Texas?" the woman asked, and it was easy to see these two were comfortable with each other. Though she didn't think their connection was sexual. They were friends, or they'd worked together for a long time. "I wouldn't try French, either. She went to a private school for much of her education, and they taught French. She switched to Spanish when she moved to a public high school. Which you would know if you ever read the files our handlers send us."

They had a file on her? Who was she dealing with? She was still thinking MI6. British intelligence rather than criminal element.

"*Jag kan inte ryska. Jag menar allvar, syster. Håll ögonen på vägen*," he replied.

So he was almost surely an intelligence operative. She wasn't sure which Nordic language that was, but she had identified one word. *Syster*.

They were brother and sister.

"*Skruva inte ihop det här,*" the sister replied with a sharp edge. She pressed a button and a wall came up, dividing the limo and leaving Lou alone with her brother.

He reached into the bar and pulled out a couple of glasses. "Don't mind my coworker. Like I said, who I am doesn't matter. I want to know why Theodore Taggart Jr. is working with The Jester."

They were back to this again. Lou took a calming breath. Well, it was supposed to calm her down. She knew from the outside she looked fairly steady, but her heart was pounding in her chest. She had to play this cool. At some point in time she would be far enough away that whatever tech he was using to jam her locator signal would fail, and she knew her team would be watching. "He's not. He has no idea who The Jester is. Are you getting intelligence from mobsters? Is that where MI6 has gone? I know your agency has been struggling to keep up, but that's sad."

She needed to shake this guy up a bit. She wasn't sure where they were going, but she had to hope she would have a chance to run again, and this time she would be ready. She was never wearing heels again. And now that she thought about it, Kala was right. She should be a walking armory at all times. If she'd thought to strap a couple of knives to her thighs, she would be in a better position.

She hadn't taken her gun because it didn't fit into the purse that went best with her dress. She needed a better excuse like oops, she dropped it or something because everyone was going to rag her for the rest of time.

Or she could die. That seemed like an actual viable option.

However, she was interested in why the Brits hadn't simply

called. Ian used to have a decent relationship with MI6. She knew at some point it had gotten tense, but she was surprised they hadn't put in a request to speak with him to Langley. Something was happening that she didn't understand, and it was her job to get as much out of this guy as she could.

He was a cool customer. He simply poured out two glasses of Scotch and offered her one. "You should know that sometimes the best intelligence comes from the oddest sources. I would never be so snobbish about gathering intel, love. Here, you should try it."

She wasn't risking taking a drink. "Like I said, it's barely ten a.m., and I'm more of a margarita girl."

"Well, when we get where we're going, I'll make you one." He downed one of the Scotches and set the empty glass back on the shelf, apparently happy to sip the second one. "You know I think we could make this whole episode interesting. We might be together for a couple of days. We shouldn't waste them. I can make things comfortable for you."

Was he flirting with her? Seriously? "You mean my kidnapping?"

He waved that off. "That's such a loaded word. I prefer to think of it as a meeting you didn't expect to take. In another country."

So they were heading to an airport. Probably a private airport where she would be driven right into the hangar, and everyone inside would be in on the plot. She wouldn't have much of a shot if she got on that plane. "I assure you kidnapping is the word my team is going to use. If you're MI6, I want to know why you didn't call Langley. What do you need to know that's so secret you couldn't use proper channels? If this Jester person is really so dangerous, I would think you would want my team helping out."

"Your team is too close to the target."

"TJ isn't The Jester, and he doesn't know who he is."

Her captor chuckled. "I certainly didn't imagine TJ is The Jester. The Jester is brilliant. Criminal, but brilliant. However, TJ could serve as a go between. I've been looking into his former commanding officer and seeing some things I don't like."

"His former CO is dead."

"Yes, I find that intriguing as well," he admitted. "He died in

Australia. I believe your team had something to do with that. And a CIA operative named Chet Whittington recently died under mysterious circumstances in prison. No one seems to know how that happened."

"Are you trying to tell me MI6 thinks TJ is working with this Jester person and he what? Is doing the dude's wet work?" It was a ridiculous thought, but the truth of the matter was she couldn't clear it up for him. What happened on the Australian op was classified, and he was a foreign agent.

"I'm not sure what to think. That's why I'm here. I have intelligence that points me in the direction of TJ. Because of his connections, I've tried to keep that quiet until I can figure out what kind of trouble he's in. However, I'm working with someone who wants answers, and he wants them now. I'm in a bit of a bind, love. That's where you come in. You're going to spend a couple of days helping us figure this out so I can either have TJ brought in or I can exonerate him."

"All right. Let me see this intelligence of yours." TJ had mentioned some pictures, but naturally he hadn't been able to take them with him so she couldn't debunk them. "I assure you I can take it all apart if you set me up with a laptop."

"I think setting the brilliant Louisa Ward up with a laptop would be the height of idiocy on my part."

"You should call my boss. This whole kidnapping thing isn't necessary. Or his boss, Drake Radcliffe."

The man snorted, an oddly elegant sound. "I doubt Ian Taggart believes Radcliffe is his boss. And I have my reasons for not involving the higher-ups. I'm working with someone who thinks you're the key to figuring this all out. He wants to avoid the rest of your team if he can."

"They will look for me." Of that she had no doubt. "There will be repercussions."

"I think I can handle anything the old man wants to throw at me," he said with all the surety of someone who had obviously not spent a lot of time with Big Tag.

What would TJ do? Would he be angry she'd let herself get kidnapped?

Or would he be the one leading the charge to find her?

"Tell me something. Do Kenzie and Kala know The Jester? Did TJ make contact for them?" the man asked.

"Who the hell are you?" How did he know about her best friends and their secrets?

"Let's say I'm an old friend," he allowed. "Which is precisely why you should trust me. Like I said, I'm hoping to clear TJ and your team before anyone can think to bring you in for more formal questioning. I don't believe for a second the twins are doing anything criminal, but my partner in this endeavor apparently got burned by them once."

That could be any number of foreign operatives. Kala could be stingy with intel. She didn't like to share, and she didn't mind stealing anything she thought her team could use.

"Here's what's going to happen," he continued. "We're going to a private airfield. We'll fly to a location where we'll meet with my partner in this endeavor. You'll be kept safe. I promise I won't let anyone hurt you. You're going to give me the information I need to make contact with The Jester, and I won't turn over the intelligence connecting your friend to an arms dealer to Interpol. Right now, they don't have any idea TJ is involved with him. If they do, he'll likely be arrested, and I doubt you'll see him again. Is that the outcome you desire? This doesn't have to be hard. Unless you're involved with The Jester, too?"

Lou glanced out and realized they'd been driving for a while. They'd left Dallas and were on the road that would eventually take them to Fort Worth, though she doubted they would go that far. There was a private airfield outside of DFW airport, and that was almost surely where they were headed to. "I barely heard the name twenty-four hours ago."

"Then he's been keeping secrets from you or you're an excellent liar. I'm not sure which. All right. Let me lay a couple of facts out for you. I came across the man known as The Jester three years ago. We believe he's responsible for the bombs used in the Jakarta terrorist attacks. I managed to connect with him via the Dark Web. It took eighteen months to get him to agree to meet with me. In Berlin."

Where TJ had said the photo of him had been taken. "And what happened at your meeting?"

"He didn't show," the man admitted. "He did, however, apparently meet with the young Taggart."

"Why are you asking me and not TJ?"

"Because I need to know if he's working for the Agency, and I don't think he'll tell me the truth. Besides, his family has a certain reputation, and I would like to avoid getting on their bad side. There are connections I would disturb. So I'm here with you."

"I assure you I can figure out exactly who you are."

He leaned forward, a serious expression on his face. "I'm sure you will, Louisa. I'm also sure there will be several arse kickings in my future. I've got a lot on the line here, and that should tell you how seriously I'm taking this threat. The Jester could lead me to someone far more dangerous."

Now they were getting somewhere. "Who are you looking for?"

He sat back, looking like a brat prince once again. "If I come to trust you, I'll let you in on the case. I have to convince my partner, though. He doesn't like your team."

So Kala probably busted his balls at some point. Literally.

"Could you tell me where we're going?"

"And ruin the surprise?" He smiled, a secretive expression that would get most girls all riled up. He had the kind of good looks that meant he could get away with murder.

And that meant he would underestimate her. He would think he could smile and flirt with her a little and get whatever he wanted.

Men. Wasn't that what TJ was doing? When she wanted a relationship, it wasn't time. When he did, she was supposed to fall in line.

"This is all useless. I don't know anything." She turned away from him. They were close to the airport, as evidenced by the wide, flat fields around them. The Metroplex was huge and filled with thriving communities, but this space around the airport still had some undeveloped land.

All the better to hide a private airfield so assholes could kidnap nice girls who just wanted to go on a date.

"What did you do to the real Miguel? Please tell me you didn't kill him. He was real, right?"

The man shrugged. "He's perfectly fine. Though likely a bit upset his date stood him up. I sent him to another café. Really, darling, the two of you wouldn't be a good match. I'm much more fun, as you'll find out."

A sliding sound caught her attention, the barrier between the front and back seats coming down.

"*Vi har sällskap,*" the driver said.

That got her captor's attention. He turned in his seat, looking out the back. "The Jeep?"

Someone was following them? She twisted to get a look.

The vehicle seemed so familiar.

"*De har legat bakom oss*," the driver began.

Lou was tired of this shit. "Okay, polyglots, can we get rid of the Finnish or Swedish or whatever you're speaking? It's kind of torture."

"Swedish," the woman replied, tension in her voice. "I would switch to Romanian but it's a Slavic language. I would bet a lot that you speak Russian."

She spoke several languages. Russian. Mandarin. Some Arabic. She was quite good with Spanish. The languages she'd learned had been about work. Russia and China were often their foes, and the Middle East was a part of the world that was always ripe for war. The Spanish was because she lived in Texas.

Why would they know Swedish? Did they spy for meatballs?

"They could be going to the airfield," her captor said.

"No. They're following us," the driver insisted.

"Well, they won't be able to follow us in unless they have the proper papers." He pulled his cell. "Yes, we're almost there and we have the package with us, but we might have a problem."

Lou was watching the Jeep. Was that Erin Taggart's Jeep?

She took a long breath. If Erin was in that Jeep, then they knew she was in here and in trouble. They wouldn't allow this limo to make it to the airfield. They wouldn't risk losing her.

But they would have to wait. They couldn't do anything in the city. They wouldn't risk it on the crowded freeway.

She saw someone moving inside the Jeep and the flash of metal in the sunlight.

TJ. TJ was in that Jeep, and he'd come for her. He was going to do whatever it took to get her back.

Shit. Lou grabbed the seatbelt and buckled herself in because this ride was about to go wild.

* * * *

TJ watched the limo pass the exit that would have taken them to DFW proper. "They're definitely headed to the private airfield. Do we have someone looking into their schedule?"

"I'm on it," Kenzie said over the line.

The twins were online over his mom's cell, so the call could be heard through the Jeep. He'd called in the minute he realized Lou was in that limo. They'd been following them through traffic cameras, looking for a place where he could try to stop the vehicle. By force, if necessary.

The Jeep was oddly calm for what was basically a high-speed chase. His mom was cool under pressure, and Liam was grumpy about not getting breakfast. He and his mom had argued over whether a protein bar passed for actual food. Uncle Liam had spent the whole time reading his paper and looking up at the restaurants they passed like he would never see them again. Lou's dad wasn't the only one with food issues.

"TJ, they have serious security out there, and I doubt you'll be allowed in. At best they'll take half an hour to clear you and by then…" Big Tag had joined his daughters about fifteen minutes in. They'd been arguing over whether to call the authorities. But they had gone through three different cities, and it would have taken a while to even sort out who to call. And then there was the problem of who had her. If it was a foreign agency, they could have all sorts of tricks to fool the police. He'd watched his cousins do it time and time again. "If they get Lou onto a plane, we'll lose her."

He'd known he would have to take a risk if he was going to get her back.

"Do you think we're far enough out?" His mom directed the question to her partner.

Liam looked up from what appeared to be the sports section. He glanced around. "Oh, yeah. I'm worried a bit that the road slopes down up ahead, but we're out of time. This is far enough away no one should see, but not close enough the airfield would get tipped off."

Fuck. He was going to have to do this. He had to stop the limo, and he couldn't use the powers of his mind. He was going to have to use the powers of his gun.

"How close do you want me to get?" His mom had been a rock. The woman knew how to tail someone. "I think they figured out we're following them."

The limo sped up.

Damn it. He didn't want to risk hurting Lou, but he couldn't let her go.

"TJ, how sure are you she's in that limo?" Uncle Liam asked. "We didn't see her actually get in."

He didn't have to. He'd heard her. He knew her voice. "I know she's in there."

"Then do it." Liam put his paper down and seemed to get serious about the job at hand. "Take a deep breath then take the shot. You can do this. You are trained for this. Lou will be okay."

Lou was about to be in a car accident. Except it wouldn't be an accident since he was going to intentionally blow the tires.

His mom kept a steady distance between them. "You're going to lose them if you don't go now. Do you want me to do it?"

Okay, maybe having his mom with him on a mission wasn't the greatest thing in the world. She was very opinionated. "I think you should keep driving."

He checked his SIG.

"You could take the wheel. Or Li can. It won't take long. I assure you I can shoot out that tire really fucking fast. Do you want Bertha? She's in the glove compartment. I think she might be better for this job."

His mom was overly attached to her Beretta. "I'll use mine, Mom."

"Erin, leave the boy be," Liam said, moving to the center of the back seat.

"Cooper and Zach should be coming in hot," Kala said over the line.

He glanced behind him, and sure enough there was a big black SUV motoring down the road. At least he would have backup. He had no idea what he was going into, but he had to stop that limo. He lowered the window and slid up, the wind blasting him. He balanced on the door, half his big body hanging out.

"Move to the left," he shouted over the wind.

His mom shifted over, giving him the view he needed. He hung out the window, a precarious position, but he wasn't about to take things easy. If he fucking fell out and died, at least Lou would know he'd come for her.

"I think you should take out the back passenger side," his mom advised.

"Erin, don't fucking distract him," Big Tag yelled over the cell.

TJ let his brain go quiet, his focus narrowing to that tire. The world went silent and he brought the SIG up, his legs the only thing keeping him in the vehicle.

Then he felt a hand on his leg. Liam had positioned himself so he could act as a balance to TJ. His uncle wouldn't let him fall. His family was annoying, and they always had his back.

Between one breath and another, he pulled the trigger.

He managed to slide back into the Jeep as the limo went skidding across the road.

Don't flip. Don't flip. Don't fucking flip.

The limo swerved, and for a moment he worried the driver would regain control.

That was when the big black car fishtailed, the awful sound of metal against concrete filling the air. And the limo veered off the road, rolling down the hill to a stop. It sat precariously on its side.

His mom managed to stop the Jeep and not roll down the hill. TJ was out in a heartbeat, his mom and uncle coming right behind him.

"Lou," he yelled out. *Let her be okay.* He kept his SIG at the ready because he had no idea how many guns he would be facing.

Just let Lou be okay. He couldn't be the reason Lou died.

"I'll take the driver, you two get whoever's in the back," his mom called out. "And we need to move because someone's going to call the cops, and I know Big Tag's going to want a word with whoever's in there."

"Take them alive if you can," Liam said quietly. He moved

around the limo so they had a gun on both sides of the vehicle.

The driver's side window opened, and two feminine hands came up. "Hello. I'm coming out. I'm not armed. Well, I am, but I'm not going to use it."

A blonde head followed the open hands, and TJ frowned because he knew that face. He hadn't seen her in a couple of years, but Samantha Knight looked almost the same as the last time he'd been in London.

"Sami?" He was confused.

"Hello, TJ. Long time no see." She gave him a brilliant smile and then frowned. "No. I'm not going to do that, Ollie. Mrs. Taggart is here. No, TJ's mom. You know I adore her. And Liam O'Donnell, if I'm not mistaken." Sami turned back to them. "Ollie wants me to try to take you out. In a nonlethal fashion, of course. He's high on something, I'm sure because that would never work. You know my brother. He thinks far too highly of himself."

"Where's Lou?" TJ didn't lower the weapon. He had no idea why Damon Knight's kids were here, but they had Lou.

"I'm here." She started to climb out of the back window. "I'm okay. I put on my seatbelt when I realized what you were going to do."

"You could have bloody well told me," a very British voice said. "I might have a concussion. And this suit is perfectly ruined. It wasn't cheap, you know."

Liam moved in, frowning. "Bloody Brits. I haven't had any breakfast, boy, so you should start talking. I'm already in a bad mood."

TJ holstered his SIG and raced to pull Lou out of the limo. He wrapped his arms around her, carrying her from the wreckage. Relief poured through him. She was alive. She didn't seem to be hurt.

"Serves you right." Sami climbed out and brushed her hands down her shirt, trying to straighten it. She seemed very peppy for someone who'd survived an accident. "It's nothing compared to what Papa is going to do to you when he finds out you kidnapped Louisa Ward and got caught doing it. Just so everyone understands, this was not my idea, but does James Bond over there listen to good advice?"

Liam offered Oliver his hand.

His mom had holstered her gun, too. She moved to the young blonde and looked her over. Their families had ties. His father was good friends with one of the London team's longest working members, a man named Russell Seeger, though he went by Robert. He and TJ's dad had survived some seriously bad shit together, and the bond had held over the years. When they visited Robert and his wife, Ariel, in London, he and his sister would often spend time with Damon Knight's kids, Oliver and Archie, and the youngest, Samantha. "You okay, kid?"

It didn't look like Archie was here.

Sami said something, but TJ was too busy checking Lou for injuries. Now that he knew she was alive, he was practically frantic. "Baby, I'm so sorry. I didn't know they were friendlies. What's going on? I didn't know you knew the Knights."

Had he made a horrible mistake?

"Knights? Like the guy who runs the London office?" Lou adjusted her glasses and tried to straighten her dress.

She was wearing her boob dress. It was the sexiest thing she owned. It showed off the swell of her breasts, and he could barely think when she wore that dress. "You wore your boob dress on a breakfast date?"

"In her defense, we didn't actually get to breakfast," a cultured British voice said. Oliver Knight had a small gash on his jawline but otherwise managed to look perfectly smooth, despite the fact he was standing in a wrecked limo.

Lou's eyes had widened. "Boob dress?"

"Yes, it's the one that shows off your boobs. Where are your shoes, baby?" TJ asked.

Liam managed to get Oliver out of the limo and onto solid ground. "I think they're in here. Oh, is that whiskey I smell?"

"Of course not, old man. That's the finest Scotch," Oliver returned.

"Damon should have spanked you more, boyo." Liam pulled his cell out. "Ian, you can stand down. It's Damon's kiddos. Either they're into kidnapping or they're following in their da's footsteps. Did you know about this?"

"Baby? Oh, shit," Sami said, looking from her brother to TJ.

"Are the two of you together?"

"Yes," TJ said.

"No," Lou said at the same time.

"It's complicated," his mom assured Sami.

TJ was stuck on that dress. "You wore your boob dress to a date with Oliver Knight?"

There was a fine flush to her face. "I wore my…this very nice dress to a date with Miguel Garza. Who apparently turned out to be Oliver Knight. And my shoes are in the car. I took them off so I could run because I didn't know this guy is some kind of friend of yours. He kidnapped me. He thinks you're in league with this Jester person."

"Oh, they're definitely MI6," Liam was saying. "Did you think you were the only one with spy kids? No, he didn't copy you. Stop yelling at me. I'm trying to listen. I think TJ might kick Ollie's arse."

"As if he could," Oliver retorted with a frown.

That was a kick in the gut. He thought they were friends. "Why the hell didn't you ask me, Oliver? You had to kidnap my girlfriend?"

An elegant shoulder shrugged. "I didn't know she was your girlfriend at the time. My intel told me Louisa Ward was single. She's also the brains of your team. I certainly wouldn't kidnap one of the twins. They can deball a man with their eyes. Also, I'm working with someone outside of my agency, and I wouldn't want to threaten the twins' secret. For heaven's sake, Mr. O'Donnell, let the big guy know I'm not a threat to his darlings. As to why I didn't call TJ, well, what was he supposed to say? Yes, Ollie, I've taken to a life of crime. I know we spent a spot of time together as children, but we're adults now."

"I wouldn't say that," his mother muttered.

"And he definitely planned on seducing her," Sami supplied.

"Well, she did look awfully lovely in that dress," Oliver said with a sigh. "I planned to make her time with us as comfortable as possible. She was never in any danger, mate."

"Except of catching a venereal disease," Sami countered.

"TJ's absolutely going to kick his arse. Yes, Lou's wearing that dress Kenzie talked her into. You know the one where her boobs hang out," Liam said.

"They do not," Lou replied, but he noticed she had to adjust the top of the dress again because they were absolutely hanging out.

"TJ, stay calm." His mother seemed intent on being the voice of reason.

"We should get back to the office. I'm sure Big Tag will want a report," Lou said.

She looked so gorgeous in that dress, but something wasn't computing. "Why would you not be able to run in your shoes?" Lou didn't wear high heels. And there was another problem with the scenario. "Why didn't you gut this guy like you did the guard?"

His baby could be deadly when she wanted to be. Had she not wanted to hurt the big, gorgeous Brit?

"I am a well-trained operative, you know." Oliver seemed disturbed at the thought of everyone kicking his ass.

"I borrowed Kenzie's shoes. She helped me get dressed. And I took too small a bag. I wasn't carrying," she admitted.

A hole felt like it opened up inside him. All the adrenaline from before was roiling into something else. Something that made him ache. She'd slept with him all night and gotten up and carefully prepared for her date. She'd done everything she could to look sexy as hell for some guy his aunt had found for her.

Somehow in the back of his head, he'd thought she was being stubborn. That the whole dating thing was payback for him being a stubborn ass for years.

She was serious. She wanted to find someone. Someone who wasn't him.

"Those shoes made your legs look a mile long." Oliver was in a three-piece suit. Dressed to kill. Dressed to seduce.

Was Oliver the kind of man Lou wanted?

"I don't know," Liam was saying. "I think he could save this if he keeps his bloody mouth shut. TJ's too freaked out by the fact that Lou dressed up all fancy for her date. Though she should have worn a bloody bra. Thank the heavens my Daisy dresses modestly."

"I'm wearing a bra," Lou argued. "It's just a low-cut one."

Oliver moved in, taking her hand in his. "Darling, don't let them shame you. You look gorgeous, and I really was going to seduce you. I've been thinking about it since I realized we were going to have to spend time together. Come with me. I've got a plane waiting. We can solve this case together and set some sheets on fire."

"There it goes," Liam said with a shake of his head.

His mom groaned.

But all TJ saw was red. He heard Cooper yelling something behind him as he came down the hill, but TJ let his beast free.

And it felt fucking good.

Chapter Eleven

"Damon, you want to explain to me why my nephew just dragged your son into my office like a lion dragging an antelope?" Big Tag growled into the phone.

They were sitting in the conference room at McKay-Taggart, and despite the fact that it was hours later, she could still feel the moment she knew TJ had come for her.

And see his face when he realized she'd worn her perfectly nice dress out on her date.

Pain. He'd been in pain.

At least now she knew he was finally back. Cooper had whisked her away while TJ had been taking out his frustrations on Oliver Knight. She'd asked to be dropped off at her office. She'd been denied, so now she'd been sitting at the conference table for over an hour and a half wondering where the hell TJ was.

And wishing she had a cardigan since apparently she was in her boob dress.

The door opened and Kala walked in, frowning her father's way before joining Lou at the table. "Has he been growling the entire time?"

Lou took a long sip of coffee. "When he's not cursing or vowing revenge. I don't know. It's been a weird day. Did you know

Uncle Li made TJ's mom stop for pancakes on the way back? Zach nearly lost his damn mind. I think they left that Oliver guy in the trunk or something."

"Yeah, they're a feisty bunch," Kala agreed.

Despite the fact that they were in a safe place, Lou leaned in, her voice going low. "Did you tell your dad that they know your secret? We probably should tell him. Unless TJ killed the British guy."

"He's alive. Mostly," Kala replied. "TJ apparently got in a couple of good kicks to Ollie's balls. He's sitting in Dad's office with a bag of ice on his dick. You think my dad's been cursing. I listened in on Ollie and Sami calling their dad."

"It was perfectly dreadful," the woman called Sami said as she entered the conference room. Big Tag had exited, pacing the halls like a wrathful tiger. "But I told Ollie it would be. Even our mum's pissed, and my mother is practically a saint. She cursed at my brother in five different languages, and then told me it was my fault too. I said if she wanted things to be my fault, she shouldn't have birthed such a stubborn wanker. Ollie mostly moaned. Your boyfriend knows how to kick a dick. I'd like to learn some of those moves."

Samantha Knight was a gorgeous woman in her early twenties, with a halo of curly blonde hair. Now that she'd studied her a bit, Lou could plainly see the two were siblings.

Where was TJ? She hadn't seen him come in. She must have been staring down at the laptop she'd logged into, trying to find anything she could on the mysterious Jester. He hadn't come to find her. He would have walked right past the conference room, but he hadn't stopped.

She was mad at him. Hurt by him. Worried about him. And he hadn't even waved as he walked in.

Kala turned to the younger woman, a cold look coming over her face. "Is it true you threatened Lou that if she didn't come with you, you would let our secret get out in the intelligence community?"

She'd told Kala the whole story.

Sami frowned. "That was Oliver. Look, none of this was my idea. I wanted to call you, but Ollie's been working with another team on this for a long time. While we're normally a team, I wasn't brought in on The Jester stuff until a few days ago. The fact that we know you is precisely why he included me. We agreed to bring Lou in without his partner because we didn't want to risk exposing the twins. That's why we were taking her to Toronto. But here's the truth—he would never have done it. He would never have told anyone. Our MI6 bosses don't even know you're twins. They don't understand our connection at all. Big Tag has been excellent at scrubbing your history clean."

"That was my aunt," Kala replied. "I can still remember the day and my mom crying about it and my dad saying there's no crying in espionage and then my mom yelling and the door closing and…ick. Lou, you and TJ should go at it in front of my dad more often. I take back everything. He deserves it."

Lou was over the whole kidnapping thing. She had other worries. "I'd like everything you have on The Jester. If you know TJ at all, you have to know he's not capable of behaving in this manner."

A brow cocked over Sami's blue eyes. "I don't know. He seemed pretty brutal when he was making sure my brother can't father children. Not that he should. He's a child himself, but still. Shouldn't there be some professional courtesy?"

"He kidnapped TJ's girl, and from what I understand had plans to seduce her. That's not the act of a friend, and you two have known TJ since you were children," Kala pointed out. "The same with me and my siblings. You knew we were Agency, but you didn't bother to mention you two had gone the same route with MI6. Should I expect Archie to show up with a team to rescue his siblings?"

One of the things Lou had recently learned was that Damon and Penelope Knight had three children, the aforementioned Oliver, the oldest, and Samantha, the baby of the family. Archie was in the middle.

"Not at all. Archie is the intellectual of the family. He's working on his doctorate in criminology. It's why I believe him when he says Ollie's a sociopath. Look, the only reason we know you're Agency is you needed help from my parents," Sami pointed out. "You ran that op in London. Your first op. My father used his connections to get you the meeting you needed, and my mother helped with the coded messages you received. Ollie and I haven't needed help, so you didn't need to know."

Kala's eyes went cold. "And you kidnapped my best friend. What do you think I'm going to do to you, blondie? I can assure you I won't go berserker on you. See, this is how TJ and I have always looked after Lou. He beats the shit out of the boys, and I plot an elaborate revenge that will ruin the rest of your posh and perfect life. You won't know what it is. You won't know when it will start. You'll just know it's going to happen."

"Kala," Lou began.

Sami frowned, seeming to think that over. "I think I'd rather do the boy thing. I'm mentally unprepared to think about what you'll do to me for the rest of my life. That's actually an excellent threat, and you have a perfect delivery. I apologize profusely. I noticed there's a sparring ring downstairs. Shall we? Only if we're friends after. I promise to never again allow my brother to talk me into something so atrocious as kidnapping Lou."

Kala stood, her decision made. "All right. Let's do this thing. No faces. Everything else is fair game. See, I don't get how they say women are the emotional ones."

Sami joined her. "Absolutely not. We're the rational ones. Hand to hand only. No knives."

"You're no fun," Kala said as she strode out the door.

Lou was about to try to stop that when suddenly TJ was at the door. He'd cleaned up and changed clothes, but there was a cut over his left eye that let her know Oliver had gotten a couple of licks in. She wanted to go over to him and check him for whatever wounds he had and baby him like she always would.

A vision of him in a baseball uniform struck her. He'd gotten hit by a pitch and everyone told him to walk it off, but Lou had found him after the game and held his hand under the bleachers while the aspirin she'd gotten from a first aid kit kicked in. He hadn't wanted his dad to know how much it had hurt, but he'd told Lou.

They weren't those kids anymore.

"Is Kala about to kick Sami's ass?" TJ asked, looking down the hall.

"I think so. They've decided to handle it like gentlemen." She forced herself to sit there, to not get up and put her arms around him and ask if he was okay.

TJ stared at her before entering the conference room. His uncle was still yelling at Damon Knight, so TJ closed the door. "I think we should talk."

"Yes, we need to figure out why all these people think you're in league with this Jester person." They should be professional. She wasn't sure she could handle another personal confrontation right now. She'd already had a lecture from first Zach, and then Big Tag on getting caught without a weapon. She was sure TJ was about to talk about how stupid it was for her to date.

"You'll figure it out. We both know I'm not going to be helpful in that situation," he said with a frown as he took the seat across from her. "You can ask me questions, but I don't know anything. However, we need to talk about why you wore that dress."

That was what it all came down to. "I was going on a date, TJ. I tend to dress up for those."

"That's not an I-want-to-look-pretty dress. That's a fuck-me dress."

It was. She knew that because she'd bought it for him. "Well, it didn't work on the guy I originally planned to use it on. He looked me over and called me a weirdo and told me to put my jeans back on."

"We were going hiking." His jaw clenched. "Lou, I can't change the past. I can't go back and say all the things I should have said. I don't think it would have worked, but it's clear to me that you're going to pay me back. That's why you put on that dress. That's why you rolled out of bed with me and got gorgeous and put on heels and did your makeup for another man."

"I fell asleep. I didn't mean to spend the night with you, and I certainly didn't cheat on you." Frustration clawed at her. She was in a corner and not sure how to get out. "I made it clear I was going to date. I told you back in Australia, and you didn't have a problem with it then."

"I didn't have to watch it then," TJ admitted. "I assure you if you'd showed up at my sister's party in a couple of days with some asshole holding your hand, I would have had a reaction."

She wasn't so sure about that, but she could go down this road with him. "So you only want me if someone else has me. How does that work? Do you dump me the minute you lock the relationship down? Do I have to find other men to tickle all your jealousy bones so you stay interested?"

"That's not what I'm saying," TJ argued. "I'm saying I finally saw a different side to you, and it made me realize our relationship can work, that it's worth risking our friendship over. I've come to the conclusion that we're not risking anything at all because we were meant to be together in every way possible."

If only he'd said those words to her even six months ago. "So I kill a dude and you get horny. That's an interesting fetish."

His eyes closed briefly, and she saw the frustration there when he opened them again. "You are twisting every word I say."

"And you are treating me like a cheating girlfriend when I've been clear that we are not together." She hated this. Hated arguing with him, but she had to stand up for herself. "You don't get to ignore me most of our lives and then snap your fingers and get everything you want."

"Ignore you?" TJ asked, utterly incredulous. "I've never once ignored you. I refused to kiss you twice because I wasn't ready. I know that hurt, but you don't get to rewrite history because I hurt your ego."

She pushed her chair back because she wasn't listening to this. "You don't have to worry about our friendship. I think you just killed it."

He was on her before she could reach the door. "And you just proved everything I was afraid of. You proved I was right. The first time I do something that you're not happy with, you want to walk away."

"I assure you it's not the first time, but it is going to be the last."

"Years, Lou. Over a decade of being friends and you want to throw it all away because I hurt your feelings? I love you," TJ said in an aching tone. "I can adore you on every level, but I'm human. I'm still going to hurt you. If we'd gotten together as kids, you would have been waiting for me to leave. It would have eaten you up because worrying is what you do, and it would have been a self-fulfilling prophecy and then we wouldn't be here."

What he was saying wasn't exactly untrue. She remembered

how insecure she'd been during those years. She'd tried to hide it, but she'd been waiting for everything to fall apart. It was kind of what she did. Years and years of watching her mom walk a knife's edge first with her bio dad, and later with his micromanaging parents. Boomer Ward had given them stability and love, but it was hard to forget the lessons those early years had taught her. "And you don't think I would worry now?"

He moved in, forcing her to back up until she was against the wall. "I know how to handle you now. I know how to make you stop thinking and focus on what's real."

Her heart rate ticked up because he was so close she could feel the heat coming off him. "Sex. You're talking about sex."

He stared down at her, every brush of his body a reminder of what had happened between them before. And a reminder that the act had been incomplete. "Yeah, baby, but it's more than sex. I'm talking about focusing on you and me. I'm talking about shutting out the rest of the world and building a place that's just for us."

She wanted that world, had felt it when they were kids. For a couple of years there hadn't been anything but a weird friendship between them that everyone chalked up to Lou being in puppy love and TJ being a nice guy. Because no one would believe he could want the odd, awkward girl. She hadn't even hoped for more until she was sixteen and tried to kiss him for the first time.

It hadn't been her ego he'd crushed. It had been her soul, but she'd gone back to being his friend after a few weeks of sulking.

Was she destined to forever be the sulky kid to his all-American hero?

He ran a hand down her arm. "And what's real is us. But we're not going to be some perfect thing. We're not going to be the vision you have of your mom and dad. I know they seem perfect, but that's because they keep their problems private like most of our parents do. Because marriage is intimate. It's not splashed across the world for everyone to see. I didn't know my parents struggled in the beginning until years later. My father pushed her away, but they got through it because she believed."

She'd heard the stories about his parents. Erin had thought Theo was dead only to find him again, but he'd lost all his memories of her. It was an epic love story.

She'd had a crush on a boy who couldn't love her back. Nothing epic about that. And he was wrong. "My parents have never fought. They knew they loved each other very quickly. I assure you my dad never once told my mom it wasn't the right time and they should just be friends."

If he had, he wouldn't be her dad because her mom would have had the self-esteem to walk away. She wouldn't have waited in the background, hoping someday that man would look her way.

God, she was pathetic.

He finally touched her, hands coming out to cup her cheeks as he forced her to look at him. "There you go. I can see it. I can see the questions and anxiety rolling through your brain, and it kills me. If I thought you would let me, I would lay you out on that conference table and eat your pussy until all those questions are gone and you have a smile on your face. I've spent years wondering what you would get out of a relationship with me, and I finally figure it out and you won't let me do the one thing I can do to show you how well this could work."

She wanted him to. That was the truly awful part. The minute he said the words, she felt her whole body go soft and willing. Traitorous. Her body didn't care that he wouldn't stay, that he would go back to work and forget about her and want to be friends when he came back because being away would remind him of all the reasons he hadn't wanted her before.

Maybe she should do it, let him fuck her brains out, and she would realize it was only sex and not some transcendent experience she would value for the rest of her life. If she did, if she spent a couple of weeks with him, maybe she would finally be able to let him go.

She was bargaining. She was at least on step two or three of Aunt Charlotte's "you've been wronged but still want to bang the person who wronged you" psychological cycle.

"It won't work."

He leaned over, his mouth so close. "I assure you it will work. Are you talking about us or sex? Because don't fool yourself. The sex will be spectacular, and I am not above using it to keep you. I'm a desperate man, Lou. If giving you a hundred orgasms before I get one is how I lock you down, I'll do it."

"I'm not changing my plans. I've got another date scheduled for two days from now. And I should try to reschedule with Miguel." But she also wasn't pushing him away.

"I'll need a schedule. I'm your bodyguard. Zach wants us to stick together, so I'll try to be unobtrusive," TJ whispered, his lips hovering over hers.

That sounded awful. "I'll talk to Zach. I don't need a… Okay, I need someone for a while, but it shouldn't be you."

His body brushed against hers, hard chest against her breasts. "There's no one else. I promise I'll be a good boy, and I won't even threaten your dates. I'll sit in the back and watch over you. I'll sit there and wish it was me you're flirting with. And if Oliver Knight tries to touch you again, I'll handle him."

"TJ," she said, but her head tilted up, uncertainty flashing through her.

"And if the only place you'll let me show you my affection is the club, then so be it. Tell me you're not planning on reneging on our deal."

She should. She should run. It was stupid, but she couldn't help herself. "I told you I would." Maybe there was a reason it was a cycle. Maybe it worked. If she went into the very compartmentalized sexual relationship with her eyes wide open and the plan to fuck him out of her system, it could work. She wasn't walking into a trap. She was smart. Everyone told her. "I'll be at the club."

"And then I'll show you," he vowed.

"For fuck's sake, this is a damn conference room." Big Tag stood in the doorway, his head shaking. "Business is conducted here. Were you raised by wolves? I'm going to talk to your mother."

Lou stiffened and started to press him away, but TJ simply kissed her softly.

"Until tonight, then." He stepped back with a shake of his head, turning to his uncle. "Yeah, like none of my cousins were conceived on that table. We have ears, you know."

"I wasn't conceived on the conference table, was I?" Kenzie walked in behind her dad, a laptop in her arms.

"No. I'm pretty sure it was my desk. Why do you think I keep it around?" Big Tag quipped.

"Is there a reason my sister and Kala are trying to kill each other?" Oliver Knight stepped into the conference room.

"Did Kala do that thing where she scares the shit out of someone by promising bloody vengeance but not today?" Kenzie asked, settling in.

Kenzie knew her twin well. "She did. Samantha decided she would rather get the vengeance over with."

"Well, I wasn't offered a choice. I like to delay vengeance whenever I can. I loved this suit," Oliver said, his full lips pouting like he was a cover model selling sex.

"It's okay. I'll jump you again at some point," TJ promised.

"You will not," Lou whispered under her breath.

He turned her way. "Are you saying that as my girlfriend or my sub? Because I'd probably do what my girlfriend told me to do."

Big Tag made a gagging sound.

She was going to start ignoring him. And TJ. "Are we having this meeting? I would like to get my hands on whatever the Knights have discovered."

So she could start taking it apart because TJ wasn't involved with an arms dealer.

"I'm afraid that's going to have to wait," Oliver announced.

"And why is that?" Big Tag frowned down at Oliver.

"I told you I've been working with someone. I need to bring him in," Oliver said. "He's getting on a plane right now. He'll be here in roughly four hours, but we need to meet him somewhere else. He's a foreign intelligence operative, and we can't have him running around an office where everyone knows the twins. How do you do this? Does one of you take meetings and the other listens in? We'll need to vet the meet spot. I was serious. I consider you family, Kenzie. I'm not about to betray you. I like Ben. He's a good man, but I don't trust anyone with this knowledge outside of my parents and siblings."

"You should keep it that…" Big Tag's expression had fallen. "Ben? Please tell me he's not Canadian."

Kenzie was practically jumping in her seat. "Ben. Lou, it's my Ben."

"Are we talking about that dude from the Australian op?" TJ asked. "The one you guys had tied to a bench? Is this his form of revenge? And why would Kenzie care?"

Because Kenz had been half in love with the handsome Canadian spy.

Kenzie grinned up at her dad, her hands clasped together. "Please, Daddy. Can I have the pretty man? Tasha got one. I need one too."

Ian's head hit the table.

Yeah, this was going to be fun.

* * * *

TJ glanced at the clock. Seven thirty. They could knock this meeting out and be on the dungeon floor in less than an hour. One hour and Lou would be at his mercy.

He didn't intend to have any.

You don't get to ignore me most of our lives and then snap your fingers and get everything you want.

Her words still haunted him hours later. Ignore her? She was always on his mind, always lurking around in the back.

If he couldn't convince her, would she haunt him forever—the future he couldn't have?

"Are we sure the roof isn't going to cave in?" His uncle looked up, squinting as though trying to see cracks in the ceiling.

Cooper groaned. "The roof is fine. The building is sound, and if you walk through my dungeon again with a safety checklist, I'm going to give you a rundown on all the scenes your spawn have run on each apparatus."

Big Tag hadn't been happy about having this meeting with the Canadian operative at The Hideout, but TJ had insisted. Oh, he'd given a bunch of reasons why it would be safer for the twins and their secret to hold this in the conference room at the small club the group had bought and was currently renovating. The Hideout had started in an unattached garage on the rambling property Cooper, Aidan, and Tristan shared. Tristan's parents had bought the place when they thought Tristan would be coming home from the Army and getting married. Years later, he still used it as his place to bunk down between assignments, though TJ had heard he hadn't been home in a long time.

And Aidan would be moving in a few short weeks because he and Carys had an apartment near the hospital they both worked at waiting for them after the wedding.

Would they offer him Aidan's old room? He didn't want it. He wanted to be with Lou, but he had to think about the fact that he could be in Dallas for a while, and though he loved his parents, he didn't want to live with them.

Big Tag sighed. "That's fair, I suppose, but you have to admit this place is a piece of crap. I would think Julian Lodge would plunk down better money for the place his kids play at. That old man has gotten stingy."

Gabriel Lodge was a founding member of The Hideout, and he preferred not to take money from his billionaire father. Not because he didn't love the man but rather he wanted to be independent. TJ kind of thought Gabe enjoyed hanging out with the regular folk. He seemed perfectly happy to spend his off time working on building the club with his own two hands.

"Be nice." Aunt Charlotte sat next to his uncle. "The club is coming along beautifully, Coop. I like what you've done with the lounge. It's tasteful and functional."

"Until it burns down because we're in a neighborhood full of meth dealers," his uncle muttered under his breath.

His uncle had gotten soft. Yes, the neighborhood wasn't great, but Sanctum hadn't exactly been located in Highland Park.

"You don't have to be here. You could conference call in," a feminine voice said.

Kenzie walked in, followed by Lou.

Every head turned because for some reason Kenzie had changed into an electric blue corset and PVC leggings. Her magenta hair was done in loose curls that flowed around her shoulders, and she had on a set of heels that would probably mean she could look TJ straight in the eyes.

God, his cousin was trouble. She must be serious about this Ben guy.

And Lou had changed, too. Lou was dressed like an Amish unicorn. She had on an ankle-length jean skirt and a sparkly unicorn sweater that covered every inch of her torso.

Brat.

"Kenzie Shay Taggart, what the fuck are you wearing?" Uncle Ian said in his best dad tone.

Aunt Charlotte was hiding a smile behind her hand.

Kenzie turned, a hand on her curvy hip. "I am in the club and I am a sub in this club, so I am properly dressed. It's the rest of you who are not respecting the club. I don't know what's up with Lou. Her boob dress is practically fet wear, but she insisted on changing."

"We're in the conference room," Lou countered. "And I'm not wearing the boob dress because everyone calls it the boob dress. And we all know why Kenz is dressed like that. Ben Parker is about to be here."

"Well, I say, that will get the man's attention." Oliver Knight perked up. He'd been sulking all afternoon, spending most of his time arguing with his parents over the phone. "As distractions go, you'll do, cos, and might I say the term cousin is affectionate. There's no blood between us. Not at all. You should think about that. I'm much more fun than the Canadian."

Samantha Knight rolled her eyes and winced as she sat back. He'd heard Kala had gotten the British operative in a choke hold that had her out for a good three minutes, but it seemed to have done the trick because the two had been talking earlier and using more than four letter words.

"You little shit," his uncle began. "What do you think I'm going to do to you for ogling my daughter?"

Oliver shrugged as though completely unworried about any possible outcome. "I don't know. You should worry about me ogling your wife. You are looking gorgeous tonight, Mrs. Taggart, and really, your daughter's right. Fet wear only for pretty subs. Does anyone have a set of leathers I can borrow?"

"I've got a ball gag you can borrow." Zach looked up from his notes. He and Cooper had been in the conference room when TJ had come in, poring over notes and reports. Now he looked up at the MI6 agent. "Look, if you think my last name not being Taggart is going to save you because I won't let them filet and eat you, you're wrong. I'm hungry, and I bet your posh ass is like Wagyu beef. So keep it up and see how long you last here, Your Highness." He glanced over at Charlotte. "Though you do look lovely, Mrs. Taggart. In or out of fetwear."

Cooper nodded his way. "Nice save, brother."

"See, that was the way you compliment a woman in a fet club," his uncle agreed. "Polite. Hello, madam, your breasts are looking luscious this evening, and I hope you have some spectacularly filthy sex with the partner of your choice. Civilized. And how does our military CO feel about his operative's clothes?"

Zach's gaze went steely. "If your sister didn't have a shiner, I would swap you out in a heartbeat. You are not here to seduce Ben Parker, and if you can't do your job, I'll find someone who can. Kara can take the night off. Lou, what the hell? Are you a professional, whole, grown-ass woman or a teen from an overly religious community who will cry if she shows a knee? Both of you need to get your shit together because this is serious. This is not a place where we should think about our love lives."

"Here, here," Samantha said, nodding approvingly Zach's way. "And Ollie's club is just as bad as this. Papa wouldn't bankroll him. Told him if he wanted a sex club, he should earn it. It's in the suburbs. It's so bad."

"Then why do you come all the time? You know what makes a sex club terrible? Having your sister in it," Oliver complained.

Lou started to pull out a chair next to Zach, a flush still on her face. "I don't think a unicorn sweater makes me less capable of doing my job. It's not like there's a dress code."

"There is absolutely a dress code, and I'm following it. And I think this is going to help me a lot," Kenzie argued. "He'll give up all the intel because he likes my boobs."

A growl came from her dad's mouth.

"Babe, she is my daughter," Charlotte reminded him.

And Lou was his sub. He stood and pulled the chair next to him out. "Louisa, have a seat."

"I'm fine here," she insisted.

"Are you in the club or not?" He deepened his voice. "Whether Zach or my uncle want to acknowledge it, this room is part of the club, and we have an agreement between us."

The room seemed to still, all eyes going to Lou.

She looked like the cutest deer in the headlights ever. "We're in a meeting."

"In the club. So you can have this seat or you can sit on my lap.

It's your choice, but you should make it quickly because the lap is going to be the only thing open to you in thirty seconds. In this club, you are my sub," he explained.

"Fuck me, this is why you drink so much," Zach said to Ian.

"This team is way more fun than ours," Samantha whispered her brother's way.

"Are you serious?" Lou ignored everyone, staring his way.

"As the heart attack my uncle is about to have. I think Zach might survive. He's young. His heart's probably pretty good, and he'll just slide into my uncle's place. He's been getting ready for that for a long time," TJ replied.

Lou frowned, but she moved to the seat beside him.

He breathed a sigh of pure relief and helped push her chair in. It was time to show her how nice it was to be his sub. And yes, he was a bastard because in this case "sub" was a placeholder for girlfriend and then wife. "Can I get you something to drink? Are you hungry? I stopped by the bakery near your place and got some of those spongy cookies you like."

Kenzie sat up, her boobs dangerously close to popping out. If she was moved by Zach's dressing down, it didn't show, but then she wasn't really dressed so it probably didn't matter. "You got madeleines? Yum. I'll take a couple."

"Can you? Can you fit anything else in that skintight catsuit?" His uncle frowned his cousin's way.

"Mom, Dad is body shaming me," Kenzie replied, her eyes narrowed.

"Sweetie, maybe you should change. I don't think it's a good idea for you to get involved with a foreign operative at this point," Aunt Charlotte said, her tone sympathetic.

TJ slid the box of cookies in front of Lou and passed her the other thing he'd prepared for her.

She picked up the coffee mug, breathing in the scent. "You made me matcha?"

"I looked it up on the Internet and figured out how to make it," he explained. It hadn't been particularly easy, but lucky for him Coop had ensured the bar had one of those fancy coffeemakers. It helped him make tea, too.

Lou smiled at him for the first time all day. "Thanks. And

thanks for the cookies. I haven't eaten today because I got kidnapped."

"You skipped lunch because you were trying to avoid me," he countered.

The smile didn't go away. "Fair."

He leaned over. "You'll find there's a turkey sandwich with barbecue chips in your locker. I want you to eat it before you get ready for the evening. You're going to need some energy."

He half expected her to argue with him, but she simply nodded and took a sip of her tea.

The discussion between his uncle and cousin came to an abrupt end as the door opened and a man with light hair and what could only be described as rugged good looks stepped in, followed by Tasha, who'd gone to pick him up at the airport, along with her fiancé, Dare. Dare was somewhere in the club getting ready for the evening, helping set up scenes and making sure things would run smoothly. TJ wondered what that car ride had been like because the last he heard, Dare still wasn't speaking to the man who'd played him for at least six months.

Benjamin Parker. He worked for Canadian Intelligence, and TJ's former team had backed him up when he was on assignment in Australia. Unfortunately, that assignment had collided with his uncle's team's assignment and everything had gotten seriously fucked up.

And his cousin had apparently been thinking about the handsome agent ever since.

Ben's eyes went right to Kenzie. Who he thought was Kara but he was certain that wasn't her real name, so he'd made one up so everything was extra confusing.

Okay, his uncle was right. The sexual tension was kind of nauseating. It wasn't like with him and Lou. That was fine, exciting even. But watching his cousin drool a little was…a lot.

"Do you ever take meetings in anything but a sex club?" the Canadian asked, his eyes still on Kenzie.

She'd been right about her boobs distracting him. He hadn't looked at anyone else in the room.

Kenzie's lips curled up. "Why would I when it works so well?"

"Mr. Parker, would you like to explain to me why you

attempted to kidnap one of the members of my team? And while you're at it, make a good argument as to why I don't send you back to your handler in pieces." His uncle got right to the point.

But TJ had spent time with Ben. He knew exactly what motivated the man. "Because he either thinks Emmanuel Huisman is The Jester, or The Jester can lead him to proof of Huisman's crimes."

It was the only explanation. TJ was sure Parker had worked a lot of ops, but his primary focus was bringing in Emmanuel Huisman, a childhood friend who he believed with all his soul was also a terrorist. If there was one thing he'd learned about Parker, it was how focused he was on bringing down that man.

It had worried him in the field, and it worried him even more seeing the Canadian looking at his cousin like he could devour her in two bites.

Lou nodded his way, a cookie in her hand. "I think you're right. And one of the things I've heard is that The Jester is the arms dealer who sold the weapons used in the Jakarta bombings. He blamed Huisman for those attacks."

There was history between Parker and the man who ran the world-famous Huisman Foundation. They specialized in neurological studies and were known for backing innovative projects like the one that had saved his cousin Tasha's life a few weeks back. He couldn't forget that it had been a drug with research funded by the Huisman Foundation that had helped Tasha recover when they thought she would die from the wounds she'd received in the field.

It could have been Lou, and he would never have told her how much he loved her. She wouldn't have known that she was the best part of him.

Lou leaned in like she was thinking the same thing, her eyes on Tasha as she sat down beside her father.

TJ leaned over and brushed his lips against her hair, loving the fact that she didn't move away from him.

"And that is why I wanted to talk to Lou." Ben pulled out the chair across from Kenzie. "If that's her real name. Like Ms. Magenta. Hello, Maggie whatever your real name is. I assume everyone lied to me."

So he was still bitter about the op. "Like you told the truth."

"I certainly did to you," Ben countered. "But it feels like you kept a couple of secrets from me. I trusted your team."

"You absolutely lied to me." Kenzie sat back, looking completely comfortable in her own skin. "And if you think Sergeant Taggart here is involved with an arms dealer, then you don't know him at all. I assume you wanted to take Lou to get information about TJ out of her. Tell me something, Ben. Did you take her because you remembered how she reacted to seeing TJ? Did you think you could convince her that he was some kind of evil go between?"

"My name really is Lou, and he's not involved with this guy," Lou said, sitting up straight and going professional.

"I wanted to talk to Lou because I thought she would be the most reasonable of all of you," Ben said, settling in. "I thought about having my boss call your boss, but the truth of the matter is my boss isn't interested in listening to my theories right now. I'm afraid he didn't appreciate the way I handled the last op."

"Are you telling me you did this without your handler's approval?" his uncle asked.

"I'm saying I am working with MI6 on this project, and they had final approval," Ben countered.

Oliver sighed. "Well, we all know I didn't handle things the way I should have, and I've certainly apologized. In my opinion, bringing in a member of Sergeant Taggart's team was necessary to ensure that an important CIA asset wasn't being used to further the interest of terrorists."

"You thought if the sergeant was bad, the rest of us were," Big Tag said.

"I thought there was a possibility that something had gone wrong," Oliver admitted.

"Look, the truth of the matter is we have a long family history of being betrayed by people we should have been able to trust," Samantha said, her expression grave. "Not only did my father's partner try to kill him, Ollie and I had a colleague who nearly cost our whole team their lives. I'm afraid we came into the situation with what you Americans would call baggage, and I apologize for that. I don't think recriminations are going to help us at this point. I think the better plan of attack is to lay our cards on the table and hope that Mr… What do you go by these days?"

Samantha was doing an excellent job keeping their ties hidden.

"Mr. Lemon works, but he can call me Ian. Everyone at the Agency does, after all." His uncle wouldn't give away his last name ever. No matter how much he trusted another operative. "Tell me how you came to the conclusion the sergeant is involved with the arms dealer known as The Jester."

"I'd like to know why it was specifically your team that rescued him," Ben countered. "I know he was kidnapped a few days ago by a German mobster who is trying to find the true identity of The Jester. I found it interesting yours was the team the Agency sent in."

"He's my boyfriend. Of course my team saved him," Lou said suddenly. "I would have done it myself if they hadn't come with me."

A brow cocked over Ben's eyes. "Boyfriend? That doesn't seem like a good idea when you have to work with him."

"Yeah, well no one listens to good ideas on this team," Big Tag muttered under his breath.

Her hand came out, covering his. "We've been off and on for a long time. It might not be a good idea, but it's the way we are, and I wouldn't leave him behind any more than he would leave me, so if you think you could turn me against him, you're wrong."

She was covering, giving them a reason beyond being childhood friends and family members for the team to come after him.

"And I help Lou since she always backs my questionable decisions," Kenzie added.

"We're a team, and I'm well aware that Lou has questionable taste," Zach said, but he gave her a wink as though he thoroughly approved of what she was trying to do.

And TJ approved because it meant whenever Ben was around, Lou had to play the doting girlfriend. He leaned over and kissed her cheek. "I thank the heavens for her bad taste otherwise I might still be in Germany getting tortured."

"Not at all," Oliver countered. "I had started making plans to get you out the minute we realized they had you. I was surprised they moved so quickly."

"Our intel came from the Dark Web," Sami explained.

"We connected the dots when we realized someone put out feelers to kidnap your sister or your mother," Ben continued. "I take it you managed to switch them out for another operative and she saved you."

"Lou saved me." He wanted to make that plain.

Suddenly he was okay with Parker hanging around for a while. In a couple of weeks, Lou would be used to him being on top of her all the time and she wouldn't feel the need to date anymore because she would have a boyfriend.

Parker turned his attention to Kenzie, who looked cool and calm with boobs half hanging out. There was no way to miss the fact that Parker had to force himself to look her in the eyes. "I would have thought they would send in the infamous Ms. Magenta. Or do you only offer saves for your boyfriend on the team?"

Kenzie frowned. "I don't have a boyfriend on the team. I don't have a boyfriend at all."

Parker nodded toward Cooper, who was already sighing. "That's not what he thinks."

Well, at least Parker proved he didn't know they were twins.

Kenzie's nose wrinkled. "Ewww, Coop is like my brother. I wouldn't touch him. Ewww."

Coop sat back. "Yeah, that was for the op, man. Lou and TJ are the only couple on the team, and TJ won't be on the team for long."

He didn't have to put it like that. "I'm still Army. I work on Special Forces teams dedicated to helping the Agency. I'm on assignment here until we figure out why someone thinks I know an international arms dealer."

"Now that we've figured out who is sleeping with whom and who is potentially available to sleep with, can we get to why we're here?" Zach asked, and his uncle grunted, obviously handing the meeting over to the captain. "If anyone needs a checklist, I'll pass one out at the end of the meeting. Until then, let's shove those hormones deep."

"No one needs a checklist. I think Mr. Parker knows what he wants," Kenzie replied. "Whether or not he'll get it is a question we can answer later."

"Oh, I'll get it," Parker promised.

"I'll get something. I'll get nauseous," his uncle said.

"Do you want a cookie?" Lou offered.

"I want some answers," his uncle replied and then frowned. "And a cookie."

It was a good thing he'd gotten two dozen. He knew his family's habit of stealing treats. TJ passed the plate around. "Now I personally would like someone to tell me how Jimmy Bond down there got involved with The Jester. I know why Tim Horton did. He sees Huismans everywhere."

His uncle and Zach snorted in perfect time, but Parker shook his head and looked almost human for a moment. He so often resembled a well-sculpted statue. "That's not the insult you think it is. Tim Horton's is delicious. It's a Canadian treasure. What do you have, Dunkin'?"

Lou laughed. "No. You have to call him Taco Bell. He doesn't eat donuts, but he will chow down on a quesadilla."

He loved it when she teased him, but he would use that as an excuse to play with her. He leaned over, whispering. "You're going to pay for that, baby."

He would have sworn she shuddered, and not in distaste.

Oliver leaned forward, his expression turning serious. "Roughly five years ago MI6 became aware of a new player in the arms dealing industry. He started, as many of them do, on the Deep Web offering small arms. At some point he got his hands on some well-made bombs. Very well made. When he started selling those, he became extremely popular in certain circles."

"In terrorist circles," Parker added. "Oliver and Samantha were working on this before I was. I became involved when the terrorist attacks in Jakarta took place."

"Because you believe Emmanuel Huisman is behind those attacks." Despite the super-tight corset, Kenzie looked somewhat professional as she glanced down at her notes. "You think Huisman, in conjunction with the group known as Disrupt Australia, coordinated the attacks. At least that was what we talked about in Sydney. I know Disrupt has groups all across the globe."

Lou opened her laptop, her hands flying across the keys. "It makes sense that it would be the Australian group. They're closest to Indonesia, but we can't substantiate those claims. As far as the Agency is concerned, Disrupt is nothing more than a think tank that attempts to solve the world's problems."

"There is a part of the group that does just that," Samantha explained. "We now believe that roughly ninety-five percent of the members do nothing illegal and are not involved in any of the planning of recent attacks. I know the Agency isn't particularly worried because so far the group hasn't touched American interests, so no real manpower has been used."

"Is that what MI6 thinks?" Zach asked. "Or do they think there are powerful Americans in the group they don't want to piss off?"

Oliver shrugged. "Either way, from what we can tell, the higher-ups at the Agency are not acting on the intel they've been given."

"I will admit that we were interested in Huisman when we first formed this group," Kenzie said slowly as though weighing her words. "There was a file on him being circulated, but we couldn't verify the information."

"There was?" Tasha had been silent up until now, sitting near Parker, taking notes. "Because I'd never heard his name before the Sydney operation. It would have been nice if someone had informed me."

"Me as well." Zach looked to the end of the table where Big Tag and Charlotte sat.

"It was a minor piece of intel someone who is no longer on the team was interested in," his uncle said. "She filed a report and the Agency closed it. We moved on to bigger cases."

Lou's hand brushed over his thigh and his cock jumped.

But she wasn't offering a repeat of the German meeting. She'd typed a single word on her screen.

Kala.

So Kala had investigated and hadn't found anything.

That didn't mean there wasn't something there.

"Why would Disrupt want to attack Indonesia?" He knew a bit about this, though he'd been left out of most of the meetings with Parker. His old CO hadn't liked him, and the Agency operative they'd been backing had problems with his last name.

Lou shifted in her seat, her sweet face turning up his way. "I think Agent Parker believes that chaos is the point. It's right there in the name. Disrupt. Though in their mission statement, that word refers to disrupting the social systems that cause human suffering and discrimination. What the inner circle wants is complete disruption of what are essentially the pillars of civilization. The attack on Jakarta's public transportation system could be seen as a trial run. If you take out public transport, make people afraid to use it, the economy of the city will suffer, and if the cities suffer, everyone does. Jakarta is an industrial hub for Southeast Asia and it's a port as well, so trade would be disrupted. That would cause potential dips in stock markets around the globe, starting with China's big three. One would assume it would affect Japan and Korea, and then it would reach outward."

"Some of it could depend on who they blame it on since we know they won't take credit," Parker continued. "I think that's why it didn't work in Jakarta. The group they blamed was able to quickly prove it wasn't them, and without a bad guy, things settled down. I think Manny's group underestimated the Indonesian government. He'll try again."

"And why would he want that?" This was the part TJ didn't get. As far as he could tell this Huisman guy was a doctor. He ran a charitable foundation and had written books on trauma and forgiveness. He had plenty of money as he was the last one left of his wealthy family.

"Because Emmanuel Huisman wants to destroy the world so he can rule the ashes," Parker said quietly. "But I don't expect any of you to believe me. MI6 doesn't, but they do think there's something going on with The Jester. Several of the bombs he sold that were used in the Jakarta attacks were next level, but they malfunctioned. I believe the loss of life would have been times a hundred if those bombs had successfully deployed."

Now he understood why they wanted The Jester. "You think it's only a matter of time before the bombmaker figures out what went wrong and fixes it. So you think if you get to The Jester, you get to the bombmaker. But the Jakarta bombings were a few months ago. Oliver said he's been working on this for longer."

"Because those weren't the first bombs," Samantha interjected. "Two years ago, RaSP discovered a small device attached to a vehicle."

Lou typed. **Royalty and Specialist Protection. They protect**

the royal family.

He nodded. It was kind of nice to have his own spy translator. The truth was up until this point he hadn't asked a lot of questions. They weren't encouraged. He was there as muscle and to follow orders.

Lou's job was more complex. A couple of days ago that might have been a problem somewhere deep in his brain—or maybe the better word was his ego. But he was over that. It was funny. Watching her work, knowing how hard she'd trained, had changed his mind about a lot of things.

Lou was special. Lou deserved everything the universe could give her.

He'd spent so much time trying to figure out where he fit into his extraordinary family, worried he was the normal one, the dumb one, the useless one.

His parents hadn't made him feel that way. Never. It was a fragility that had been born inside him.

It was something he could overcome because he'd found his real place. He was Lou's support. He could be the strong center of whatever family they built.

"You mentioned something about anti-monarchists back in Australia," Kenzie prompted.

"I believe that's a group the inner core of Disrupt is working with," Ben replied. "I believe my boss sent your boss some intelligence."

Big Tag shook his head. "It's a lot of conjecture and not enough clean lines to connect the two. I want to know about the bombs and why this is new information if they've been around for a while."

"You should talk to your boss," Sami said. "We've given the Agency the information. We believe that this bombmaker is close to building what we call small arms nuclear weapons. We think he's trying to target specific areas while leaving others standing and without worry about nuclear fallout. It could change urban warfare in ways we can't imagine."

"And make genocide easy and fun," his uncle muttered under his breath. "Lou, look into this. I want a report on how this would work and how far along the research is."

"You could read my report," Ben offered, sounding slightly

offended.

"I want Lou's analysis," his uncle insisted. "What I will take from you is any and all intelligence that leads you to believe Sergeant Taggart is involved." His uncle looked his way. "I'm going to ask you again. Do you know anything about this situation?"

He was so happy he could be open and honest. "Nope. I know they have a picture of me they say is a meeting with The Jester in Berlin. Only thing I did in Berlin was get a briefing on an op and drink a lot of beer. I know nothing, but I'm willing to answer questions. Most of the answers will be I don't know."

His uncle gathered the papers in front of him. "I'm going to read this and call Langley, however I'm going to do it from the comfort of my home so I don't have to be in this rat hole where things happen that I shouldn't have to watch."

"That sounds good to me," Kenzie said, her eyes on Ben.

His uncle shuddered and started to stand.

Lou stood as well. "I should come with you, boss. I need to get you that research."

Whoa. "I think Lou needs a break."

Lou turned his way. "This is too important. I'd also like some time with this evidence they have."

"That has to wait until the higher-ups give my handler the go ahead," Oliver announced. "So we should feel free to enjoy the club this evening. Say, I was wondering if anyone is putting us up for the night? We're supposed to be in Toronto."

"Yes, where you would have taken my kidnapped sub." TJ stood beside Lou. "Who hasn't had a break in days."

Charlotte was beside her husband, whispering in his ear. His uncle sighed, blue eyes rolling. "Fine. Lou, despite the fact that we're in the middle of something dangerous and important, please take the evening off to play with my…with the sergeant. See if your vagina can get any answers out of him. As for you…" He looked at Kenzie. "This is a mistake."

"But it's mine to make," she replied steadily.

His uncle sighed and took his aunt's hand. "Zach, you deal with the Brits however you see fit. I'm out of here for the night. We'll get back together tomorrow when hopefully I've got all the intel I need."

"Knight, you got a credit card?" Zach asked, not looking up from his notes.

"Of course," Oliver replied.

"Good, there's a motel a couple blocks over. They charge by the hour." Zach stood, gathering his things. "Have fun. And take the Canadian with you."

TJ wasn't sure the Canadian wouldn't be staying with his cousin. Who was walking a fine line.

But none of that meant a damn thing because he was about to play with Lou, and no matter what happened he knew he would remember the night forever.

Chapter Twelve

Lou looked at herself in the mirror and wondered what the hell she was doing. She should be on her computer waiting for the intel to come in so she could take it apart and get TJ off the hook so he could go back to his job and she could go back to hers and they would normalize again.

Instead, she'd poured her body into a corset and skimpy boy shorts and let Kala do her makeup.

"Hold still." Kala had a curling iron in her hand now, giving Lou beachy waves. "I do not know what my sister is thinking."

Kala had been raging about her twin the whole time she'd been helping Lou get ready.

"Oh, I know what she's thinking." They had friends. Or an audience. Daisy O'Donnell and Brianna Dean-Miles had been hanging around the locker room. They'd returned from New York but TJ's sister had stayed because of work. Daisy flashed an angelic smile. "She's thinking she can boost our relationship with Canada through her vagina."

Brianna gasped and lightly tapped her friend on the arm. "Dais, you're terrible."

Daisy tended to call things like she saw them. Unless her dad was around, and then she said whatever would convince the man she was the sweetest angel on earth and all the bad stuff that happened to her was a tragedy and not something she often brought on herself by being the most reckless woman Lou had ever met.

"Well, I got a glimpse of the man." Daisy had on jeans and a sweatshirt that proved she had no intention of playing this evening. She'd been curled up on one of the sofas working on her laptop when Lou had walked in. She was apparently studying for her real estate license test.

And Brianna had been helping her by eating chocolate chip cookies and holding the timer while she watched a movie on her phone.

The Hideout was for more than play. It was a place they came to when they needed to hang out, to be together the way they had when they were kids.

Well, except for all the sex toys. Those were new.

"I don't get it." Kala tugged on her hair, twirling around the iron. "I mean, he's fine and all, but he's obviously a douche."

Daisy and Bri shared a look, some silent conversation going on between them.

"You don't have to get it," Lou replied. "It's Kenzie's thing. I think it's good you're not attracted to the same guys. She's got zero interest in Cooper."

"Cooper isn't…" Kala stopped, her jaw tightening. "All I'm saying is I think the guy's trouble."

"Because he's a foreign operative?" Daisy asked, her eyes lighting up with curiosity.

Damn. A curious Daisy was a dangerous Daisy. "Operative? I don't know what you're talking about."

Kala groaned. "They're not dumb, Lou. Dad had a meeting in the conference room when he barely likes to set foot in here unless he's complaining about the place. The Brits show up and then a weird Canadian? They're going to put two and two together."

"So it is an op." Brianna breathed the words like they were magic. "Right here in our club."

"You understand you're not supposed to know about the spy stuff, right?" Kala asked.

Daisy's eyes rolled. "Yeah, because you would be this happy working for your dad doing security checks. Everyone knows. No one is talking. We're family. We don't gossip. Well, with outsiders that is. Besides, Aunt Charlotte came through and told us we should avoid talking to Kenzie and the hot guy tonight. She asked if we wouldn't mind sticking to the locker room. I wasn't planning on playing so it was no biggie, but Chloe Lodge is out there and probably spitting bile Seth's way. What is up with that?"

Lou shrugged. "No idea. They rubbed each other the wrong way once long ago, and they've been weird enemies ever since."

"Like Seth doesn't want her," Kala said with a sigh. "But back to the relevant point. I know everyone suspects, but it's important not to blow our cover."

"My brother is on your team," Brianna pointed out. "And Daisy's brother has been my brother's best friend forever. Of course we know. I think you should view this whole club as an asset. If you listen to my parents, the world has been saved many times because someone took someone else to a club and fixed the problem with proper use of BDSM."

Kala snorted.

"It happens more often than you would think," Daisy added.

"Do you have any idea where Tris is?" Lou was curious.

Brianna sighed and sat back in her chair. "I don't know, but I did overhear my dads talking. I think Papa knows more than he's telling, and Dad is mad about it. Mom…well, my mom believes in true love, and there's nothing my brother could do to hurt her more than walking away from the love of his life."

"Yeah, it's not doing my brother any good either," Daisy admitted.

But there was something about the way Daisy said the words. When Daisy believed something, she said it with her whole being. This was said under her breath.

It was funny because Kala seemed to pick it up, too, her head swiveling in precise time with Lou's as they both looked at the brunette beauty.

Daisy's eyes widened. "Uhm, wow, see sometimes I forget you're like deadly and stuff, but then you look at me like that."

It was good she had a killer stare. She was so often underestimated. "What do you know?"

"Know? I know a lot of things." Daisy looked a little flustered.

Kala held that curling iron like it was a weapon. "What do you know about Tristan?"

Brianna frowned her friend's way. "You're supposed to be better at this. You are the queen of looking innocent."

Daisy shrugged. "Well, they throw me off when they go all predatory. Especially Lou. And honestly, I wouldn't hate them looking into it because I don't know what's going on. Aidan and Carys are acting like they're so mad at Tris and they're going through with the wedding without him, but I swear I've heard them talking. I was out at my brother's place last week and it was super late. I got up to grab some water and he was out on the porch, pacing and talking, and I swear it had to be Tristan. He was asking him when it would be over. I don't know what *it* is. Then he saw me and hung up. He said he was talking to someone at the hospital, but I know what I heard."

Brianna seemed to come to some kind of decision. "I think my brother might be in over his head. I know my dad is worried about him. I can't tell if he knows what's going on, but he knows something, and he's not even telling my mom."

Lou looked up at Kala, who nodded.

They were thinking the same thing. Tristan was working a job. A dangerous one, and they needed to figure out how deep he'd gone.

"We'll take care of it," Lou promised.

Still, both women looked to Kala.

"We will," Kala confirmed.

She was going to have to work on her street cred.

"See, I told you we should put it all in the hands of our spy girls," Brianna said.

"She did," Daisy agreed. "But I was worried. I don't want to betray my brother, but I think he's getting in over his head. And I should know because I'm always in over my head. So now that's out of the way, is it true you're finally doing TJ?"

Lou felt a flush go through her system, and she turned back to the mirror. "It's part of the op. You know how the Brits are here? Well, they know about our team, but Ben Parker doesn't. I can't talk about it, but it was necessary for the op that he believes we're dating."

"Ooo, you're fake dating," Brianna said with a whistle. "It's my mom's third favorite trope, only defeated by enemies to lovers and friends to lovers. I think she mostly wants the characters to be lovers."

Brianna's mom was a legend in the romance publishing industry. Serena Dean-Miles had been writing happily ever afters for more than twenty years, and she'd built an empire around it.

"How does your mom feel about the dumbasses who can't get their timing right trope?" Kala snarked.

She turned on her best friend, narrowing her eyes. "Seriously? Mirroring much?"

Kala shrugged. "Not mirroring at all. Cooper and I will never have a right time, but you and TJ obviously do."

"I thought Lou was dating around," Daisy said, obviously confused. "I talked to Aunt Charlotte about some of the guys I know. They're all awful players, and I wouldn't let them anywhere near Lou. Ooo, I heard a rumor that Nate Carter is coming to Dallas. He used to be kind of cute."

The big Aussie they'd worked with in Sydney was more on the gorgeous side, but she didn't see that happening. "I think he's coming for a job. Not to date."

"You know she's only dating because TJ's being an ass," Brianna replied.

She had to stop that. "He's not. He wasn't interested in me that way. It's okay. He's always been a good friend."

"Well, I suppose that fits," Daisy said with a sigh. "I'm going back to studying. Real estate. I'm going to be good at selling real estate."

Daisy flounced off. Brianna shook her head as she stood. "Last week she was going to be good at party planning. At least there wasn't a test for that one. Let me know if you find anything out. I'm worried about my brother. I'm worried about all of them."

When they were safely away, Kala looked at Lou in the mirror. "Fake dating? Oh, bestie, do you want to go there? Because we've been quiet about this up until now, but I have to worry that you are moving into self-delusion. Are you really going to sit here and tell our friends you're getting ready to play because of an op?"

It was good that Kala understood what she was doing. "Yes."

Kala sighed, her eyes rolling. "I don't like this. You're supposed to be the reasonable one. If you insist on being this stubborn, we're going to end up living together at eighty with a bunch of cats. I kind of…"

Now Lou was worried because Kala sounded almost…wistful. Kala didn't do wistful. "What?"

"I don't know. I kind of thought if you and TJ could work things out…"

If she and TJ could work things out, maybe there was hope for her and Cooper? Is that what Kala was saying? "It's not the same. My problems aren't your problems."

Kala sank down to the bench beside her. The Hideout was kind of DIY and on a budget, but there was one space Cooper and the guys had spent real cash on. The women's lounge. It did not escape Lou that the whole place had been done in deep blues and greens, with hints of gold and red.

Kala Taggart's favorite colors. Cooper wasn't some design guy, but he'd insisted on those colors.

Lou was pretty sure the guys' locker room was a piece of crap with a bunch of folding chairs and a barely working shower.

"Aren't they?" Kala asked. "Let's see. You fell for TJ and he rejected your physical affection. But he still wanted to be around you. He didn't want to keep you a secret because he didn't want to upset his friends."

"Kala, he was fifteen." She knew this story, and it always made her heart break. "You can't hold that against him forever. TJ wasn't fifteen the last time he told me he didn't want me. He was like three weeks younger than he is today. Cooper makes every attempt to get close to you. From what I can tell, he's not dating, and he only tops subs in a nonsexual fashion. I think he's doing that because he hopes you'll forgive him."

"There's nothing to forgive." Kala's voice went stony. "He wanted normal and that's fine. I'm not normal and I never will be, and have you forgotten that we're not exactly compatible when it comes to D/s?"

"I don't know as much about it as you do. My parents never got into it. They mostly went to Sanctum to hang out with friends, but I do know there are some married tops. They find a way to make it work." She didn't see the problem unless Kala absolutely had to have a lover who submitted to her.

She rather thought her friend might enjoy the fight.

"Well, like I said, if you and TJ can't make it work, there's not a lot of hope for the rest of us. You've always loved him, and I believe that dumbass deep down loves you. I don't know what happened, but something clicked in his head and he wants you now. Can't that be enough?"

She wasn't sure. But it was going to be enough for tonight. When she'd realized what it meant to have Ben Parker running around the club, she'd known she had a unique opportunity. She didn't have to give herself away. It was for the mission. They could play and pretend for a couple of days, and when TJ inevitably changed his mind, she would shrug and tell everyone well at least she got a couple of orgasms out of it and she would move on.

No one would have to know how broken she was. Because she knew beyond a shadow of a doubt that this time would break her, and she was still going to do it.

"I don't know." She had to be honest. "I think it might be too late, but I also can't seem to help myself."

Kala put the curling iron on the counter and sank down on the padded bench beside Lou. She had the start of a serious shiner because apparently Sami had accidentally gotten a good one in. Kala leaned over, resting her head on Lou's shoulder. "Maybe it's okay if it's you and me and cats. I want to be okay with that, but I also hate the thought."

"Which makes you human." She rubbed her cheek against Kala's hair. When Kala was affectionate like this, Lou tended to shower her with love. Kala could be so withdrawn, and Lou understood she was one of very few who ever got to see this side of the woman. "You deserve love, too."

Kala groaned but didn't move. "I hate that word. I don't understand that word."

"Yes, you do. I should know because you have loved me for a long time, and that changed my life," Lou whispered.

"I do love you," Kala replied. "And I've been your best friend for a long time. So I'm not going to ask you to give my dumbass cousin a second chance."

That was a relief.

But Kala wasn't finished. "I am going to ask you to give you a second chance. Lou, you've loved him since you were a kid. Don't let your current and his younger self's insecurities cost you more time. The last thing in the world I want is to not get to spend all my time with you. But I do know how to love even if I hate the word, and part of that is wanting the best for you, wanting you to get everything you need out of life. Think about it, okay. You don't have to make decisions tonight because you put yourself in a corner neither of you can get out of. Smart play, by the way. Gives you some time."

Time with TJ. Time to build some memories for when he was gone.

Time to decide if she was brave enough to ask him not to leave again.

"I'll think about it," she promised. She was fairly certain she wouldn't think about anything else.

She stared at herself in the mirror and hoped she was ready.

* * * *

TJ stood outside the women's locker room, his eyes on the door that Lou would soon walk through.

"Are you sure about this?" Cooper leaned against the wall. He was lean and muscular in his leathers. Cooper was elegant.

TJ was well aware he looked like a linebacker. He was kind of bulky and didn't look great in a suit the way Coop did.

What kind of guys was Lou dating? Maybe he needed to do some research. He'd checked into the real Miguel Garza's profile and he seemed more like a Cooper.

"Am I sure about Lou? Yes. Am I sure this is going to go well? Absolutely. The sex part is going to be spectacular. The rest? No idea, man." He was fairly certain that despite the fact Lou had placed them in a position where they had to look like they were together, she was still wary of him.

Which was why tonight was so fucking important.

Cooper chuckled. "Well, at least you're going into this with some confidence." He sobered, crossing his arms over his chest. "All right, I'm going to ask. What changed between the two of you? I mean why now? I know Lou's been telling certain people that she thinks it's a response to what happened to you."

TJ groaned. "It's not. Or maybe it is. Does it matter why the wake-up call happened? I think all that should matter is that I am awake now, and I know what I want."

"Yeah, well knowing what you want doesn't always make her want you back," Cooper replied, and then shook his head. "Forget I said that. I don't want to talk about that right now."

"You sure? Because we can go there. I probably know her better than any of the other guys," TJ offered. Kala was tight with him because they shared Lou's friendship.

"I know my mom's an actual psychologist, but I do not see the need to talk shit out," Cooper admitted. "I guess I'm more like my dad. Well, not biologically, of course."

"I don't think your dad gives a shit about biology." Sometimes he had to be reminded that both Cooper and his younger brother, Hunter, had been adopted. His parents had never hidden that from either of them, and there was zero evidence the boys had been treated differently than their sister, who had been born to their parents. Vivian didn't see them as anything but her big brothers. Still, TJ often thought Cooper tried to be perfect in order to make sure he fit in, to ensure his parents never regretted adopting him.

"I know. Again, nothing I want to talk about tonight." Cooper seemed to close himself off, staring at the door with every bit of focus TJ had.

But TJ was waiting on Lou to walk out and offer herself up to him for the night. Kala wouldn't be doing that for Cooper.

So a change of subject was needed because he knew when a wall had gone up.

There were a few things he needed to talk to Cooper about while they were waiting for their women. Kala could pretend all she liked, but he knew she was still in love with Cooper. It was kind of sad watching them play with other people when what they really wanted was to find a sub to torture together before going at each other hard in a privacy room. "Hey, I had a talk with Aidan earlier today, and I'm almost certain he lied to me."

A brow rose over Coop's eyes. "Aidan? Why would he lie?"

Normally he wouldn't. Normally Aidan was a tell-it-like-it-is guy. As a doctor, TJ wasn't sure it made for a great bedside manner, but it was the truth. And that meant something was wrong. "I asked him if he'd talked to Tristan recently. Didn't you have the feeling they've cut off contact?"

Cooper nodded. "Yeah. Tristan gives this whole song and dance about how they've grown apart since Aidan and Carys started their residencies. But I don't understand because they got through medical school with him being halfway around the world most of the time. Why now?"

That was a question he was asking a lot lately. "Something's going on that we don't understand. I think he knows something about whatever it is Tris is doing. I'm not even sure I buy the whole breakup thing. I'm not saying this to gossip…"

Cooper put up a hand. "You're worried that something's going on with Tris we don't know about. I am, too. I love the guy, but he can be a reckless motherfucker. I'm worried about you, too, though. I'll feel better once Lou's gone through whatever they have. Though I have to admit, it's something I wish Tris was in on, too. I've called his cell and told him what's happening and I've gotten nothing back."

"If he's working an op with either the military or another team, you know he might not have access to his phone." TJ felt the need to defend his friend. Family, really. Though there wasn't blood between them, he'd grown up with Tristan. "You have to know whatever he's doing, he believes he's helping."

"Or he's trying to prove himself," Cooper said under his breath. "You know he's always trying to live up to his dad. Though it's not like Adam ever demanded it. I don't get his hang-up about his dad."

And TJ didn't get Cooper's hang-up about being adopted. "I don't know. I think we find problems where there aren't any. I know I've cost me and Lou a lot of time. I did it because I was more worried about losing her than I was making her happy. My parents didn't teach me that. No matter how great our families are, we'll still have problems, and there's nothing wrong with that."

Cooper turned his way, shaking his head. "Sometimes I wonder if Aunt Erin is truly your mom, and then I remember who your dad is."

TJ gave him a grin. "Hey, I've got my dad's willingness to talk and my mom's willingness to shoot. Best of both worlds."

He heard a door opening down the hall and watched as Tasha's fiancé walked out, escorting the new guy. Ben Parker was wearing a set of leathers and looked slightly uncomfortable in them. He glanced down the hallway, and his eyes locked on Cooper.

"I was hoping to avoid this. Kala better stay in that room or we're going to have trouble," Cooper said quietly. "If you…"

"I'll handle it." He would make sure Parker never realized there were two "Karas."

"Hey, Cooper. I was hoping we would get a chance to talk," Parker began.

Cooper's expression went bland. It was obviously not his night. "About Kara?"

"Is that even her name?" Parker asked. "She knows mine. I'm not sure why I can't know hers."

"Just because you play these things fast and loose doesn't mean she does," Cooper replied.

Damn. There was no small amount of jealousy in his friend's tone.

Because Parker wanted Ms. Magenta. At least he wanted her when she was played by Kenzie, but the trouble was at any given time she could actually be Kala.

"Zach told you," Dare began. He'd been playing with Tasha for the last couple of weeks. Rumors had it they'd started out gently at first and gotten more hardcore as they went. He'd helped set up a suspension scene for them earlier. And no matter what his damn uncle said, it wouldn't bring the roof down. "You can call her Kara or Ms. Magenta. You know how it is in this business."

"But only with her," Parker argued. "I buy it from the rest of you. You're really Cooper and he's TJ and Lou is Lou. So that makes me think you're the support team."

"You can think whatever you like, man," Cooper shot back. "And if you're here to ask if I have a problem with you playing with Kara, I told you. I don't. What you saw in Australia was nothing but a front for the op. You think you caught us together, but we knew you were there."

Oh, he didn't know this story.

Cooper turned like he'd read TJ's mind. "Kara and I might have presented as a couple when we were in the club in Sydney. Dare saw us and apparently mentioned it to his friend."

"He didn't," Parker countered. "He's barely talked to me since the minute he figured out I was an operative."

"Since I found out you'd lied to me for months," Dare corrected.

"Tasha did that, too, and she's now your fiancé." Parker's expression tightened as though he wished he hadn't said anything. "No, I saw you two together, and I doubt that kind of chemistry is all for an op. I won't lie. I can't stop thinking about her. I'm not going to do anything tonight. It would be the height of idiocy to fuck around in the middle of an op."

He didn't think it was the height. Maybe like the middle of idiocy. It was obvious to him that Parker wasn't a fan of true freaking love.

"I am not Kara's lover." Cooper said the words with a gravity that kind of kicked TJ in the guts. He wasn't, and he was pretty sure he never would be. Cooper loved Kala and she wouldn't give him more than the occasional glance, a touch here or there. Just enough to keep him coming back.

Fuck.

Had he done that to Lou? He hadn't meant to. He'd never meant to hurt her.

"I wanted to make sure I'm not stepping on any toes if I spend some time with her," Parker said. "Though I wonder if she's merely looking for some intel."

Kala would be. Kenzie, not so much. He kind of hoped Kenzie remembered there was a mission.

"Hey, baby," a feminine voice said, and TJ realized Tasha was walking in from the dungeon. "I didn't realize you guys would take so long making yourselves pretty. I thought that was our job."

Kenzie was right behind her sister, and Zach stood at the end of the hallway, his massive body cutting off most of the blue lights coming from the lounge area of the dungeon. So that was their play. Parker and Kenzie were getting a babysitter for the night. Maybe more than one set since Zach looked like he wasn't about to take his eyes off them.

The poor subs who tried to kneel at that man's feet would be disappointed tonight since it looked like he was working.

Dare's expression lit up as he saw Tasha walking toward him. He held out a hand, which she took. "You know I want to be pretty for you, baby. Hey, I missed you."

Tasha's lips turned up in a soft smile. "I've only been gone for an hour."

"Too long," Dare said before pulling her in for a kiss.

Parker and Kenzie were staring like they were going to devour the other, but Parker held back.

"Kara, Parker here still thinks we're involved." Cooper seemed to force the words out.

"We're friendly but nothing more," she reiterated. "Come on, Ben. Let me show you our little slice of perverted paradise. If it's not your cup of tea, we can sit in the lounge and get a beer."

The door to the women's locker room started to open, and absolute disaster was sitting behind it because Kala was right there in the doorway following Lou.

TJ jumped into action, hauling Lou out and into his arms even as he slammed the door on a frowning Kala, who better have the good sense to not open it again.

He had Lou in his arms, backed against the wall in a heartbeat.

"Hey, baby. You look gorgeous," he said.

Her eyes widened as she took in the crowd and likely figured out how close they'd come to disaster. She tilted her head up. "You've barely seen me. How would you know?"

He shook his head. "Don't need to. You're always gorgeous, and tonight you're all mine."

He lowered his head and felt a deep sense of gratitude when she softened beneath him and let him kiss her. Her hands went under his leather vest to brush up his sides as he stroked inside her mouth with his tongue. Fuck, she felt good. She felt perfect and right, and he was going to show her tonight that they were good together.

"So I guess I'll be seeing more of that," Parker said.

"Don't go to sex clubs unless you want to see some sex," Kenzie countered. "And if you'd like to slut shame me, I can show you the sparring ring. It's upstairs, though we don't normally talk about fight club. Rules and all. There's no shame allowed here."

"No shame," Parker said. "I kind of like the idea of no shame."

Not that TJ was really listening because he was busy stroking his tongue over Lou's, getting his arms around her and pressing his suddenly desperate cock against her belly. She was such a sweet bundle in his arms, and he needed to know what it would feel like to have her curvy body wrapped around him.

He had no shame when it came to this woman. None. He would do anything to keep close to her.

He realized in that moment that he truly meant it. He would give up his career, his future plans. He would take everyone calling him a kept man and smile proudly because she was worth it.

Nothing in his life was worth more than being Lou's man.

"Uh, I think we're good now," Cooper said, clearing his throat. "They left so you can stop. I mean unless you want to do it here. You need a condom, man? You do not want to take Travis's crown."

Lou pulled back, and TJ kind of wanted to smack Cooper. "No. We don't. There's actually a crown, and it's made of condoms. Big Tag made Travis wear it to Colton's baby shower."

Lou straightened up and seemed to try to look presentable to the suddenly empty hallway.

"Yeah, we wouldn't want to screw anything up," Cooper said a bit louder than he needed to.

There was a banging sound from the other side of the door and then the sound of combat boots thudding across the floor.

Cooper shook his head. "I'll go get the beast something to sink her teeth into. And a bottle of wine. That might soothe her."

Cooper sighed as he walked away, and TJ stared down at Lou. She was adorably sexy in a corset that showed off her breasts and boy shorts that clung to her hips.

He might be willing to wear that crown. He wasn't Travis, who'd had a one-night stand go wrong. If he made a baby with Lou, it would be their future. Their family.

But he had to convince her first.

"You ready to play?" He stepped back and held out a hand.

"This is more than showing Ben we're a couple, right?" She seemed hesitant, her lower lip disappearing behind her teeth.

"This is real for me, Lou. This is everything to me, and I know you don't believe me, but you will," he vowed.

She put her hand in his. "All right, then. I'm ready, Sir."

He led her down the hall and into the club, eager to begin.

Chapter Thirteen

TJ led her down the hall but stopped before they entered the lounge because there was something he hadn't thought of. "I didn't get you a collar. Lou, baby, I'm so sorry."

Her head tilted up, a quizzical expression on her sweet face. "When were you supposed to do that? Before or after my kidnapping?"

He should have known she wouldn't insist on anything at all. "There was a thirty-minute period somewhere in there. I got the cookies and your sandwich instead."

She moved in slightly, her body almost brushing his. "So you thought about feeding me before securing an outward sign of your possession around my throat?"

Suddenly, that didn't seem like a bad thing. He put a hand on her hair, gently pushing his fingers through so he could feel that soft silkiness. "I didn't want you to be hungry. Sometimes you forget to eat when you're anxious or you're working through a problem."

"And if you're around, you put food in front of me," she said, her lips curling up slightly. "And now you know how to make matcha tea."

"Now I know." He studied her for a moment. She seemed softer than she'd been before, more centered and ready to accept what he was offering. "Are we pretending to live in the moment, or can I tell you I want to know everything about the care and feeding of Louisa Ward?"

"I don't know. That sounds like a very Dom thing to say, at least in our part of the world." She leaned into his hand, her eyes closing. "I talked to a friend. She seems to think I should give this a real try. I have to admit, this is something I've dreamed about. I don't like admitting that."

"Why? I have. I don't mind telling you. You want to know what my fantasy is?"

"I want to know how you see us working in this club."

Of course she was still only talking about the club, but he wasn't going to push her. Not tonight. He had a couple of weeks before he had to worry about being apart from her. If he was close, he would bet she wouldn't be able to help herself. So he had to show her how good it could be here. It was a start.

He let his hand sink into her hair, twisting lightly so she had to come up on her toes. "How it's going to work in this club is I'm in charge, Lou. I know you're used to being the smartest person in the room and that meaning something, but here it's nothing more than a truth about yourself. The world doesn't depend on you here. Here there is you and me, and nothing else matters. Here your brain gets a rest because your only responsibility in this club is to obey and honor your Dom. Now tell me that's what you wanted from me before. Tell me you could see us in this club as a serious D/s couple, because I'm going to be honest. I need this to feel complete in a sexual sense."

She bit her bottom lip, looking at him like she'd never seen him before. "I guess I didn't think about D/s when it came to us. I guess I didn't think about sex beyond it meant we would be together."

"You didn't think about your own pleasure. You didn't think about what me topping you might give you."

She shook her head. "I guess I didn't think you could top me."

Ah, now they were making progress. He tightened his grip and heard a gasp puff from her mouth. "See, baby, you saw us making love, quickly and in the dark, and then me holding you all night. I'll do that last part, and it won't be some reward for pleasing me sexually. I want to hold you. I want to wrap myself around you and sleep like a fucking baby because I'm finally home. But before that I want to fuck you. I want to fuck your mouth and your pussy, and I want to fuck your ass one day. We have to build up to that, but I'm going to so enjoy watching you when I work a plug in there."

"TJ." She sounded scandalized.

"I'll give you time, but you'll want it eventually. There won't be a part of you I haven't touched with my hands and mouth and cock. You want my fantasy? It's you. This you. I've loved you Lou, but I fell in love with this you, with the one you hide from the world. I want all of you, but here I want that alpha bitch who took out the guard and coolly moved on to the next part of her mission. I want to give her a place to relax. I want to reward her with pleasure like nothing she's ever had before, but I also want her to trust me enough to submit, to turn off that big brain and let herself feel."

Her eyes had gone soft. "I think I want that, too."

"With a Dom? Any Dom?" Maybe he would push her.

"With you, Sir. Only you. I wouldn't trust anyone else. I've never seriously been topped. I want to experience it. I know you think I went on with my business after taking that guard out, but I didn't feel right again until you spanked me."

"And you got put in a dangerous situation today. You need someone to take you out of your head, Louisa. You should understand that I won't let you stew. Even if we say this is only for the club, if I see you struggling, it won't matter. I'll take you somewhere private and deal with the situation. I'll be discrete, but I'll fuck you calm, baby. And I will get you a collar before the next time we walk into this club."

"Whoa, Lou. You look hot. Hey, I heard something's going down tonight. TJ, is it true you two are like undercover and shit?"

TJ turned and saw Lucas Taggart standing in the hallway, a grin on his face like all the world was his fucking stage or something. Normally he loved his cousin. Now all he could do was release Lou's hair and get in Lucas's space. "Keep your fucking voice down. Do you understand what it means to our cousins if you give away vital information when we have foreign operatives running around? We've talked about this, known eventually we would probably use this club, and we all agreed to take it seriously."

Lucas's eyes widened, and he held up his hands. "Shit, man.

Sorry."

"TJ, he's only asking questions." Lou stepped beside him, and he expected her to take Lucas's side. She would lecture him on how he needed to be polite and shit. Then her voice went cold, and her inner alpha bitch made an appearance. "Questions that could get one of us killed. Is that what you want to do, Lucas?"

Lucas's voice went low. "Sorry. I was… I'll keep my mouth shut. But you really do look hot, Lou. Like damn, baby. When you're done with the undercover…"

That was when TJ had enough. He put his hand around his cousin's throat and shoved him up against the wall. Lucas might be one of America's up and comers in the cooking world, but TJ knew how to kill a man with his hands, and not merely by giving him salmonella. "Stay away from her. Do I make myself clear? You look at her again and I'll forget we're related. She's mine."

Lucas managed to nod. "Yep. All yours. Got that now, but you have to admit this is new information. Now how about you let me breathe and I will never look at Lou again, you crazy motherfucker."

He felt a hand on his shoulder. Lou. "I think he understands, Sir."

And his rage was gone. He let his cousin go and stepped back.

Lucas pointed his way. "You have serious anger issues, cousin. I like it. Makes you way more interesting. If you go around beating up a bunch of people, maybe my dad will stop talking about my perfectly normal for my age sex drive." He put a hand on his chest. "Louisa, you look lovely this evening, and it's obvious you've pleased your Dom. Now I'm going to go find a pretty sub and bitch about how my cousin tried to kill me." He grinned, looking every bit the young Viking his father had once been. "Sympathy sex is awesome."

Lucas strode into the dungeon.

Lou stepped in front of him, her hand going to his jaw, brushing along it as she gave him what seemed like every bit of her softness. "Are you all right, Sir? You had a day, too."

He had. "I felt helpless, and I still feel a bit of that. They took you. They put hands on you, and Oliver being alive right now required an act of restraint on my part."

She was so pretty as she went on her toes and kissed his cheek.

"I thought it was an act of restraint on Zach's part, but I don't mind rewriting a little history. Thank you for not killing him, Sir. I appreciated the lack of blood. Now what do you say you show me what you have in store for me."

She would be able to manipulate him so easily. All she would ever have to do was turn those big doe eyes on him and he would give her anything she wanted. And if she would give him the power here, it would all work out. He would worship her with all parts of his being satisfied by one woman.

He kissed her forehead and took her hand, leading her into the dungeon. Soft industrial music thudded through the place. It wasn't the greatest sound system, but it worked for them. LED lights gave the space a moody vibe, painting the subs and Doms in pretty greens and reds and blue. The main stage was taken up by Gabriel Lodge, who had not one, but two subs tied to St. Andrew's Crosses as he used dual single tails on them.

Kenzie and Parker stood on the edge of that crowd with their babysitters close by. They passed by the lounge where Lucas was obviously telling Seth Taggart the story of how TJ had tried to kill him, which earned him a thumbs-up from Seth before he went back to staring at the woman sitting at the bar. Gabriel's sister, Chloe.

So much sexual tension, and he didn't care about any of it. He didn't want to be on the main stage or in the middle of gossip. He'd planned this evening, and it was going to be a private one.

"A privacy room," Lou said when he started up the stairs. There was another stage on the second level, along with the space they sometimes used for what they referred to as fight club, though now it held a couple of chaise lounges where members seemed to be getting warmed up for the privacy rooms. Or they might do it right there. The second floor was a free for all outside of the rooms.

"I want you to myself. I don't think this first time should be in public. You're not the exhibitionist my cousins are, but we can explore later if you like," he explained. "Unless you don't want to be alone with me. Are you scared of what I might do to you?"

Bratty, gorgeous eyes rolled. "No. I'm not scared."

The dungeon monitor stood watching over the room. The big guy nodded his way. Ross Brighton. He was roughly TJ's height and had recently been promoted. He was one of the DPD's youngest detectives working homicide. He knew how to keep his mouth shut. His sister was another issue.

"Hey, Ross. Is your sister here?"

Ross shook his head. "Naw. She's helping Lou's mom with some wedding this evening. They spent three days making the cake. Why?" He seemed to suddenly understand. "Ah, you want to make sure she doesn't tell Lou's mom that you're finally doing it." He leaned in. "Because it's like one of those fake situations for whatever op the team is running here tonight. Not to worry. She won't know anything about it, so you're safe. Lou, you want me to bring you up a book or something? How long do you two have to hide? I can keep watch if you're worried about the newbies seeing you and blowing your cover because you're not blowing each other. Though I was surprised at how thorough TJ here was. There's some crazy shit in that room. You are really dedicated to playing out this undercover thing."

He was going to have to make an announcement. Maybe he could put it in the club's weekly newsletter.

"No book. I think we'll find something to do," Lou said, her eyes sparkling like she enjoyed having a secret.

He could work with that, and now he didn't have to worry about her parents finding out before she was ready. The last thing he wanted to do was put pressure on her through her family. He gripped her hand. "Just make sure the privacy room stays private."

Ross nodded. "Sure. You two take a nap or something. It must be weird."

Yep. He was going to make a whole announcement. Maybe he would have like cards printed or something because the idea that he and Lou were together seemed shocking to his friends and family.

Lou was stifling a laugh as he got her into the room. "No one believes you would actually top me."

What he heard was no one believes you *can* top me. He knew what she'd said, but he'd had a fucking day. It had started out shitty, and now he had to realize no one thought he could do this.

He was a joke to most of them. He was the funny fuckup who hadn't gone to college like his sister, who hadn't been as deadly as his cousins.

He could handle that from anyone but her.

He shut the door as she laughed.

"It's kind of funny, if you think about it," Lou said, still grinning. "They think we're in here playing board games or something."

TJ took her wrists in his hands and had her shoved up against the wall before she could take another breath. He loomed over her, hauling her wrists above her head, which made her breasts swell against the corset she wore and brought her on her tiptoes. That was where he wanted her. Slightly uncomfortable and fully aware of him. "Is this a joke to you, Louisa?"

Her eyes had gone wide, mouth open slightly as she tried to find a way to balance herself. "No. It's just… I thought it was funny that we're both all freaked out, and the truth is everyone who knows us thinks we're pretending."

"Are you pretending?" He was on the edge. He'd managed to keep it pretty together until they'd walked into the dungeon. Or until Lucas had flirted with her. It didn't matter what had caused the break, he was there, and what she said next would either send him over the edge or calm him down.

"No." Her chin came up. "No, I'm not pretending. You're mad that they think we're pretending. Why?"

"Because not a one of those fuckers out there thinks I'm serious, and I don't think you do either. But you'll understand how serious I am about this. I can be the happy-go-lucky guy who watches TV with you and who will haul his ass out to get you whatever you're hungry for and I'll be happy to do it. I'll be every sappy fucking thing you want me to be out of this space. But here it's going to be different."

"Different?" Lou asked.

He nodded. "Yes, I told you how this was going to work. I told you I'm a different person here. Or rather I let this side of me out here."

"I've watched you with subs. I know how you top them, and it's still pretty much TJ."

"Because they weren't *my* sub," TJ explained. "You're mine. Unless you want to go downstairs and join the many women who float in and out of my cousin's bed."

She huffed. "You can't think Lucas was serious."

"I think my cousin is always serious about sex, and if he could get you into bed, he would do it."

"That's ridiculous. Lucas is…" Her mouth closed, and that bottom lip was behind her teeth as she seemed to realize she'd stepped on a landmine.

Oh, he thought she should probably finish that thought. "Lucas is?"

Her mouth became a stubborn line. "Lucas is no one I would ever sleep with."

He didn't buy that. "That wasn't what you were going to say, baby. Tell me the truth."

"It doesn't matter."

"Then we'll start with a spanking."

"Fine. Lucas is practically a Greek god. Why would he look at me?" Her jaw went tight, and he could see her stubborn side was making an appearance.

Excellent. He'd had plans to ease her into this, but if she wanted to jump into the deep end, he could do that, too. Luckily he'd planned for a lot of different scenarios, unsure of exactly what would work on her.

Now he would simply give her what she deserved.

He brought her hands down but didn't let her wrists go. He could hold them both in one hand, controlling her easily since she wasn't fighting him.

It was odd, but knowing if she decided to fight him she could give him real trouble made him more confident that this could work.

"TJ, you don't have to be jealous. I don't know where this is coming from."

He reached over and casually grabbed the length of rope he'd prepped. He'd thought a little bondage would work for her. Now it was going to work for him. He eased one side of the restraints over her right wrist. "You think this is a new thing? Maybe the ferocity is new. Like everything, now it has a sexual component, and I'm rapidly discovering that while my heart can reason, my dick wants to murder anyone who touches you. I'm not joking. I would have pulled Oliver's heart out of his chest if Zach would have left well enough alone."

She frowned down at where he was tightening the restraints.

He'd tied the rope this afternoon so all he had to do now was pull to get it to the right pressure that would keep her immobile while not harming her circulation. "That's overkill. I wasn't about to sleep with Oliver Knight. I certainly wouldn't sleep with Lucas."

"But he's a Greek god of a man, according to you." That rankled, and he was letting his inner bastard off the leash tonight. Hiding his stupid jealousies would do nothing but make him act out on them. This was the space where they could be honest and work through their problems.

Her eyes rolled. "Yes, and that's my point. He was joking. He certainly wasn't about to flirt with the nerd of the group."

He hissed, his frustration coming out. This was part of the problem, and he was going to correct it. Now. He tugged on the short length of rope that formed the middle of her bindings.

"Come on, TJ. We don't have forever in here, and I thought we were going to play," she said, dragging her heels as he tried to get her to the middle of the room.

"No, you thought I would get on my knees and get my face in your pussy again. Were you planning on letting me fuck you tonight?"

A flush told him everything he needed to know. "I don't know. Probably."

"All right, Lou. We'll play that part your way," he conceded. "I won't get my cock anywhere near you unless you beg me for it."

"That doesn't feel fair."

"I've been begging for days, and you don't listen to pleas. So I think it's perfectly fair. I'm not a Greek god. I'm just a man, and at least tonight I'm your Dom, so while we play that part your way, everything else is mine." He lifted her hands over her head and slid them over the hook in the ceiling. It was rigged to be adjustable. He'd fixed it so it would keep her right on her toes, making her body bow beautifully.

Now there was some worry in her expression. "What are you doing? I thought we were going to play."

"This is playing. We're playing my way. I know you've done a couple of demos with Cooper and Zach, but do you know how many other tops have asked about you?"

"What?" Lou asked the question with a gasp.

It was time she understood how ruthless he could be. “You can’t imagine you’ve been coming here for almost two years and no Dom wanted to play with you.” She looked so fucking pretty. Her tits strained against the confines of her corset, swelling over the edges so he could almost see her nipples. “I made it clear to every single hetero Dom in this club that no one plays with you without my consent.”

“You did what?” She sounded indignant.

He liked that she understood. He let his fingertips brush from her neck down to where the corset held her in. “I kept all the other men off you, baby. And one woman who I thought would be too handsy with you. I’ve also heard she’s excellent at oral, and that might be enough to turn you.”

She ignored his sarcasm. “So I wasn’t ever going to play with anyone? I had to wait around for you. That’s the fucking story of my life.”

And that was where he wanted her. “Yeah, you were so invested in the lifestyle.”

“Maybe I would have been if some Dom had taken an interest in me. I’ve only ever scened with two men who are like my brothers, and that’s why you allowed it. You don’t allow things, TJ.”

“In this club I sure as fuck do,” he vowed. “I’ll follow you around outside of here. I’ll let everyone call me pussy whipped and happily take the label. I’ll watch the movies you want to watch and rub your feet and basically be your errand boy. I won’t care what anyone thinks, but in here, I’m the Dom, and that’s what you need from me. You need me to take control from time to time and you always have. So spit your bile, baby, but this all ends one way. Now I know it was always going to come to this.”

“But on your timetable.” There was bitterness in her words.

“Yes, we have to both be ready. And I didn’t stop you from dating.”

“Really?”

He shrugged. “Unless the dude was an asshole, and then I took care of it. Now I’m ready to take care of you. In every way.”

“You’re ready to take me down from the shelf now? TJ Taggart has figured out that the pathetic girl who followed him around might make for a convenient lay?”

He stepped back, feeling his skin heat. This privacy room was a suite with a big bed on one side and several pieces of equipment, including a spanking bench and a sex swing. And a nice table where he'd prepped a whole lot of toys. He selected a cane, taking it out and testing it against his palm. It smacked, the sound satisfying to him. "If that's how you want to play it, we can do that."

Her eyes were on the cane. "Play it? I'm not playing. I got tired of waiting for you to see me, and you can't stand the thought of not having your sad little crush on a string. What does that make you? I know what it makes me."

He crossed the space between them, that cane in his hand. "Don't use the word *pathetic* in my presence again."

Her eyes narrowed. "It makes me pathetic."

"You know your safe word. I wanted this to be fun, but if this is what you need, baby, then I'll give it to you." He brought the cane down on her ass. There was a whooshing sound and then a gasp from Lou. He brought it down again. "You are not pathetic. I've spent a hell of a lot of time ensuring every fucking Dom in a ten-mile radius stays off you. You think Lucas wouldn't have scooped you up and gotten you on a stage tonight if you would have let him?" This stroke hit the underside of her ass and had her cursing. But he did not hear her safe word. "He would have taken you on that stage and gotten you naked and fucked you in front of everyone, and the truth of the matter is if that had happened while I was gone, I would have dealt with it. You having sex wasn't the problem. You wanting what Lucas can give you, craving him, that's what I fucking feared."

"I've never craved anyone but you, asshole."

Sweet words. He brought the cane down again, right across that pretty ass. "Excellent. Then the next sixty or seventy years should work out for you because while I craved your attention before like a fucking lost little boy who didn't want to lose his only friend, it's different now, and it's not going to change. I crave your naked body against mine. I crave that wet pussy of yours. I crave this round ass that one day I'll spread wide and work my cock inside. I haven't done that, Lou. I've never been all that interested in anal, but I want your ass, baby. I want to put my mark on every fucking inch of this gorgeous body. This body I haven't even had a proper chance to inspect yet. I've given you a couple of orgasms, sub. Now I want to see what's mine in this club."

He stepped in front of her, her gaze meeting his, and he could already see the need there. She'd cried a bit, but he was sure the way her pulse was beating at her throat had nothing to do with pain and everything with anticipation. He took a step back, looking her over. He brought the cane out, touching the tip to her chin and bringing her head up.

"I'm going to take these clothes off you, Louisa. They're nothing more than armor meant to keep me away. Eventually you simply won't wear any when we're playing and it will be okay because it pleases me."

"I thought you were jealous."

"Oh, I am righteously possessive is what I am. I always have been when it comes to you. You're the prize. You're the thing I can't give up no matter what. How does it feel? You think you're the little mouse no one notices and yet you have two of the biggest predators in our world who made a deal a long time ago to share you, to protect and shelter you. Little mouse? You're the fucking center of the universe."

"Are you talking about Kala?" Lou asked.

How had Lou never seen this? "Baby, if she swung that way, she would have stolen you away a long time ago, but she's honest and knows herself. She wants what's best for you, and that's why we work as a team to protect you. Except she doesn't give you good advice. You should have gone to prom with me. I stood outside your house watching all night long in case you changed your mind."

"It would have been a sympathy date. I didn't want your sympathy."

"It wouldn't have been sympathy. It would have been a good memory," he corrected. "Now hush unless you're going to force me to stop."

"What are you going to…" Her question was cut off by him gripping the top of her corset and pushing the sides together so he could get the hooks out of their resting places.

It was a move he'd perfected at The Club when performing scenes with exhibitionist partners. Like Lou, he'd done a lot of demos, and that practice was going to pay off now. Her breasts spilled out as he worked the bottom half free and he was able to drag the corset off her.

Pretty tits. Lou's breasts were full, with perky nipples. Nipples that needed some attention. He stood back, taking in her beauty. He brought up the tip of the cane.

Her whole body went tight as though waiting for him to bring the cane down on her sensitive flesh. Instead he drew a line from the curve of her neck down to her right breast, tracing the areola and watching her shiver at the sensation.

"Such a pretty sub. Tell me about your sexual experience, sub. I want to know how hard and fast I can go. Or if I need to be gentle because you're such a soft, sweet thing. I can go slow, but we'll get to the hard and fast one day."

"TJ," she began.

That wouldn't do. He took the cane away from her breasts and smacked her ass with it, eliciting a low moan from her. "Sir. We've talked enough about the past. We're going to spend the next few hours in the now, and that means putting our problems to the side and being a Dom and a sub. Now you will answer my questions, and no other talk is needed from you. If you can't comply, I have a lovely ball gag I can use on you. I think you would look awfully hot with drool coming out of that luscious mouth of yours."

"Yeah. That would be so hot."

She was a stubborn sub. Another three lashes of the cane had her panting. "I can do this all day and you'll spend tomorrow with a sore ass. And yes, it is hot because it means your mouth would be warm and wet and ready to suck my cock. I would ease the gag out and give you something else to suck on. Have I made myself clear or do we need to do this again?"

He held the cane against her ass, and she shook her head. "No, Sir. I understand, Sir."

Excellent. Then they were making progress. Something settled inside him. Some restless piece that never seemed to fit suddenly found its place as he stared at her. "Do you like a man to play with your breasts?"

"I don't know. Maybe not. It can be weird."

"Because you get in your head and think too much. I'm not going to let you do that. Has anyone clamped these pretty tits? Ever had someone nip them with their teeth, squeeze them between their fingers, or suck on them until you feel it in your pussy?"

She shook her head, her breath in gasping pants. "No."

He reached out and palmed a breast. "Then we can start there."

* * * *

Lou was dying. Her whole body was desperate with an aching need she'd only ever felt for this man.

What the hell had she done?

She was hanging from a hook in a ceiling half naked, and she'd never felt more alive.

It had been a perfectly dreadful day, and she was no longer certain anything she was doing was right, and all those questions and anxieties flew out of her head the minute TJ started touching her and all she could think about was him.

He'd been jealous of Lucas? Lucas might be beautiful, but he couldn't touch TJ's masculinity. It wasn't Lucas's face that haunted her every dream. And it wasn't Lucas's eyes on her breasts right now.

She'd always thought they were a bit too big, awkward. They didn't sit as nicely in a bra as Kala's did, but now as he looked at her with hot anticipation in his eyes, she could see the beauty in them. Her nipples puckered as his fingertips traced her areola, and he was right. She felt that touch deep in her core.

The way she'd felt every slash of the cane. She'd thought it was only spanking that did it for her because of the physical connection, but she'd been wrong. The cane took her to a new place altogether. It hurt, the initial lash of pain making her groan, and then it was quickly replaced with heat and sensitivity.

She'd laughed about Ross's misconception, but now she could admit it had hurt that no one thought they could be a serious D/s couple. Especially when he was proving them wrong with every touch of his hand, with every deep, timbred command.

Blue eyes stared into hers as he palmed her right breast. "These belong to me. In this club, they're mine, and you should understand that I'm going to have you naked, sitting at my feet in that lounge very soon."

"Because you want them all to know?" Lou asked.

"Because I don't ever want to hear anyone question my rights to you again. Because I want the whole fucking world to know you belong to me, and that's why I'm getting you a collar. You can take it off in the daytime, but know I'll get it around your throat every second I can."

She wanted to believe him, wanted to have some faith that this change in him was permanent and she could relax and hold onto him with both hands. That felt impossible, so she was going to live in this moment. Only this one. Everything else would or wouldn't happen, but for now she was going to be exactly what he wanted. His sub, whose only thought was obeying her Master and taking what he had to give her. "I'll wear your collar here, Sir."

He stepped back, his eyes still on her chest. "Your breasts are beautiful, Louisa. You look beautiful in fet wear but so much better naked. When we're alone, when it's you and me and the rest of the world doesn't matter, I want you to pretend we're in this club. When we're alone, you don't wear a bra. I want to be able to touch your breasts without anything coming between my hands and lips and your nipples."

He was pushing her. It was supposed to stay in the club, but she was honest with herself. If they started a real sexual relationship this evening there was no way she kept him out of her bed. He was staying in the room next to hers. It was too easy for one of them to sneak into the other's room. Did she want this feeling put in a corner and only allowed a couple of times a week?

"Yes." She wasn't strong enough to deny him. She'd meant the things she'd said before. There was a deep bitterness in her about the timing, a distrust that came from long rejection. Even if the rejection had been soft, it had been there, and she'd developed walls that didn't crumble easily.

"Good. When we're alone, we're a Dom and sub. That means your body is mine, and I want you as close to naked as possible." He turned back to the table he'd had the rope laid out on and came back with a knife.

Surprise flared through her but not fear. He would never harm her. Not physically. His intent became clear. He would definitely harm her lingerie. "TJ, these aren't cheap."

"I'll buy you more." He slit the silky fabric up one side and then down the other before sliding them pointedly from between her legs. He fisted the material and was careful and slow in drawing it out so the softness slid between her labial lips and over her clitoris in a way that made her pant. Then he brought them straight up to his face and breathed in the scent.

"You smell like sex. Are you sure you want to keep me out tonight?"

"No." She wasn't in any way. She kind of wished he would spread her legs and take her then and there, but she couldn't ask him for it.

"Good. Because I intend to make it impossible for you." He put the knife and her now defunct undies on the table and picked up the cane again. "Spread your legs."

She wasn't sure how she was supposed to do that. "I'm barely standing."

His eyes narrowed, a certain wickedness she'd never seen before glinting there. "Are you telling me no?"

She suddenly didn't want to find out what would happen if she was telling him no. She bit her bottom lip and forced her legs to spread an inch or two. There. That was it. She was still balanced here. "Not at all, Sir."

A brow rose over his eyes. "That's the best you can do? Well, I'll have to help you out then, sub."

He turned and walked to the back of the room. What was he doing? What was in the closet that he suddenly needed? Oh shit. This was what Kenzie meant when she talked about a good mind fuck. Lou hadn't truly understood the idea of not knowing what a Dom was going to do to her. It wasn't fear because again she trusted him. But this TJ could do something nasty and smutty and glorious to her.

He wanted to fuck her ass. As a concept it didn't hold a ton of appeal, but the idea of giving this man every part of her sent a sizzle along her spine.

He came back with a thick slat of wood.

Spreader bar. He was going to lock her ankles into a spreader bar, and she would be completely at his mercy.

He wasn't going to have any, and suddenly she could feel how wet her pussy was.

"I'll try again," she offered.

"Too late." He knelt down and pulled one ankle tight to the edge of the spreader, locking her in. Then the other. She was spread so wide. Every part of her was on display. He'd spread her legs so wide she could feel cool air on her backside, on that part of her he'd promised he would shove his cock into someday.

She'd dreamed about being with TJ, and now she realized she'd never gotten past those twelve-year-old fantasies of kisses and touches and being held.

This was intimacy, raw and powerful. It was discovery, and there wasn't anything soft and sweet about it and yet it was a part of them, too. The part she hadn't even understood was missing.

The cane caressed the inside of her thighs. He'd planned this perfectly because she was balanced on the floor and the strain was off her shoulders. She could still feel the pull in her hands, but there was nothing painful about how he'd tied her up.

"Fuck, you're beautiful like this, Lou." He ran the cane up one leg and down the other, the hard tip leaving a path of arousal. He brought the cane up again, brushing it over her clit. "How are you feeling, sub?"

"Open. Exposed. Vulnerable."

"Excellent. Then we're halfway there." He studied her for a moment. "You shaved your pussy. Did you do that for me? Or is it part of your normal grooming routine?" He tossed the cane to the side and moved in close, getting on his knees in front of her. His fingertips moved over her mound. "It's smooth. You did this today or maybe yesterday. Did I mention how fucking good you smell?"

His face was right there. So close. It should be awkward, but all she wanted to do was shove her pussy at him and beg him to eat her right then and there. Her backside still burned from the cane, but all she could think of was getting his mouth on her. "Yes, Sir. And yes, I did it in the shower before I got dressed, though I do shave it normally. Fet wear can be unforgiving."

She liked the way a smooth pussy felt and the confidence that she didn't have wild hairs pushing through whatever fet wear she had on. But now she realized the real joys of being hairless. Sensitivity.

"Like I said, you shouldn't wear anything at all." He leaned forward, and she gasped as he put his nose right against her. "You should always be like this. This pussy is mine. Tell me who it belongs to, Louisa."

"You." The word came out without a thought because it was simply true. They might not work out, and her fear was she would always belong to him, to a man who loved her, but it wasn't enough.

It felt like enough in this moment. It felt like everything.

"Me. This belongs to me."

She felt a big finger teasing at her entrance, sliding around in all that cream he'd drawn out of her.

"TJ, please." She no longer cared how pathetic she sounded. She needed him. He was right. They'd started something, and no matter how it ended, she needed to see where this path led to.

He didn't move, simply eased his finger in and out and then around, as though learning her like he would a game. He was treating her like a toy he wanted to play with for a long time. "Yes, love, this is pleasing TJ enormously. Hush. I want to look at you."

He was going to make her crazy, but she bit her bottom lip to keep from begging him again.

He finger fucked her gently and leaned over to give her clitoris a brush of his lips that did nothing but make her want more. She squirmed when he let his fingers trace over her skin toward her ass.

"TJ, please. Please." She couldn't hold back.

His head finally came up. "Please what? Are you begging me to fuck you, baby?"

Did she even try to spare her pride? What was the point in that? She would have to pay later whether she got tonight or not. Would it be easier or harder to let him go if she knew what it meant to be his woman?

Those questions didn't mean a damn thing because pride was gone, laid bare and meaningless in the face of her desire.

"Yes. Please. Please." She couldn't stand another second of not being able to touch him.

He cursed and then he was releasing her ankles, standing to lift her off the hook and carry her to the bed. "I should torture you more. I get the feeling you're going to do a lot of that to me before you give in, but I can't. Not tonight. Tell me you want me."

"I've always wanted you." Though not like this. She wanted him inside her more than she wanted to breathe.

He cradled her against his chest. "I've never wanted anything more than I want to be with you. In every way. No matter what happens between us, you should know that is true." He sat on the big bed, forcing her to sit up as he moved in close. He unwrapped the ropes that bound her hands, freeing her. "Undo my leathers."

He thought she could think long enough to follow orders? She was going to see him naked. They were going to be naked together in the same room at the same time. She forced her shaking hands to go to the ties of his leathers while he tossed aside his vest.

Her eyes caught on his chest. Such a freaking beautiful chest. Her head came up, staring at him, and she placed a hand there, feeling his silky-smooth skin and a light dusting of hair covering all those muscles.

A low rumble came from his chest. "I should spank you, but when you look at me like that I feel… Fuck, baby. I've never felt as good as I do when you look at me like you could eat me up. I want to feel like this every day. I want to feel how much you want me because I want you."

Sweet words, and she loved the way his hand moved over her hair, stroking it back as she leaned forward and pressed a kiss to his chest. He smelled so good. Like soap with the faintest hint of arousal. Or that could be her. Their scents were mixing and mingling until there was no him or her. Only their. Only us.

She worked her way down to the ties on his leathers and managed to get them undone, his cock springing free. Hard and long, his cock was as perfect as the rest of TJ. She couldn't help herself. All of the protocols of D/s were out the window, and while she might lie to herself in the morning, she wasn't playing a role. She wasn't his sub. She was simply, in this moment, his. Lou took his cock in her palms, getting the feel of all that aching hardness covered with the sweetest silk. TJ's lean hips pressed forward, forcing her to stroke him.

"Harder, baby," he commanded.

She squeezed with gentle but firm pressure and felt him get even harder in her hand. A bead of arousal seeped from his cockhead and she started to lean over, wanting to take him in her mouth.

He growled and pressed her back against the mattress. “I won’t last. I want inside you tonight. I want us to be together. Spread your legs for me.”

She backed up and did as he commanded, spreading herself wide while he kicked out of his boots and pants. He was so beautiful. She’d always known he would be, but reality far exceeded her expectations. Or maybe when she’d thought of him before it had been as her sweet, supportive boyfriend and nothing more. When she’d thought of him before, she wasn’t looking at him down her own body, waiting for him to crawl on top of her and shove his cock in. She would have been perfectly shocked had anyone suggested it. But now it felt right. It felt primal and real and like what they’d been born to do—fit together in every way.

“You’re so fucking gorgeous, baby.” He reached over and grabbed a condom, rolling it on his cock with shaking hands. He stroked himself as he stared down at her. “And there is no going back. This is the point of no return. You can run from me if you want, but it’s you and me in the end.”

He covered her body with his, and she wrapped herself around him. Lou took a long breath in as she felt his cock at her pussy, starting to penetrate.

“Hold on to me. Dig your nails in, baby. I’ll love having that mark on my skin,” he whispered as he pulled out and then invaded another inch.

Lou tilted her hips, forcing him deeper inside her. “Don’t hold back. I want you as much as you want me.”

His jaw clenched, and a savage groan came from his throat as he pushed forward, stroking inside her until there was nothing more she could take.

Her heart threatened to stop as he dropped his head to hers. “I love you, Lou.”

Tears threatened because it was all she’d ever wanted and nothing she could trust.

“I’ll show you. I’ll make you believe,” he promised then kissed her before twisting his hips and rubbing his pelvis over her clit.

He pulled out and plunged back in, his cock filling her and stroking hard, making her body start to pound with anticipation.

Something was happening. Something that hadn't happened before. Sex had been fine, pleasurable even, but nothing compared to this feeling.

Transcendence.

Lou felt her whole body tense, nails grasping at his shoulders as he fucked her hard. Every stroke and movement brought her higher and higher until there was nowhere left to go, and the world seemed to explode around her.

The orgasm made her shake and beg him for more. She clutched him while he stiffened and held himself tight against her, his arms wound around her.

He rolled to the side, dragging her with him. "That was better than a board game."

Normally nothing was better than a good board game. Lou laid there, her body warm and satiated in a way she'd never felt before. TJ kissed her forehead.

And she knew the heartbreak—when it came—was going to be devastating.

Chapter Fourteen

Lou came awake to a gentle knock on her bedroom door.

The events of the previous night came slamming back into her mostly because she had a big, muscular arm wrapped around her waist.

TJ. He was in her bed. When they'd come home from the club, TJ hadn't bothered going into the room he'd been assigned to. Nope. He'd walked right in with her and had her on her back before she could ask him what he was doing.

Then there had been no doubt what he was doing because he'd shoved his cock deep and had her crying out his name.

Damn it. She'd meant to keep it to the club. Oh, she'd known it would be hard, but it was just supposed to be sex. Nothing more. A way to get him out of her system.

She was pretty sure she was addicted to him now.

"Lou, we have company," a familiar voice whispered. "The kind you need to talk to. Oliver and Sami have gotten authorization to give us some intel. I'm afraid this is a you thing."

"What?" Lou had to blink to focus. The door to her bedroom was open and a big white and brown dog was smiling at her.

Bud 2. Even more Bud. The twins loved a big, dumb, adorable and cuddly rescue. They'd adopted the massive mutt when they'd moved into this place. He was some kind of St. Bernard/Great Dane mix. He sounded impressive. He looked like he would lick an intruder to death.

Kala stuck her head in, her nose wrinkling when she saw TJ in bed with her. "Ewww. Get dressed and come out to the dining room. Let Sleeping Beauty get his rest."

"I'm trapped," Lou whispered back. His arm was heavy.

"Just roll out," Kala advised. "And don't worry about waking him up. Everyone jokes about how dead he is when he's sleeping. Especially…well, at the time we were talking about him playing sports really hard…"

Her best friend was never going to let her live this down.

Of course, if he was telling her the truth and nothing changed between them except that they were together in every way, Kala would get used to it. The question was would TJ get used to sometimes waking up with Kala in their bed because she didn't believe in a lot of privacy. If she had a story to tell Lou at the ass crack of dawn, she would crawl in beside her.

Which she might do now if Lou didn't move fast enough.

Lou eased from under his arm, causing TJ to mutter in his sleep. Something about hot dogs and how he couldn't find one. She wasn't sure. She had a momentary revelation that he was more like her dad than she should be comfortable with. "I'll be there in a minute. Unless I should pull a Kenzie and go to a briefing with my boobs hanging out."

"I think all that would do is make Zach's head explode. Come on. I put coffee on, and the Brits brought donuts. They're acting like it's an exotic food to them. They're weird," Kala said with a shake of her head. She leaned over to put a hand on Bud's head. "Try not to wake him up. I'd like Oliver to forget he's here. I think they still suspect him, and they're going to until you tear their evidence apart. Come on, buddy. Let's grab some breakfast."

Lou closed the door and took the world's fastest shower, dressing in clothes she would normally wear to the office. It depended on what they handed over, but she would likely spend the afternoon at her office using the ridiculously high-powered systems she kept there.

It might be good to spend some time away from TJ. She needed to get her head on straight.

Lou quietly closed the bedroom door behind her and wondered

if he planned to move his stuff straight in to her room or if they would keep up the pretense of him staying in Tasha's.

Kala had been right. TJ had simply turned over and was now hugging her body pillow, a smile on his face.

God, he was so gorgeous. And weird, and that did something for her.

She had to get her head in the game. She forced herself to walk out.

"Well, hello, Lou." Oliver was sitting at her dining room table, a mug of something hot in front of him. Despite the early hour, he was in a button-down and slacks, his hair messy in that way that had probably taken him hours in front of a mirror. "You seemed to have fun last night."

"Hey, I told you not to tease her." Zach walked in wearing his normal jeans and black T-shirt. "Lou, you okay this morning? Last night was pretty intense."

Lou felt her face heat. "You heard something? Who talked about us? I was under the impression everyone thought it was an undercover thing."

For their first baby op at the club, it seemed to have gone well. Kenzie hadn't disappeared with Ben, though the sexual innuendo had been heavy when she and TJ had joined them in the lounge. There had been a lot of longing looks between the two of them when Dare and Tasha had taken Ben to his hotel.

Zach winced and took the seat at the head of the table. "Uh, unlike the big guy, my eyes work even if you guys are doing sex stuff. TJ was pretty handsy in the bar, and apparently he threatened to murder Lucas, which I can understand. I'd like to murder him half the time and then he sticks a plate of something in front of me and I think he's a national treasure. Anyway, I heard a lot of speculation that one of you is using this undercover thing to get what he's always wanted."

"Don't you mean what she's always wanted?" Lou asked, well aware she'd always been the one chasing.

"That's not what I saw." Sami had her curly blonde hair up in a ponytail and looked far more casual than her brother. "I saw a possessive Dom, and I don't think that man is capable of that level of acting. I haven't seen TJ in years, but it's hard to believe he would have changed so much."

"Yet you think he's capable of working with an arms dealer." It was time to get down to real business. Now that he wasn't here, she realized how much they'd left out the night before to spare TJ's feelings. "If you know him, you know he's not capable of this."

"I have been around long enough to know that most people are capable of anything given the right pressure," Sami replied. "Like I said before, we've been betrayed, Ollie and I. I'm afraid the only people we truly trust are each other, our parents and brother, and the men and women who've worked with our parents for years."

"Speak for yourself. I don't trust Archie as far as I can throw him, and he's getting a little tubby," Oliver quipped.

Sami's eyes rolled, and it was good to know family was family no matter where they came from.

"I don't trust anyone." Kala strode in, putting a big mug of coffee in front of Lou and giving her a wink because Kala actually trusted a lot of people. She didn't like to admit it. Bud strolled alongside her, sitting when she did.

"I think we can trust Ben." Kenzie still had a dreamy look on her face.

Everyone in the room groaned.

"Bloody hell, I do trust the bloke, and I'm sick of hearing about him." Oliver gave her a shudder. "You need to start thinking with the head on your shoulders, cos."

"That seems boring." Kenzie pouted as she sank into her chair.

"It's not boring. It's sensible." Cooper was the last to join them.

"Where's Tash?" She was usually at every meeting.

"She and Dare are taking Parker out to breakfast," Zach explained.

"So they're distracting him," Lou concluded. "And TJ is sleeping, so all the people we don't trust are out of earshot."

"Lou, you know we trust TJ," Cooper argued, a donut in one hand. In the other he had a plate with two cinnamon twists on it. "Hey, I got you the last two."

Cooper always made sure Kala got what she liked. Often Kala would try to make do with whatever was in front of her because she knew she had odd tastes and didn't want to make a big deal out of it. But Cooper would swoop in and change things so she had the most atrocious pizza on earth. Even when they were in rural Europe he would find a way to feed her what she liked.

I want to know everything about the care and feeding of Louisa Ward.

Hadn't TJ been doing that for her for a long time?

Kala took the plate with a subdued smile. "Thanks, and he's right. We trust TJ, but we can't make MI6 do the same. What we can do is prove them wrong. So what do you have?"

Sami opened her laptop. "We have intelligence that puts The Jester in Germany at the same time this photo was taken. It was uploaded to a tip site we have asking for help finding The Jester. It's run through Interpol and talks only about him moving arms in the Middle East. We don't want to tip off that the intelligence community is looking for him because of his connections to the bombmaker."

"And this is the first tip you've gotten?" Lou leaned over, studying the picture. Well, there was no way to argue that wasn't TJ, however the other man's face was down, a hood over his head. They were walking down a street in Berlin that led by the Brandenburg Gate and eventually to the US Embassy.

"Not at all." Oliver was all business now. "We've had several. Most of them didn't pan out. Here's the truth. Something changed a little over two years ago. The Jester had been small time before then, and suddenly the man was everywhere, but no one is willing to confirm his identity."

"This is the best picture you have?" Kenzie asked. "Because that seems weird. I know Berlin isn't as packed with CCTVs as London, but there should have been more than one picture. If you were following him…or were they following TJ?"

"That's the question," Sami agreed. "Why would anyone have been tracking them? And if they were, why this grainy, tells-us-nothing photograph? It's frustrating, but I believe it's real enough that this is the reason TJ was targeted the way he was. I also find it interesting that they were smart enough to know TJ was vulnerable. I would bet he usually went out on the town with members of his team when they have downtime."

"You're right," Zach agreed. "If they'd waited even another day, he likely would have been called back in, or he would have caught a flight back to the States. That night was the perfect one to take him."

"I don't like coincidences," Oliver admitted.

"So all you have is that picture." Lou was getting angry. One picture was all it took to put TJ's whole career at risk?

"Of course not. Along with the picture, we received proof that someone has been paying the sergeant. He received five thousand in an offshore account three days after that picture was taken," Oliver explained. "There was also an eyewitness report placing TJ in close proximity to one of The Jester's recent large sales. We have intelligence that proves The Jester recently sold a hundred thousand dollars' worth of small arms to several groups in Eastern Europe."

That part of the continent was on the edge, Russian saber rattling causing all the old Soviet bloc countries to take sides and stash arms.

The money was the key. It wouldn't be the first time someone had put money into an account to frame another person. She shook her head. "Five thousand is nothing in that world."

Oliver's shoulder shrugged. "It's enough for an errand. Or to purchase some intelligence."

She didn't like Oliver Knight. "He wouldn't sell his country out for any amount, much less five grand. You know his family is well off, right?"

"His uncles are," Sami mused. "His parents, not so much. Theo and Erin are relatively middle class. I know they didn't pay for their daughter's college."

"No. My dad and uncles did that," Kenzie said, her eyes narrowing. "And they offered to pay for TJ's, too. Devi wanted to go to a private school. Most families can't afford that, but there's not a lot Uncle Case's money can't buy. Which is why it's ridiculous to think TJ would take five grand to do something that could ruin his career when all he has to do is ask his uncles and they'll pay for anything he needs."

"Case Taggart's money belongs to his wife," Oliver pointed out.

"I assure you Aunt Mia would disagree," Kala argued. "Look, none of this matters because you're not going to believe us until we tear apart your evidence. Which Lou's going to do."

Zach stared at his screen, his hands working the keys. "I need a date. When was this sale TJ was supposedly close to, and when was the money transferred?"

"We believe The Jester was in Bulgaria to finalize a sale on this date. Two days later, the money went into the account." Sami wrote on a piece of paper and slid it Zach's way. "You have to understand why we've been so cautious. If your team is involved in any way, we have to be careful. Honestly, we haven't wanted to work with the Agency since we realized TJ was potentially involved. The Taggart name opens some doors we would rather stay closed."

"Meaning the Agency would come in and take control and cover things up if they needed to," Kala said, polishing off one of the cinnamon twists.

"We all know they would," Oliver agreed. "And that's why some of our bosses in MI6 don't even know how far down the rabbit hole we've gone. Like your team, we're considered young, and our parents give us some cover. We get left out of some intel that would be helpful, but we also fly under the radar when we need to."

Something about the way his eyes narrowed made Lou wonder. "Do you think The Jester has contacts in more than one intelligence agency?"

Kenzie nodded, picking up on what Lou threw down. "They think MI6 is involved, too. I can tell you Ben doesn't trust everyone in his agency. He thinks CSIS might be compromised."

"By Huisman," Cooper prompted.

Kenzie's eyes flared, the light of battle coming into them. "I know we haven't been able to prove Ben's theories, but I didn't like Huisman. I know he presents as this inspirational, rational man, but that's a mask."

"Says the woman who wants to get into Parker's pants," Zach replied, his eyes still on the screen.

"Don't." Kala frowned Zach's way. "I'm with my sister on this one. I've watched the man, and something is off about him. He's not the person he pretends to be. I'd like to know more about him before we shrug off the Canadian's concerns."

Lou leaned over, watching what Zach was doing. He cursed, and she realized he was in a military database, pulling up information.

"TJ was in Sofia, Bulgaria, that day," Zach said. "I've got him and his whole team in the city, so that piece of the intel checks out. If that is indeed The Jester in the Berlin picture, then we can place TJ in relative proximity to The Jester twice. Whatever the team was doing there is classified. I can probably find out."

"Or we could ask him," Cooper shot back. "I don't like that we've left him out of this."

Lou had been planning on doing exactly that, though she wouldn't admit it in front of the Brits. Or Zach, who had to be careful. If he knew TJ was talking about classified assignments, he would have to turn him in. Lou did not.

"I'll look into it. I bet I can find out," Lou promised.

Zach sat back, groaning. "Just don't tell me about it. I'll pretend you have access."

"I'll have something for you this afternoon, but I need to use the system at the 4L office," Lou explained. "It's got better security than anything the Agency has. I get the feeling I'm going to need to break into some fun systems. Like Interpol. That should be easy, right?"

"Why would you break into Interpol?" Oliver asked, though the question wasn't tinged with outrage, merely curiosity.

Lou started to pack up her laptop. "Because I want to know who sent you that intel."

"It's anonymous," Oliver pointed out.

Sami snorted. "You know nothing is truly anonymous, and that girl right there is one of the best hackers in the world."

Lou glanced back at the hallway and halfway wished TJ would come walking out, yawning and ordering her to stay with him all day. The other half thought she should move and fast. Otherwise, she wouldn't be able to think. "Who's coming with me because I suspect TJ will be upset if I go to the office alone."

Kala stood and stretched. "I'll babysit you, bestie. I'm sure we'll find something to talk about since you fell asleep in TJ's lap in the lounge last night and then ran to your room when we got back here. I was promised gossip."

What she really wanted to know was if Lou was okay.

Was she okay? Something had changed inextricably between her and TJ the night before.

"Kala, you going to stay with her at the office?" Zach asked.

"Because I don't want her alone. That was precisely why I put TJ on her. He's got nothing better to do than stare at her and ensure she doesn't die."

Kala's eyes rolled, and she pushed her chair back. "I think I can manage it. I'll send him a text so he doesn't lose his shit the way he did yesterday."

"She was kidnapped yesterday," Cooper pointed out.

Kala shrugged. "And we got her back. Besides, if I hang with Lou, I don't have to listen to my dad bitch at Kenzie about the Canadian. So it's a win-win."

Kenzie frowned. "I don't understand why. Tasha's marrying a Canadian. We could have a double wedding."

Kala made a vomiting sound. "I think you'll find there was only one Canadian slot available, and your sister took it. So sad. Now, someone drive the Brits to the office. I'm not leaving them here. They might kidnap Bud 2, and then I would have to kill them."

Lou gave Bud a pet and grabbed her laptop. As everyone was breaking up, she decided to text TJ, too. Maybe he would think she wasn't running away.

But she kind of was. It would be good to focus on work because if she sat here another second longer, she would crawl back into bed with him.

Yes, work was what she needed. She followed Kala out and tried not to think about the man in her bed.

* * * *

TJ woke to warmth and a soft feeling.

Lou. He was in bed with Lou, and she was getting frisky. He'd always known once they got together she would be so affectionate. But with his feet?

That didn't feel right. He could see Lou waking him up by pressing kisses all over his chest or even getting handsy with that part of himself that was irrevocably hers. But his feet?

TJ forced his eyes to open, and sure enough Bud was at the foot of the bed, licking his exposed feet since they'd demolished the bedding the night before. It was all fucked up because he hadn't gone easy on her. He'd pretty much tossed her on the bed and been inside her. Then they'd fought in the best way. She'd twisted until she was on top and riding his cock, and then he'd flipped her so he could drive into her pussy. It had been everything he'd never even thought he could dream of with her. The best sex he'd ever had. They'd connected in all ways. The only thing that even came close to actually fucking Lou had been sitting in the lounge with Lou on his lap, talking to his friends while she rested her head on his shoulder. He'd been surrounded with warmth and love.

And once again she was gone. TJ sighed and sat up. He'd thought she would stay since this was her room, after all.

"Where's Lou, Bud?" He glanced over at the clock and groaned. It was ten a.m. He was going to spank the hell out of her if she'd gone into the office without him. Damn it. He would spank her for leaving their bed.

Their bed. He was going to be in this bed with her every night until she gave up trying to kick him out of it. That was a good plan.

He scrubbed a hand over his head and yawned. The place was shockingly quiet. If the twins were here, there would be some noise. There was always music on or the TV playing or Kala and Kenzie arguing about something.

Damn it. She'd run. Oh, she wouldn't have gone far, and she would have been smart enough to take someone with her—probably Kala—but she'd run. He'd felt so close to her the night before, like something had slipped permanently into place for them and this was the rest of their lives, but she couldn't have felt the same thing if she'd gotten out of bed and left him behind.

A weariness settled over him.

He could get up and get dressed and find out where she was, but would that change anything? He had to face the fact that she might not want him long term. That the idea of being with him for the rest of her life was a reality she'd realized she couldn't handle.

Bud roamed over and set his big head on TJ's knee, doggy eyes looking up at him with sympathy.

"You don't like the fact that all the girls are gone either, do you, Bud?" TJ felt a deep connection to the dog. He sat around and waited for the girls to come home. He didn't get to go on dangerous ops. He got babysat by Travis and spent his time staring at the door, waiting for them to come back.

Was that what TJ had to look forward to? Would Lou walk out at some point, and he would spend the rest of his life waiting for her to come home? Would she build another home, one that didn't include him?

Damn it, she shouldn't have run. They deserved to have time, intimate time that wasn't simply about fucking. How did he have a shot if she refused to give him her time?

He sighed and grabbed his phone. Sure enough, there were two texts. The first was from Kala.

Hey, Sleeping Beauty. I'm taking Lou to her office. I'll hang with her until you get there. Make sure Bud's got water before you head out. Sometimes he tips the damn thing over.

And then Lou.

I'm going to the office to work on some stuff. No need to worry. Kala's with me. See you later.

That was all. No heart emojis. No thanks for last nights. No I love yous.

What the hell was he going to do if he couldn't convince her?

A chiming sound went through the house. Likely some package. The twins had an active Prime account. He reached over and grabbed his jeans, shoving his legs in. He would save whatever the twins had bought from porch pirates and then shower and shave and figure out how to get to Lou. Bud followed behind him as he walked down the hall. If she was with Kala, she was safe, so he could stop somewhere and get some cheese and crackers and fruit and tempt her with a picnic.

Or he could stop somewhere and pick up some exotic lube and make her asshole burn so she didn't leave him a freaking text again.

Bud raced ahead and started his doggy dance at the front door, letting him know someone was there.

Not a package, then. TJ glanced at the video screen attached to the security system so he could decide if he wanted to open that door or if he needed to grab a gun.

TJ's stomach dropped. He didn't want to answer that door.

Nope. He also would never pull a gun on the man standing there.

Bud barked and jumped at the door, and there was a sharp bark echoed back.

So the big man hadn't come alone, but then he rarely did. He always had some combo of his never-ending menagerie with him. He'd shown up at Thanksgiving last year with a potbellied pig in tow because the little guy had separation anxiety.

Actually, from what TJ had heard, he'd adopted a bunch of pigs. Didn't pigs make for easy body disposal? Would he end up as pig chum? That probably wasn't the right word, but it properly described what the big guy might do to him.

The chime rang again.

There was nothing for it. The man had a freaking key, after all. Was he going to hide in Lou's shower and pray her father didn't find him there, or was he going to man up and act like the future son-in-law he wanted to be?

He opened the door and Boomer Ward stood there, frowning in a way he almost never did. Boomer was the happiest of his honorary uncles, though he'd stopped using the honorific around fifteen when he knew for absolute certain that he didn't even want to pretend there were blood bonds between him and Lou. Boomer's vibrant blue eyes laser focused on TJ in a way that made him remember that Lou's dad had once been the best sniper in the US Army. He could kill a man from over a mile away.

But he could do it up close and personal, too.

He also had a bird on his shoulder and a tiny elderly chihuahua on a leash. Bud was going crazy dancing around the other dog, who barked and tried to sniff his way-too-high-for-a-chihuahua butt.

"TJ," Boomer said. "Are you going to invite me in? I think we should talk. Lou's at the office according to her tracker, so I thought this would be a good time to have a discussion."

"I thought the tracker thing was strictly for CIA use." He needed to get a new one since the last asshole who'd kidnapped him had cut the tracker out of his bicep. And if everyone could track Lou, he wanted to as well, damn it.

"Oh, I assure you Big Tag shares that shit with me. It was part of our agreement when Lou joined up. He keeps me informed about her movements even though they're classified," Boomer allowed.

"Which is how I know she recently went to Germany to rescue you, and I've been waiting for her to come home to inform us about the change in your relationship status. She hasn't updated her socials, so I suspect she thinks we won't find out. You should both have clicked that *in a relationship* button by now. So are we going to do this or should I head over to your parents and we can come up with something way more embarrassing?"

"I wasn't trying to put you off. I was wishing I had a way to track her since she seems to slip away so easily. Please come in." He was well aware he was inviting Boomer into the house Lou owned part of. He didn't own a house. Didn't keep an apartment. Just hung out here when he wasn't on assignment. Was there a casual way to bring up the subject of his savings account? It was pretty healthy since he didn't spend a lot on himself. He wanted to be able to buy a house when he got out of the Army. A house for him and Lou.

"Sorry to bring the crew with me, but they're getting up in years, and Molly doesn't like to be alone."

The seemingly immortal monk parakeet on his shoulder perked up. "*Hope you wore a condom.*"

TJ stepped back and let the man in. Well, at least there was zero question he knew what was going on. Molly tended to parrot back the things she heard, and she was excellent at picking up on the embarrassing shit. "I did, sir."

Boomer stopped and stared. "You did what, son?"

Damn, but the man could be intimidating, which was weird because Boomer was the dude who took in all the strays and who was always kind and patient.

"I…" What was he supposed to say? Maybe the truth would work. "I'm in love with your daughter and I think she might be using me for sex, and I'm trying everything I can to make her see that this can work, but I think she's going to leave me and I don't know what to do."

That seemed to throw Boomer off. His frown suddenly didn't seem so menacing. "All right. Let's put some coffee on and talk about it. But please go take a shower. You…"

"*Smell like sex*," Molly said.

Sometimes he hated that bird. Still, he locked the door and ran off to do the man's bidding.

Twenty minutes later he was clean and dressed in clothes that were mostly clean. He needed to do some laundry. He would throw a load of his and Lou's clothes in before he left. He settled across from Boomer and Molly, the bird eyeing him like she had none of her owner's sympathy.

Sprinkles was cuddled up with Bud, the dogs taking this time for a nice nap.

"So you're serious about her?" Boomer set a mug of coffee in front of him. His cell phone went off. He checked it and then placed it back down on the table.

"Is it Lou?" There was no question she would have gotten a notification that the doorbell camera had gone off. If she'd looked, she would have seen it was her dad.

His cell started ringing again. "Yes. Hang on." He slid his finger over the screen and brought it to his ear. "Hey, sweetie. Yes, I'm here and I'm talking to him. I was happy to know he wore a condom. Don't worry about it. This is between me and TJ. Have a good day at work, and you should know that your mom wants a word." Then he hung up and settled into his seat. "So?"

Boomer had asked him a question. "I'm always serious about Lou."

"Then why did she cry over you so much?"

So they weren't pulling punches. This was probably a talk that had always been inevitable unless TJ wanted to fade out of her life. "It wouldn't have worked back then. If I'd gotten physical with her back then, I don't know that we would even be friends today. She had work to do."

"And you?"

"I had to figure out how I could possibly add to her life," he admitted. His cell buzzed. He glanced down. Lou was calling him now.

"You should answer her," Boomer offered. "She won't stop until you do."

He answered and brought the phone to his ear. "Hey."

A long sigh came over the line. "I need you to tell my dad that it's all for the op. Nothing happened. We're the same as always. It's going to be okay. We can get out of this. I don't know what the condom thing was about, but tell him you were joking. Hey, there's half a cheesecake in the fridge. Offer him some."

She thought she could get everything she wanted out of this? Sex with him, but she didn't have to admit that she was in a relationship with him? She could have the orgasms but spare herself the shame of slumming?

"And I need you to stay in our bed." He didn't want to pretend. He was done with that, and anyone who thought last night was acting was going to get an announcement. "For once I would like to wake up with you actually in bed beside me. We can't always get what we want, baby. Now you get back to work and I'll handle your dad. Also, Molly is very interested in us having safe sex. I'm going to go over all the ways we won't be making anyone a grandparent until you agree to marry me."

A chuckle came from the other side of the table. "That makes me feel so much better."

"Is he sitting right there?" Lou practically screamed the question.

"Where else would he be? I gotta go. What do you want for lunch? I should be there before then. Or we can go out," TJ offered.

Lou hung up on him.

"I guess that means no lunch." He set the phone back down. "See, I keep screwing up with her."

Boomer stared at him for a moment. "What changed? I have to ask because you've been insisting there was nothing between you for years."

He needed to figure out how to make anyone understand. "What if you had met Daphne right after her husband died?"

"I met her a couple of years after he died, so I get your point. She would have been raw then. She wouldn't have given us a chance. She almost didn't anyway. I had to kind of sneak date her for a couple of weeks," Boomer explained. "She had the mistaken impression that I was involved with someone and therefore safe. But that's not the case with Lou. Lou's been in love with you since she was twelve. I think her feelings for you have cost her every relationship she's been in."

"No, sir." He was going to own up to this. "It wasn't her

feelings most of the time. It was me because she kept picking guys who were not worthy of her."

Boomer bristled, his shoulders squaring. "That's not your call."

TJ matched his energy. "It sure as hell is when they're planning on stealing her research. Then there was the prom date that was really a bet with a bunch of jocks to see how fast he could get her in bed."

Boomer's face went a nice shade of pink. "What?"

"Lou knows. About all of it. About how either Kala or I would deal with problems so she didn't have to. So she could just be Lou. Like I said before I love your daughter. I'll do anything I need to do to protect her. When she was dating that asshole, too-old-for-her professor, I didn't do anything."

"Because you couldn't find anything on him?" Boomer asked.

TJ shrugged. "We tried. You should understand that Lou's dates have been vetted since she was able to date."

Boomer let out a long sigh. "Then why, son? Why not love her the way she should be loved?"

"Because up until now I didn't think I could," TJ replied. "What was I supposed to do? Should I have gotten some minimum wage job and been her dead-end boyfriend? Should I have slept with her knowing I was going into the Army and we would be apart for years at a time? Should I have asked her to give up her dreams and marry me? What would you have had me do, sir?"

Boomer sat back, his anger obviously deflating. "Well, I would have liked a heads-up that someone was trying to steal my daughter's research. Did you think about bringing an adult into any of this?"

"Don't raise independent kids if you expect them to cling to you. We took care of things. They were our problems to deal with," TJ insisted. "And honestly, what would you have done that Kala and I didn't do? We didn't want Lou to know. She wasn't ready then. She is now, and it's not about wanting her to be grateful to me. I don't want her gratitude. I want what I've always wanted. I want her to love me. It *is* right now."

"It's right for you," Boomer pointed out. "What if it's not right for Lou?"

"Then I should go back to Europe and rejoin my team and not

come home unless she asks for me." It was his fucking nightmare. "I don't know how I'll watch her fall in love with someone else. See, this is why I pushed it off. I knew the minute we got physical the friendship part was over and I would be alone."

"You have a massive family around you," Boomer pointed out.

TJ shook his head. "I got nothing if I don't have her."

"All right. I can see where you're coming from, but you have to understand that Lou's been doing the whole watching you from afar thing for a long time. What you describe as the worst outcome for you now has been her reality for years. I understand not getting physical with her during high school and college. I actually think that was a mature decision."

TJ wasn't so sure. "It wasn't. It was fear."

"Sometimes fear is a good thing, but it's time to put that away now," Boomer advised. "If you want to try a relationship with Lou, you have to be brave."

"I want to marry her. I know it seems fast…"

Boomer's head shook. "Nothing about this has been fast. Not a damn thing, and that's why you have to understand you're on her timeline now. She's been on yours for years. Can you give her some time to adjust? I'm not telling you to leave her alone. I think that would be the worst thing you can do, but can you back off on having everything your way?"

"I'm not…"

"You are," Boomer argued. "You're upset with her because you crooked your finger and she didn't fall in line. I know that sounds harsh and it's probably not what you meant, but it's how it has to feel to her. What you feel right now, she's been going through for years."

He felt his gut twist. "I never meant to hurt her."

"And she's not trying to hurt you. I know my girl, and that big brain of hers is working overtime to try to solve the equation. She's asking a million questions you and I wouldn't think to ask. Why now? What did I do to finally make him see me, and what will happen when he realizes I'm still the same old Lou? How can I give in when everyone will know it won't work in the long run? How will I hold my head up when he leaves me?"

"She wouldn't have to because Kala would murder me. She

made that plain a long time ago. Our partnership when it comes to Lou only goes so far." He sighed and sat back. "I can tell her I won't leave, that this is forever, but I can't make her believe it."

"So give her time. Sit back, take care of her. Put her first," Boomer advised. "And think, really think, about the future. I understand you went through something hard. You might not always feel this way. I don't know how a relationship with her will work if you're both in such high-stress jobs. You'll be apart more than you're together. That's a lot of strain on a relationship."

"I'm going to ask my uncle to have me moved onto the team as part of their military detail." He'd made the decision as he'd sat in the lounge the night before. Cooper and Zach had been joking around and he'd felt like part of them, more than he'd felt on any team he'd ever been on. "And I'm going to take some language classes so I can help out more. Lou can bring me up to date on tech, and I'll find a way to be more than cannon fodder. I know I shouldn't ask for favors, but…"

"Your mother will be thrilled." Boomer's head shook and Molly's with him. "I don't understand why you kids won't accept that we did a lot of work so you would have it easier than we did. I know the word *privilege* gets kicked around a lot, but I assure you your mom and dad didn't do what they did, make the sacrifices they made, so you would be out there on your own. Your uncle wants to help."

"*Dumbass*," Molly said.

Such a judgmental bird. "Well, I'm going to take every advantage I can get, but what if Lou doesn't want me on the team?"

"Ask her. I think you'll be surprised. You making that step might give her some solid ground to stand on." Boomer looked him over. "Are you sure, TJ?"

"I've never been more sure of anything in my life. I know what I can give her now. I thought I had to be as smart as her or as ambitious. I think she's my ambition, making sure Lou has what she needs to do the work she does—that's my ambition. If what she needs is me staying home with the kids and figuring out how to cook for all of us, then I'll be the best stay-at-home dad I can be, and I'll make my cousin teach me how to handle myself in a kitchen. I know people will look down on me and I let that affect me for a long time, but now I have one question. Why? Why should anyone look down on people who are trying to figure out what's right for them? What's best for their partnership and their family? Lou has so much to give the world and I have so much to give her. That's enough for me, and if anyone thinks differently, they can fuck right off."

"Your uncles will tease the hell out of you."

TJ waved that off. "They do that no matter what. They'll also be proud of me for knowing how to love my wife and my family. After all, they're the ones who taught me. You and Daphne are good examples."

A smile crossed Boomer's face. "I'm afraid we revolve around Lou, too. She's special. But if Daphne had asked me to quit my job and join her in the bakery because she needed me, I would have done it and not looked back. I would have done it because loving her is the best thing I ever did. Lou is complex, and you're going to have to navigate that."

"I can't give up on us," TJ replied. "But I can go easier on her. I was wondering how I should play this afternoon. I figured I could bring her a bunch of food she likes or I could top the hell out of her."

Boomer's head shook, and he pushed back from the table. "Nope. Too much information. I don't want to know anything about what you two choose to do in the club or out of it. Just use protection…"

"*Wear a condom*," Molly added.

"…and be safe. And I think the food is the way to go. That's definitely the way you should handle her this afternoon."

He'd forgotten how fragile the older generation could be. Probably because his mom would have given him advice on exotic lubes and his dad would have been right beside her. Not everyone had such tough parents. "I will definitely feed her. Hey, Lou wanted you to know there's a half a cheesecake in the fridge. I could get you a piece…or get you a fork. We can talk about the Cowboys. I think they're looking good this year."

Boomer sat back down. "I guess I could eat."

TJ got up and headed to the fridge. At least he knew how to handle one Ward.

Now he just had to figure out the most important one.

Chapter Fifteen

Lou stared down at the phone and thought seriously about grabbing her things and heading back home so she could stop the absolute disaster that was apparently occurring there.

"Did you tell TJ about the cheesecake? It's turtle. Your dad's favorite," Kala called from the couch where she was currently reading a magazine. She twisted her body so she was looking Lou's way. "You know I wish we had the whole place wired for video and sound. I would like to see how TJ's handling your dad."

"Apparently he's telling him everything." She'd thought he might deflect, maybe use the op to keep her dad calm. That did not sound like what he was doing.

They'd talked about condoms?

"You know if it was my dad, he would make TJ show him the condoms and then no matter how good the condoms are, he would complain about them. You should count yourself lucky that your dad is just going to be happy he's wearing them." A brow cocked over Kala's eyes. "He is wearing one, right?"

"Not right now he isn't." Lou was feeling… She wasn't sure what she was feeling, but it wasn't a nice, peaceful thing. It was anxiety and anger and guilt and anticipation because TJ would be coming up here after he was done screwing things up with her dad, and what would she do about that? "He might never have to wear one again."

Kala sighed and sat up. "It was inevitable. At some point in time my dad was absolutely going to tell your dad that you're sleeping with TJ. We all told you to cut him off at the pass. You didn't want to because you didn't want to lie to your parents."

"I wasn't going to lie."

"You were if you were going to tell them that it's all about an op, and that's all I'm going to say about it because you are going through a delusional stage." Kala stood and crossed the big room that contained her office space and what she called her workshop. She technically took up what they referred to as a lab here at 4L. There were several floors that were divided into quarters for the scientists and teams who worked here. She shared this floor with Dr. Madeline Murphy, who worked on satellite tech, and Dr. Noelle LaVigne-Hutchins, whose work centered on helium conservation. The fourth large space was security, including a couple of Agency plants.

Needless to say she felt safe here in this building. Which is why it would have been great if Kala had been willing to drop her off so she wouldn't have to talk about her delusions. Because she knew damn well her friend was right.

"So what do we have?" Kala asked, moving behind her so she could look over Lou's shoulder at the screen of her laptop.

Before she'd figured out her dad was paying TJ a visit, she'd been taking apart the "evidence" MI6 had sent over.

The problem was that photo was well done. She was fairly certain it was real. "Nothing tells me it's a deep fake, and I've isolated some background items that can help me pinpoint the day it was taken. There's a restaurant in the background, and I can get a closeup on the menu they have on a sign outside. After I checked with their website, I can confirm that this picture was taken on the day MI6 thinks it was taken on. It's not just the menu. If you look at the club across the street, the only night they had live music that month was the day MI6 believes the picture was taken."

She'd looked for anyway to disprove the picture.

"And all of that lines up with when TJ was in Berlin. Zach placed TJ in Bulgaria when MI6 believes The Jester was making a deal. So that's two times they have him in close proximity," Kala murmured. "Still mere coincidence. Also, there's no decent picture of the man they claim is The Jester. I still don't know how we can't find a single picture where we get this guy's face. What can you tell about him from his clothes?"

"I would say he's American. Those shoes he's wearing were brand new at the time. Basketball shoes. They hadn't been released outside the US at that point. The rest of his clothes are typical American," Lou explained. "I want TJ to look at it again because I think this is someone he knows. Maybe someone on his team."

"Someone who knows how to hide his face? Maybe if they were on an op, but TJ is obviously not," Kala pointed out. "How about the money? You know how little money five grand is in that world."

It was good they were on the same page. "I tracked it down, and like most crap with crypto it's hard to pinpoint who owns what. I can tell you that the transfer got pinged around the globe. No surprise there."

"But you can unravel that thread, can't you?"

Her head was starting to hurt. She shouldn't have skipped breakfast. "Given some time. I think that's the way to go. Follow the money. You're right—the rest could be coincidence, or it could be someone who wants to fuck with TJ. Who would do that? Everyone loves TJ."

"I wouldn't say everyone, but I do get your point. Besides stringing you along for years he's fairly unproblematic. More importantly, what would they get from framing TJ?" Kala stared at the screen. "Unless the point is to hurt our team. I can think of a lot of people who would love to get me in a bad position. If fucking Chet was alive, I'd point the finger at him, though he said he was coming specifically after my dad."

Chet Whittington.

Who hadn't liked having to deal with Taggarts.

Chet, who worked for the Agency and might have known about The Jester.

"I need to talk to Zach," Lou said. He might be able to figure out if Chet had worked with any team that might have known about The Jester.

"I was hoping you would talk to me for a little bit, sweetheart," a familiar voice said.

Kala whistled under her breath. “Damn, they teamed up on you, Lou. Your dad was a distraction.”

Oh, she doubted that. Her dad would absolutely be doing that staring thing he did when he was disappointed. For a man who hadn’t come into her life until she was twelve, he quickly picked up on the dad thing, as TJ was currently learning.

But there was someone she wanted to talk to less than her dad.

Her mom stood in the doorway, a bag in one hand and her brother, Jayce, at her side. He was adorably gangly at twelve years old. He was all long limbs and blonde hair that matched his father’s.

He grinned at her. “Hey, Lou. I heard you’re going to marry TJ. That’s awesome. I love TJ.”

A flash of anger went through her. This was why she’d wanted to keep the whole thing under the radar. She looked at her mom. “Who told him that?”

A brow rose over her mom’s eyes. “I think he’s making a leap that you can’t be surprised he would make. Jayce, I told you it’s early days.”

“But they’ve mostly been together for years. And all her other boyfriends suck,” Jayce said.

Kala grinned. “We should discuss this, little dude. Come on. I’ll take you down to the cafeteria so your mom can talk to your sister.”

“But…” Jayce began.

“They are serving chicken tenders and fries.” Kala knew how to deal with her brother. Her kid brother looked like a younger version of their dad, and he had Boomer Ward’s appetite. And metabolism. “Also, there’s going to be a lot of feelings discussed.”

“We should talk about our feelings,” Jayce told Kala, but he was already moving behind her.

“Daphne, you ruined this child,” Kala said with a shake of her head as she held the door open. “Come on, buddy. We’ll get lunch and talk about how to properly shove all your feelings down deep.”

Her mom frowned. “Maybe I should stop that.”

“Or maybe you should say what you’ve come here to say so I can get back to work.” Lou winced. She hadn’t meant to sound so cold.

“Okay.” Her mom set the bag she was holding down on Lou’s

workstation. There were several of them through the suite, this one containing the smart watch she was playing around with. The Daphne's Delights bag sat right next to her tool kit. "I don't think macarons are going to solve this. I came by to see if you're okay, and I can see plainly that you're not. What's he done to you this time?"

Wow. This was a problem she hadn't counted on. All this time she'd worried that TJ would leave her, and she hadn't thought about the ramifications if he stayed. Her mom was always circumspect. When she had a problem, her mom gave her reasonable advice on how to handle it, and for years when it came to TJ it was all about getting out there and finding someone else.

She'd never thought about the fact that her mom might not like TJ. Her mom liked everyone. "It's not a big deal. We kind of fell in bed together, and he'll be gone in a couple of months. We're working on an op and it's…"

"Classified." Her mom knew the drill. She sighed and moved in, a frown on her face. "So much about your life is classified. Sometimes I think I would resent Kala if I hadn't known her as a kid, hadn't watched how closely she protected you."

"Mom, she's my best friend."

"And she pulled you into a world I can't understand," her mom pointed out.

"Dad does."

Her mother's head shook. "Well, Dad lived it, but he didn't have a wife and kids. He wasn't close to his family, so he made one out of the men and women he worked with. I assure you he feels it now, though I know Big Tag tells him what he can. All I'm saying is sometimes I wonder what your life would be like if you hadn't met Kala Taggart. If Boomer hadn't been involved with the Taggarts, and we were a family of four."

The word actually hurt. "You can't ever let Kala hear that. She loves you. You're one of the only people she actually will listen to, and if she knows you don't like her…"

"I didn't say that," her mom argued. "I love Kala. I adore her, but I wonder where you would be without her."

"Alone. Lonely is what I would be. I have no idea where this is coming from."

Her mom stared at her for a moment. "If you'd never met Kala, you would be working at a university and you would have met a nice man and started your life."

Her mother was forgetting a few facts. "If I'd never met Kala, I wouldn't have figured out what I want in a man because I would have curled in on myself and become everything my grandmother wanted me to be. Do you honestly think Dad would be the same person if he hadn't worked at MT and become part of that family? What about you? You have friends. You never had friends. You didn't trust anyone, and now you want to wish that away so you know where I am twenty-four seven? You think I would be some successful professor you could point to and be proud of? I would be lonely. I would be sad. I would never have learned how to be a sister to Jayce because I would never have seen it, been surrounded by it. I'm sorry my friends annoy you, but I am who I am because of them. You and Dad had a lot to do with it, but so did they."

Her mom sank down to the couch, her expression going a careful blank. "Does the 'they' include TJ?"

"Of course it does. He's been my friend since I was a kid."

"Excellent. Now do him. Tell me where you would be without him because I personally think your life would be so much better if you'd never met him."

Never met him? "He was one of my first friends. I didn't know you were so into rewriting history. Do you remember who I was at that age?"

"You were a brilliant child who didn't fit in anywhere and who wanted so badly to have people she could count on because the ground never felt stable to you." Her mother's tone went soft.

"He was stable ground. He didn't care that I was weird and talked about things he didn't understand. He didn't care that some of his friends thought I was a nerd. When they came at me, he wasn't their friend anymore. I can't tell you how often he's protected me."

"And yet you've cried over him more times than I can count."

She didn't like the way this conversation was going. Anger was starting to build, and she was never angry with her mom. "Because I loved him. Because I didn't want to lose him. Because even when he didn't want me physically, he still showed up when I needed him. Yes, I cried because I didn't get what I wanted, but he was still my friend. So you can shove your judgment, Mom."

A low smile crossed her mom's face, and she realized her mom was playing chess. "Then why is your brother wrong? Are you telling me you and TJ finally got together and you're…what? Playing around? Please don't try to tell me this is all for an op or something. And like I said, I adore Kala and know damn well you're better for having her in your life. I will admit there are times I wondered about TJ, but you can't blame me for questioning the kid who made my daughter cry. Even if he didn't mean to."

She slumped on the couch beside her mom. "He didn't. I don't think he ever meant to make me ache the way I do sometimes. I think that's the price of unrequited love."

"Well, if what Big Tag says is true, it feels pretty requited to me," her mom shot back. "Also, Marley was talking about something happening at the club last night, but she was getting it secondhand from her brother. Something about you and TJ playing games in a privacy room. She wasn't sure if the games were board games or something else."

So at least one of her plans had worked. Her friends were unsure if she was making a fool of herself or working.

And she needed to go over the meaning of the word *classified* with her boss.

"We were running an op last night at The Hideout," she replied.

"Really?" Her mom sounded like she didn't believe her.

"Really."

"And the stuff in Germany?"

"Was a mistake." Lou wanted to wrap it all up and send her mom on her way and go back to work, forgetting everything except the task in front of her.

It was always her first instinct—to satisfy her brain and leave the rest of it locked behind some door she never had to open.

She could easily have been Kala's friend and soaked herself in Kala's dark view of the world. She could have been Kala's operational wingman, sitting in the shadows and pursuing directives with no thought beyond getting the job done. It would have been easy. Simple.

Kala had given her confidence, but it had been TJ who dragged her out of her head and convinced her life wasn't life without joy and fun and yes, even heartache.

Why was she holding back? Why was she reverting to a her that hadn't existed in years? The one who shut down so she didn't have to listen to criticism, the one who walked a tightrope so she tried not to feel anything or need anyone.

"Mom, I don't know what I'm doing."

Her mom sniffled and moved over, wrapping her arm around Lou. "Oh, baby, you're not supposed to. Not about something like this. Something like this, you follow your instincts. You let yourself feel everything because this is important. Do you know why I love TJ?"

It was Lou's turn to sniffle since she found herself on the verge of tears. "It sounds like you hate him."

"Never," her mom vowed. "I might have wished you weren't so hurt, but I do know how he's been a friend to you over the years. You and your dad concentrated on what he did wrong, but I was able to sit back and consider the situation. Do you know what it takes for a twelve-year-old boy to pick the weird new girl over his friends?"

Lou nodded.

"I loved that kid when I overheard him telling a guy from his baseball team that if you weren't welcome at his party, then he wasn't coming either," her mom continued. "I think he wanted to go but he came home with us that night and helped your dad with the dogs and watched TV with you until his parents picked him up. I know he worries he's not smart enough for you, but there are different levels of intelligence."

"What do you mean? Is this the whole he didn't want to mess up my college career thing? We've had this discussion." She'd had it over and over again. Was she supposed to reward the man for rejecting her so she could get an education? Like she would have passed it up.

Her mom seemed to consider how to proceed. "But have you really thought about it? Have you thought about it from his point of view? Would you have followed him if he'd asked you to?"

She snorted at the thought. "I had a full ride to MIT, Mom. No, I wasn't going to follow TJ and be a good military wife. But we could have tried. We could have seen if it could work long distance, or he could have changed his plans since he should have gone to college. Someone we know could have gotten him into a college close to me. His family has crazy connections."

"Maybe, but could they make him comfortable in it?" Her mom sat back. "I want you to think about what you've said because you've used the pronoun *you* an awful lot."

She was confused. "What was I supposed to do? You think I should have followed him?"

"No. I think you have to consider the fact that he did what he thought was best for you and for him at the time. And he did it at the age of eighteen. He was a boy who you would have happily slept with who decided that if he couldn't be all in, he would wait to pursue a physical relationship with you. I know that was frustrating at the time, but it showed me he could put your best interests in front of his own wants," her mom explained.

She was ignoring a few salient facts. "And after? Mom, a few weeks ago I tried to kiss him and he wouldn't. Why the hell should I believe that he's changed?"

Her mom blushed. "Well, the video alone proves that he's changed. I would say the whole actually sleeping together is a sign of change."

Lou shook her head, a familiar stubbornness invading her veins. "He got scared and he held on to me like a teddy bear. That's what he does. When he needs something, he comes to me."

Her mom sat back, a skeptical look on her face. "Really? What has he ever asked you to do for him?"

The question stopped Lou in her tracks. "I've done a lot for him."

"I know you've cooked meals for him and been his plus one to things he didn't want to go to alone, but what have you sacrificed for him?"

"Uhm, my youth." She'd pretty much wasted her twenties mooning over the guy.

"No, you dated," her mom argued. "You chose to stay in the friendship with TJ because you got something out of it. What worries me is that your friends have the wrong idea about that relationship. I think your friends believe TJ's used you over the years, and you've played a part in that. You talk about him stringing you along. How did he do that? When he skipped the end of the summer blowout the kids were having to drive you up to Massachusetts so you would have your car? When he used his only leave nine months later to drive you back home?"

Lou went quiet. She'd never thought about it like that. Those days had been precious. Just her and TJ in a car, driving across the country. They'd sang along to music they both loved and ate greasy diner food and stopped at dumb tourist sites to take pictures. In every one of them, he was smiling like he was having the time of his life. When they stopped at a motel for the night, he would cuddle up with her and watch TV until she fell asleep and then she would wake up with him in the bed next to hers.

At the time she'd taken it as proof that he couldn't love her, but what if that was the wrong conclusion? Life wasn't an equation where everything balanced perfectly. The math of any relationship was messy, with shifting inequalities that—if the relationship was right—somehow balanced out in the end.

Her mother wasn't finished. "During your senior year, he called your father and I when he was worried you were overloaded academically. It's why we skipped Thanksgiving and took you and your brother to Hawaii."

Tears pricked her eyes because she remembered that semester. Senior year in college, and she'd taken on way too much. She'd been ready to break, but TJ called her every chance he got. He sent her letters and gifts for her to open when she completed the assignments she'd needed to. It had given her the push she needed, a reminder that she wasn't alone. It hadn't been much. A book she wanted to read. A stuffed penguin. A bracelet with tiny diamonds that now that she thought about it probably cost him a lot. And then he'd called her parents. She'd needed that week away from everything. "I thought you wanted to surprise me."

Her mom put a hand over hers. "I wanted to give you what you needed. He came home that year and I know how much he wanted to see you, but he wanted you healthy and happy more."

He'd sent flowers to her hotel room with a card wishing her the happiest Thanksgiving, and she'd wondered if he was relieved he hadn't had to spend time with her that holiday. She'd spent her time wondering if he was bringing home a woman to meet his family. Or if he was just hooking up with whoever was around.

She'd thought of herself and put the worst spin on anything he did.

He never forgot a birthday. Always knew what presents would make her happy.

Everyone called him Fucking TJ, the guy who just kept stringing her along.

What if he was TJ, the guy who really couldn't stand the thought of losing her?

"I know you're scared, and I would bet you've come up with a million ways this ends poorly. You're sitting there asking all the wrong questions. Or you keep asking questions you know the answer to. You think he's clinging to you like a teddy bear because something bad happened to him. Well, sometimes we need a push. He could have viewed his kidnapping as proof that his life was too dangerous for you."

Lou snorted.

Her mom shrugged. "Men can ignore the truth a lot. Your dad still thinks all you do is sit behind a computer, so if you want to be mad at TJ for that, throw your father in that jail, too."

"He found out how well I can handle myself. I showed him how capable I am."

"Before or after he tossed you on a bed and made a meal of you?"

She was right, but did she have to put it that way? "Mom, really?"

Her mom shrugged. "I've been around lifestylers for long enough to become comfortable with sex. It's important, and that's a lesson I never learn if I didn't meet your dad. I think about it a lot, you know. When you guys first came to Ian and the Sanctum board with your plans for your own club, I had to sit with it for a while. Do you want to know what I decided?"

Did she? "Sure."

"I decided that I would rather have you in a club that takes sex seriously with a bunch of people who watch out for you than on a single dating app rolling the dice. I would rather you had good sex and learned to appreciate your body and value yourself than sleeping with guys because you hoped the connection was right when you have no real idea what their intentions are. The club is a place for honesty. You can make proper decisions because you'll have the data you need."

"Mom, I never had sex in the club until last night, and even then it was a private thing," Lou admitted.

"He took you to a privacy room because it was your first time, baby. Again, that boy knows how to do things properly. I assure you if he's anything like his father he'll be parading you around soon enough."

She blushed. "Mom."

Her mom shrugged, a grin tugging her lips up. "Well, I've never played at Sanctum, but I have spent many an evening sitting in the lounge gossiping while wearing fet wear. You know we should go shopping."

"Absolutely not. Boundaries, Mom." They needed to find a few of those.

"Well, was it bad? Did he not take care of you?"

"You know he did and it was…" Magical. Life changing. "The sex doesn't matter."

"But it does," her mom insisted. "It's the only thing you've been lacking. You've had an attentive boyfriend for a long time. What you lacked was a situation he felt like he could add to, not take away from. He couldn't fit into your academic career. And then you joined the team and he was on his own team and couldn't spend time with you the way he should. Now you're in his world and he's had to face the idea of losing you and what's he doing?"

"Talking to my dad, for one thing." Her stomach turned at the thought.

"I bet he handles your dad spectacularly. I bet your dad finally comes to the conclusion I came to a long time ago."

"What's that?" Lou asked.

"That you and TJ were one of those couples who were meant to be," her mom said softly. "The road might not have been to your liking, but that part is over if you want it to be. If you can look past your ego and see what he's offering you, you can start this part of your life, and baby, it is the best part. I'm not saying everything magically gets easy, but knowing you have someone watching your back, someone who will never leave you, who will always listen, that's everything. Now I want you to look back and tell me what he kept from you all these years? It wasn't love. He gave that to you. It wasn't his help. He moved mountains to get you the things you needed. What did he deny you?"

Lou struggled to see through the tears that pooled in her eyes. "Sex. That was all. Just sex."

Her mom nodded sagely. "And he's offering you that now. He's ready because he sees the place he can have in your life now. You have a man who thinks of you before himself. Grab him with both hands and honor that love. Take it into your soul, baby girl, and let it warm you for the rest of your life. I did. I never regretted it even once. Now, that is all I'm going to say. The rest is your decision, and I need you to understand if you decide you can't risk it with TJ, I'll honor that and I won't ever bring it up again. The only thing I'll ask you to do is to be kind to him. Maybe help rehab his image because it has to bug him that everyone sees him as the villain and you as the innocent thing he's taking advantage of."

She hadn't thought about how it would be for him. She'd halfheartedly pushed back when their friends talked about how he treated her. She'd seen herself as a doormat he wiped his feet on every now and then. That was her problem, not his. That was her damage, and he'd done his best to help her.

"I'll talk to them," she promised. "And I'll think about everything you've said. But there's still the problem of distance. TJ works on the best team. We rarely get that team as backup. We would still be apart most of the time."

Her mom stood up. "I would bet he'll fix that problem for you, too. You need a keeper, my sweet girl, and I'm happy he's finally decided he can do the job right. Give it some time. Give yourself some grace. I know it's hard, but stop thinking about what it could cost you and start planning your future."

Lou stood and hugged her mom. "I'll try. It's pretty scary."

"Well, then it's good you're a badass," her mom whispered. "Another reason for me to love this family we found. I know you think I wanted you to have some spectacular academic career where you stacked up honors, but this is a great adventure. This is what I wanted for you. Do I worry you're in danger? Yes. But I never worry that you aren't living a life that's big enough for you. It's big enough for the both of you. You were brave enough to put your life on the line for the world you want to live in. Be brave enough to risk your heart on a boy who's literally loved you half his life."

Lou's heart clenched because she knew this talk should soothe something inside her, but it merely made her gut twist. Could they make it work? Could she believe him?

"I've got to get to the bakery. Marley Brighton can bake like an angel, but she's not so great with customers," her mom said with a grimace. "She threatened to shove an éclair up a guy's ass because he didn't understand that pastry cream isn't whipped cream. She's like the baking equivalent of her mom. I left you macarons. Don't worry about your dad. He's letting TJ know that we're here for you both."

Sure. That was what he was doing. "Don't plan a wedding yet."

Her mom stopped at the door, a glint in her eyes. "Me? Would I do that? Would I get together with Theo and Erin at a nice restaurant where we can plan out the rest of your lives and talk about grandbabies? Would I? I doubt it. By the way, if you need me on Friday night, I'll be at Top. Maybe you and TJ could take Jayce to a movie or out for pizza?"

"Mom," she began.

But she was already gone, and Lou was left with a dozen perfectly crafted macarons and a million questions.

* * * *

TJ practically ran into the 4L building, stopping only to show his security badge. He'd been given one a year ago when he'd helped Lou work on a big project. She'd modified the twins' cell phones so they were basically mini laptops with features no one outside of the spy world would ever need or think to put on a phone.

He'd held her spare tweezers as she'd worked on the microchips and got her lattes and snacks.

It had been a good time.

He was worried he was in for a not so good time this afternoon, but he was ready. He'd picked up pad see ew from her favorite Thai place along with a cold brew that would fuel her through the afternoon. He would sit on her couch while she worked and probably fumed his way, and hopefully she would let him sit in the front seat with her when they drove home.

He was taking his badge back from the guard when something knocked into him, wrapping long arms around his waist.

He looked down and couldn't help a smile. Jayce Ward. Lou's kid brother was one of his favorite people in the world. Probably because he seemed to be one of the only people who thought he deserved Lou. He wrapped an arm around the kid. "Hey, Jayce, how are you doing? I just saw your dad."

Jayce's head turned up. "I thought he was taking Molly and Sprinkles to the vet."

So that was the excuse he'd given. "I'm sure he is, but he wanted to stop by and make sure everything was okay at your sister's place."

Jayce stepped back and looked so much like his dad. "I bet he wanted to ask you if you're planning on marrying my sister."

"Jayce." Daphne Ward caught up to her son. "I told you to be patient."

"But he's with Lou, right?" Jayce looked from his mom to TJ. "I heard you're Lou's boyfriend now. I kind of thought you were always Lou's boyfriend, but Mom told me no and then she said a bunch of stuff that I didn't understand."

Before his talk with Boomer he would have said yes, he was Lou's boyfriend and plowed right through, but now he wondered. He'd spent the last hour thinking about how she had to feel. He had to be patient. He got on one knee so he could look Jayce in the eyes. "Your sister is my best friend and always will be, but we're talking about maybe taking it to another level. But you need to know that no matter what happens between us, I'll always love her, and I'll always be here for you, buddy."

"Cool," Jayce said. "Because Mom says you're taking me for pizza on Friday."

"I am." He'd learned to simply agree with the Ward women. Although there was something Daphne hadn't thought about. "Unless your sister needs me. I'm sticking close to her for the time being."

"Oh, she'll be with you." Daphne gave him a soft smile as she stood next to her son. "Her dad and I are having dinner with your parents, so I thought it would be fun for you to spend some time with Jayce."

TJ stood, staring at the woman he wanted as a mother-in-law. "That sounds like you're planning something. Don't push her, Daphne. She needs time."

"She needs to change her mindset." Daphne leaned over and pressed a kiss on his cheek. "Don't worry, sweetie. Everything is going to work out. Was Boomer hard on you?"

"Of course not. I can't say the same about Molly."

Daphne chuckled. "Well, then all is right in the world. Come along, son. Let's go save the customers from Marley's rage. You can have all the sandwiches that didn't sell from lunch."

"Awesome. I hope there's peanut butter and jelly. Bye, TJ." Jayce raced for the door.

Daphne shook her head. "So like his dad. He ate the equivalent of three adult meals and he's looking forward to a snack. And I meant what I said. This is all going to be all right, and I am going to make you the most beautiful wedding cake."

"I thought we were being patient." He watched her go. Well, shit. Lou was going to be in an awful mood if her mom had been pushing her.

He rushed to the elevator, punching in the code that took him to the top floor, where his baby worked to change the world. Or at least to make it easier to protect the world. Every time he watched her work, he was in awe of her.

Because she was the smartest person he knew, would ever know. Because she was transcendent. The truth of the matter was no one would know her. They might know the things she invented, the enhancements she created that made the world work better. They wouldn't stand and cheer for her in a stadium, but she was every bit as special and gifted as a Michael Jordan or Meryl Streep. She was unique and special, and she would figure it out even if she rejected him. She would find what she needed.

Was he talking himself out of it again?

Psyching himself out was more like it.

He was a grown man who was now hearing his mom in his head. Telling him he could do this, that he was good enough.

If he wasn't then he would change and make sure he was

because he loved Lou, and no one in the world was going to love her the way he did.

The elevator doors opened, and he forced himself to walk through. Patience. He wasn't going to think about what Daphne had said. Boomer had advised patience, and he was following the plan. They'd been on his timeline and now they were on Lou's, and he had to chill and hope she came to her senses before they were too old to enjoy their lives.

Because he would be sitting here waiting for her.

He strode down the hall as Lou's door was opening. Kala walked out and sighed when she saw him.

"I'm so glad you're here." Kala sounded like she meant that, which made him wonder what terrible thing was about to happen.

"You are?"

Kala nodded, walking toward him. She settled her big bag over her shoulder. "Yep, because I'm pretty sure Daphne broke her. I don't know what she said because I was feeding a young Boomer. I'm not joking. Something's wrong with him. Anyway, Daphne came down to the cafeteria when Jayce was ready for dessert, and I came back up here and Lou is all fucked up."

Damn it. He'd known it. He had to calm Lou down, and that meant denying himself everything he wanted. But he would do it for her. "I'll handle it. You taking off?"

"I figured you would stay with her the rest of the day." Kala started for the elevator. "I've got some stuff she wants me to talk to Zach about. Timelines and such. He's picking me up in a couple of minutes because Kenz is hanging with the foreigners, and I have to hide. Sometimes this job sucks." She stopped in front of him. "You know you look guilty to the outside eye."

His gut threatened to twist. She was talking about The Jester. "Lou thinks I did it?"

He still wasn't sure what "it" was, but he didn't want Lou to think he did it.

Kala's eyes rolled. "Not even for a second, and if my opinion is important, neither do I." She reached up and put a hand on his cheek. "Take care of her. You know I love you, TJ, right?"

"Shit. Am I about to die?" It felt a little like that moment in the *Godfather* when Corleone knew it was Fredo.

"I am not that bad, cousin." She stepped back. "And I am perfectly capable of love. Also, you need to talk to my dad about joining the team. This isn't going to work if you're on a different continent."

"Uh, I already planned to do that."

She strode away. "Well, I'll tell everyone it was my plan anyway. Wear a condom, TJ. I'm not ready to be an aunt again."

He watched her disappear and then used his key card to enter what he thought of as Lou's paradise lab. It was big and sleek, with every technological feature Drew Lawless's money could buy. He walked through the entryway with its small reception desk for an assistant Lou never hired. Many a time he'd sat at that desk and played games while waiting for Lou to make her latest breakthrough.

He made his way to the main lab where Lou was sitting at one of the long tables, carefully studying her laptop.

He stared at her for a moment, loving every inch of her. The way her hair brushed the top of her shoulders and the lines of her nose and lips and chin.

He had no idea what he would do with the rest of his life if he couldn't convince her to take a chance on him.

"I brought you lunch. Pad see ew with chicken and extra egg."

Her face turned, and he saw tears in her eyes.

Shit.

"Lou, we should talk," he began, placing the bag and the coffee on the end of the table.

She shook her head. "No. I can't talk about this a second longer. This morning was precisely why I wanted to avoid my parents finding out."

"I'm sorry," he offered. "I told your mom not to push you, and I explained to Jayce that we're not anything but friends. I know I've pushed you, Lou, but I'm not going to do that anymore. We're on your timeline. However long you need. If having me as a bodyguard bothers you, I'll talk to Zach and we can bring in an MT guard."

"I told you I can't talk about this." Her hands were in fists at her side, a sure sign she was emotional and fighting it.

"Baby, you're killing me. Do you want me to leave? I can catch Kala. I don't want to be the guy who makes you cry. I'll go if that's what you need."

"And if what I need is for you to stay?"

What was she… Fuck. She was wound up and had no idea how to get out of her own head. When they'd been younger, he would take her for a walk or sit with her while they watched some silly movie.

Now he knew exactly what she needed. "This doesn't have to mean anything, baby. Like I said, we're on your timeline, but when you need me, I'll always be here. Do you need a spanking?"

"I need you." Tears spilled over her cheeks. "But I don't want to need you."

The words hurt, but he couldn't argue with her. She needed something from him, and it wasn't softness. "That sounds like a you problem, sub. Take your clothes off."

His heart started to pound as he moved to the door and made sure it was locked in a way that not even keycards would get through. Security would call if anyone from outside the building was coming up without a card. Lou had a few people who got to breeze through security, but they'd mostly already been here today.

This wasn't how he wanted to be with her. He wanted to kiss her and be gentle and loving, but she didn't need that. She felt out of control and needed to know he could take the whole situation in hand.

He turned back and she was standing there, her jaw a stubborn line.

So she wanted this to get nasty. "Lou, I gave you an order. If you want me to handle this situation, you have to submit. Otherwise, I'll call Kala back. Unless your plan is to punish me. Do you think that will make you feel better? Yelling at me for whatever thoughts your mom put in your head? Is railing at me going to get you back to normal? I don't think it's going to work. I think if you yell at me, all that's going to do is add anger to the fear you're feeling."

"I'm not afraid."

"Oh, yes, you are," he countered. "You're terrified, and now that I'm thinking about what your mom said, I might have a long conversation with her. I'll handle Jayce on Friday. You can do whatever you like as long as you take a guard with you."

Her head shook. "You'd like that, wouldn't you? Knowing I'm

out on a date and I can't really do anything because I've got someone watching my every move? Is that your plan? Are you going to keep a guard on me until I decide to give you whatever you want?"

Maybe he'd been wrong and there was already a shit ton of anger in there. What the hell had they talked about? "Nope. The minute Zach says it's safe, you're an independent woman again. How about I find you a woman bodyguard who'll high five you when you screw your date for the evening?"

Her eyes flared, and he realized he'd made a huge mistake. "You want to slut shame me, Romeo?"

He shook his head. "I've never once done that to you, but I think you've done it to me. You know I've probably slept with as many women as you have men. Meaning two, Lou. I know I've dated, but I've only had sex with two of them. I'm sorry. I'm sorry I wasn't capable of cutting that part of myself off. If it helps, every single person who knows the two of us thinks I'm some kind of player, fucking every girl I see with the exception of the sweet one who loves me."

"I never told anyone that."

"But you didn't defend me, did you?" He didn't want to do this. "Lou, I'm sorry. I don't want to fight."

"What if I do?" Lou asked between clenched teeth. "You know what else we never do, TJ? Besides have actual sex, we never fight. Because I always back down and you always know that I'll fall in line."

"Fall in line?" He breathed out a long sigh because his heart ached. "I can't do this with you. We don't fight because the last thing I want to do is hurt you, and it feels like me being around is hurting you. I didn't mean to do that. I know you don't believe me, but I love you. I love you so fucking much, and I'm going to prove it by doing the only thing I can do."

Her arms crossed over her chest as she watched him with wary eyes. "What's that? What can you possibly do that would make things better for me?"

His heart ached. "Leave, baby. I thought I could push my uncle to let me on the team and play a long game to convince you to take a chance on us, but if this is what me being close does to you, it's time for us to call it."

Her face flushed. "One fight? I get mad once and you're walking out? Yeah. It's time for us to call it."

She turned and went back to her computer.

He stood there, utterly at a loss. TJ took a long breath, letting the last few minutes sink in.

She was afraid and she was pushing boundaries, and he'd done the one thing he shouldn't have. He'd given in. He'd been so determined not to push her that he hadn't realized she might need to push him. She might need to shove against him to see if he would crack.

She didn't need him to be a freaking martyr in this moment. She needed him to be her Dom.

"Louisa, I told you to take off your fucking clothes. If you aren't naked in one minute, we'll move straight to the spanking."

She turned, her eyes wide. "What? You said we're over. You don't get to spank me."

He needed to make something plain to her. "I had a moment of weakness, but Lou, you need to understand that it will never be over between us. If you shove me out, I'll be waiting for you to come home to me, and it won't matter who you've been with or what you've done. I will be standing there and I'll greet you with open arms and I'll spend whatever time we have left loving you. If you don't, I'll spend that time missing you, wishing you were here with me. You do not have to make a decision today. You can take what I give you and find comfort in it and go right back to being mad at me. You can date whoever you want to date, and I will be waiting. So take off your clothes or say your safe word and I'll go sit on the couch until you're ready to go home."

Her jaw was a stubborn line. "What if I don't want you in my house?"

"Then I'll sit outside in the rain the same way I did when we were seventeen and you wouldn't go to prom with me."

They stood there for a moment, staring at each other, the distance mere feet, but it felt like miles to TJ. It felt like there was a mountain between them, but he suddenly knew he was going to climb it. "I'm human, Lou. You think you're afraid I'll leave. I'm afraid you'll figure out I'm not worthy of you. But I'm done being afraid. You might change your mind someday, but I'm going to do everything I can to make sure you never regret being with me and yes, that means when you're ready marrying me. Living with me. Having kids with me, if you want them. Having a bunch of overly anxious dogs with me. Growing old with me. I'll do anything to make that happen, but right now all that matters is the next hour. Let me take all that worry away. Let me top you."

When her hands when to the hem of her shirt, he knew he still had a shot.

Chapter Sixteen

Lou wasn't even sure what she was doing, but she pulled her shirt over her head and let it fall to the floor.

Every word her mother had said, Kala had said…fuck, everyone over the last twelve years of her life had said about her and TJ was rolling through her system. It had always been so simple. She loved TJ and he couldn't love her back, and everyone knew the universe had somehow wronged her. Unrequited love. She was its victim.

But her mother was forcing her to reframe those years, to look at them through a different filter, one where she wasn't innocent. One where she did let the people around her make assumptions about TJ that weren't true.

She couldn't face that right now any more than she could face the idea that this would be over soon.

She was stuck between wanting to believe him and still being that girl who saw the world as a knife's edge she had to walk or everything would fall apart. It was all still there despite the fact that she'd had beautiful stability for half her life now. Those first years had indelibly marked her, and if she couldn't get over them, she might lose the best thing that ever happened to her.

TJ. He stood, his eyes dark and jawline tight. She'd pushed him but she'd needed to. She'd needed to test them because she'd known so fully that they would break. And he'd done it. He'd said the words, though they hadn't been cruel. They'd been what she'd feared most of all. That she wasn't worth the trouble. That she was difficult and hard to love.

But he was still here. He was staring her down like an angry Dom who meant every word he'd said.

She needed that Dom every bit as much as she needed the sweet boy who'd been her friend for years. She accepted that now. Maybe the sweet boy wouldn't be able to handle her damage, but the man in front of her could, and that meant they might be okay.

She sniffled, emotion running wild through her. "I didn't defend you."

His head shook slightly. "I don't care, Lou. I don't care about what anyone thinks of me except you, and your time is running out. If you force me to spank you, you won't be able to sit tomorrow, I promise you. You'll feel my hand on your ass for the next couple of days. I would so rather punish you in another way."

A shiver went up her spine that had nothing to do with fear. Honestly, the thought of the spanking did something for her. Feeling his hand on her skin for days wasn't the deterrent he thought it was. Or maybe he knew her and this was a mind fuck.

And still, she rather thought it would be better for him if she followed his orders. If she needed the big bad Dom, maybe he needed her unquestioning submission from time to time. What if he was telling her the truth and he didn't care about mistakes made in the past, didn't give a damn what anyone thought of him. Only needed her.

She kicked out of her flats and shoved her slacks down, cool air hitting her skin and contrasting with the sun that streamed in from the big windows that formed the walls of her lab. She'd opened the screens when she'd come in and didn't think about closing them now. No one could see in, and even if they could, she didn't care in the moment.

In this moment all that mattered was being what he needed. The anxiety melted away as she fell to her knees and let her head fall submissively forward. He'd been right the night before. She hadn't truly wanted to play. She'd hoped he would fall on his knees and eat her pussy and she could hold parts of herself back from him.

That wasn't what either of them needed.

He'd tried to make a safe space for them, a place where they didn't have to worry about the past or the future, and she'd fought him because worry seemed to be the thing she did best. She'd done it because she'd been thinking of herself.

He wasn't a prize to be won or an object to pine after. She loved him, and it was fucking time to show him that. Even if they didn't work out. Even if somewhere down the line she lost him. Loss was inevitable, so she suddenly wanted to make that loss as big as it could be. Her mother had told her to live a big life. There was no big life without risk. She hated the word, but it was time to start using it.

She wished she had a bed in this monstrosity of a place. Some of the other labs had small cots for overnight experiments. She didn't do those, so she'd never seen the reason for it. However, looking at the big bulge in her Dom's jeans, she could see the appeal.

She rather thought she was about to get tossed over one of her chosen-for-their-aesthetics couches that dotted the space. They damn straight hadn't been made for rough sex with a big guy.

Lou dropped to her knees, hoping she could remember what she'd been taught. It had been over a year since she'd taken the class that allowed her membership to The Hideout. Normally when she let a Dom run a scene with her, there wasn't a lot of formality. Half the time she high fived them at the end.

This was serious. Everything about TJ was serious.

She let her head fall submissively forward and held herself still.

She heard TJ crossing over to her desk. The impulse to look up and see what he was doing was a whole damn mood, but she held back. Patience. He'd had it with her, and now it was her turn. She kept her eyes on the floor in front of her, listening as things shuffled around, and then finally she heard the thud of boots getting closer.

"You have some interesting things in here, Louisa." His well-worn boots moved into her field of vision. "I know you're the innovator, but I play in that field, too. I don't need my kit to handle you."

The edge of the ruler she used to draw straight lines came to rest under her chin. He lifted her head gently, bringing her eyes up so she could look at him.

This was a different version of the man she loved, and she understood why he'd held it back from her. This TJ was hungry, staring at her like he could devour her whole and make her beg for more. She needed him, and he needed the side of her she rarely accessed. The one who was confident enough to take care of her Dom.

She could do this. She could be what he needed.

"Do you have a safe word?" he asked.

"I don't need one. Not with you."

His lips curled up slightly. "I could make you regret those words. Do you think I'm not capable of it?"

"I don't think you're capable of willingly hurting me in a way I won't enjoy. I think the minute you realized it was more than I could handle, you would do anything you can to make it right for me."

"I'm glad you learned that, but we're still going to have a safe word because I don't want to be careful today. I want to let my beast out a bit, and that means you have to tell me if I'm going too far." That was when she realized there was electrical cord in his hands. He held it up. "Starting with this. Hands behind your back, spine straight. I want your tits thrust out for me, and tell me your safe word for the day."

"Ridiculous." That could be her word because she was getting ridiculously turned on. He was going to tie her up, make her vulnerable. Arousal shot through her at the thought. This was a place only he could take her to, and she couldn't wait to be there again. It was frightening, but that was part of the sensation. She got to experience it all because he was safe.

Though he didn't feel safe when he wrapped the cord around her wrists. He bound her tight, and then she felt the edge of the ruler against her backside, reminding her she was completely naked, the afternoon light streaming into the office.

She held her breath as he scraped the ruler over her skin, teasing her, and then when she thought he was through, a loud slap filled the air and she gasped as the little pain bloomed over her. Another slap to the other cheek made her pussy clench. She was going to make a mess, but she rather thought he wouldn't like the fact that she was thinking about that. It didn't matter. It was a problem for not-submissive sex doll Lou.

And suddenly that was okay because that near future her would handle the cleanup perfectly.

How was it only now hitting her that she could count on herself, that the future wasn't something to fear but to explore, to be ready for because she had a good base. Those early years could be overwritten with love and friendship and stability.

"Are you with me, Lou? Where's that big brain of yours?"

"Switching off, Sir. It's not my brain's time. It's my body's, and that seems to belong to you."

"It's good that you understand that, but you should know the big brain is mine, too," TJ insisted. "I'm a greedy bastard. I want all of you. I'll be happy to share you with the world, but in this space, I don't share you at all. In this space, you're all mine, every delicious inch of you. Every idea you have. Every piece of your soul."

The words were a balm to that soul he seemed to want. "Yes, Sir. And you're mine."

A hand came up, circling her neck from behind. TJ's callused hand was so big he could grasp her neck fully. "What part of me is yours?"

"Every part, Sir. The boy and the soldier and the Dom. The friend. The lover. I want all of it."

"Is there a specific part you would like, Louisa?"

Her name came out of his mouth like a filthy promise. It made her nipples hard and core heat up. She could feel how wet and hot he was making her. And she knew exactly what he wanted. He hadn't allowed her to take care of him. Nope. He'd been way too interested in blowing her mind, but she wanted this intimacy between them, wanted to know she could make her Dom lose his cool, too "I want your cock, Sir. I want it in my mouth. I want to wrap my lips around it and lap up everything you give me."

He cursed behind her, and his hand fell away. "I'm not going to make it easy on you."

"Well, you've already taken away my hands. I'd like them back because I want to stroke your cock. I want to roll those big balls in the palm of my hand while you fuck my throat." She didn't normally use that word, but it felt right.

"There she is. There's my dirty girl." He ran the edge of the ruler up her spine, making her sit up straighter, her breasts thrusting out. "When you decide to do something, you go all in. I always knew if I could get you invested in this lifestyle, I would have the sweetest, nastiest little sub in the world. You're going to let me do dirty things to you, aren't you, baby?"

"Yes." She would pretty much let him do anything. "I'm not going to hold back on you when it comes to this. I want this."

"You know if I have this, I'll likely have you. You won't be able to hold yourself back, and I know deep down that you love me. At least I think so."

"I know, but I need the time." Despite the revelations, she couldn't make the decision in that moment, couldn't do more than live in this space and let herself be. That was a decision for future Lou, too.

"I'll give it to you," he vowed. "But you're going to give me everything today." He moved around to her front, kneeling down and fishing into his pocket. He brought out a binder clip, the kind she used to keep reports together.

What the hell was he planning on doing with that? He played with it for a moment, forcing it open so there was a bit of give to it.

"Uhm, I thought we were going to let me give you a blow job." Maybe he forgot.

The wicked look in his eyes told her he hadn't. "We'll get there. But first I need to make my toy look even prettier. Lean back."

She bit her bottom lip, as she suspected where he was planning to put that thing and that he likely had a matching one in those pockets of his. "Maybe we should talk."

"Maybe I should slap your pussy with this ruler."

Lou leaned back.

A savage grin crossed her Dom's face, lighting him up in a way that made Lou's blood pound. He was the sexiest man in the world, and he was hers if she was brave enough to take him. "It's good to know you have some self-preservation skills. Don't worry. This won't hurt." He leaned over and let his hand brush against her right breast, stopping to play with the nipple. He caught it between his thumb and forefinger, rolling it. "Much."

He slid the clamp over her and it bit into her flesh, making her squirm. He ignored her discomfort and moved to her left breast, giving it the same rough-and-tumble treatment.

It hurt, and it woke something inside her because she liked the pain. The pain freed some piece of her that had been bound up and shoved away. The piece that didn't fit into the life she'd been supposed to lead.

She'd made the decision to allow that side of herself out when she'd given up her cushy professorship to work for the Agency, but now that part still inside came roaring to life. She was bowed back, her body on display for him, and she suddenly felt so fucking powerful.

This was a choice. She chose to explore this with him, to let herself figure out what worked and what didn't, and to not flinch from any of it. This was her right. Her sexuality wasn't something to push to the side. It was one of the pillars of who she was, as much as her smarts or her loyalty.

And she wanted to give it all to him, to the only man who could bring this out of her.

"You got a third one in there, TJ?"

His eyes narrowed. "You think you can handle it, sub? You kind of sound like you want me to slip a clamp on your clitoris. Is that what you want? You want your Dom to clamp your clit and fuck your mouth?"

"Yes." She'd never been more sure of anything. Even as she could feel her nipples pulsing with the clamps, she wanted it on her clit, wanted to show him how savage she could be. She could be enough for him. Enough for her.

He reached in and pulled out a small clamp. "I wasn't sure if I would use it, but I'm ready for you. Hold still." He leaned in and slid the cold clamp over her hot flesh. "You're so fucking wet, baby."

She'd never been so wet, so ready for something that she knew was going to take a while. Her Dom seemed determined to make this torture session last. Old TJ would have thrown her over the couch and had his way with her.

No. Not old TJ. The TJ in her head, the perfect TJ her twelve-year-old self had loved.

She let him go in that moment because the real TJ was a magnificent mystery, and she wanted to solve him.

He pinched her clit, making her eyes close as pain and pleasure warred in her veins. It was a fight she couldn't possibly lose because both sensations were out of this world. And then her breath heaved as he clamped her, trapping her clit with the binder.

"And you taste so fucking good." TJ sat back, licking his fingers as he stared at her, his eyes dark and hot with desire. He rose and dragged his shirt over his head, revealing that magnificent chest of his. He tossed it aside and undid the fly of his jeans. "You look ready now."

She wanted to argue with him, to tell him she'd always been ready, but that was pure stubbornness. She hadn't been. If he'd tried to clamp her breasts a few years before she would have pushed back, not eagerly accepted the experience. The same way she would have pushed back on any thought of giving up making all her own decisions. She was ready for compromise now. For partnership. "I am, Sir."

She thanked Kala for all the abs workouts because it took a surprising amount of strength and balance to lift herself up and get into position to take his cock in her mouth. She managed it without a protest, rising gracefully even as the clamps did their job, forcing her focus on them.

He grinned, a sign that her cuddly TJ was still in there. "That was sexy, Lou."

She winked at him because she liked thinking of her badass self as sexy. Hopefully when she was his mom's age she could still kill a man with the strength of her thighs. Goals. "I'm glad you think so, Sir. Now show me. You know you've never let me stare at your cock. It's not fair because you stare at me a lot."

"I need my staring time," he acknowledged, "but I'm a fair man. You can stare all you like."

He shoved his jeans down, freeing his cock. It was a thing of beauty. Lou sat there, her body aching with need, and took him in. Every inch of him was precious. She really did want to take him in her hands, but that wasn't happening now.

TJ moved in, invading her space and looming over her. His hand found her hair, sinking in and twisting lightly. She could feel him everywhere. Her ass still stung slightly from the slaps he'd given her. His "rope" was wrapped around her wrists, and she definitely couldn't ignore what he'd done to her nipples and clit. He was everywhere, and that was probably his point. He surrounded her with his will and dominance, and she gave him her submission.

All in all, not a bad exchange.

"Take me," he demanded.

She could do that. She felt her whole body go on full alert as she leaned forward, ready to make her Dom happy.

* * * *

She looked like his every fucking wet dream. Not merely because she was gorgeous and naked and wearing his marks, but because she was Lou. She was the right one. The only one.

And she was so beautifully trussed up and ready for him. Something had changed when she'd shed her clothes this time. She was always so worried, her mind always thinking, but this time he'd watched as she'd found her power.

It was so hot on her.

He kept a hand on her hair. The other stroked his cock, though he didn't need to. He was pretty much as hard as he could get and had been since the moment he'd realized she was going to take off her clothes. He'd gone from the fucking depths of despair to not being able to think because all the blood in his body was in his cock.

Her tongue came out, swiping over his cockhead and making him bite back a groan. He wouldn't be the Dom he wanted to be if he immediately came all over her face. There would be time for nasty quickies later on, but now he needed to make this last and make it meaningful for them both.

Watching his big dick disappear behind those lips of hers wasn't helping. He could feel his balls threatening to draw up and wondered how they would feel in Lou's soft hands. "You're killing me, baby."

"Not my plan."

He loved the sass she seemed to have found since she'd joined the Agency. The confidence she'd developed was beyond sexy. It was everything.

They could make this work.

He held himself still as she explored his cock with her tongue, sending darts of heat all through his system. She rubbed her tongue along the underside of his head until he was sure he wouldn't be able to take another breath. All the while she watched him, her brown eyes shining with desire and power.

"Yes, baby. You're the one in control and you know it. We can pretend, but it's always you," he whispered.

She responded by sucking his cockhead past her lips.

Damn, but he'd always known she would be good. Lou was good at anything she set her mind to. If she wanted to make him crazy in a sexual fashion, he should be ready to lose his mind.

He tightened his hold on her hair, well aware he was also acting as a balance to her somewhat precarious position. The binder clips shook as she moved, and he wondered what the one on her clit was doing. Fuck, Louisa Ward had a clamp on her clit and he'd put it there. He'd take it off, too, and show her how nice that could be.

He could show her what he knew, and they could learn everything else together. Like they should. If he could convince her.

He would convince her. Starting now. "Take me deep."

He held her hair and pressed his hips forward, forcing his cock into her mouth. She seemed to struggle for a moment, but that kind of did something for him, too. Her body moved as she settled her mouth around him, sending heat shooting through him.

He was almost certain that she wasn't thinking about anything but him now, anything but the two of them. She needed this, and he would convince her that he was the only man in the world who could give it to her. He would be fucking ruthless.

"Your mouth feels like heaven. Just like that."

Lou was a people pleaser. She needed praise, thrived on it, and he planned to give it to her.

Her tongue fought to swirl around his cock, the pleasure threatening to drown him. He pulled out to the edge of her mouth, letting her take a breath before shoving inside again. "That's right, baby. I'm going to do this to your pussy in a couple of minutes. I'm going to fill you up, and I'm not going to hide in some privacy room the next time we go to the club. Those fuckers won't question my rights to you once they've watched me tie your gorgeous body up and play with you all night. They'll back off or I'll make them."

He toyed with her hair, feeling her gasp when he gave her a hard tug, the sound resounding over his cock and making his whole body tighten.

He couldn't handle it. If she kept going, he would come straight down her throat, and he wanted more. This was all about helping Lou focus, and swallowing him down would only work for him. He needed to overload her with a killer orgasm, and he knew how to do it.

He pulled back, loving how swollen her lips looked from taking him deep. She looked like sex and sin and the sweetest treat he'd ever been offered.

"I want to finish," she said with a rare pout. His Lou never pouted. She was practical and reasonable, and he kind of loved that she was doing it now.

How could they have any real fun if she was never a brat?

He reached down and twisted one of the clamps, sending a shudder through her body. "My way, Louisa. Today is my way, and I want to play with these toys I put on your body. Did you think they're there for decorative purposes?"

"I don't know. I've seen it, but I didn't know how it would make me feel," she admitted.

"How does it make you feel?"

"Like you're everywhere. Touching me everywhere. Playing with me. Like I belong to you."

Then they were doing their jobs. "You do belong to me. Maybe not outside of this space, but in here, you're fucking mine, and that means you obey me. Get on your feet."

Her eyes widened. "I don't know that I can do that."

"I'm going to talk to Zach about your training. Since I'll be working with you for a while, maybe I can take it over. We'll start with cardio and flexibility."

"You are an evil man." Her jaw firmed stubbornly, and she managed to bring one knee up before she gasped. "Oh, I can feel it."

He bet she could. "It'll be the best two hours of your day, Lou. I promise. We're going to weight train."

She shoved herself off the floor. It wasn't the most graceful move but she did it, proving how far she would go to avoid a workout.

She didn't know it, but that was coming. Zach was too easy on her. If she was going to be risking her life, TJ would make sure she was as strong as she could be.

She was his whole fucking world.

He kicked out of his shoes and ditched his jeans and boxers so he was as naked as she was. Though not anywhere near as pretty. He stared at her breasts, the nipples a deep ruby red. “Excellent. We’ll work on balance, too. You’ll be able to rise from any position I put you into.”

“TJ,” she began with a frown.

He wasn’t arguing with her. He simply moved in, backing her up against the tall workspace. Her head tilted up as her ass hit the edge of the desk. His chest brushed against hers, the clamps cool against his skin. She squirmed, trying to find a comfortable position. He didn’t want her comfortable.

He rubbed his cock against her belly as he lowered his lips to hers. Her mouth opened, and he took the invitation to devour her. His tongue swept over that plump bottom lip of hers before invading her mouth. He stroked inside, gliding along her tongue until he could feel his cock pulsing and desperate. That was the moment he leaned back, picked her up, and set her pretty ass on the edge of the desk. He spread her legs and stared down at the glorious ruby red jewel of her clit.

“This has to be uncomfortable, baby,” he cooed.

“I actually don’t feel it anymore. Is that okay?”

Not at all. It meant his timing was going to be perfect. He spread her legs wide and toyed with the small clamp he’d placed on her, enjoying how she gasped and squirmed as he twisted the handles.

“Okay, I can feel that,” she managed to say.

“How about this?” He twisted the clamp, opening it and pulling it off.

She practically screamed, but before she could get the outraged sound out, he had his mouth on her, his tongue laving her clit with the affection it desperately needed. He brushed his tongue over and over her, feeling her body shake beneath his. Her feet found his broad shoulders and her hips came up, offering her whole core to him. He would take it. He settled into eating her pussy with abandon right there on the desk where she researched and innovated. Now when she sat here she would remember what it meant to have his face in her pussy.

Her body shook as arousal coated TJ's tongue, and she called out his name as she came.

Then it was his turn. He picked her up again, her body completely limp in his arms as he carried her across the room to one of the big leather couches she kept there. Many a time he'd spent sitting on that damn couch while she worked. Never again. Not that he wouldn't let her work, but only after he'd fucked her thoroughly and she was in a calm headspace. Then he would sit on the couch and wait for her.

He set her on her feet and released her hands. "Bend over. Hold on to the back of the couch and spread your legs."

Her head fell forward as she complied.

He found his jeans and ripped open the condom he'd put in his pocket because he was nothing if not an optimist. He rolled it on and gripped her hips, bringing his cock to her pussy and filling her with one hard thrust.

"You feel so good," he groaned. And then he was off. He didn't have to go easy on her. She was so fucking wet, she could take everything he gave her. He thrust in and dragged his cock back out, angling up to find her sweet spot. He let his hands play with the clamps on her nipples, loving every moan that escaped from her mouth.

When her whole body seemed to tighten around him, he couldn't hold out a second longer. He held himself against her, giving up everything he had.

A blissful peace replaced the perfection of that orgasm, and he hauled her up so he hugged her from behind. "Better, baby?"

Her head fell against his shoulder. "So much better. But now I get the need for a shower in here. I'll have to go down to the locker room to clean up."

She didn't need to clean up at all. Not yet. "I'll go down with you later and sneak in and we can do it in the shower. After you have lunch and get some work done. You smell perfect to me."

The sweetest smile hit her face, and she looked a little drugged. Like she might get addicted to him. He hoped so because he was helplessly addicted to her. "You're going to cause a scandal."

Oh, he could show her a scandal. He was about to start round two when a sound from outside the office stopped him in his tracks.

"Don't force that door open," a deep voice said. "I'm not joking, brother. I don't want to see what they are doing behind that door. It's not some science experiment."

"How can you tell? You know they could be in trouble in there," another voice.

Damn it. His dad and uncle were here. "Go away."

Lou winced, biting her bottom lip as she moved. She was so fucking pretty with ruby red nipples. He hadn't sucked on them enough yet. He needed to ease the clamps off and suck on her pretty nipples until she came again. "What are they doing here?"

She'd whispered, but he'd called out in a strong voice.

"We can't, sweetie." And his day was complete because that was his mom. If his mom wasn't willing to leave him alone, it was serious. His dad and uncle could be overly dramatic, but his mom was super solid.

He groaned and forced himself up. "I'm sorry, baby. We're going to have to get dressed."

Lou pouted and he kissed her.

"Yes, dressed. Dressed is best," his uncle shouted. "I'm too old for this shit."

Except he knew the man wasn't since he paraded his wife around a couple of times a week at his sex club. "You're not old. You're soft."

He heard his dad bark out a laugh.

"I'll show you soft, kid," his uncle said, a hint of menace in his tone.

Luckily he knew how to handle that old man. "Give me a second. I need to take the clamps off."

"TJ," Lou hissed.

"Fuck me," his uncle groaned.

And TJ wished they could spend the afternoon cuddling, but it looked like the world was pushing its way back in.

Chapter Seventeen

Lou felt oddly calm as she opened her laptop and connected to the screen. The big boss was here, and so were TJ's parents. It had been that kind of day. Once she'd longed for a large family. Careful what you wish for…

Of course if she'd stayed in bed with TJ this morning, she would only have been forced to see her dad, and he was easily handled with cheesecake.

"Is this…" Big Tag began as he looked down at the couch closest to the screen she'd pulled down.

Theo and Erin had already taken seats on the couch, but Big Tag was staring at it like it might bite him.

"Where I just fucked my sub? Is that what you're asking?" TJ was a menace. He seemed determined to break his uncle.

Lou groaned and decided to put the man out of his misery. "We didn't do it on the couch. You can sit down."

Big Tag tossed his body on the couch beside his brother. "Excellent."

TJ gave her a smirk, letting her know he approved of the half-truth.

Her whole body hummed with satisfaction, and yet there was still a place inside her that couldn't fully submit to joy.

She settled her glasses on her nose as she regarded the three parental units currently occupying the couch where she'd absolutely gotten railed. Just not on the actual seat. They'd used it more as a balance. "Is there a reason my parents weren't invited to this… I'm not sure what this is."

She did not want to have to do this twice. Luckily she'd set some programs running this morning after the breakfast meeting, and it looked like they were ready. Of course the fact that she couldn't definitively prove that TJ was innocent had made her anxious.

Maybe that's why he's doing it. Maybe he's pretending to be into you so you'll find the evidence to keep him out of Agency jail.

Lou sighed. That voice was still there. Might always be.

Big Tag gestured his brother's way. "Theo has clearance. He's done some work for Drake over the years, so he's got the go ahead to sit in on meetings. Erin's scary enough that no one will question it."

"And I'll tell Boomer and Daphne whatever I find out," Erin said with a nod that let everyone know she did not care. "We're here because the Brits told us they turned over their intel, and we thought you would have already gone over it."

"Well, we thought that, but then we found out you discovered boys and now you're ruined," Big Tag quipped.

Erin frowned his way. "You sound like the grandmother from a Regency romance. You do know your daughters have had…"

Big Tag shook his head. "Nope. They are perfect angels who would never even consider having sexual relations. Tasha and Dare are committed to celibacy."

TJ snorted and moved in behind her, wrapping an arm around her waist. "Leave the old guy his delusions."

"They aren't delusions. He's literally been inside the sex club they play at. He's being…he's being Big Tag." She couldn't call the man an ass. He'd been too good to her over the years, and she knew exactly what he was doing. She'd seen him do it to a lot of people. People who usually ended up as happy couples. "He's also trying to push me into your arms. If he acts like a weirdo, it gives us a villain we can unite against. I assure you he would be the first one cheering a wedding."

"Hah, she's got you down, brother," Theo said.

"Well, I hope if there's a wedding, they'll start having sex in not-public places," Big Tag explained.

TJ didn't seem to care that he was playing right into his uncle's hand. He leaned forward and kissed her earlobe, his voice going low. "Are your nipples sore, baby? I can get rid of these guys."

She had the sudden insight that TJ getting rid of them would not necessarily lead to her getting back to work. And did he have to mention her nipples? Which were absolutely sore, but in a weirdly pleasant way. It was also kind of odd that she felt way more focused with TJ so close to her. When he touched her, she couldn't work up the will to question him. "They'll just come back."

"Not if we barricade the door," he whispered.

"TJ, let her work. You know this is all about you," his mother pointed out. "She's trying to figure out who's after you. Give her some room."

"She doesn't need room," TJ shot back. "Go on, baby. Tell them what you've found."

"Well, the photo is real," she announced.

"But I didn't meet with an arms dealer," TJ insisted. "I met with my team leader and a couple of my Army buddies."

Lou managed to get the picture in question on the screen. "I've verified this photograph, but it proves nothing. I'd like to know who the man with him is."

"It's Zach," Erin said, squinting. "I bought him that jacket for Christmas. I got his name for Secret Santa."

TJ's head came up, and he was suddenly interested in something other than how her nipples felt. "It's a nondescript black jacket. How can you tell?"

His mom's red hair shook. "Because this is what I do. I look at details and search for patterns. Do you honestly not remember walking around Berlin with this guy?"

TJ sighed. "No. I don't remember every second of every day. I probably had a couple of beers. It's what we do in our off time. It's freaking Germany. Do you remember every second of every day?"

Theo shook his head like that was a mistake.

"Yes," TJ's mom replied.

"Well, some of us have normal memories. Now, what I do

remember is that Zach wasn't in Berlin at the time." TJ stepped back, and Lou realized she kind of liked having an emotional support soldier while she worked. She was a little cold now.

"It's not Zach. He's not tall enough." Lou had already gone through these scenarios. "Although he was in Europe. We all were, but in Prague."

"And there's a high-speed rail that could get him from Prague to Berlin in four hours," Big Tag pointed out and held up a hand. "Not that I'm saying it's him. I believe you on the height. But that is a nondescript jacket, and they've done what they could to hide their face."

"Are we thinking this is a setup?" Theo asked.

"It's obviously a setup." Lou clicked a couple of keys that brought up the receipts for the bank account with TJ's name on it.

TJ's eyes went wide. "What is that? I don't have an account like that. I barely have a regular account."

"Well, this one was set up right before The Jester closed a sale of small arms in Bulgaria. Sofia, to be precise, and while the arms were small, the shipment was not," Lou pointed out. "The payment was made in crypto."

Erin snorted. "Like he knows how to deal with crypto. Whoever did this didn't think the plan through."

"I assure you this kind of proof will work on agencies that don't know him." Big Tag had gotten serious. "Someone has been setting TJ up for quite a while. I wonder who that could be."

TJ shrugged. "I have no idea. I kind of thought most people liked me."

"Sure. All the people you screwed over to get Lou probably think you're a great guy," Big Tag said.

Erin winced. "I hadn't thought of that, but how would they be able to track him around Europe?"

Lou had some theories, but she didn't want to put them out there yet since they led back to the person who set this all up using TJ to screw over someone else. She needed proof before making that accusation since it could hurt one of the Taggart sisters. "I don't think this is someone who is so angry they lost my love that they're willing to hack into classified systems."

"I would," TJ assured her. "I mean I would totally have Kala do it, but I would be super upset if I had you and lost you. What's that professor doing?"

She barely managed to not roll her eyes. "The last I heard he was getting married, so he's probably not trying to figure out how to screw you over. Besides, you said you didn't do anything to him."

TJ nodded way too fast. "That's right. Because he seemed like he would be good for you. But what about Dennis? He's back in your life now."

Again with the need to roll her eyes. "Sure. He's so desperate he's coming after you over ten years later."

"The best revenge is served cold and years after anyone would be looking for it," Theo said. "What does this guy do?"

She winced because this fact wasn't going to help her case. "He's in banking."

Erin sat up. "So he would know how to move crypto around."

"But I seriously doubt he would know how to track a Special Forces soldier," Lou argued. "He would have to have serious contacts."

"If it's him, then you definitely aren't seeing him again," TJ said, arms crossed over his chest.

"Wait, she's still dating after what she did with you on this couch?" Erin asked. "Son, we need to talk about your technique."

Big Tag shook his head. "Lou said they didn't do it on the couch."

"They obviously did it on the couch," his brother shot back.

"It's not Dennis." Lou could only deal with one Taggart at a time, and in this case TJ had her attention.

"You don't think it's pure coincidence that he comes back into your life at the same moment someone is trying to set me up to take a fall?" TJ returned, his eyes steady on her.

She didn't see the logic behind it. "What does he get out of it?"

"Revenge." TJ obviously did.

"Brother, if you can't smell sex, then we need to get you to a doctor," Theo was saying. "Isn't loss of smell a sign of a stroke?"

"No, it is not," Erin replied, but she was watching Ian and Theo with a grin on her face like she lived for this.

Which she did. "We did it on the back of the couch." She turned to TJ. "Aren't you forgetting that there were a couple of people on your team who didn't like you at all?"

She didn't want to get into this, but she didn't think spending time checking into Dennis Sims would be a good use of resources. And why Zach? It was too much of a coincidence that the person walking with TJ was wearing an identical jacket to one Zach owned.

Who would know he wore that jacket? Not Dennis Sims.

"The only people who didn't like me are dead because Kala killed them," TJ replied.

"The back of the freaking couch counts, Louisa Ward." Big Tag was on his feet and staring her down with his best mad-dad expression. It was one she knew well.

"No lady parts touched the couch," Lou argued.

"Well, none today," Erin said with a nod.

"And just because someone is dead doesn't mean the plans they put in motion before they died… Wait, what does that mean?" Lou frowned as she remembered the reception she'd had up here because there was a lovely view and Drew Lawless threw an amazing holiday party that he invited the MT group to every year. "Whose lady parts would touch my pristine couch where I sit every day?"

TJ was shaking his head like it was his damn job.

"None ever," Erin agreed with the confidence of a woman who knew how to lie.

"On my couch?" Lou had mooned over TJ on that couch. His parents shouldn't be livening up their long-term marriage on it. It didn't feel fair.

"I'm pretty sure Kala and Cooper almost did it there," TJ admitted. "But then she got mad and punched him in the face."

"Good for Kala," Big Tag said.

Erin threw him a nasty look. "Yeah, because it's so healthy."

Another thought hit her. "I left Tasha in here when we were working a couple of weeks ago, and when I got back Dare was here. But it was only a couple of minutes."

"And that is all they need," Theo said with a sigh.

She didn't want to know. She was calling the cleaning crew. Big Tag was pacing like a lion in a cage, and if she didn't take control, this meeting would devolve. "It doesn't matter." It was natural. Well, natural for the people in her family. Actually, when she thought about it, bringing anyone else in would be problematic.

She probably should stay with TJ because at least she wouldn't have to explain his uncle to someone new. "I'll send you everything I have so far. And I'm pretty sure I found something on the files Kala managed to get out. It's what we thought it was."

Big Tag seemed to get serious. "They taped his interrogation?"

She'd spent a couple of hours this morning listening to them torture TJ. "Yes."

Erin's jaw tightened. "I'd like to hear it."

"Mom, there's nothing on there that would help," TJ countered. "It's torture and me screaming when I couldn't hold it in. Also, there's a point where I kind of threw you under the bus. They basically told me they would go after you or Devi or Lou. I pulled a whole 'not my sweet, elderly mom' thing."

Erin stood and crossed the space between her and her son, putting her hands on his cheeks. "You should always send them my way because I am your mother and I will slay every monster for you."

Tears pricked Lou's eyes because Erin was a good foot shorter than her son and he weighed a hundred pounds more, and Erin meant every word. She would stand between her son and whatever came his way. The way Lou's mom would.

The way Lou would.

It didn't matter. The revelation came upon her suddenly. She loved TJ and she always would. She wasn't sure why. Maybe it had been his sweet smile combined with his tender heart when he was a boy. Maybe it was the friendship they'd formed. It didn't matter. Her love wasn't selfish, and she made it less when she allowed it to be.

Theo joined his wife and son, forming a circle around TJ.

That was what she wanted. What she had, in a way. She was the center of that circle for her parents, and she was so grateful, but she wanted more. She wanted to be the strong arms protecting their kids.

She wanted everything with him, and she had to be brave enough to risk disaster.

"I love you guys, and this is one of those moments," TJ was saying. "One of those family moments that I'll never forget. But it's not complete."

For a moment she thought he was talking about the fact that his sister wasn't here, but then she realized he was looking at her. He opened his arms, giving her entry to the circle. "It's never complete without you, Lou."

"It's not, sweet girl," Erin agreed. "It hasn't been since he was twelve years old. He's a late bloomer. Forgive him."

Forgive him. Was there anything to forgive? They hadn't been ready if one of them hadn't been ready. If he'd given in, would they still be together or would they be broken like Kala and Cooper? Did she want that for them? No. She wanted this. She wanted inside that beautiful circle, and with tears blurring the world, she walked to them, letting them surround her utterly.

"We're going to get through this," Theo promised. "It's going to be okay."

"We can get through anything together," Erin added, and Lou felt her tighten her arms around her.

Then there was another body behind her as Big Tag joined in.

Theo looked up at his brother, a brow cocking.

"Hey, I like a good hug and this one is a long time coming," Big Tag said. "Now we have to find a way to fix the rest of them. Also, I like how TJ called his mom elderly and got this big hug out of it. Erin's mellowing."

"I'll get him back," Erin promised, but leaned her head against her son's.

"And we shouldn't forget that she killed that monster with the power of her thighs," Big Tag added.

Theo laughed and hugged them all tighter. "That's my baby."

"And you're mine," TJ whispered, nuzzling against her.

A sense of peace settled over Lou.

And she was buying a thigh master because she was going to be as fierce as her mother-in-law.

* * * *

TJ wanted the moment to never end because when Lou had joined them, it had felt like forever, but like all things, time moved on and his parents pulled away.

Damn, but he loved them.

He prayed that had been more than a moment for he and Lou.

She had to see how much love was waiting for her.

"All the familial love aside," his uncle began, his voice softer than before, "was there anything interesting on the tapes?"

Lou's eyes widened as though she was remembering they had a job to do. He wished they could go to lunch and sit with his parents and maybe afterward go over and hang out with hers. He would toss whatever ball Jayce was playing with this season—football, baseball, basketball—he could do any of them. He liked having a younger brother to mentor. They would have dinner with her parents and then he would take her home to their bed where his cousins would gag and pretend it was all too much for them, but he would know how happy they were he was finally able to properly take care of Lou.

Endless days of being with Lou was all he wanted. He'd proven himself, found a place where he belonged, and that was at her side.

Which he couldn't do if he was in prison.

She wiped at her eyes as she walked back to the desk where half an hour ago he'd eaten her pussy.

He moved in beside her, unable to stay away.

She gave him a watery smile and squeezed his hand before turning back to her laptop. He watched as she took a long breath and seemed to try to get professional again. But when he put a hand on her hip and got close, she didn't push him away.

He wanted to be in that moment where she'd joined them and he finally fucking felt complete.

"TJ mentioned he thought someone was behind the scenes," Lou began. "This isn't intel we got from MI6. This is what Kala and Cooper managed to get from the mercenary base. I've had the AI working on it for hours."

"You talking about the man who was interrogating TJ?" his father asked.

TJ shook his head, a chill coming over him where he'd been so warm mere moments before. "No. You should be able to hear him clearly. I didn't see his face, but he spoke openly to me. He was the guy giving instructions and leading the interrogation. Almost certainly German. There was someone else. I'm sure of it. He showed up late the first day I was held."

"I think the man who interrogated you is Huber," Lou said, her eyes on the screen. "The accent is German, and the tape even catches him ordering security around in German. If I could find another tape of his voice, I could confirm it, but that feels right to me. He absolutely acts like the boss until the second man shows up."

"I'll contact some friends of mine at Interpol," his uncle offered. "I suspect someone in that part of the world has taken him in for questioning. The good news is German police know how to document. If they have tapes, we can get them and put aside all doubt."

"You could reach out to Damon," his mom prompted.

His uncle's eyes narrowed. "I'm still not sure if I'm killing that son of his."

His dad sat back on the couch with a smile. "Oliver is still hitting on Charlotte. And Genny Rycroft."

"And me," his mom added. "The boy seems to have a thing for older women. Mommy issues."

His dad frowned and looked to his uncle. "Maybe we should talk…"

Nope. He wasn't letting the OGs devolve again. His dad and uncle could sit around for hours talking about how to torture a dude they didn't like, and they would throw around fantasies like drawing and quartering and evisceration. His mom would toss in her two cents. No way. "I'm almost certain there was someone else there, someone asking questions in the background. I know this sounds weird, but he was the one I was afraid of. I could barely hear the man, but something was wrong with him. He was…felt…I hate to use this word, but he felt evil."

"I think I've managed to isolate what TJ is talking about, but the language isn't German," Lou was saying. "I'm using a program I worked on with Tristan that identifies background sounds. The AI behind it studies the sound and attempts to reconstruct it if it can't simply amplify it. It couldn't in this case, so what we're going to hear isn't the actual voice but what the AI decided is its best guess about what's being said."

"Yes, we used it recently on a corporate case," his mother explained. "We couldn't use it in court, but it gave us the right account numbers to prove the CEO was stealing from the shareholders. It's a good piece of work, babe."

Lou's lips curled up. Praise. She flourished in it.

He wanted to make sure he understood. "So the computer can pick up stuff the human ear can't hear."

She nodded his way. "Yep. It's all there on the tape in some capacity, but at a level we can't make out. The AI can usually identify what it is. In this case, I've isolated what it thinks is a voice, and from there it uses logic and what it can hear to extrapolate what's being said. In other cases, it would simply tell me what it thinks the sound is. Like this one."

She hit a button, and he heard the sizzle of the taser coming on. Then an artificial voice came over the speakers.

This is the sound of some dude getting hit by a taser, and I don't think that was the way he planned his day.

"Sorry," Lou said, flushing slightly. "Tris programmed the AI to sound like a surfer guy. He thought it was funny."

"It's annoying, and that was his point," his uncle said. "He is so like his father."

"Well, it's right. I did not put get tortured via cattle prod on my daily schedule, so that point goes to surfer guy," TJ snarked. "What does it think that voice said?"

"This is what I was able to pull off the original recording." Lou pressed some more keys and then something like scratchy humming came out. "That's the isolated sound. If you listen closely, you can hear a word every now and then."

His mom nodded. "It's not English."

"No, it's not," Lou agreed. "It's not German either. Here's what the AI came up with."

Demande-lui s'il connait le fabricant de bombes.

"Fuck," his uncle cursed. "It's French. He wants to know if TJ knows who the bombmaker is."

Lou nodded. "That was my translation as well. I also picked up on this."

Tue-le s'il ne sait rien. Ça pourrait être un piège. Il pourrait être envoyé par le Jester.

"He says the whole thing could be a trick from The Jester and to kill TJ," Lou announced.

His uncle nodded. "That's what I got, too."

Lou took a long breath as though bracing herself. "This is the one I'm worried about. We need to remember that the AI isn't always right. It's making a best guess."

TJ felt his whole body tighten. "What is it, Lou?"

She shook her head. "It's not about you, babe."

The *babe* totally made his heart warm even as she hit the button and the AI spoke again.

Comment sais-tu que c'est la bonne personne ? Je ne crois pas qu'il soit proche du fabricant de bombes.

His uncle frowned. "He's looking for someone close to the bombmaker."

"There's more, but it's all along the same line. They argue about whether TJ is the one they were looking for. Whoever was behind Huber, he wanted to get to The Jester to get to the bombmaker. But the other guy thinks TJ should know the bombmaker personally if he's the one they're looking for. There's one place where he talks about finding the bombmaker before something in Nepal. The AI got confused," Lou admitted. "I actually think we should let the Brits hear it. They might make some sense of it."

His parents looked to his uncle as though seeking his counsel.

"I don't know if we should involve the Brits." His uncle looked grim. "And it's not about Oliver, the little shit. Despite the idiot-lothario thing he has going, he's Damon Knight's son, and I trust that family. Sami has a good head on her shoulders."

"But they're working with Ben Parker." TJ understood exactly what his uncle was saying. "And if he hears someone is speaking French in the background, looking for this bombmaker, his brain is going to one place."

Emmanuel Huisman.

"Can we consider that he might be right and this person we're listening to might be Huisman?" Lou asked. "He's speaking French. I wish I could hear more and figure out if the French he's speaking is proper or more Canadian, but the AI wasn't able to differentiate."

"As far as I can tell he wasn't in Germany that day," his mother said. "When I found out Parker was involved, I started looking. I've read those files and knew what Parker would think, so I looked into Huisman's movements for that last day. I can tell you he was in Montreal at a gallery opening at eight p.m. the night the team recovered TJ. So he would have to get to the airport and go straight from the Munich airport to Montreal, and still manage to make the gallery opening looking perfect in roughly eight hours. The flight time from Munich to Montreal is eight hours and twenty-five minutes. We were at least an hour from the nearest airport."

"Only if he flew directly from the airport," his dad mused. "If he had a private plane or a helo waiting, it could have been faster, and some of those new private jets are faster than you would suspect."

New technology was constantly pushing the boundaries of what was possible, and Huisman had the money to have that cutting-edge jet if he wanted one.

"It's still tight," his uncle allowed. "But it doesn't take him off the board. However, if the Canadian finds out, he won't look at anyone else. I'd like more time with what we have before Parker blows up and potentially goes after the doctor." He held up a hand Lou's way. "I'm not making a judgment call. I'm not saying he's clean. I'm saying I want time. Parker is a bomb that's set to go off. Look what he's already managed to do. He put our team in direct conflict with an MI6 team we should have a good working relationship with."

"It wasn't Ben's fault that we didn't know Damon Knight's team existed," Lou argued.

"I don't care about that. I understand what Knight was doing. I need more intel about Ben Parker, and I don't know that I can trust either of my daughters to get it," his uncle replied, a grim expression on his face. "Kenzie is half in love with the guy and Kala wants to murder him. I know. Kala wants to murder most people, but she really has it in for this guy."

"Kenzie will do her job," Lou assured him. "If you tell her to get the dirt on him, she'll do it."

"That's the problem, Lou. I don't want to hurt her that way." His uncle looked a bit weary, and he sat on the sex couch without a single protest. "I'm not sure this is going to work, and I have no idea how they'll handle failure."

Kala and Kenzie wouldn't handle it well. This was their dream, and they'd worked so hard to achieve it. Hell, it was Lou's, and he could see that now. He was pretty sure Cooper and Zach and Tris wouldn't be happy if they broke up the team.

"Have we considered sending Dare in?" TJ asked. "Parker seems like a lone wolf, but he took Dare's friendship seriously. I was on his detail during the Australian op. He made it clear he didn't want Dare hurt. If he could have gotten away with it, he wouldn't have ever let Dare know who he really was. Now that's not to say he wouldn't have walked away. I think Parker's a guy who always gets the job done, but he cared about Dare. He valued that friendship."

His uncle seemed to consider it. "That's an astute observation. Let's see where this goes."

"Has anyone considered the fact that our whispering man thinks someone is close to this bombmaker?" Lou asked. She bit her bottom lip. "He accuses Huber of getting the wrong guy. I think we have to consider that someone is setting up TJ in order to cover their own tracks."

"And that would mean it's someone close," his mother mused. "Maybe someone on his team or someone close to his team."

"Or someone close to our team," Lou said quietly. "I don't like the fact that someone was wearing a coat Erin bought for Zach in that picture. I worry they might be trying to set up more than TJ."

His uncle groaned. "Shit. Zach… There's a lot you don't know about Zach. I can't talk about it right now, but he has some connections that have always worried me."

TJ shook his head. "Zach wouldn't do this."

"I don't think so, either, but I have to consider that someone might be setting him up too, and for entirely different reasons," his uncle said. "I need to talk to Drake and do some research. Until then, you two stick together and watch yourselves until I get the Canadian back on a plane. Send me what you have and I'll try to figure out if I can trust MI6 with it." He stood and turned to TJ. "But you need to be ready to run if the time comes. If I lose control, they might try to take you into custody. The actual authorities will mean to question you, but…"

His uncle left the threat dangling. But in a holding cell, anything could happen. They'd already talked about getting rid of him once. If they thought he knew something and might talk, they would get rid of him fast.

All of this reeked of an inside job. Things were starting to happen around him, puzzle pieces flying about, waiting to be put together.

"I'll go wherever you tell me to." He wasn't going to put any of them in danger.

Even if it meant leaving Lou.

"I'll get everything to you," Lou promised. "And I'll work the logistics in case TJ needs a safe house.

"I'll be careful until we figure out what's going on," TJ promised. "And by *we*, I mean Lou. I'll be here getting her lattes and making sure she eats."

And relaxed.

"Then she's in good hands," his uncle said. "Come on, brother. Let's get a couple of beers and let the kids handle this part. Theo, you can come, too."

His father snorted but he followed his uncle out, and after his mother hugged them both soundly, he was left alone with Lou.

She stared up at him as though memorizing his face. "You might have to run."

"It won't happen," he promised. "We're going to figure this out. I still think this is all one big hoax. I'm not saying there couldn't be a military contact to the bombmaker, but that doesn't mean someone's not fucking with me."

She shook her head as though she knew what he was about to say. "It's not Dennis."

"It could be Dennis." He wanted it to be Dennis. Real bad.

She sighed and leaned against him. "I'm going to prove to you it's not Dennis."

"How are you going to do that?" He kissed her hair and reveled in how close she was.

"We're going to a reunion," she announced.

He was sure that was going to be fun.

In an awful way.

Chapter Eighteen

"We're doing this, why?" Kala asked as they walked down the street toward the little bar in the middle of Deep Ellum. "Did we want to practice dodging bullets or drunk frat guys?"

Lou kept walking, though her bestie was right. It could be either. This wasn't the best part of town, but it also wasn't the weekend, and when she'd texted Dennis to ask where the group was meeting yesterday afternoon, he'd quickly sent her this address.

Along with a flurry of emojis that had made the veins in TJ's neck stand out. To his credit, he hadn't complained, merely tied her up and forced a plug up her ass and blown her mind in ways that had Kenzie and Kala calling a house meeting about loud sex.

TJ had been all about the plug the last couple of days. Just this morning he'd convinced her to sit through a whole meeting with the team with a small butt plug lodged in her even smaller rectum. While she'd listened to Kenzie discuss why Ben Parker couldn't possibly be a bad guy and Tasha talk about why her fiancé shouldn't be used to gather intel, she'd fought the urge to squirm.

And the urge to tell everyone that if TJ had to go on the run, she was going with him. Because she was. She'd spent the last day and a half sitting with the decision.

"I'm trying to show TJ that his past isn't coming back to haunt him," Lou explained. "And it might be fun to catch up."

"There is absolutely no one from high school that I feel the need to catch up with," Kala complained. "They were terrible then. They'll be terrible now. And I don't even get to tell everyone what an awesome job I have. I'm supposed to say I work for my dad. Everyone thought I would end up working for my dad because no other human on earth would hire me."

Lou bit back a laugh because that had been a whole thing.

"I was voted most likely to end up in prison," Zach countered. "It wasn't like in the yearbook or anything, but everyone knew."

They all stopped to look at Zach. He was the only member of the team they hadn't grown up with, so sometimes the man was a mystery.

He shrugged. "My family had some unsavory connections. The military did me some good. I'm just saying I wouldn't mind showing all those assholes I didn't end up doing twenty to life."

"I don't care how they're doing except for Dennis." TJ was thoroughly single-minded.

Cooper snorted from behind her. "Well, they can't be doing too well if they're meeting at this rattrap bar."

"Isn't The Hideout three blocks from here?" TJ pointed out.

"Hey, it's a city. Things change very quickly," Cooper said firmly. "You can walk a block or two and it's a whole new neighborhood."

It could be, but not in this case, though she wasn't about to point that out to Cooper. He had an irrationally inflated sense of the club's monetary worth. Probably because every dime he had was invested in it.

Though Lou loved it all the same, and she was looking forward to playing there tonight. Although she would probably have to take another plug. She'd tried to argue with TJ, but he'd started talking about exotic lubes, and she'd decided this was one of those times he was in charge and she needed to follow.

She was pretty sure he viewed watching endless episodes of *Selling Sunset* with his cousins as just as painful. Reality TV was TJ's butt plug, and he managed to smile through it.

"I'm up for either. The bullets or the frat guys, though I probably want to fight the latter." Zach moved beside Kala. "It's been a while since I got the old adrenaline up."

Kala rolled her eyes. "You're not getting anything up tonight. I know these assholes. They were awful in high school. They'll be awful now. Although you sometimes have terrible taste in women."

Lou stopped at the corner, waiting for the crosswalk light to turn green. She was sure Kala would plow through, but this was her mission. Her probably dumb mission that had exploded in a way only her team could manage. "You know you don't have to come along. I meant for this to be me and TJ. I'm not sure why the rest of you are here."

Oh, she knew. They were nosy. So nosy and always in her business, and they formed a chain. Kala had decided to go, so naturally Cooper had to tag along to make sure Kala didn't get like murdered or something or commit murder that wasn't sanctioned by the Agency, and then Zach hadn't had anything to do and Kenzie had argued that she should be allowed to come along, but Ben Parker was somewhere in Dallas with the Brits, and in a city of one point two million, they couldn't risk him running into two Ms. Magentas. Tasha had stayed behind with Kenzie to monitor a couple of things before they headed to the club, and Tristan was still doing whatever Tristan did. Otherwise, the gang would all be here.

"We don't have to be." Zach was dressed in jeans and a black T-shirt, looking like just another guy out to have some fun after work. "Personally, I think we should head to the club and have fun there instead. I'm with Lou. This dude is meaningless to what we're working on."

Kala frowned. "You're not the one who has to hide in the locker room because your twin is panting after a possibly deranged Canadian. God, even saying those words feels weird. What does a rabid beaver look like?"

Not like gorgeous Ben Parker. The signal finally changed, and Lou started across the street. The lights were beginning to come on, neon illuminating the way as evening turned to night.

She and TJ had never been to a club together. Not one that didn't have a bunch of St. Andrew's Crosses on the walls. They'd never been dancing and drinking. Instead, they'd sat at home and watched TV and talked and played games. They went to family gatherings together and walked the dogs.

They'd had a life together, just not the one TV shows told her equaled romance.

What if it had been a romance all along? A slow burn, take their time until it was right because they valued each other romance? She might never have the crazy passion of Tasha and Dare or the angsty pain of Kala and Cooper, but it was enough.

Their story was enough.

"People change." TJ strolled alongside her, his hand in hers. It felt right. It felt real this time. "They grow up. I'm actually a little excited to see what happened to some of them. But mostly I want to prove that Dennis Sims needs to be assassinated."

Lou groaned.

"Yes, that's why I'm here, buddy." Zach gave him a pat on the shoulder. "To make sure you don't kill anyone."

Kala gave Zach a smile. "I thought you were here to make sure we didn't have any fun."

Zach nodded. "That's what I said. Where is this place? I feel like we've been walking forever."

There wasn't a lot of parking in this part of town. "It's just around the corner, if my GPS is right."

"I'm starting a timer," Cooper announced. "We spend exactly one hour so Lou can convince TJ her old… What are we calling him? He wasn't a boyfriend."

"Her ex-asshole," Kala offered.

"We're giving her an hour to prove her ex-asshole isn't some weird criminal mastermind who's been plotting his revenge for years and then we're heading to the club," Cooper said. "Parker's coming in again tonight, and Dare's agreed to spend time with him. And yes, I know Tash is going to kill us all, but Dare's our best bet at figuring out if Parker's a rabid beaver."

Kala's grin was as bright as all the neon signs. "Thanks, bab…" She seemed to straighten up. "Thanks, man. I appreciate the support."

Kala had been all for the send Dare in plan, while Kenzie had taken Tasha's side. They'd agreed to let Dare decide, and he had not decided the way Tash had wanted him to. So they were arguing and Kenzie was on Tasha's side and the guys had sided with Dare, and Big Tag had opened a bottle of Scotch and Lou was feeling anxious again.

Because she might lose them all. Because her decision was made.

She looked down at her phone again, trying to figure out if they were going the right way.

"Hey, guys, keep smiling but I think we might have a tail," Zach said, his smile totally masking what was likely his awareness heightening. "The tall guy in black parked close to us, and he's stayed a block back since we started walking."

They huddled around Lou, looking for all the world like they were trying to figure out which way to go.

"I can circle around and get behind him," Kala offered.

Cooper sent her a Dom stare that would not work on Kala. Lou gave him credit, though. He kept trying. "Yeah, because he won't notice the pink-haired bombshell walking behind him. You kind of stand out, babe."

He placed an emphasis on the word Kala hadn't been able to say. Her nose wrinkled. "I can blend when I want to."

She actually could, but she didn't have time to tone it down.

"It's probably Parker," Zach said. "If I were him, I would set someone up to watch us. It's why we've been so careful not having Kala and Kenz together in public. We just need to be aware we're being watched. Act like nothing's out of the ordinary, and we move on. Kenzie's in lockdown until we can switch her out at the club."

But now they had a complication. "They'll see Kala go in and wonder why she enters a second time."

A groan came from Zach's throat. "All right, we'll go into this bar, and I'll call her. We need another plan. But I'm with Coop. One hour, tops. I hope you can soak in all the nostalgia you can in that sixty minutes because after we're all going into lockdown until the Canadian's gone."

Lou didn't mind the idea. She and TJ could curl up on the couch with Bud 2 and watch movies when they weren't working.

When she wasn't trying to find a way out of the trap someone was trying to put him in.

Of course, they would all be waiting to see if she could solve the mystery before the Agency dragged TJ in for questioning. Tried to, because they had plans in place to get him out before it could happen.

"Hey, it's going to be okay." TJ leaned in and brushed his lips over hers. "We'll cuddle up and catch up on some TV."

They were really in synch when she let them be. She gave him a half smile because even if they ran, there was no guarantee someone wouldn't catch them. "Sounds good. And I think we can cut down this alley and it should be on our right."

TJ's hand found hers as Kala took the lead.

Cooper joined Kala, and Zach took up their six.

She'd noticed that TJ had checked the back of his jeans where he'd loaded a holster with a semiautomatic before they'd left the office.

Maybe they should have stayed at home, but she needed him to take this seriously, and investigating Dennis Sims was going to waste time. Time they might not have.

Lou glanced behind her and sure enough, the man in black was there. He stopped at the entrance to the alleyway and seemed to make a decision, pausing briefly before walking past like he wasn't following them.

Yeah, she didn't believe that at all, and she noticed the man suddenly had a cell in his hand and he was talking as he walked away.

"All right," Zach said, moving them all along. "So we have to consider he's calling in reinforcements. We need to split up."

"Kala and I are going to sit in that coffee shop right there and keep watch on the door," Cooper offered. "You go in with TJ and Lou."

"*I* should go in with TJ and Lou," Kala argued, but her hand was already in Cooper's like she was always waiting for the moment she had an excuse to touch him.

"Nope." Cooper tugged on her hand. "I'm nervous, and we're going to watch for a little while and then head back to the office where we can do a clean exchange between you and Kenz. Have you thought about what could happen if Parker finds out the secret? We can't trust him, and someone following us feels like a play on his part. Guys, get whatever you need done and fast."

Zach nodded. "I agree. Actually, I think I'm going to call this." He had his cell phone out. "I'm going back to get the car, and I'll pick everyone up right here. Lou, do what you need to do in the next ten minutes because we're leaving."

How was she supposed to convince TJ in ten minutes? She put a hand on her hip and glared Zach's way. "You know you're not in charge of my private life, right?"

TJ frowned down at her. "I am. The same way you're in charge of mine, baby. I don't want to be here, but I'm following you mindlessly because I'm so crazy in love with you. I'm walking into a bar where you want to meet a dude who's trying to date you, and no, I don't honestly believe he's involved in this. I believe he got one look at you and wants a real taste. I'm still the idiot who's walking in there without any kind of claim on you. However, things have changed and we're going to follow the CO's orders."

"He is so not the CO," Kala argued.

But he was in this situation. Tasha ran the team on the intel side, while Zach was in charge of any military operations. Which meant TJ would look to Zach, and she kind of should, too. Zach was here to balance out the fact that the rest of the team had deep ties and history. Zach was supposed to look at things with an unbiased eye.

"Fine, one drink, and we'll meet you out here." Lou took TJ's hand. It would be smarter to leave with Zach, but she wanted to prove a point. She'd been quiet for days, letting the decision sink into her soul. She'd needed the time, but now she wondered what it had cost the man she loved.

"Fine," Kala said as she followed Cooper across the street. "I hate that Canadian. I was hoping to watch TJ eat Dennis's innards."

He wouldn't do that. He might play with them a little, but TJ was a gentleman.

Zach jogged away, and she could hear him talking to Tasha about trying to hook into the CCTV cameras in the area so they could get an ID on the man following them.

Things were happening much too fast.

One drink. A quick hello and sorry, I won't be seeing you again and they would be on their way, and they would face this unsure future together. Side by side.

She would never leave him again.

She pushed into the dark little bar. It wasn't the kind of place she thought Dennis would pick, but it had an odd ambiance to it, she supposed. It was quiet as she walked into the lobby. Soft music played through the place.

It was fairly empty. There was a bartender and a woman who could be a hostess, but she didn't see the crowd that should inhabit a place like this at this time of the evening. Deep Ellum was coming to life, with nightclubs and bars all filled to the brim, and it looked like no one was here.

Were they in the right place?

"I don't like this, Lou," TJ whispered.

"Hey, you're here." Dennis stepped out, and he was wearing a three-piece suit, his hair perfectly slicked back. He looked good if one liked the sleek, master-of-the-universe look.

She preferred the dressed down soldier at her side, and she always had. Since the day she'd met him, TJ had been the only boy in the world for her. Boy, guy, man. They were all TJ.

"Yeah, are we early?" Lou glanced into what appeared to be the pub-like bar. There were high-top tables and a dart board, TVs on the walls, though none were turned on.

Dennis frowned as he looked TJ over. "No, but I didn't expect a *we* at all. I thought you were coming alone. Is that Taggart?"

TJ dropped her hand and stepped to her side. "Hello, Dennis. It's good to see you again."

"It's unexpected to see you," Dennis replied somewhat sourly.

"I'm just an escort," TJ said, pulling his hand back when it was clear Dennis wasn't going to shake it. "Lou's job can lead to her needing bodyguard services from time to time. I can sit at the bar."

She rolled her eyes because this was probably the time his alpha Dom should take over. They needed to work on his instincts. "Babe, there's obviously something wrong here, and you're not my bodyguard. You're totally my boyfriend, and apparently Dennis didn't take my whole let's-be-friends thing seriously."

This whole thing felt like a setup to get her alone.

"Boyfriend?" Dennis and TJ managed to say the word at the same time, though one said it with a satisfied smile and the other's frown deepened.

Lou went on her toes so she could look TJ in the eyes. "Boyfriend, though I suspect that won't last long. My mom really is hankering for a wedding."

The smile on his face lit up the dark room. "Oh, I'll give her a wedding. Am I off the leash?"

She sighed. It wasn't how she'd planned to celebrate her almost engagement. "He didn't know about you."

TJ stepped in front of her, his shoulders suddenly straight. "No, but this isn't some reunion, is it, Dennis?"

Dennis's hands went to his hips, and he looked bereaved. "No. I thought it would be a nice way to get to know Louisa again."

"This is supposed to be a date?" TJ seemed to need confirmation.

He was never going to let her live this down.

"Yes," Dennis shot back. "Sue me. She's hot and smart, and I wanted a chance with her."

But Lou was getting a weird vibe.

She'd been kidnapped way too often lately, and it was starting to feel like that again.

"Why here?" Lou asked.

"It doesn't matter where," TJ argued. "He's an asshole."

Dennis ignored him. "A friend of a friend told me I could rent out this entire place for next to nothing. He'd heard I was looking for a cool date idea and gave me a call. I thought it would impress you." He glanced around. "I'll admit, I should have come to have a look at it before tonight. I thought it would be nicer than this."

TJ reached for her hand. "So someone called you at the last minute and you didn't think to question it? How well do you know this person?"

Dennis shrugged. "I don't really. He's a friend of a friend."

"Lou, we're leaving."

Yes, it was time to get out of here and regroup.

But when they turned, the door was blocked.

"I'm afraid you won't be going anywhere," a deep voice said. "*Schnappt sie euch*!"

German. Take them.

Lou prepared to fight for their lives.

* * * *

TJ tried to put Lou behind him, but they were quickly surrounded.

"Stay calm," he whispered.

They weren't alone, and these men had no reason to want him dead. They wanted him talking, and he was about to start a new career in storytelling. It wouldn't have to be long. Zach would show up. Though when they didn't appear, he would likely walk into the freaking bar and potentially get caught, too.

Lou put her back against his, and he could feel her shifting against him.

"Don't move, Ms. Ward. I know who you are now." The obvious boss stepped out of the shadows. He was in all black, a middle-aged man who kept up a gym routine and looked like he shopped at paramilitary stores. "I'm afraid I'm more of an arms dealer than someone who traffics in information, and that was where I made my mistake. You're an interesting partner for someone like the sergeant. I said don't move."

"I'm sorry. I'm just adjusting my glasses. I've got really bad eyes, and it's a nervous habit," she replied. "I'll try to stop."

Her glasses. She'd turned them on. She would have had to brush the right side to open the signal that would go to Kala's phone. Hopefully his cousin wasn't lost in Cooper's eyes or something because she now had a direct line to everything that was happening.

"What is going on?" Dennis seemed to understand his day had taken a deep dive. "I'm not really with them, you know. I barely know her."

So he was just a freaking pawn. Awesome. He'd still gotten them in this position, so TJ was going to kill the fucker.

"No one is going to hurt you, Dennis," Lou said carefully, as though she could call Kala off. He was absolutely certain Kala was in her ear now, making the same threats that TJ couldn't verbalize.

His predator cousin wouldn't listen to reason, and he would let her take care of Dennis because Lou would yell at Kala less. And Lou couldn't cut Kala off sexually. As threats went, it was definitely one that would work on him for the rest of his life.

"I wouldn't say that," their captor replied, a serpentine smile crossing his face. He had a deep scar across his right cheek that matched the pictures they had of Huber. And TJ recognized the voice. “You’ll find with me, everything is negotiable. But first I would like to know who rescued you. I’m not normally in a position where I don’t understand the ground I walk upon, but I do with you, Sergeant Taggart. I rather thought you were a soldier who aided a rival arms dealer, but you’re something more, aren’t you?”

That was where he was wrong. “Well, you got the soldier part right, man. I’m also a really nice guy whose team likes him. I don’t know what the German army is like, but we have a whole thing in the US military where we don’t leave a man behind.”

Huber tsked as he moved closer. Now TJ could see the gun in the holster at his side. He was sure they were all carrying. Were they planning on interrogating him here? That would lead to a gun battle because one way or another, Zach, Kala, and Cooper would be walking into this bar guns blazing.

He would have to make sure he protected Lou.

“They never leave a single man behind,” Lou agreed. “Not one or two or even seven. Those guys always have each other’s backs.”

Not exactly subtle, but she wasn’t in the best situation, and she’d managed to let Kala know how many dudes they were dealing with. It was obvious they hadn’t picked up on Lou herself being the one who’d actually rescued him.

“They’ll come after him this time, too,” Lou promised.

“Well, maybe I don’t need him,” Huber mused. “Maybe I’ve decided to play this a different way. I’ve done what I should have done before—a little research. You, Ms. Ward, might be the actual prize.”

That made the hair on TJ’s arms stand up straight. He shifted around to keep Lou behind him.

“And you should take her,” Dennis offered. “No harm, no foul, right?”

Prick. “Lou’s got nothing to do with it, and don’t think I’ll forget that you said that, Sims. I protected her before. I’ll sure as hell protect her now. Mr. Huber, if you let Lou go, I’ll tell you everything you want to know about The Jester.”

“What?” Lou kind of screeched out the question.

TJ tried to turn, but one of the seven bad guys waved a gun in his face and muttered something in German that he took to mean stay still. He held his hands up to show how harmless he was. For now. "I meant what I said. I lied to you in Germany. I know a lot."

Huber waved him off, choosing to stare at Lou. "I think perhaps knowing The Jester's identity is not the best way to go about things. It's recently been pointed out to me that whoever wears that mask is ruthless and has even less care for human life than I do. However, there is something I need. You see, I have an associate who wants some very specific information that he believes only The Jester knows. But I think I've found another way to get him what he needs."

Lou.

Whoever had been pulling Huber's strings back in Germany wanted to contact the bombmaker. Lou couldn't contact the bombmaker, but what she was excellent at was reverse engineering. "You want to see if Lou can recreate what the bombmaker did."

His baby was a genius and she used it for good, but if she could be twisted, oh, the chaos she would cause. And they could twist her with the right pressure—that pressure being him.

"Yes, I think that would be an even better gift to my associate than giving him the name," Huber explained. "What if I could just give him the bomb he so clearly needs? Wouldn't that be infinitely more helpful? That was when I realized the woman who could do it was inside my compound. She's so much more valuable than you."

"That has always been true."

"TJ," Lou said, his name an obvious warning.

One he couldn't take at this point.

Huber said something in German to one of the men, and then TJ had a gun in his face. He took a deep breath to calm the panic that threatened. His first instinct was to punch out, take the gun, and start killing these fuckers.

But he had to think of Lou. They were outnumbered, and she could get caught in the cross fire. The space was too small for a gunfight. He had to wait for the team and then cover Lou with his body and try to get her out while Kala, Coop, and Zach took care of business.

"Hands up," the man in front of him said, his English almost unaccented. He was likely in his thirties, with dark hair and eyes and bland good looks.

TJ held his hands up as the man looked him in the eyes and then nodded to the dude on his right. That man holstered his weapon and ran his hands down TJ's sides, a routine pat down before they likely tied him up and he lost the opportunity to do anything at all.

He took a deep breath, trying to decide if he should take the chance.

And then the man's hand ran over the gun at his back. Ran over it like it wasn't there.

He straightened up again and nodded to his boss.

He couldn't have missed the gun, yet he'd just told everyone that TJ didn't have a weapon on him.

Why the hell would he do that?

Something was wrong. Or right. He wasn't sure. Could the Agency have someone on the inside?

"I don't have a gun on me." Dennis was moving beside him, trying to shift away.

"Just stay still and let him verify it," Lou advised. "Stay calm."

If the Agency had someone embedded, they would have done something in Germany. They certainly would have at the very least informed his uncle of what they were doing so he wouldn't ride in and fuck everything up. Sometimes the Agency held back intel, however he couldn't see it happening here.

But the Agency wasn't the only interested party. No. TJ's mind started to race as he put some very valuable pieces together.

Was this how it felt to be Lou all the time? Because he was feeling all smarty pants and crap.

"Lou, baby, do you smell maple syrup?" The fucker had already put Lou at risk once in his never-ending pursuit of his white whale, who in this case was a Canadian doctor who might or might not be a sociopath with apocalyptic ambitions.

"What?" Lou shifted so she was beside him. The guns were still trained on them, but they seemed more relaxed now that they'd done the whole pat-down thing and verified no one was carrying a deadly weapon.

Or would have been if the dude hadn't been lying. They wanted him to be able to defend himself. Something was about to go down, and he needed Lou ready. "I was just wishing we'd gone to Tim Hortons instead of a bar, baby. It's always the better bet."

Lou's little gasp let him know she'd picked up on what he was saying.

"What the fuck are you talking about, Taggart?" Dennis's suit didn't look so great now. It was wrinkled, likely because the guy who'd done his pat down hadn't been as careful. "There's no Tim Hortons here. That's a Canada thing. You know I always thought you were a moron and now, here I am."

Huber frowned. "Kill that one. He annoys me."

"If you kill him, Dr. Huisman won't get the bomb he needs," Lou said suddenly.

Huber went stock-still. "Where have you heard that name?"

Dennis pushed at his guard, obviously panicking.

That was the moment the door cracked open and Kala moved in, flanked by Zach and Cooper.

TJ reached around, one hand going to grab Lou's and the other his gun.

"Get down," Kala yelled as the bullets started flying.

The guy who'd left him the gun cursed and shoved Dennis down.

TJ took out the guy to his left, hoping Ben Parker didn't have more than one agent embedded, and started for the bar.

Huber fired off a couple of rounds but managed to take cover.

He had to get Lou out of there. "Stay close, baby."

Lou followed, clutching his hand. "You think Ben Parker's here?"

"I would bet my life on it," he replied as he slid behind the bar, ducking down. "If he's not physically here, then he's the one who set this up."

"He's right about Huisman," Lou whispered as the bar went disturbingly quiet. "You saw how he reacted."

"It seems we're at a standoff." Huber's voice still sounded steady, and it was coming from TJ's left. "If you don't drop your weapons, I will kill this man."

"Dude, I've wanted him dead for years. Have at it," Kala replied.

Damn it. "Stay here."

TJ stood, taking in the scene in front of him. Kala and Zach had guns trained on Huber, who stood in the middle of the bar, his body covered by Dennis's.

The Canadian embedded operative was on the ground next to one of the Germans. It appeared that the team had taken out everyone except Huber, and that would make him infinitely more dangerous.

"Don't kill him."

TJ's heart damn near shot out of his chest because Lou had said the words, and she was standing at the end of the bar, her hands up in the air.

He was going to spank her until she couldn't stand up. And then he would find an elephant plug, lube it up with the nastiest ginger he could find, and shove it in her rectum, and maybe then he would find some calm again. "Louisa Ward."

"Don't," she said, shaking her head. "I can't let anyone else die."

She couldn't do this to him. She couldn't sacrifice herself. "Fine, I'll go with you."

"I'm only taking the girl," Huber said. "I think you might be more than I can handle on my own, Sergeant."

If he thought he could handle Lou, then he hadn't properly done his research. Still, he couldn't risk it. They would torture her. He knew how strong and brave she was, but he couldn't let that happen if he could stop it.

"This deal is only for me," Lou said, looking back at him. "You let me do this, TJ. You have to trust me the way I promise from this moment on I will always trust you. I've learned that. I trust you, Theodore Taggart."

Fuck. She was pleading with him. Trust her. He hadn't, and it had cost them years. Or maybe things had played out the way they always should have. Maybe that was the trust she was talking about. Maybe she was giving him everything he'd hoped for, and all he had to do was shove his fear aside.

All he had to do was risk it all.

His instinct was to go over that bar, cover her with his own body, and let the rest of the team finish the job.

Oh, fuck. They couldn't finish the job without proof. That was what his Lou was doing.

"When I get you back, your ass is mine, baby," he growled and brought his gun down. It would be red. So red. He could trust her fully and still spank her ass over this stunt.

The look on Lou's face was everything. She looked at him like he was the sun in the sky. "I love you, TJ." She turned to the arms dealer, who was still hiding behind a trying-to-cower Dennis. "I'll go with you. I'll get Dr. Huisman what he needs, but you have to let Dennis go."

"Lou," Kala said. "TJ might have lost his fucking mind, but I haven't. If you think I'm letting him walk out with you, you're wrong."

Lou's shoulders went straight as she moved in between Kala and her target. "I'm going to do what I have to. I'm not letting anyone else die."

TJ's gut was a tight knot as he forced himself to stay still. He should shoot Dennis himself and take the problem out of play, but he knew what Lou was doing. The Canadian team wouldn't have set this up without video or audio recording. Likely both. She was going to give Parker what he wanted. Proof.

Neither Zach nor Cooper had let down their guards. Kala was practically vibrating with rage as Huber managed to exchange Dennis for Lou in one smooth move that proved he was a man used to covering his own ass. He wrapped an arm around Lou's waist and dragged her back against him.

TJ's hands twitched with the need to kill the man. Dennis scrambled away, hiding behind one of the overturned tables.

Where Dennis had been a blubbering mess, Lou was calm and cool.

"You better be able to deliver, little girl," Huber said in a raspy voice as he held his gun at her side.

"I can do it," Lou promised him. "I can get him what he needs."

Huber's gaze took in the rest of the room, trying to figure out his best plan of action. "You better or he'll kill us both."

"Emmanuel Huisman will kill us," Lou said plainly.

Huber cursed. "Yes. That crazy fucker will kill us all if he doesn't get what he wants. Now move with me and we'll leave out the back."

Lou held her ground. "Is it enough, Agent Parker?"

A line of red light came from the second floor, streaming down behind Huber.

The arms dealer couldn't see that thin red line. He simply stared at what he thought was the threat. "You better stay…"

Whatever he was going to say was lost as his head jerked forward, a bullet lodging in his brain. Lou pushed away as Huber started for the floor. Dennis screamed and started running. Right into Kala, who caught him neatly.

"Hello, old friend. We're going to have a little chat," she said with a predatory smile.

Dennis's eyes rolled to the back of his head, and he passed out.

Ben Parker stood on the second-floor landing, a sniper rifle in his hands.

Dennis wasn't the only one who was getting a talking to.

Chapter Nineteen

Four hours later, Lou's backside still felt like it was on fire, but she wasn't going to complain because TJ hadn't yet found a plug. And it was possible that he could easily find one since they were in the conference room at The Hideout.

To say TJ had taken exception to her plan to end the conflict would be putting things mildly.

But he'd let her do it. He'd trusted her. He'd shoved his fear and insecurity aside and let them be the badass couple they could be. Not that it saved her ass, but it felt like a good exchange.

After she'd managed to get Parker to show himself, TJ had lost his cool utterly. First, he'd tried to kill Parker. While those two had been beating on each other, Lou had taken time to assure herself Dennis hadn't suffered a heart attack from sheer fear. Then Zach and Cooper had broken up the fight and called the whole fiasco in to base.

While they'd been awaiting the cleanup crew, TJ had taken his anxiety out on her poor backside. Right in front of everyone.

And then he'd wrapped her in his arms and told her again and again how much he loved her.

"We didn't know what he was planning." Samantha Knight looked earnest as she turned to face the big boss. Her curly blonde hair was down, and she looked young and not at all like a person who routinely stole state secrets.

"We didn't know he'd set up that young man," her brother continued. "I assure you I wouldn't have put your team in that situation without your full backing."

"I had a man in place." Parker sat at the end of the table, his right eye only a little swollen.

"A man who died," Big Tag pointed out.

Ben's expression shuttered. "Yes, and I'll have that blood on my hands, but that happened because your team rushed in without understanding the situation at all."

The fact that Kala wasn't sitting in on this meeting was a blessing because she would likely have tried to finish the job TJ had started. Her dad had asked Kala to sit in on the debrief with Dennis. Drake Radcliffe had sent in a bunch of lawyers to ensure Dennis understood what he could and couldn't talk about. Charlotte was there so everything ran smoothly and her daughter didn't murder anyone.

At least she wouldn't have to worry about Dennis coming around again. "I assure you my team knew what was going on. I had the comms on my glasses on. Not only could the team see what was happening, they could hear, and I gave them plenty of verbal cues. What did you expect to happen?"

"Yes, Parker, illuminate us." Big Tag sat at the front of the conference table, his gaze on the Canadian.

Maybe Charlotte had picked the wrong member of her family to watch over so they didn't end up in jail.

"I know I'd like to understand the thought process behind that clusterfuck of a situation." Zach was the only team member besides her and TJ at this meeting. Cooper had gone with Kala, and Tasha was meeting them at the club. Kenzie was probably fuming in the locker room.

Of course, if she was in here, she would likely be trying to convince everyone Ben had the best of intentions.

Lou understood why he'd done what he'd done, but she had to think there could have been another way.

"The operative I had embedded couldn't get me the proof I needed. Huisman was very careful about coming and going. Terry hadn't even been able to get eyes on him," Parker explained. "I'm on a tight leash with this op. My boss gave me two more weeks to prove my theory or he was going to reassign me and close the case. I know what Manny's planning, and I knew I couldn't let that happen."

"You knew they'd taken TJ," Big Tag accused.

Parker nodded tightly. "Yes. I also knew they weren't planning to kill him. I had control. I had a man who was going to get him out, but I needed to give him time. Huisman was there, wasn't he?"

TJ's gaze was steely as he took in the Canadian operative. "Someone was there."

Lou turned his way. "Babe, you know what happened. Huber confirmed that he was there. Let's not have gone through all of this and not get crucial intelligence."

"He put you in danger," TJ said stubbornly.

"And I'm fine," she replied, taking his hand. It was good to be able to do that whenever she liked. "Well, except for my backside."

"One thing TJ gets right," Big Tag said under his breath.

It was good to know that Big Tag approved of how TJ handled his anxiety.

TJ sighed and squeezed her hand before getting back to staring down the Canadian operative. "I'd like to know how you planned this mission. Dennis said he'd originally had a different location in mind. I'm going to assume your embedded agent is the one who tipped off Huber as to the location of Dennis's date."

"Oh, I had Terry deal with all of it. I never contacted Huber at all. After your team raided the German compound, Terry told me that Huber was suddenly more interested in Lou than he was in the sergeant. That's when I decided to work with MI6 to bring her in for questioning."

"That bit of intelligence was one of the reasons I thought it was a good idea to bring her in," Oliver admitted. "If Huber thought she could be a stand-in for the bombmaker, then we needed to take her off the board."

"Sharing that bit of intelligence and sitting down with us so we could all work together would have been the right play, but Parker over there doesn't like to share," Big Tag said, menace plain in his tone.

"I think you know the reputation your team has when it comes to sharing," Parker countered. "Miss Magenta doesn't play fair, and that's exactly why I didn't call you up. We're not friends. Your team literally tied me to a damn spanking bench in Australia and left me out of whatever intel you picked up. So yeah, I wasn't about to offer to work together."

Big Tag stared at the Canadian. "We can discuss politeness at another time. When did you decide to set up Lou again?"

Parker sat back with a weary sigh. "I had the idea when I was sitting in the lounge here with Ms. Magenta. She was teasing Lou about the Dennis guy, and I got her to tell me the story. She told me she was almost certain Dennis would try again. I found him, and Terry convinced Dennis to change his plans. We needed the whole thing to go down in a place where we could control the comings and goings. That particular bar has been closed for weeks in preparation for a renovation. We simply reopened it. But I wasn't going to let Huber walk out with Lou. She wasn't supposed to bring TJ with her. According to the DMs she sent to Sims, she was going to attend alone."

"Yeah, he was setting up a freaking opportunity to molest her," TJ said under his breath.

He was very dramatic. "Given all the things going on, I wasn't about to go on a date. I thought it was a get-together with some people from high school, and TJ would have known almost everyone there. I wasn't ever going to meet with Dennis alone. Not until this situation resolved."

TJ growled.

"Not ever now." Her boyfriend was a very growly top. She had to admit it did something for her.

"I was watching the whole time, and Terry handled things properly. He made sure he was the one who checked you for weapons. He left you the gun," Parker pointed out. "All I wanted was to hear the name. I needed Huber to acknowledge the name on tape. Terry was going to get close enough to Lou to ask her to talk to Huber, but he didn't need to. She brought it up herself."

"Because TJ pointed out that he thought you were there." She gave her guy a bright smile. "That was brilliant. I didn't pick up on it."

He grinned. "You would have figured it out. I only did because the guy let me keep my gun. It was logic from there. I knew *we* didn't have an agent embedded, so it made sense that it was the Canadians."

"Working missions on American soil without informing the Agency," Big Tag pointed out.

"Says the man who started it all." Parker slapped at the table. "Years ago you ran an op in Toronto, and that's precisely why we're here. The CIA killed Huisman's father."

"I wasn't working for the Agency at the time," Big Tag pointed out. "And somehow I think Emmanuel would have found his dark side one way or another. He's good, though. He played things beautifully in Australia. I wasn't able to give the Agency anything on him. Now we can talk."

"Will what we've found be enough for your boss to keep the case open?" Lou asked.

Ben nodded. "Yes. I've already sent Joseph what I got, and he's handling Terry's body." Ben's jaw clenched. "I'm really… Damn it, it shouldn't have gone down like that."

"I'm going to give you some advice, Parker." Big Tag closed the folder in front of him and stood, looming over the room. "Ditch the guilt. The way you play, there's no place for it. You were willing to risk everyone's lives for one answer. If I was your handler, I would be perfectly happy to send you on any op because you'll get the job done. That blood on your hands is nothing. It's a speck. You'll bathe in it before you're done. You keep down the path you're on and there won't be an inch of your soul that resembles what you started with. What you did today is one of the most ruthless things I've seen in a long time. There's a part of me that's impressed. There's a part of me that thinks I should take you out now because Terry isn't the only person you're going to get killed."

"I didn't mean for that to happen," Ben insisted.

"But you would do it again," Big Tag said quietly.

"You don't know what Manny's capable of." Ben sat up, his jaw going stubborn.

"No, but I damn straight know what you're capable of." Big Tag walked to the door. "I'm going back to Langley with the lawyers where I've been told I'll have a chance to meet with your boss and have a long chat about how we're going to handle the situation with Huisman."

Oliver sighed and pushed back from the table. "Yes, I think my boss is planning on being at that meeting as well. If Sami and I could catch a ride with you, we would appreciate it. Perhaps you could yell at me some more and get it out of your system before you meet with my boss."

Big Tag snorted. "Not on your life, Oliver. Your boss will be getting the full brunt of my rage, but you're welcome to a seat on the plane. Zach, we're wheels up in two hours. Make sure the Brits are where they're supposed to be."

Zach nodded. "I'll get them to the airport on time."

"Shouldn't I be on that plane?" Parker stood, his expression going blank. Like he knew what the answer was going to be.

"You've got a one-way ticket back to Toronto," Big Tag informed him. "Take it up with your boss. And Parker, while there's a part of me that understands why you did what you did, know that if you ever put my team at risk again without my consent, I'll take you apart myself and then you'll see what it means to truly play unfair."

Oliver whistled. "That man is intimidating. I rather thought all the stories I'd heard were overblown."

"I didn't," his sister said. "I wouldn't want to be on his bad side, so let me handle him when we're in the air. You irritate him."

Probably because Oliver hit on every woman in a five-mile radius.

Parker stared at the door Big Tag had walked out of.

"I'll take care of you right now," Zach offered. "I'll play fair and everything. We have a boxing ring. I won't even carry a weapon."

"Zach." Lou thought the Canadian had been through enough.

"He's all mine, Zach," TJ argued.

"Fuck you both," Parker replied, flushing slightly with obvious anger. "The two of you would do the same thing if you knew what I know. You're about to. You're about to have to deal with a monster unlike anything you have before, and he's already cost me everything, so don't think I wouldn't do it again. I would give my own life if it meant taking him out. Lou, I wasn't going to let anything happen to you."

She felt sympathy for the man.

"You said the same thing about Terry." TJ obviously did not.

"I understand." She squeezed her boyfriend's hand. "I'd like to know more about what kind of threat Huisman poses. I'll be honest. I got bad vibes off the man in Australia. I was willing to listen to you, but the rest of the team thought we should wait until we had proof."

"He's good at hiding who he really is," Ben said.

"So are you, asshole."

Lou stood because Kala was in the doorway, her eyes tight as she stared at Ben.

Had she been waiting for her dad to leave so she could get her murder on?

The whole room seemed to go still.

"Maggie," Ben began.

Kala strode up to Ben and slapped him right across the face, whipping his head around.

His eyes closed, and TJ stood up as though ready to defend his cousin.

Who had tears in her eyes.

Who wasn't Kala.

Kenzie had swapped clothes with her sister to preserve the illusion that they were one person, and she was looking at Ben like he'd ripped her heart out. "You stay away from my team. You should be happy that I didn't want to have to clean up another body today. I won't make the same mistake again."

She turned to stride away, but Ben caught her by the wrist, turning her around. For a moment the air was charged with emotion, and Lou wasn't sure which way this was going to go. TJ was tense beside her.

Ben stared at Kenzie for a moment and then brought the hand she'd slapped him with up to his lips. "Until next time."

Kenzie pulled her hand away and walked out.

Ben sighed and watched her.

"You should be careful, Parker," TJ said. "I think she meant that."

"I do, too." Parker's expression shuttered. "Thanks for

everything, Lou. I'm sorry it got so fucked up. You, too, Oliver and Samantha. Maybe when you understand what's at stake you can forgive me."

He walked out of the room, the door closing firmly behind him.

"That was Kenz," TJ whispered.

"That was a whole lot of drama," Sami announced, sitting back and looking Zach's way. "You have your work cut out for you, mate."

Zach shook his head. "You have no idea."

TJ wrapped an arm around her, pulling her close. "We should go find her."

"I think she needs a minute." Lou knew she would. "I think we should get this club ready. She's going to need some time in subspace. I know I could use some. Though in a way that's easier on my backside."

Zach groaned. "I'm actually happy I'm going to miss that. And let's not forget we still haven't figured out who set TJ up."

But she was almost sure she knew. She only needed one more piece of information and then she could set the question to rest. "I think that's going to be okay now."

TJ's brow rose. "Oh, you do?"

"Trust me," she said. Her heart ached for Kenzie, but she couldn't help but feel hope.

TJ brought his lips down to cover hers. "Implicitly. See. I properly used a big old vocabulary word."

She grinned and wrapped her arms around the love of her life.

* * * *

"But he's dead."

An hour later, TJ sat back, staring at Lou's laptop screen.

The Brits were gone, and no one knew exactly where Parker had gotten to. He'd left The Hideout and hadn't looked back. Big Tag, Charlotte, and Zach were on their way to DC with Oliver and Sami. It was the core team sitting in the conference room, knocking back a couple of beers and bemoaning the events of the day.

Kala wasn't in a good mood having dealt with Sims and a bunch of Agency lawyers. "Fucker causing trouble even after death.

Tash, you know how to pick 'em, sister."

Tasha's jaw had dropped, but she looked up to stare at her sister. "I have excellent taste in men."

"Now she does," Dare said, looking cheerful.

Cooper shook his head. "Okay. Explain this to me. So Tasha's ex-and-now-dead fiancé set all of this up. How did you figure it out?"

His smarty pants, soon-to-be wife pointed to her screen. "Well, I had a suspicion. Knowing that TJ had absolutely nothing to do with some arms dealer made me wonder why anyone would try to set him up. I know he can be annoying at times, but the truth is most people find him adorable."

He found her adorable. "This wasn't about me at all, was it?"

Lou shook her head. "Nope. It was all about Big Tag."

Tasha sat back, her face flushing. "He told me he was going to find a way to make my dad look bad. I didn't think he could do it. I certainly didn't think he'd already set the plan in motion. Asshole. I really hate him. I wish I could kill him again."

Tasha hadn't killed him the first time. He'd died in prison, and Lou wondered if part of that wasn't to cover up some of the crap he'd pulled. "I think Chet was in deep with a lot of scary people. But I can absolutely prove that he's the one who moved the crypto. I managed to hack a couple of old systems. Also, I'm pretty sure the guy in the photo is TJ's old CO, the one Kala killed."

Kala tipped her beer Lou's way. "Good times, man."

"So this was something Chet set in motion even before the Australia op." Kenzie had a glass of wine in front of her. The club was open and they could hear the thud of industrial music outside, but the team had decided to lock themselves in for now.

"About six weeks before, from what I can tell," Lou explained. "He worked with TJ's old CO to start the ball rolling, and I have to believe at some point he would have subtly pointed out to someone that Interpol was looking for a man who looked an awful lot like this guy he knew on one of the Special Forces teams."

"But Huber picked it up first," Cooper mused. "That was something Chet couldn't have counted on. He wanted suspicion on TJ because suspicion on him puts it on Big Tag, too."

"When we broke up, Chet was afraid my father would do

something to fuck him over career-wise," Tasha admitted. "He even told me he had plans in place to ensure that didn't happen."

"And it wouldn't have been hard to convince Mike." TJ shook his head at how things had played out. "He hated me. He loathed the fact that when we worked with this team, my uncle insisted on me being the liaison and not him."

"Well, it goes against all military rules, and Big Tag knew that," Cooper pointed out.

"My dad doesn't care about rules. He would say he's not in the military anymore, and Taggart rules are in play," Kenzie said. "And that means we only trust family. A truth I should have remembered."

"Kenz," Kala began. "You're being overly dramatic. I'm pissed at Parker, too, but I also get why he did what he did. I just got the file he's worked up on Huisman, and if that fucker is half as bad as Parker says he is, I would have done the same thing."

Kenzie shook her head. "He put Lou in danger. He could have told us."

"And we could have trusted him in Australia," Kala countered. "We're fucking spies, Kenz. Look, I know it goes against everything I believe in to defend that asshole, but if you're going to be pissed at him for that, you need to find some nice dude with a white hat to ride into the sunset with. I would have done the same thing."

"No, you wouldn't," Cooper argued.

Kala turned his way, her expression grim. "Yeah, I would, and that's why you should walk out there and find your perfectly wholesome little sub to top and build a white picket fence with so she can pop out your two point five kids."

"Kala," Cooper said, his mouth in a frown. "You wouldn't put someone's life on the line. I know you."

"If you can say that, then you don't." She took a long drag off her beer. "And my sister should remember it, too. Though, hey, if you want me to take Parker out, I'll be happy to."

"He could have talked to me," Kenzie said quietly.

"Or he could have talked to me," Kala replied. "I think the fact that he doesn't trust us proves he's got a brain in his head."

"Well, it's over now." Kenzie finished her drink and seemed to steel herself. "We won't be the ones on the Huisman case if he's really that dangerous. And now that we know Tasha's ex set TJ up, we should be able to clear everything with Interpol and The Jester can be someone else's problem."

"But I want to deal with The Jester," Kala complained. "Not only does he sound like a massive asshole since he calls himself The Jester, but I kind of want to figure out who the bombmaker is. I don't think we should let this go. Dad won't. He'll lobby to keep us in play."

"Even if we manage to clear things up with Interpol, that doesn't mean everyone will get the memo," Dare pointed out. "It's still out there that TJ is somehow connected to this guy. Shouldn't we be worried about that?"

"Yes, we should."

TJ looked up, and a familiar figure stood in the doorway. He'd moved with the silence of his father. One of them, anyway. When Jacob Dean had been in the Green Berets his call sign had been Ghost because he'd moved like one. Though Tristan Dean-Miles looked like Adam, there was a lot of Jake in him, too. "Hey, man. You missed all the fun."

Lou turned her gaze Tristan's way. "Yes, you did. I suppose you can't tell us where you've been."

Cooper frowned. "How many teams are you working for, man? We needed you here."

"Yeah, Lou hasn't been able to figure out who The Jester is yet," Kala said.

"I think I know," Lou said quietly. "But I haven't put all the pieces together."

Tristan walked into the conference room, closing the door behind him. "Don't worry about The Jester. I've got it handled. And yes, I'm working with another team on some highly classified ops, but I think it's time to come clean. I'm sorry I wasn't here. My handler kept me out of the loop, and I'm starting to wonder if he's not keeping me in the dark about a lot of things. I'm afraid I might have fucked up my whole life for nothing. TJ, Dare's right. You can try to clean up the mess Chet made, but not everyone out there will believe it. They'll still think you have a connection to The Jester."

Kenzie sat up, focusing in. "So, the Agency is aware of the problem, and you're working with the team that's trying to find The Jester?"

Lou shook her head, and TJ knew what she was going to say two seconds before she said it. After all, it only made sense. Something about The Jester had changed two years before. The same time Tristan started disappearing for long periods of time.

"He is The Jester," Lou said quietly.

Tristan sank down in his seat. "I am, and now I need your help because we're all in trouble."

Lou's hand found his as Tristan started talking.

The future was suddenly dangerous, but it would be okay because she would be at his side.

Epilogue

Some time later

Erin Taggart looked out over the dance floor where her son was smiling down at his new bride. Louisa Ward Taggart looked beautiful in her wedding dress, her hair in soft curls.

The night was illuminated with twinkle lights and the stars above, and she had to admit this was one hell of a wedding.

Her kids were surrounded with love and family and joy.

She glanced over where her daughter was laughing at something Brianna Dean-Miles was saying. She had a whole group of girls who were her crew. Devi might not have gone into the military and formed a team, but those girls knew how to take care of each other.

A laugh from behind her reminded Erin that she had a girl gang of her own. Her sisters-in-law were sitting together at one of the big tables in the white tent set up for the reception. It was being held about thirty miles outside of Fort Worth, just far enough away that it seemed like they were surrounded by nature.

She'd never had sisters before she'd married Theo. Well, it hadn't truly been marrying Theo that had made her one of them. It had been loving him. Losing him. Before she'd found him again, she'd discovered she wasn't alone the way she'd thought she'd been.

Sometimes those words her father used to hurt her seemed like they'd been heard with different ears. In another life.

Somewhere along the way she'd set aside her anger at the man who hadn't been able to love her. She'd forgiven her brothers for being mini versions of her dad, though she would shoot any of them who came close to her kids, but that wouldn't be about what they'd done to her.

Her rage had been utterly overtaken by the love she'd found.

"You good?" Boomer Ward offered her another glass of champagne. He looked stunning in his tuxedo. Almost as good as her man, though no one on earth looked like Theo Taggart.

But Boomer's smile had lit up the night as he'd walked his daughter down the aisle after the strangest, most adorable wedding party she'd ever seen. Every bridesmaid had been escorted down the aisle by a groomsman and one of the many animals the Ward family had rescued. Her own daughter had grinned as she'd walked beside her cousin Lucas and a potbellied pig named Jarvis. Devi had claimed Jarvis was far better behaved than her cousin.

"Well, no one tried to blow up the place, so I think we're good." The last wedding they'd all attended had been…eventful, to say the least, so she was counting this one going off without a hitch as a win.

Especially since Daisy O'Donnell had been involved in the planning, and that girl was a chaos magnet. Though she'd calmed down since she'd found her balance in the form of a hunky boyfriend she was madly in love with.

But those were other stories for other days. She was concentrating on the here and now, and the here and now felt really amazing.

"The cake Daphne made was spectacular." Lou's mom had outdone herself with the seven-tiered elegant cake she'd made.

"She's made a lot of wedding cakes over the years. This one was the most special," Boomer said, a smile on his lips. "They make a beautiful couple. I always knew they would end up together."

Erin chuckled. "Really? I thought you might kill my boy a couple of times in there. It was a long road."

"Yeah, but sometimes those are the best roads to travel," Boomer said. "I know they struggled, but they were always going to end up right here. Which is why I'm going to have faith when it comes to the rest of them."

"You mean our completely fucked up nieces and nephews?" The twins were excelling at the spy game, but their romantic lives were a big old mess. Still, she'd seen miracles happen…

"Yep." Boomer snagged a beer from the waiter walking by. "That is what I mean. They'll figure it out and save the world at the same time."

A slow song played, and TJ swayed with his new bride, staring down at her with a look she'd seen in his father's eyes. It was how Theo looked at her.

"You ever think we'd be here?" Boomer asked.

"I had my doubts. You're the one who seemed to see the future, buddy."

Boomer laughed. "I didn't mean Lou and TJ. I meant you and me. I think a lot about who I was when I first came to McKay-Taggart. We were a lot alike."

Ah, she knew what he meant. They had been a lot alike. "Shitty parents. No family. Work was the only thing that mattered."

"Yeah," he agreed. "I think a lot about that guy who just wanted to fit in somewhere."

Damn, she was soft.

And it felt good to be soft. She reached out and gave her old friend a half hug, leaning into his massive body. "You fit in here just fine, Boom. I personally couldn't imagine this family without you."

He leaned into her. "You either. Sometimes I want to go back and tell that guy to just hold on, that he won't believe how good it can get. I thought I was happy when I had my friends, but tonight, watching Lou start this part of her life and knowing my son will be here one day…"

Erin straightened up and punched him in the arm. "Asshole. You're trying to make me cry. I spent an hour in a chair with a teenager painting makeup on me, and I am not going to ruin it."

Boomer got the softest look on his face and reached out to wipe away a tear clinging to her cheek. "Too late, sister. I'll give you something else to ruin that perfect face of yours. Thank you."

"Don't." She shook her head.

"Thank you for raising that kid," he said solemnly. "Thank you for making him into the man he is. He's worthy of my girl, and I'm proud to have him as a son-in-law."

Yep, she was crying. And that was good, too. She'd never fucking cried before she'd met Theo Taggart. He and his amazing, unusual family had cracked her wide open, and it had made all the difference.

They'd taught her how to love. How good it was to be loved.

"Thank you for raising the smartest girl I've ever met. The kindest. I'm so proud to be her mother-in-law."

"We're going to be the best grandparents," he said with a smile.

"Boomer, stop making Erin cry." Daphne grabbed her husband's hand. "I'm sorry. He's been very emotional the last couple of days. He's done a lot of talking to his younger self."

Boomer shrugged. "I've heard it's healing."

"Enough with the healing. Let's get to dancing," Daphne declared.

Grandparent. She was going to have grandbabies. She was going to watch her son settle in with the love of his life, and one day her daughter would do the same.

She'd come to this place angry at the world, closed down and sure she would be alone.

She was so surrounded by love.

And Daphne was right. It was time to dance.

She downed the rest of her champagne and walked up to the DJ, taking the microphone. "Hey, Theo Taggart, this guy's about to play some Taylor Swift and we're going to dance the night away because I am so in love with you."

A loud whoop went up, and she saw Big Tag laughing as he pushed his brother forward. The Taggart brothers had been ribbing each other all day.

Her husband was suddenly front and center, looking deliciously sexy with his tuxedo coat off, the white sleeves of his dress shirt rolled up. His smile was brighter than any sun, and he filled her whole fucking soul with joy.

"You know I never turn down a Taylor Swift song," he said as he lifted her up and twirled her around. "And I never, never turn down you, gorgeous."

He hauled her onto the dance floor as the song began.

A long road. That was what Boomer had called it. Such a long road to get here, and she wouldn't change a single turn or curve, even the worst ones.

Erin leaned against her husband and realized the world was still opening. There were still glorious adventures to be had.

She danced under the stars and looked forward to every single day she had with these people.

With her family.

Tristan, Carys, Aidan, and the whole New Recruits crew will return in *Sweet Little Spies*, coming September 17, 2024.

Sweet Little Spies

Masters and Mercenaries: New Recruits, Book 3
By Lexi Blake
Coming September 17, 2024

Since he was a kid, Aidan O'Donnell has known two things about the world. Tristan is his best friend, and Carys is the love of his life. Sharing her with Tristan was oddly easy. They both loved her deeply, and they never cared what anyone else thought. They were a team and everything was wonderful. Until the day it ended.

Carys Taggart has spent the last year and a half of her life living a lie. A lie Tristan forced on them all. She understands that it was meant to protect her and Aidan, but lately when Tristan says he doesn't love her, it feels more like the truth. The wedding she's dreamed of has been put off far longer than he promised. When he asks her and Aidan for another delay, she's ready to move on without him.

Tristan Dean-Miles has a good plan and the best of intentions. Go undercover as a ruthless arms dealer so he can find a deadly bombmaker at the top of the agency's wanted list. It might be taking longer than expected, but he's so close he can taste it. Unfortunately, getting this close meant getting in way too deep. He knows he will succeed, but if he can't convince the love of his life and his best friend that he's worth the wait, his victory will cost him everything.

Author's Note

I'm often asked by generous readers how they can help get the word out about a book they enjoyed. There are so many ways to help an author you like. Leave a review. If your e-reader allows you to lend a book to a friend, please share it. Go to Goodreads and connect with others. Recommend the books you love because stories are meant to be shared. Thank you so much for reading this book and for supporting all the authors you love!

About Lexi Blake

New York Times bestselling author Lexi Blake lives in North Texas with her husband and three kids. Since starting her publishing journey in 2010, she's sold over three million copies of her books. She began writing at a young age, concentrating on plays and journalism. It wasn't until she started writing romance that she found success. She likes to find humor in the strangest places and believes in happy endings.

Connect with Lexi online:

Facebook: Lexi Blake
Twitter: authorlexiblake
Website: www.LexiBlake.net
Instagram: authorlexiblake

Sign up for Lexi's free newsletter at
www.LexiBlake.net/newsletter

Made in the USA
Columbia, SC
22 March 2024